THE HYPNOTIST

THE
HYPNOTIST

LARS KEPLER

Translated from the Swedish by Ann Long

blue door

Blue Door
An imprint of HarperCollinsPublishers
77–85 Fulham Palace Road,
Hammersmith, London W6 8JB
www.harpercollins.co.uk

Published by Blue Door 2011

2

Originally published in 2009 by Albert Bonniers Förlag,
Sweden, as *Hypnotisören*

Lars Kepler assert the moral right to
be identified as the authors of this work
A catalogue record for this book
is available from the British Library

ISBN: 978-0-00-735910-3 (hardback)
ISBN: 978-0-00-735911-0 (trade paperback)

Printed and bound in Great Britain by
Clays Ltd, St Ives plc

Mixed Sources
Product group from well-managed
forests and other controlled sources
www.fsc.org Cert no. SW-COC-001806
© 1996 Forest Stewardship Council
FSC

FSC is a non-profit international organisation established to promote the responsible
management of the world's forests. Products carrying the FSC
label are independently certified to assure consumers that they come
from forests that are managed to meet the social, economic and
ecological needs of present and future generations.

Find out more about HarperCollins and the environment at
www.harpercollins.co.uk/green

In Greek mythology, the god Hypnos is a winged boy with poppy seeds in his hand. His name means sleep. He is the twin brother of Thanatos, death, and the son of night and darkness.

The term *hypnosis* was first used in its modern sense in 1843 by the Scottish surgeon James Braid. He used this term to describe a sleeplike state of both acute awareness and great receptiveness.

Even today, opinions vary with regard to the usefulness, reliability, and dangers of hypnosis. This lingering ambivalence is presumably owing to the fact that the techniques of hypnosis have been exploited by con men, stage performers, and secret services all over the world.

From a purely technical point of view, it is easy to place a person in a hypnotic state. The difficulty lies in controlling the course of events, guiding the patient, and interpreting and making use of the results. Only through considerable experience and skill is it possible to master deep hypnosis fully. There are only a handful of recognized doctors in the world who have truly mastered deep hypnosis.

THE HYPNOTIST

Like fire, just like fire. Those were the first words the boy uttered under hypnosis. Despite life-threatening injuries—innumerable knife wounds to his face, legs, torso, back, the soles of his feet, the back of his neck, and his head—the boy had been put into a state of deep hypnosis in an attempt to see what had happened with his own eyes.

"I'm trying to blink," he mumbled. "I go into the kitchen, but it isn't right; there's a crackling noise between the chairs and a bright red fire is spreading across the floor."

They'd thought he was dead when they found him among the other bodies in the terraced house. He'd lost a great deal of blood, gone into a state of shock, and hadn't regained consciousness until seven hours later. He was the only surviving witness.

Detective Joona Linna was certain that the boy would be able to provide valuable information, possibly even identify the killer.

But if the other circumstances had not been so exceptional, it would never even have occurred to anyone to turn to a hypnotist.

1

Erik Maria Bark is yanked reluctantly from his dream when the telephone rings. Before he is fully awake, he hears himself say with a smile, "Balloons and streamers."

His heart is pounding from the sudden awakening. Erik has no idea what he meant by these words. The dream is completely gone, as if he had never had it.

He fumbles to find the ringing phone, creeping out of the bedroom with it and closing the door behind him to avoid waking Simone. A detective named Joona Linna asks if he is sufficiently awake to absorb important information. His thoughts are still tumbling down into the dark empty space after his dream as he listens.

"I've heard you're very skilled in the treatment of acute trauma," says Linna.

"Yes," says Erik.

He swallows a painkiller as he listens. The detective explains that he needs to question a fifteen-year-old boy who has witnessed a double murder and been seriously injured himself. During the night he was moved from the neurological unit in Huddinge to the neurosurgical unit at Karolinska University Hospital in Solna.

"What's his condition?" Erik asks.

5

The detective rapidly summarizes the patient's status, concluding, "He hasn't been stabilized. He's in circulatory shock and unconscious."

"Who's the doctor in charge?" asks Erik.

"Daniella Richards."

"She's extremely capable. I'm sure she can—"

"She was the one who asked me to call you. She needs your help. It's urgent."

When Erik returns to the bedroom to get his clothes, Simone is lying on her back, looking at him with a strange, empty expression. A strip of light from the streetlamp is shining in between the blinds.

"I didn't mean to wake you," he says softly.

"Who was that?" she asks.

"Police . . . a detective . . . I didn't catch his name."

"What's it about?"

"I have to go to the hospital," he replies. "They need some help with a boy."

"What time is it, anyway?" She looks at the alarm clock and closes her eyes. He notices the stripes on her freckled shoulders from the creased sheets.

"Sleep now, Sixan," he whispers, calling her by her nickname.

Carrying his clothes from the room, Erik dresses quickly in the hall. He catches the flash of a shining blade of steel behind him and turns to see that his son has hung his ice skates on the handle of the front door so he won't forget them. Despite his hurry, Erik finds the protectors in the closet and slides them over the sharp blades.

It's three o'clock in the morning when Erik gets into his car. Snow falls slowly from the black sky. There is not a breath of wind, and the heavy flakes settle sleepily on the empty street. He turns the key in the ignition, and the music pours in like a soft wave: Miles Davis, "Kind of Blue."

He drives the short distance through the sleeping city, out of Luntma-kargatan, along Sveavägen to Norrtull. He catches a glimpse of the waters of Brunnsviken, a large, dark opening behind the snowfall. He slows as he enters the enormous medical complex, manoeuvring between Astrid Lindgren's understaffed hospital and maternity unit, past the radiology and psychiatry departments, to park in his usual place outside the neurosurgical unit. There are only a few cars in the visitors' car park. The glow of the streetlamps is reflected in the windows of the tall buildings, and blackbirds rustle through the branches of the trees in the darkness. Usually you hear the roar of the motorway from here, Erik thinks, but not at this time of night.

He inserts his pass card, keys in the six-digit code, enters the lobby, takes the lift to the fifth floor, and walks down the hall. The blue vinyl floors shine like ice, and the corridor smells of antiseptic. Only now does he become aware of his fatigue, following the sudden surge of adrenaline brought on by the call. It had been such a good sleep, he still felt a pleasant aftertaste.

He thinks over what the detective told him on the telephone: a boy is admitted to the hospital, bleeding from cuts all over his body, sweating; he doesn't want to lie down, is restless and extremely thirsty. An attempt is made to question him, but his condition rapidly deteriorates. His level of consciousness declines while at the same time his heart begins to race, and Daniella Richards, the doctor in charge, makes the correct decision not to let the police speak to the patient.

Two uniformed cops are standing outside the door of ward N18; Erik senses a certain unease flit across their faces as he approaches. Maybe they're just tired, he thinks, as he stops in front of them and identifies himself. They glance at his ID, press a button, and the door swings open with a hum.

Daniella Richards is making notes on a chart when Erik walks in. As he greets her, he notices the tense lines around her mouth, the muted stress in her movements.

"Have some coffee," she says.

"Do we have time?" asks Erik.

"I've got the bleed in the liver under control," she replies.

A man of about forty-five, dressed in jeans and a black jacket, is thumping the coffee machine. He has tousled blond hair, and his lips are serious, clamped firmly together. Erik thinks maybe this is Daniella's husband, Magnus. He has never met him; he has only seen a photograph in her office.

"Is that your husband?" he asks, waving his hand in the direction of the man.

"What?" She looks both amused and surprised.

"I thought maybe Magnus had come with you."

"No," she says, with a laugh.

7

"I don't believe you," teases Erik, starting to walk toward the man. "I'm going to ask him."

Daniella's mobile phone rings and, still laughing, she flips it open, saying, "Stop it, Erik," before answering, "Daniella Richards." She listens but hears nothing. "Hello?" She waits a few seconds, then shrugs. "Aloha!" she says ironically and flips the phone shut.

Erik has walked over to the blond man. The coffee machine is whirring and hissing. "Have some coffee," says the man, trying to hand Erik a mug.

"No, thanks."

The man smiles, revealing small dimples in his cheeks, and takes a sip himself. "Delicious," he says, trying once again to force a mug on Erik.

"I don't want any."

The man takes another sip, studying Erik. "Could I borrow your phone?" he asks suddenly. "If that's okay. I left mine in the car."

"And now you want to borrow mine?" Erik asks stiffly.

The blond man nods and looks at him with pale eyes as grey as polished granite.

"You can borrow mine again," says Daniella, who has come up behind Erik.

He takes the phone, looks at it, then glances up at her. "I promise you'll get it back," he says.

"You're the only one who's using it anyway," she jokes.

He laughs and moves away.

"He *must* be your husband," says Erik.

"Well, a girl can dream," she says with a smile, glancing back at the lanky fellow.

Suddenly she looks very tired. She's been rubbing her eyes; a smudge of silver-grey eyeliner smears her cheek.

"Shall I have a look at the patient?" asks Erik.

"Please." She nods.

"As I'm here anyway," he hastens to add.

"Erik, I really do want your opinion, I'm not at all sure about this one."

2

Daniella Richards opens the heavy door and he follows her into a warm recovery room leading off the operating theatre. A slender boy is lying on the bed. Despite his injuries, he has an attractive face. Two nurses work to dress his wounds: there are hundreds of them, cuts and stab wounds all over his body, on the soles of his feet, on his chest and stomach, on the back of his neck, on the top of his scalp, on his face.

His pulse is weak but very rapid, his lips are as grey as aluminium, he is sweating, and his eyes are tightly closed. His nose looks as if it is broken. Beneath the skin, a bleed is spreading like a dark cloud from his throat and down over his chest.

Daniella begins to run through the different stages in the boy's treatment so far but is silenced by a sudden knock at the door. It's the blond man again; he waves to them through the glass pane.

"Fine," says Erik. "If he isn't Magnus, who the hell is that guy?"

Daniella takes his arm and guides him from the recovery room. The blond man has returned to his post by the hissing coffee machine.

"A large cappuccino," he says to Erik. "You might need one before you meet the officer who was first on the scene."

Only now does Erik realize that the blond man is the detective who woke him up less than an hour ago. His drawl was not as noticeable on the telephone, or maybe Erik was just too sleepy to register it.

9

"Why would I want to meet him?"

"So you'll understand why I need to question—"

Joona Linna falls silent as Daniella's mobile starts to ring. He takes it out of his pocket and glances at the display, ignoring her outstretched hand.

"It's probably for him anyway," mutters Daniella.

"Yes," Joona is saying. "No, I want him here . . . OK, but I don't give a damn about that." The detective is smiling as he listens to his colleague's objections. "Although I *have* noticed something," he chips in.

The person on the other end is yelling.

"I'm doing this my way," Joona says calmly, and ends the conversation. He hands the phone back to Daniella with a silent nod of thanks. "I have to question this patient," he explains, in a serious tone.

"I'm sorry," says Erik. "My assessment is the same as Dr. Richards'."

"When will he be able to talk to me?" asks Joona.

"Not while he's in shock."

"I knew you'd say that," says Joona quietly.

"The situation is still extremely critical," explains Daniella. "His pleural sack is damaged, the small intestine, the liver, and—"

A policeman wearing a dirty uniform comes in, his expression uneasy. Joona waves, walks over, and shakes his hand. He says something in a low voice, and the police officer wipes his mouth and glances apprehensively at the doctors.

"I know you probably don't want to talk about this right now," says Joona. "But it could be very useful for the doctors to know the circumstances."

"Well," says the police officer, clearing his throat feebly, "we hear on the radio that a caretaker's found a dead man in the toilet at the playing field in Tumba. Our patrol car's already on Huddingevägen, so all we need to do is turn and head up towards the lake. We figured it was an overdose, you know? Jan, my partner, he goes inside while I talk to the caretaker. Turns out to be something else altogether. Jan comes out of the locker room; his face is completely white. He doesn't even want me to go in there. So much blood, he says three times, and then he just sits down on the steps . . ."

The police officer falls silent, sits in a chair, and stares straight ahead.

"Can you go on?" asks Joona.

"Yes . . . The ambulance shows up, the dead man is identified, and it's my responsibility to inform the next of kin. We're a bit short-staffed, so I have to go alone. My boss says she doesn't want to let Jan go out in this state; you can understand why."

Erik glances at the clock.

"You have time to listen to this," says Joona.

The police officer goes on, his eyes lowered. "The deceased is a teacher at the high school in Tumba, and he lives in that development up by the ridge. I rang the bell three or four times, but nobody answered. I don't know what made me do it, but I went around the whole block and shone my torch through a window at the back of the house." The police officer stops, his mouth trembling, and begins to scrape at the arm of the chair with his fingernail.

"Please go on," says Joona.

"Do I have to? I mean, I . . . I . . ."

"You found the boy, the mother, and a little girl aged five. The boy, Josef, was the only one who was still alive."

"Although I didn't think . . ." He falls silent, his face ashen.

Joona relents. "Thank you for coming, Erland."

The police officer nods quickly and gets up, runs his hand over his dirty jacket in confusion, and hurries out of the room.

"They had all been attacked with a knife," Joona Linna says. "It must have been sheer chaos in there. The bodies were . . . they were in a terrible state. They'd been kicked and beaten. They'd been stabbed, of course, multiple times, and the little girl . . . she had been cut in half. The lower part of her body from the waist down was in the armchair in front of the TV."

His composure finally seems to give. He stops for a moment, staring at Erik before regaining his calm manner. "My feeling is that the killer knew the father was at the playing field. There had been a soccer match; he was a referee. The killer waited until he was alone before murdering him; then he started hacking up the body—in a particularly aggressive way—before going to the house to kill the rest of the family."

"It happened in that order?" asks Erik.

"In my opinion," replies the detective.

Erik can feel his hand shaking as he rubs his mouth. Father, mother, son, daughter, he thinks very slowly, before meeting Joona Linna's gaze. "The perpetrator wanted to eliminate the entire family."

Joona raises his eyebrows. "That's exactly it . . . A child is still out there, the big sister. She's twenty-three. We think it's possible the killer is after her as well. That's why we want to question the witness as soon as possible."

"I'll go in and carry out a detailed examination," says Erik.

Joona nods.

"But we can't risk the patient's life by—"

"I understand that. It's just that the longer it takes before we have something to go on, the longer the killer has to look for the sister."

Now Erik nods.

"Why don't you locate the sister, warn her?"

"We haven't found her yet. She isn't in her apartment in Sundby-berg, or at her boyfriend's."

"Perhaps you should examine the scene of the crime," says Daniella.

"That's already under way."

"Why don't you go over there and tell them to get a move on?" she says, irritably.

"It's not going to yield anything anyway," says the detective. "We're going to find the DNA of hundreds, perhaps thousands, of people in both places, all mixed up together."

"I'll go in a moment and see the patient," says Erik.

Joona meets his gaze and nods. "If I could ask just a couple of questions. That might be all that's needed to save his sister."

3

Erik Maria Bark returns to the patient. Standing in front of the bed, he studies the pale, damaged face; the shallow breathing; the frozen grey lips. Erik says the boy's name, and something passes painfully across the face.

"Josef," he says once again, quietly. "My name is Erik Maria Bark. I'm a doctor, and I'm going to examine you. You can nod if you like, if you understand what I'm saying."

The boy is lying completely still, his stomach moving in time with his short breaths. Erik is convinced that the boy understands his words, but the level of consciousness abruptly drops. Contact is broken.

When Erik leaves the room half an hour later, both Daniella and the detective look at him expectantly. Erik shakes his head.

"He's our only witness," Joona repeats. "Someone has killed his father, his mother, and his little sister. The same person is almost certainly on the way to his older sister right now."

"We know that," Daniella snaps.

Erik raises a hand to stop the bickering. "We understand it's important to talk to him. But it's simply not possible. We can't just give him a shake and tell him his whole family is dead."

"What about hypnosis?" says Joona, almost offhandedly.

13

Silence falls in the room.

"No," Erik whispers to himself.

"Wouldn't hypnosis work?"

"I don't know anything about that," Erik replies.

"How could that be? You yourself were a famous hypnotist. The best, I heard."

"I was a fake," says Erik.

"That's not what I think," says Joona. "And this is an emergency."

Daniella flushes and, smiling inwardly, studies the floor.

"I can't," says Erik.

"I'm actually the person responsible for the patient," says Daniella, raising her voice, "and I'm not particularly keen on letting him be hypnotized."

"But if it wasn't dangerous for the patient, in your judgment?" asks Joona.

Erik now realizes that the detective has been thinking of hypnosis as a possible shortcut right from the start. Joona Linna has asked him to come to the hospital purely to convince him to hypnotize the patient, not because he is an expert in treating acute shock and trauma.

"I promised myself I would never use hypnosis again," says Erik.

"OK, I understand," says Joona. "I had heard you were the best, but . . . I have to respect your decision."

"I'm sorry," says Erik. He looks at the patient through the window in the door and turns to Daniella. "Has he been given desmopressin?"

"No, I thought I'd wait awhile," she replies.

"Why?"

"The risk of thromboembolic complications."

"I've been following the debate, but I don't agree with the concerns; I give my son desmopressin all the time," says Erik.

"How is Benjamin doing? He must be, what, fifteen now?"

"Fourteen," says Erik.

Joona gets up laboriously from his chair. "I'd be grateful if you could recommend another hypnotist," he says.

"We don't even know if the patient is going to regain consciousness," replies Daniella.

"But I'd like to try."

"And he does have to be conscious in order to be hypnotized," she says, pursing her mouth slightly.

"He was listening when Erik was talking to him," says Joona.

"I don't think so," she murmurs.

Erik disagrees. "He could definitely hear me."

"We could save his sister," Joona goes on.

"I'm going home now," says Erik quietly. "Give the patient desmopressin and think about trying the pressure chamber."

As he walks towards the lift, Erik slides out of his white coat. There are a few people in the lobby now. The doors have been unlocked; the sky has lightened a little. As he pulls out of the car park he reaches for the little wooden box he carries with him, garishly decorated with a parrot and a smiling South Seas native. Without taking his eyes off the road he flips open the lid, picks out three tablets, and swallows them quickly. He needs to get a couple of hours more sleep this morning, before waking Benjamin and giving him his injection.

4

Seven and a half hours earlier, a caretaker by the name of Karim Muhammed arrived at the Rödstuhage sports centre. The time was 8:50 p.m. Cleaning the locker rooms was his last job for the day. He parked his Volkswagen bus in the car park not far from a red Toyota. The soccer field itself was dark, the floodlights atop the tall pylons surrounding it long since extinguished, but a light was still on in the men's locker room. The caretaker retrieved the smallest cart from the rear of the van and pushed it towards the low wooden building. Reaching it, he was slightly surprised to find the door unlocked. He knocked, got no reply, and pushed the door open. Only after he had propped it with a plastic wedge did he spot the blood.

When police officers Jan Eriksson and Erland Björkander arrived at the scene, Eriksson went straight to the locker room, leaving Björkander to question Karim Muhammed. At first, Eriksson thought he heard the victim moaning, but after turning him over the police officer realized this was impossible. The victim had been mutilated and partially dismembered. The right arm was missing, and the torso had been hacked at so badly it looked like a bowl full of bloody entrails.

Soon afterwards, the ambulance arrived, as did Detective Superintendent Lillemor Blom. A wallet left at the scene identified the victim as Anders Ek, a teacher of physics and chemistry at the Tumba High School, married to Katja Ek, a librarian at the main library in Huddinge. They lived in a terrace house at Gärdesvägen 8 and had two children living at home, Lisa and Josef.

Superintendent Blom sent Björkander to notify the victim's family while she reviewed Eriksson's report and cordoned off the crime scene, both inside and outside.

Björkander parked at the house in Tumba and rang the doorbell. When no one answered he went around to the back of the row of houses, switched on his torch, and shone it through a rear window, illuminating a bedroom. Inside, a large pool of blood had saturated the carpet, with long ragged stripes leading from it and through the door, as if someone had been dragged from where they'd fallen. A child's pair of glasses lay in the doorway. Without radioing for reinforcements, Erland Björkander forced the balcony door and went in, his gun drawn. Searching the house, he discovered the three victims. He did not immediately realize that the boy was still alive. While hastily radioing for backup and an ambulance, he mistakenly used a channel covering the entire Stockholm district.

"Oh my God!" he cried out. "They've been slaughtered . . . Children have been slaughtered . . . I don't know what to do. I'm all alone, and they're all dead."

5

Joona Linna was in his car on Drottningholmsvägen when he heard the call at 22:10. A police officer was screaming that children had been slaughtered, he was alone in the house, the mother was dead, they were all dead. A little while later he was radioing from outside the house and, calmer now, he explained that Superintendent Lillemor Blom had sent him to the house on Gärdesvägen alone. Björkander suddenly mumbled that this was the wrong channel and stopped speaking.

In the sudden quiet, Joona Linna listened to the rhythmic thumping of the windscreen wipers as they scraped drops of water from the glass. He thought about his father, who had had no backup. No police officer should have to do something like this on his own. Irritated at the lack of leadership out in Tumba, he pulled over to the side of the road; after a moment, he sighed, got out his mobile, and asked to be put through to Lillemor Blom.

Lillemor Blom and Joona had been classmates at the police training academy. After completing her placements, she had married a colleague in the Reconnaissance Division and two years later they had a son. Although it was his legal right, the father never took his paid paternity leave; his choice meant a financial loss for the family as it held up Lillemor's career progression, and eventually he left her for a younger officer who had just finished her training.

Joona identified himself when Lillemor answered. He hurried through the usual civilities and then explained what he had heard on the radio.

"We're short-staffed, Joona," she explained. "And in my judgment—"

"That's irrelevant. And your judgment was way off the mark."

"You're not listening," she said.

"I am, but—"

"Well, then, listen to me!"

"You're not even allowed to send your ex-husband to a crime scene alone," Joona went on.

"Are you finished?"

After a short silence, Lillemor explained that Erland Björkander had only been dispatched to inform the family; he had decided on his own to enter the house without calling for backup.

Joona apologized. Several times. Then, mainly to be polite, asked what had happened out in Tumba.

Lillemor described the scene Erland Björkander had reported: pools and trails of blood, bloody hand- and footprints, bodies and body parts, knives and cutlery thrown on the kitchen floor. She told him that Anders Ek, whom she assumed had been killed following the attack on his family, was known to Social Services for his gambling addiction. While his official debts had been written off, he still owed money to some serious local criminal types. And now a loan enforcer had murdered him and his family. Lillemor described the condition of Anders Ek. The murderer had started to hack his body to pieces; a hunting knife and a severed arm had been found in the locker room showers. She repeated several times that they were short of staff and the examination of the crime scenes would have to wait.

"I'm coming over there," said Joona.

"But why?" she said in surprise.

"I want to have a look."

"Now?"

"If you don't mind," he replied.

"Great," she said, in a way that made him think she meant it.

6

Fourteen minutes later, Joona Linna pulled up at the Rödstuhage sports centre, parking a few yards from a Volkswagen bus with the logo JOHANSSON'S CARE HOME emblazoned on the side. It was dark out, and snowflakes whirled around in the biting wind. The police had already cordoned off the area.

Joona gazed across the deserted soccer field. All of a sudden, an eerie noise — vibrating, humming — kicked on. Off to his left, Joona could hear shuffling sounds and quick footsteps. Turning around, he could make out two black silhouettes walking in the high grass along the fence. The humming escalated — and then abruptly stopped. Spotlights encircling the soccer field exploded with light, flooding the centre, while casting the surrounding area in even more impenetrable winter darkness.

The two figures in the distance were uniformed policemen. One walked quickly, then stopped and vomited. He steadied himself against the fence. His colleague caught up with him and placed a comforting hand on his back, speaking soothingly.

Joona continued on towards the locker rooms. Flashes of light from cameras burst through the propped-open door, and the forensic technicians had laid out stepping blocks around the entrance so as not to contaminate any prints during their initial crime scene investigation. An older colleague stood guard out front. His eyes were heavy with fatigue, and his voice was subdued. "Don't go in if you're afraid of having nightmares."

"I'm done with dreaming," Joona replied.

A strong scent of stale sweat, urine, and fresh blood permeated the air. The forensic technicians were taking pictures in the shower, their white flashes bouncing off the tiles, giving the entire locker room a strange pulsating feel.

Blood dripped from above.

Joona clenched his jaw as he studied the badly mauled body on the floor between the wooden benches and the dented lockers. A thin-haired, middle-aged man with greying stubble.

Blood was everywhere—on the floor, the doors, the benches, the ceiling. Joona continued into the shower room and greeted the forensic technicians in a low voice. The glare of the camera flash reflected on the white tiles and caught the blade of a hunting knife on the floor.

A squeegee with a wooden handle stood against the wall. The rubber blade was surrounded by a large pool of blood, water, and dirt, with wisps of hair, plasters, and a bottle of shower gel.

A severed arm lay by the floor drain. The bone socket was exposed, lined with ligaments and torn muscle tissue.

Joona remained standing, observing every detail. He registered the blood's spatter pattern, the angles and shapes of the blood drops.

The severed arm had been thrown against the tiled wall several times before being discarded.

"Detective," the policeman posted outside the locker room called out. Joona noted his colleague's anxious expression as he was handed the radio.

"This is Lillemor Blom speaking. How soon can you come to the house?"

"What is it?" Joona asked.

"One of the children. We thought he was dead, but he's alive."

7

Joona Linna's colleagues at the National Criminal Investigation Department will tell you they admire him, and they do, but they also envy him. And they will tell you they like him, and they do, but they also find him aloof.

As a homicide investigator, his track record is unparalleled in Sweden. His success is due in part to the fact that he completely lacks the capacity to quit. He cannot surrender. It is this trait that is the primary cause of his colleagues' envy. But what most don't know is that his unique stubbornness is the result of unbearable personal guilt. Guilt that drives him, and renders him incapable of leaving a case unsolved.

He never speaks about what transpired. And he never forgets what happened.

Joona wasn't driving particularly fast that day, but it had been raining, and the rays of the emerging sun bounced off puddles as if they were emanating from an underground source. He was on his way; thought he could escape . . .

Ever since that day, he's been plagued not only by memories but also by an unusual form of migraine. The only thing that's proven helpful has been a preventive medicine used for epilepsy, topiramate. Joona's supposed to take the medicine regularly, but it makes him drowsy, and when he's on the job and needs to think clearly, he refuses to take it. He'd rather submit to the pain. In truth, he probably considers his punishment just: both the inability to relinquish an unresolved case, and the migraine.

The ambulance, lights blinking, rocketed past him in the opposite direction as he approached the house. Leaving a ghostlike silence, the emergency vehicle disappeared through the sleeping suburb.

Waiting for Joona, Lillemor Blom stood smoking under a streetlamp. In its glow, she looked beautiful in a rugged way. These days, her face was creased with fatigue, and her makeup was invariably sloppy. But Joona had always found her to be wonderful-looking, with her high cheekbones, straight nose, and slanted eyes.

"Joona Linna," she said, almost cooing his name.

"Will the boy make it?"

"Hard to say. It's absolutely terrible. I've never seen anything like it— and I never want to again." She let her eyes linger awhile on the glow of her cigarette.

"Have you written up your report?" he asked.

She shook her head and exhaled a stream of smoke.

"I'll do it," he said.

"Then I'll go home and go to bed."

"That sounds nice," he said with a smile.

"Join me," she joked.

Joona shook his head. "I want to go in and look around. Then I have to determine whether the boy can be interrogated."

Lillemor tossed the cigarette to the ground. "What exactly are you doing here?" she asked.

"You can request backup from National Murder Squad, but I don't think they will have time, and I don't think they'll find answers to what happened here anyway."

"But you will?"

"We'll see," Joona said.

He crossed the small garden. A pink bicycle with training wheels was propped against a sandbox. Joona headed up the front steps, turned on his torch, opened the door, and walked into the hallway. The dark rooms were filled with silent fear. Just a few steps in and the adrenaline was pumping through him so hard, it felt like his chest would explode.

Purposefully, Joona registered it all, absorbing every horrific detail until he couldn't take any more. He stopped in his tracks, closed his eyes, felt back to guilt deep inside him . . . and continued to search the house.

In the bleak light of the hallway, Joona saw how bloody bodies had been dragged along the floor. Blood spattered the exposed-brick chimney, the television, the kitchen cabinets, the oven. Joona took in the chaos: the tipped-over furniture, the scattered silverware, the desperate footprints and handprints. When he stopped in front of the small girl's amputated body, tears began to flow down his face. Still, he forced himself to try to imagine precisely what must have happened; the violence and the screams.

The driving force behind these murders couldn't have been connected to a gambling debt, Joona thought. The father had already been killed. First the father, then the family; Joona was convinced of it. He breathed hard between gritted teeth. Somebody had wanted to annihilate the whole family. And he probably believed he had succeeded.

8

Joona Linna stepped out into the cold wind, over the shivering black-and-yellow crime tape, and into his car. The boy is alive, he thought. I have to meet the surviving witness.

From his car, Joona traced Josef Ek to the neurosurgical unit at Karolinska University Hospital in Solna. The forensic technicians from Linköping had supervised the securing of biological evidence taken from the boy's person. His condition had since deteriorated.

It was after one in the morning when Joona headed back to Stockholm, arriving at the intensive care section of Karolinska Hospital just past two. After a fifteen-minute wait, the doctor in charge, Daniella Richards, appeared.

"You must be Detective Linna. Sorry to keep you waiting. I'm Daniella Richards."

"How is the boy, doctor?"

"He's in circulatory shock," she said.

"Meaning?"

"He's lost a lot of blood. His heart is attempting to compensate for this and has started to race—"

"Have you managed to stop the bleeding?"

"I think so, I hope so, and we're giving him blood all the time, but the lack of oxygen could taint the blood and damage the heart, lungs, liver, kidneys."

"Is he conscious?"

"No."

"It's urgent that I get a chance to interview him."

"Detective, my patient is hanging on by his fingernails. If he survives his injuries at all, it won't be possible to interview him for several weeks."

"He's the sole eyewitness to a multiple murder," said Joona. "Is there anything you can do?"

"The only person who might possibly be able to hasten the boy's recovery is Erik Maria Bark."

"The hypnotist?" asked Joona.

She gave a big smile, blushing slightly. "Don't call him that if you want his help. He's our leading expert in the treatment of shock and trauma."

"Do you have any objections if I ask him to come in?"

"On the contrary. I've been considering it myself," she said.

Joona searched in his pocket for his phone, realized he had left it in the car, and asked if he could borrow Daniella's. After outlining the situation to Erik Maria Bark, he called Susanne Granat at Social Services and explained that he was hoping to be able to talk to Josef Ek soon. Susanne Granat knew all about the family. The Eks were on their register, she said, because of the father's gambling addiction, and because they had had dealings with the daughter three years ago.

"With the daughter?" asked Joona.

"The older daughter," explained Susanne.

"So there is a third child?" Joona asked impatiently.

"Yes, her name is Evelyn."

Joona ended the conversation and immediately called his colleagues in the Reconnaissance Division to ask them to track down Evelyn Ek. He emphasized repeatedly that it was urgent, that she risked being killed. But then he added it was also possible that she was dangerous, that she could actually have been involved in the triple homicide in Tumba.

9

Detective Joona Linna orders a large sandwich with Parmesan, bresaola, and sun-dried tomatoes from the little breakfast bar called Il Caffè on Bergsgatan. The café has just opened, and the girl who takes his order has not yet had time to unpack the warm bread from the large brown bags in which it's been delivered from the bakery.

Having inspected the crime scenes in Tumba late the night before, and in the middle of the night visited the hospital in Solna and spoken to the two doctors Daniella Richards and Erik Maria Bark, he had called Reconnaissance once more. "Have you found Evelyn?" he'd asked.

"No."

"You realize we have to find her before the murderer does."

"We're trying, but—"

"Try harder," Joona had growled. "Maybe we can save a life."

Now, after three hours of sleep, Joona gazes out the steamed-up window, waiting for his breakfast. Sleet is falling on the town hall. The food arrives. Joona grabs a pen on the glass counter, signs the credit slip, and hurries out.

The sleet intensifies as he makes his way along Bergsgatan, the warm sandwich in one hand and his indoor hockey stick and gym bag in the other.

"We're playing Recon Tuesday night," Joona had told his colleague Benny Rubin. "We have no chance. They're going to kill us."

The National CID indoor hockey team loses whenever they play the local police, the traffic police, the maritime police, the national special intervention squad, the SWAT team, or Recon. But it gives them a good excuse to drown their sorrows together in the pub, as they like to say, afterwards.

Joona has no idea as he walks alongside police headquarters and past the big entrance doors that he will neither play hockey nor go to the pub this Tuesday. Someone has scrawled a swastika on the entrance sign to the courtroom. He strides on towards the Kronoberg holding cells and watches the tall gate close silently behind a car. Snowflakes are melting on the big window of the guardroom. Joona walks past the police swimming pool and cuts across the yard toward the gabled end of the vast complex. The façade resembles dark copper, burnished but underwater. Flags droop wetly from their poles. Hurrying between two metal plinths and beneath the high frosted glass roof, Joona stamps the snow off his shoes and swings open the doors to the National Police Board.

The central administrative authority in Sweden, the National Police Board is made up of the National Criminal Investigation Department, the Security Service, the Police Training Academy, and the National Forensic Laboratory. The National CID is Sweden's only central operational police body, with the responsibility for dealing with serious crime on a national and international level. For nine years, Joona Linna has worked here as a detective.

Joona walks along the corridor, taking off his cap and shaking it at his side, glancing in passing at the notices on the bulletin board about yoga classes, somebody who's trying to sell a camper, information from the trade union, and scheduling changes for the shooting club. The floor, which was mopped before the snowstorm began, is already soiled with bootprints and dried, muddy slush.

The door of Benny Rubin's office is ajar. A sixty-year-old man with a grey moustache and wrinkled, sun-damaged skin, he is involved in the work around communication headquarters and the change-over to

Rakel, the new radio system. He sits at his computer with a cigarette behind his ear, typing with agonizing slowness.

"I've got eyes in the back of my head," he says, all of a sudden.

"Maybe that explains why you're such a lousy typist," jokes Joona.

Benny's latest find is an advertising poster for the airline SAS: a fairly exotic young woman in a minute bikini suggestively sipping some kind of fruit-garnished cocktail from a straw. Benny was so incensed by the ban on calendars featuring pin-up girls that most people thought he was going to resign, but instead he has devoted himself to a silent and stubborn protest for many years. Technically, nothing forbids the display of advertisements for airlines, pictures of ice princesses with their legs spread wide apart, lithe and flexible yoga instructors, or ads for underwear from H & M. On the first day of each month, Benny changes what he has on the wall. The variety of ways that he avoids the ban is dazzling. Joona remembers a poster of the short-distance runner Gail Devers, in tight shorts, and a daring lithograph by the artist Egon Schiele that depicted a red-haired woman sitting with her legs apart in a pair of fluffy bloomers.

Moving on, Joona stops to say hello to his assistant, Anja Larsson. She sits at the computer with her mouth half open, her round face wearing an expression of such concentration that he decides not to disturb her. Instead, he hangs up his wet coat just inside the door of his office, switches on the Advent star in the window, and glances quickly through his inbox: a message about the working environment, a suggestion about low-energy lightbulbs, an inquiry from the prosecutor's office, and an invitation from Human Resources to a Christmas meal at Skansen.

Joona leaves his office, goes into the meeting room, and sits in his usual place to unwrap his sandwich and eat.

Petter Näslund stops in the corridor, laughs smugly, and leans on the doorframe with his back to the meeting room. A muscular, balding man of about thirty-five, Petter is a detective with a position of special responsibility and Joona's immediate boss. Everyone knows that Joona is eminently more qualified than Petter. But they know, too, that he is also singularly disinterested in administrative duties and the rat race involved in climbing the ranks.

For several years Petter has been flirting with Magdalena Ronander without noticing her troubled expression and constant attempts to switch to a more businesslike tone. Magdalena has been a detective in the Reconnaissance Division for four years, and she intends to complete her legal training before she turns thirty.

Lowering his voice suggestively, Petter questions Magdalena about her choice of service weapon, wondering aloud how often she changes the barrel because the grooves have become too worn. Ignoring his coarse innuendoes, she tells him she keeps a careful note of the number of shots fired.

"But you like the big rough ones, don't you?" says Petter.

"No, not at all, I use the Glock Seventeen," she replies, "because it can cope with a lot of the defence team's nine-millimetre ammunition."

"Don't you use the Czech?"

"Yes, but I prefer the M39B," she says firmly, moving around him to enter the meeting room. He follows, and they both sit and greet Joona. "And you can get the Glock with gunpowder gas ejectors next to the sight," she continues. "It reduces the recoil a hell of a lot, and you can get the next shot in much more quickly."

"What does our Moomintroll think?" asks Petter, with a nod in Joona's direction.

Joona smiles sweetly and fixes his icily clear grey eyes on them. "I think it doesn't make any difference. I think other elements decide the outcome," he says.

"So you don't need to be able to shoot." Petter grins.

"Joona is a good shot," says Magdalena.

"Good at everything." Petter sighs.

Magdalena ignores Petter and turns to Joona instead. "The biggest advantage with the compensated Glock is that the gunpowder gas can't be seen from the barrel when it's dark."

"Quite right," says Joona.

Wearing a pleased expression, she opens her black leather case and begins leafing through her papers. Benny comes in, sits down, looks around at everyone, slams the palm of his hand down on the table, then smiles broadly when Magdalena flashes at him in irritation.

"I took the case out in Tumba," Joona starts.

"That's got nothing to do with us," says Petter.

"I think we could be dealing with a serial killer here, or at least—"

30

"Just leave it, for God's sake!" Benny interrupts, looking Joona in the eye and slapping the table again.

"It was somebody settling a score," Petter goes on. "Loans, debts, gambling . . ."

"A gambling addict," Benny says.

"Very well known at Solvalla. The local sharks were into him for a lot of money, and he ended up paying for it," says Petter, bringing the matter to a close.

In the silence that follows, Joona drinks some water and finishes the last of his sandwich. "I've got a feeling about this case," he says quietly.

"Then you need to ask for a transfer," says Petter with a smile. "This has nothing to do with the National CID."

"I think it has."

"If you want the case, you'll have to go and join the local force in Tumba," says Petter.

"I intend to investigate these murders," says Joona calmly.

"That's for me to decide," replies Petter.

Yngve Svensson comes in and sits down. His hair is slicked back with gel, he has blue-grey rings under his eyes and reddish stubble, and, as always, he's in a creased black suit.

"*Yngwie*," Benny says happily.

Not only is Yngve Svensson in charge of the analytical section but he's also one of the leading experts on organized crime in the country.

"Yngve, what do you think about this business in Tumba?" asks Petter. "You've just been having a look at it, haven't you?"

"Strictly a local matter," he says. "A loan enforcer goes to the house to collect. Normally, the father would have been home, but he'd stepped in to referee a soccer match at the last minute. The enforcer is presumably high, both speed and Rohypnol, I'd say; he's unbalanced, he's stressed, something sets him off, so he attacks the family with some kind of SWAT knife to try and find out where the father is. They tell him the truth, but he goes completely nuts anyway and kills them all before he goes off to the playing field."

Petter sneers. He gulps some water, belches into his hand, and turns to Joona. "What have you got to say about that?"

"If it wasn't completely wrong it might be quite impressive," says Joona.

"What's wrong with it?" asks Yngve aggressively.

"The murderer killed the father first," Joona says calmly. "Then he went over to the house and killed the rest of the family."

"In which case it's hardly likely to be a case of debt collection," says Magdalena Ronander.

"We'll just have to see what the postmortem shows," Yngve mutters.

"It'll show I'm right," says Joona.

"Idiot." Yngve sighs, tucking two plugs of snuff under his top lip.

"Joona, I'm not giving you this case," says Petter.

"I realize that." He sighs and gets up from the table.

"Where do you think you're going? We've got a meeting," says Petter.

"I'm going to talk to Carlos."

"Not about this."

"Yes, about this," says Joona, leaving the room.

"Get back in here," shouts Petter, "or I'll have to—"

Joona doesn't hear what Petter will have to do, he simply closes the door calmly behind him and moves along the hall, saying hello to Anja, who peers over her computer screen with a quizzical expression.

"Aren't you in a meeting?" she asks.

"I am," he says, continuing toward the lift.

10

On the fifth floor is the National Police Board's meeting room and central office, and this is also where Carlos Eliasson, the head of the National CID, is based. The office door is ajar, but as usual it is more closed than open, as if to discourage casual visitors.

"Come in, come in, come in," says Carlos. An expression made up of equal parts of anxiety and pleasure flickers across his face when Joona walks in. "I'm just going to feed my babies," he says, tapping the edge of his aquarium. Smiling, he sprinkles fish food into the water and watches the fish swim to the surface. "There now," he whispers. He shows the smallest paradise fish, Nikita, which way to go, then turns back to Joona. "The murder squad asked if you could take a look at the killing in Dalarna."

"They can solve that one themselves," replies Joona. "Anyway, I haven't got time."

He sits down directly opposite Carlos. There is a pleasant aroma of leather and wood in the room. The sun shines playfully through the aquarium, casting dancing beams of undulant refracted light on the walls.

"I want the Tumba case," he says, coming straight to the point.

The troubled expression takes over Carlos's wrinkled, amiable face for a moment. He passes a hand through his thinning hair. "Petter Näslund rang me just now, and he's right, this isn't a matter for the National CID," he says carefully.

"I think it is," insists Joona.

"Only if the debt collection is linked to some kind of wider organized crime, Joona."

"This wasn't about collecting a debt."

"Oh, no?"

"The murderer attacked the father first. Then he went to the house to kill the family. His plan from the outset was to murder the entire family. He's going to find the older daughter, and he's going to find the boy. If he survives."

Carlos glances briefly at his aquarium, as if he were afraid the fish might hear something unpleasant. "I see," he says. "And how do you know this?"

"Because of the footprints in the blood at both scenes."

"What do you mean?"

Joona leans forward. "There were footprints all over the place, of course, and I haven't measured anything, but I got the impression that the footsteps in the locker room were . . . well, more lively, and the ones in the house were more tired."

"Here we go," says Carlos wearily. "This is where you start complicating everything."

"But I'm right," replies Joona.

Carlos shakes his head. "I don't think you are, not this time."

"Yes, I am."

Carlos turns. "Joona Linna is the most stubborn individual I've ever come across," he tells his fish.

"Why back down when I know I'm right?"

"I can't go over Petter's head and give you the case on the strength of a hunch," Carlos explains.

"Yes, you can."

"Everybody thinks this was about gambling debts."

"You too?" asks Joona.

"I do, actually."

"The footprints were more lively in the locker room because the man was murdered first," insists Joona.

"You never give up, do you?" asks Carlos.

Joona shrugs his shoulders and smiles.

"I'd better ring and speak to the path lab myself," mutters Carlos, picking up the telephone.

"They'll tell you I'm right," says Joona.

Joona Linna knows he is a stubborn person; he needs this stubbornness to carry on. He cannot give up. Cannot. Long before Joona's life changed to the core, before it was shattered into pieces, he lost his father.

Maybe that's when it all began.

Joona's father, Yrjö Linna, was a patrolling policeman in the district of Märsta. One day in 1979 he happened to be on the old Uppsalavägen a little way north of the Löwenström Hospital when Central Control got a call and sent him to Hammarbyvägen in Upplands Väsby. A neighbour had called the police and said the Olsson kids were being beaten again. Sweden had just become the first country to introduce a ban on the corporal punishment of children, and the police had been instructed to take the new law seriously. Yrjö Linna drove to the apartment block and pulled up outside the door, where he waited for his partner. After a few minutes the partner called; he was in a queue at Mama's Hot Dog Stand, and besides, he said, he thought a man should have the right to show who was boss sometimes.

Yrjö Linna never was one to talk much. He knew regulations dictated that there should always be two officers present at an incident of this kind, but he said nothing, although he was well aware that he had the right to expect support. He didn't want to push, didn't want to look like a coward, and he couldn't wait. So, alone, Yrjö Linna mounted the stairs to the third floor and rang the doorbell.

A little girl with frightened eyes opened the door. He told her to stay on the landing, but she shook her head and ran into the apartment. Yrjö Linna followed her and walked into the living room. The girl banged on the door leading to the balcony. Yrjö saw that there was a little boy out there, wearing only a nappy. He looked about two years old. Yrjö hurried across the room to let the child in, and that was why he noticed the drunken man just a little too late. He was sitting in complete silence on the sofa just inside the door, his face turned towards the balcony. Yrjö had to use both hands to undo the catch and turn the handle. It was only when he heard the click of the shotgun that Yrjö froze. The shot sent a total of thirty-six small lead pellets straight into his spine and killed him almost instantly.

Eleven-year-old Joona and his mother, Ritva, moved from the bright apartment in the centre of Märsta to his aunt's three-room place in Fredhäll in Stockholm. After graduating from high school, he applied to the Police Training Academy. He still thinks about the friends in his group quite often: strolling together across the vast lawns, the lull before they were sent out on placements, the early years as junior officers. Joona Linna has done his share of desk work. He has redirected traffic after road accidents and for the Stockholm Marathon; been embarrassed by football hooligans harassing his female colleagues with their deafening songs on the underground; found dead heroin addicts with rotting sores; helped ambulance crews with vomiting drunks; talked to prostitutes shaking with withdrawal symptoms, to those with AIDS, to those who are afraid; he has met hundreds of men who have abused their partners and children, always following the same pattern (drunk but controlled and deliberate, with the radio on full volume and the blinds closed); he has stopped speeding and drunken drivers, confiscated weapons, drugs, and homemade booze. Once, while off from work with lumbago and out walking to avoid stiffening up, he'd seen a skinhead grab a Muslim woman's breast outside the school in Klastorp. His back aching, he'd chased the skinhead along by the water, right through the park, past Smedsudden, up onto the Västerbro bridge, across the water, and past Långholmen to Södermalm, finally catching up with him by the traffic lights on Högalidsgatan.

Without any real intention of building a career, he has moved up the ranks. He could join the National Murder Squad, but he refuses. He likes complex tasks, and he never gives up, but Joona Linna has no interest whatsoever in any form of command.

Now Joona sits listening as Carlos Eliasson talks to Professor Nils "The Needle" Åhlén, Chief Medical Officer at the pathology lab in Stockholm.

"No, I just need to know which was the first crime scene," says Carlos; then he listens for a while. "I realize that, I do realize that . . . but in your judgment so far, what do you think?"

Joona leans back in his chair, running his fingers through his messy blond hair. So far he does not feel any tiredness from the long night in Tumba and at Karolinska Hospital. He watches as Carlos's face grows redder and redder. Joona can hear The Needle drone faintly on the other end of the line. When the voice stops, Carlos simply nods and hangs up without saying goodbye.

"They . . . they—"

"They have established that the father was killed first," supplies Joona.

Carlos nods.

"What did I tell you?" Joona beams.

Carlos looks down at his desk and clears his throat. "Fine, you're leading the preliminary investigation," he says. "The Tumba case is yours."

"First of all, I want to hear one thing," says Joona. "Who was right? Who was right, you or me?"

"You!" yells Carlos. "For God's sake, Joona, what is it with you? Yeah, you were right—as usual!"

Joona hides a smile behind his hand as he gets up.

Suddenly he turns grave. "Reconnaissance hasn't been able to track down Evelyn Ek. She could be anywhere. I don't know what we're going to do if we can't get permission to talk to the boy. Too much time will pass, and it'll be too late when we find her."

"You want to interrogate the wounded boy?" Carlos asks.

"I have no choice."

"Have you spoken to the prosecutor?"

"I have no intention of handing over the preliminary investigation until I have a suspect," says Joona.

"That's not what I meant," says Carlos. "I just think it's a good idea to have the prosecutor on your side if you're going to talk to a boy who is so badly injured."

Joona is halfway out the door. "All right, that makes sense. You're a wise man. I'll give Jens a call," he says.

11

tuesday, december 8: morning

Erik Maria Bark arrives home from Karolinska Hospital. As he quietly lets himself in, he thinks about the young victim lying there and the policeman so eager to question him. Erik likes Detective Joona Linna, despite his attempt to get Erik to break his promise never to use hypnosis again. Maybe it's the detective's open and honest anxiety about the safety of the older sister that makes him so likeable. Presumably somebody is looking for her right now.

Erik is very tired. The tablets have begun to take effect; his eyes are heavy and sore; sleep is on the way. He opens the bedroom door and looks at Simone. The light from the hallway covers her like a scratched pane of glass. Three hours have passed since he left her here, and Simone has now taken over all the space in the bed. Resting on her stomach, she lies there heavily. The bedclothes are down by her feet, her nightgown has worked its way up around her waist, and she has goose bumps on her arms and shoulders. Erik pulls the covers over her carefully. She murmurs something and curls up; he sits down and strokes her ankle, and she moves slightly.

"I'm going for a shower," he says, but he leans back against the headboard, overwhelmed by fatigue.

"What was the name of the police officer?" she asks, slurring her words.

Before he has time to answer, he finds himself at the park in Observatorielunden. He is digging in the sand in the playground and finds a yellow stone, as round as an egg, as big as a pumpkin. He scrapes at it with his hands and sees the outline of a relief on the side, a jagged row of teeth. When he turns the heavy stone over he sees that it is the skull of a dinosaur.

Suddenly, Simone is screaming. "Fuck you!"

He gives a start and realizes that he has fallen asleep and begun to dream. The strong pills have sent him to sleep in the middle of the conversation. He tries to smile and meets Simone's chilly gaze.

"Sixan? What is it?"

"Has it started again?" she asks.

"What?"

"What?" she repeats crossly. "Who's Daniella?"

"Daniella?"

"You promised. You made a promise, Erik," she says. "I trusted you, I was actually stupid enough to trust—"

"What are you talking about? Daniella Richards is a colleague at Karolinska. What's she got to do with anything?"

"Don't lie to me."

"This is actually getting ridiculous," he says, and despite her clear anger he feels a smile spreading involuntarily across his face. He is so tired.

"Do you think this is funny?" she asks. "I've sometimes thought . . . I even believed I could forget what happened."

Erik nods off for a few seconds, but he can still hear what she's saying.

"It might be best if we separate," whispers Simone.

He snaps awake at this. "Nothing has happened between me and Daniella."

"That doesn't really matter," she says wearily.

"Doesn't it? Doesn't it matter? You want to separate because of something I did ten years ago?"

"*Something?*"

"I was drunk, Simone. Drunk, and—"

"I don't want to listen. I know all about it. I . . . Fuck it! I don't want to do this, I'm not a jealous person, but I *am* loyal and I expect loyalty in return."

"I've never let you down since, and I'll never—"

"Prove it to me. I need proof."

"You just have to trust me," he says.

"Yes," she says with a sigh, and collecting a pillow and duvet she shuffles out of the bedroom and down the hallway.

He is breathing heavily. He ought to follow her, not just give up; he ought to try to calm her down and persuade her to come back to bed, but right now sleep exerts the stronger influence. He can no longer resist it. He sinks down into the bed; feels the dopamine flood his system, the tension flow out of his body as relaxation spreads pleasurably across his face, his neck and shoulders, down into his toes and the tips of his fingers. A heavy, chemical sleep enfolds his consciousness like a floury cloud.

12

Erik slowly opens his eyes to the pale light pressing against the curtains. He rolls over with a grunt and glances at the alarm clock; two hours have passed. Immediately, his mind begins to replay the images from the night before: Simone's angry face as she made her accusations, the boy lying there with hundreds of black knife wounds covering his glowing body.

Erik thinks of the detective, who seemed convinced that the perpetrator had wanted to murder an entire family: first the father, then the mother, the son, and the daughter.

An older daughter is out there somewhere, in extreme danger, if Joona Linna is right.

The telephone on the bedside table begins to ring.

Erik gets up, but instead of answering he opens the curtains and peers across at the façade of the building opposite, trying to gather his thoughts. The dust glazing the windowpanes is clearly visible in the morning sunshine.

Simone has already left for the gallery. He doesn't understand her outburst, why she was talking about Daniella. He wonders if it's about something else altogether: the drugs, maybe. He knows he's very close to a serious dependency on them, but he has to sleep. All the night shifts at the hospital have ruined his ability to sleep naturally. Without pills he would go under, he thinks. He reaches for the alarm clock but manages to knock it on the floor instead.

The telephone stops, but is silent for only a little while before it starts ringing again.

He considers going into Benjamin's room and lying down beside his son, waking him gently, asking if he's been dreaming about anything. He picks up the telephone and answers.

"Hi, it's Daniella Richards."

"Are you still at the hospital? It's a quarter past eight."

"I know. I'm exhausted."

"Go home."

"No chance," says Daniella calmly. "You have to come back. That detective is on his way. He seems even more convinced that the perpetrator is after the older sister. He says he has to talk to the boy."

Erik feels a sudden dark weight behind his eyes. "That's a bad idea, given his condition."

"I know. But what about the sister?" she interrupts him. "I'm considering giving the detective the go-ahead to question Josef."

"It's your patient. If you think he can cope with it," says Erik.

"Cope? Of course he can't cope with it. His condition is critical. His family has been murdered, and he'll find out about it under questioning from a policeman. But I can't just sit and wait. I don't want to let the police at him, but there's no doubt that his sister is in danger."

"It's your call," Erik says again.

"A murderer is looking for his older sister!" Daniella breaks in, raising her voice.

"Presumably."

"I'm sorry, I don't know why I'm in such a state about this," she says. "Maybe because it isn't too late. Something could actually be done. I mean, it isn't often the case, but this time we could save a girl before she—"

"What do you want from me?" asks Erik.

"You have to come in and do what you're good at."

Erik pauses, then answers carefully. "I can talk to the boy about what's happened when he's feeling a little better."

"That's not what I mean. I want you to hypnotize him," she says seriously.

"No."

"It's the only way."

"I can't. I won't."

"But there's nobody as good as you."

"I don't even have permission to practise hypnosis at Karolinska."

"I can arrange that."

"Daniella," Erik says, "I've promised never to hypnotize anyone again."

"Can't you just come in?"

There is silence for a little while; then Erik asks, "Is he conscious?"

"He soon will be."

He can hear the rushing sound of his own breathing through the telephone.

"If you won't hypnotize the boy, I'm going to let the police see him." She ends the call.

Erik stands there holding the receiver in his trembling hand. The weight behind his eyes is rolling in towards his brain. He opens the drawer of the bedside table. The wooden box with the parrot and the native on it isn't there. He must have left it in the car.

The apartment is flooded with sunlight as he walks through to wake Benjamin.

The boy is sleeping with his mouth open. His face is pale and he looks exhausted, despite a full night's sleep.

"Benni?"

Benjamin opens his sleep-drenched eyes and looks at him as if he were a complete stranger, before he smiles the smile that has remained the same ever since he was born.

"It's Tuesday. Time to wake up."

Benjamin sits up yawning, scratches his head, then looks at the mobile phone hanging around his neck. It's the first thing he does every morning: he checks whether he's missed any messages during the night. Erik takes out the yellow bag with a puma on it, which contains the factor concentrate desmopressin, acetyl spirit, sterile cannulas, compresses, surgical tape, painkillers.

"Now or at breakfast?"

Benjamin shrugs. "Doesn't matter."

Erik quickly swabs his son's skinny arm, turns it towards the light coming through the window, feels the softness of the muscle, taps the syringe, and carefully pushes the cannula beneath the skin. As the syringe slowly empties, Benjamin taps away at his cell phone with his free hand.

"Shit, my battery's almost gone," he says, then lies back as his father holds a compress to his arm to stop any bleeding.

Gently Erik bends his son's legs backwards and forwards; then he exercises the slender knee joints and massages the feet and toes. "How does it feel?" he asks, keeping his eyes fixed on his son's face.

Benjamin grimaces. "Same as usual."

"Do you want a painkiller?"

Benjamin shakes his head, and Erik suddenly flashes on the unconscious witness, the boy with all those knife wounds. Perhaps the murderer is looking for the older daughter right now.

"Dad? What is it?"

Erik meets Benjamin's gaze. "I'll drive you to school if you like," he says.

"What for?"

13

The rush-hour traffic rumbles slowly along. Benjamin is sitting next to his father, the stop-and-go progress of the car making him feel drowsy. He gives a big yawn and feels a soft warmth still lingering in his body after the night's sleep. He thinks about the fact that his father is in a hurry but that he still takes the time to drive him to school. Benjamin smiles to himself. *It's always been this way*, he thinks: *when Dad's involved in something awful at the hospital, he gets worried that something's going to happen to me.*

"Oh, no!" Erik says suddenly. "We forgot the ice skates."

"Right."

"We'll go back."

"Doesn't matter," says Benjamin.

Erik tries switching lanes, but another car stops him from cutting in. Forced back, he almost collides with a dust cart.

"We've got time to turn around and —"

"Just, like, forget the skates. I couldn't care less," says Benjamin, his voice rising.

Erik glances at him in surprise. "I thought you liked skating."

Benjamin doesn't know what to say. He can't stand being interrogated, doesn't want to lie. He turns away to look out the window.

"Don't you?" asks Erik.

45

"What?"

"Like skating?"

"Why would I?" Benjamin mutters. "It's boring."

"We bought you brand new—"

Benjamin's only reply is a sigh.

"Fine," says Erik. "Forget the skates." He concentrates on the traffic for a moment. "So skating is boring. Playing chess is boring. Watching TV is boring. What do you actually enjoy?"

"Don't know," Benjamin says.

"Nothing?"

"No."

"Movies?"

"Sometimes."

"Sometimes?" Erik smiles.

"Yes," replies Benjamin.

"I've seen you watch three or four movies in a night," says Erik cheerily.

"So what?"

Erik goes on, still smiling. "I wonder how many movies you could get through if you *really* liked watching them. If you *loved* movies."

"Give me a break." Despite himself, Benjamin smiles.

"Maybe you'd need two TVs, zipping through them all on fast forward." Erik laughs and places his hand on his son's knee. Benjamin allows it to remain there.

Suddenly they hear a muffled bang, and in the sky a pale blue star appears, with descending smoke-coloured points.

"Funny time for fireworks," says Benjamin.

"What?" asks his father.

"Look," says Benjamin, pointing.

A star of smoke hangs in the sky. For some reason, Benjamin can see Aida in front of him, and his stomach contracts at once; he feels warm inside. Last Friday they sat close together in silence on the sofa in her narrow living room out in Sundbyberg, watching the movie *Elephant* while her younger brother played with Pokémon cards on the floor, talking to himself.

As Erik is parking outside the school, Benjamin suddenly spots Aida. She's standing on the other side of the fence waiting for him. When she catches sight of him she waves. Benjamin grabs his bag and, sliding out the car door, says, "'Bye, Dad. Thanks for the lift."

"Love you," says Erik quietly.

Benjamin nods.

"Want to watch a movie tonight?" asks Erik.

"Whatever."

"Is that Aida?" asks Erik.

"Yes," says Benjamin, almost without making a sound.

"I'd like to say hello to her," says Erik, climbing out of the car.

"What for?"

They walk across to Aida. Benjamin hardly dares to look at her; he feels like a kid. He doesn't want her to think he needs his father to approve of her or anything. He doesn't care what his father thinks. Aida looks nervous; her eyes dart from son to father. Before Benjamin has time to say anything by way of explanation, Erik sticks out his hand.

"Hi, there."

Aida shakes his hand warily. Benjamin sees his father take in her tattoos: there's a swastika on her throat, with a little Star of David next to it. She's painted her eyes black, her hair is done up in two childish braids, and she wears a black leather jacket and a wide black net skirt.

"I'm Erik, Benjamin's dad."

"Aida."

Her voice is high and weak. Benjamin blushes and looks nervously at Aida, then down at the ground.

"Are you a Nazi?" asks Erik.

"Are you?" she retorts.

"No."

"Me neither," she says, briefly meeting his eyes.

"Why have you got a—"

"No reason. I'm nothing. I'm just—"

Benjamin breaks in, his heart pounding with embarrassment over his father. "She was hanging out with these people a few years ago," he says loudly. "But she thought they were idiots, and—"

"You don't need to explain," Aida interrupts, annoyed.

He doesn't speak for a moment.

47

"I . . . I just think it's brave to admit when you've made a mistake," he says eventually.

"Yes, but I would interpret it as an ongoing lack of insight not to have it removed," says Erik.

"Just leave it!" shouts Benjamin. "You don't know anything about her!"

Aida simply turns and walks away. Benjamin hurries after her.

"Sorry," he pants. "Dad can be so embarrassing."

"He's right, though, isn't he?" she asks.

"No," replies Benjamin feebly.

"I think maybe he is," she says, half smiling as she takes his hand in hers.

14

tuesday, december 8: morning

The Department of Forensic Medicine is located in a redbrick building in the middle of the huge campus of the Karolinska Institute. And inside the department is the glossy white and pale matt grey office of Nils Åhlén, Chief Medical Officer, aka "The Needle."

After giving his name to a girl at reception, Joona Linna is allowed in.

The office is modern and expensive and comes with a designer label. The few chairs are made of brushed steel, with austere white leather seats, and the light comes from a large sheet of glass suspended above the desk.

The Needle shakes Joona's hand without getting up. He is wearing white aviator-framed glasses and a white turtleneck under his white lab coat. His face is clean-shaven and narrow, the grey hair is cropped, his lips are pale, his nose long and uneven.

"Good morning," he says, in a hoarse voice.

On the wall hangs a faded colour photograph of The Needle and his colleagues: forensic pathologists, forensic chemists, forensic geneticists, and forensic dentists. They are all wearing white coats, and they all look happy. They are standing around a few dark fragments of bone on a bench; the caption beneath the picture states that this is a find from an excavation of ninth-century graves outside the trading settlement of Birka on the island of Björkö.

49

"New picture," says Joona.

"I have to stick photos up with tape," says The Needle discontentedly. "In the old pathology department they had a picture sixty feet square."

"Wow," replies Joona.

"Painted by Peter Weiss."

"The writer?"

The Needle nods; the light from the desk lamp reflects off his aviators. "Yes. He painted portraits of all the staff in the forties. Six months' work, and he was paid six hundred kronor, or so I've heard. My father is in the picture among the pathologists; he's down at the end." The Needle tilts his head to one side and returns to his computer. "I'm just working on the postmortem report from the Tumba murders," he says.

"Yes?"

The Needle peers at Joona. "Carlos rang up to hassle me this morning."

Joona smiles sweetly. "I know."

The Needle pushes his glasses back. "I gather it's important to establish the time of death of the different victims."

"Yes, we need to know the order."

The Needle searches on the computer, his lips pursed. "It's only a preliminary assessment, but—"

"The man died first?"

"Exactly. I based that purely on the body temperature," he says, pointing at the screen. "Erixon says both locations, the locker room and the house, were roughly the same temperature, so my estimate was that the man died just over an hour before the other two."

"And have you changed your mind now?"

The Needle shakes his head and gets up with a groan. "Slipped disc," he mutters, as he sets off down the hall.

Joona follows him as he limps slowly toward the postmortem unit. They pass a room containing a freestanding dissection table made of stainless steel; it looks like a drain board but with rectangular sections and a raised edge all around. They enter a cool room where bodies being examined by the forensic unit are preserved in drawers at a temperature of forty degrees Fahrenheit. The Needle stops and checks the number, pulls out a large drawer, and sees that it's empty.

"Gone," he says, and they return to the corridor. As they walk, Joona notices that the floor is marked with thousands of scuffs from the wheels of trolleys. They reach another room and The Needle holds the door open for Joona.

They are in a well-lit white-tiled room with a large hand basin on the wall. Water is trickling into a drain in the floor from a bright yellow hose. On the long dissection table, which is covered in plastic, lies a naked, colourless body marked with hundreds of black wounds.

"Katja Ek," states Joona.

The dead woman's face is remarkably calm; her mouth is half open and her eyes have a serene look about them. She looks as if she is listening to beautiful music, but her peaceful expression is at odds with the long, vicious slashes across her forehead and cheeks. Joona allows his gaze to roam over Katja Ek's body, where a marbled veining has already begun to appear around her neck.

"We're hoping to get the internal examination done this afternoon."

Joona sighs. "God, what a mess."

The other door opens and a young man with an uncertain smile comes in. He has several rings in his eyebrows, and his dyed black hair hangs down the back of his white coat in a ponytail. With a little smile, The Needle raises one fist in a hard rock greeting, pinkie and index finger aloft like devil's horns, which the young man immediately reciprocates.

"This is Joona Linna from National CID," The Needle explains. "He comes to visit us now and again."

"Frippe," says the young man, shaking hands with Joona.

"He's specializing in forensic medicine," says The Needle.

Frippe pulls on a pair of latex gloves, and Joona goes over to the table with him; the air surrounding the woman is cold and smells unpleasant.

"She's the one who was subjected to the least amount of violence," The Needle points out. "Despite multiple cuts and stab wounds."

They contemplate the dead woman. Her body is covered in large and small punctures.

"In addition, unlike the other two, she has not been mutilated or hacked to pieces," he goes on. "The actual cause of death is not the wound in her neck but this one, which goes straight into the heart, according to the computer tomography." He indicates a relatively unimpressive-looking wound on her sternum.

"But it is a little difficult to see the bleeds on the images," says Frippe.

"Naturally, we'll check it out when we open her up," The Needle says to Joona.

"She fought back," says Joona.

"In my opinion she actively defended herself at first," replies The Needle, "based on the wounds on the palms of her hands, but then she tried to escape and simply tried to protect herself."

The young doctor studies The Needle intently.

"Look at the injuries on the outer arms," says The Needle.

"Defensive wounds," mutters Joona.

"Exactly."

Joona leans over and looks at the brownish-yellow patches that are visible in the woman's open eyes.

"Are you looking at the suns?"

"Yes."

"You don't see them until a few hours after death; sometimes it can take several days," The Needle says to the young doctor. "They'll turn completely black in the end. It's because the pressure in the eye is dropping."

He picks up a reflex hammer and asks Frippe to see if any idiomuscular contractions remain. The young doctor taps the middle of the woman's biceps and feels the muscle with his fingers, checking for contractions.

"Minimal," he says to The Needle.

"They usually stop after thirteen hours," The Needle explains.

"The dead are not completely dead," says Joona, shuddering as he detects a ghostly movement in Katja Ek's limp arm.

"*Mortui vivis docent*—the dead teach the living," replies The Needle, smiling to himself as he and Frippe ease her onto her stomach.

He points out the blotchy reddish-brown patches on her buttocks and the small of her back and across her shoulder blades and arms.

"The hypostasis is faint when the victim has lost a lot of blood."

"Obviously," says Joona.

"Blood is heavy, and when you die there is no longer any internal pressure system," The Needle explains to Frippe. "It might be obvious, but the blood runs downward and simply collects at the lowest points; it's most often seen on surfaces that have been in contact with whatever the body was lying on."

He presses a patch on her right calf with his thumb until it almost disappears.

"There, you see . . . you can press them and make them disappear up to twenty-four hours after death."

"But I thought I saw patches on her hips and chest," says Joona hesitantly.

"Bravo," says The Needle, regarding him with a faintly surprised smile. "I didn't think you'd notice those."

"So she was lying on her stomach when she was dead, before she was turned over," says Joona.

"For two hours, I'd guess."

"So the perpetrator stayed for two hours. Or he came back to the scene. Or somebody else turned her over."

The Needle shrugs his shoulders. "I'm a long way from finishing my assessment at this stage."

"Can I ask something? I noticed that one of the wounds on the stomach looks like a C-section."

"A C-section," says The Needle, smiling. "Why not? Shall we have a look at it?" The two doctors turn the body once again. "This one, you mean?" The Needle is pointing to a large cut extending about six inches downward from the navel.

"Yes," replies Joona.

"I haven't had time to examine every injury yet."

"*Vulnera incisa*," says Frippe.

"Yes, it does look like an incision," says The Needle.

"Not a stab wound," says Joona.

Frippe leans over so that he can see.

"In view of the fact that it's a straight line and the surface of the surrounding skin is intact." The Needle pokes inside the wound with his fingers. "The walls," he goes on. "They're not particularly blood-soaked, but—"

"What is it?" asks Joona.

The Needle is looking at him very strangely. "This cut was made after her death," he says. He pulls off his gloves. "I need to look at the computer tomography," he says worriedly; he walks over, opens up the computer on the table by the door, clicks through the three-dimensional images, stops, moves on, and alters the angle. "The wound appears to go into the womb," he whispers. "It looks as if it follows old scars."

"Old scars? What do you mean?" asks Joona.

"You're the one who called it." The Needle smiles faintly. "An emergency C-section scar."

He points at the vertical wound. As Joona looks more closely, he can see that all along one side there is a thin thread of old, pale-pink scar tissue, from a C-section that healed long ago.

"But she wasn't pregnant?" asks Joona.

"No." The Needle laughs, pushing his aviators back.

"Are we dealing with a murderer who has surgical skills?" asks Joona.

The Needle shakes his head; Joona thinks about the fact that someone killed Katja Ek in a frenzy, with considerable violence, and came back two hours later, turned her over, and carefully cut open her old C-section scar.

"See if there's anything similar on the other bodies."

"Do you want us to make that a priority?" asks The Needle.

"Yes, I think so."

"You're not sure?"

"I'm sure."

"So you want us to prioritize everything."

"More or less." Joona is smiling as he leaves the room.

But as Joona gets into his car, he starts to shiver. He starts the engine, pulls out into Retzius Väg, turns up the heater, and keys in the number for Chief Prosecutor Jens Svanehjälm.

"Svanehjälm."

"Joona Linna."

"Ah. Good morning. I've just been talking to Carlos. He said you'd be in touch."

"It's a little difficult to say what we're dealing with here," says Joona. "I've just left the forensic unit, and I'm thinking of heading to the hospital; I really need to question the surviving witness."

"Carlos explained the situation to me," says Jens. "Have you got the profiling group started?"

"A profile won't be enough," replies Joona.

"No, I know; I agree. If we're to have any chance of protecting the older sister, we absolutely have to speak to the boy."

Joona suddenly sees a firework explode in complete silence: a pale blue star, far away above the roofs of Stockholm. He clears his throat. "I'm in touch with Susanne Granat at Social Services, and I was thinking of having Erik Maria Bark, the psychiatrist, with me during questioning. He's an expert in the treatment of shock and trauma."

"That's perfectly in order," says Jens reassuringly.

"In that case I'll go straight to the neurosurgical unit."

"Good idea."

15

Hurrying along the hospital corridor after dropping Benjamin off at school, Erik thinks how stupid he had been to comment on Aida's tattoo. He has just made himself look self-righteous and critical in their eyes.

Two uniformed police officers let him into the unit. Joona Linna is already waiting outside the room where Josef Ek is lying. When he sees Erik he gives a little wave, like a small child might, opening and closing his hand.

Erik looks in at Josef through the window in the door. A bag of blood, almost black, is suspended above him. His condition has stabilized somewhat, but there's still a risk of new bleeds in the liver. The nurse prepares an infusion of morphine.

He is lying on his back, his mouth tightly closed; his stomach is moving rapidly up and down, and his fingers twitch from time to time.

"I was right when I said the perpetrator started at the soccer field," says Joona. "He murdered Anders Ek first. Then he went to the house and killed Lisa, the little girl, thought he killed the boy, and killed Katja, the mother."

"Has the pathologist confirmed that?"

"Yes," replies Joona.

"I see."

"So if the killer's intention is to eliminate the entire family," Joona goes on, "only the older daughter remains. Evelyn."

"Unless he's found out the boy is still alive," says Erik.

"Exactly, but we can protect him."

"Yes."

"We have to find the killer before he can get to Evelyn," says Joona. He looks Erik directly in the eye. "I need to find out what the boy knows."

"And I need to do what's in the best interests of the patient."

"Perhaps it's in his best interests not to lose his sister."

"That occurred to me as well; I'll have another look at him, of course," says Erik. "But I'm fairly sure it's too early. That said, I believe the patient will regain consciousness quite soon, within just a few hours, at least to the extent that we'll be able to start talking to him. But after that point, you have to understand that we have a lengthy therapeutic process ahead of us. An interrogation could damage the boy's condition."

Daniella walks over briskly, wearing a snug red coat. She hands the patient's file to Erik.

"Erik, it doesn't matter what we think. The prosecutor has already decided that special circumstances apply."

Erik turns and looks inquiringly at Joona. "So you don't need our consent?" he asks.

"No," answers Joona.

"So what are you waiting for?"

"I think Josef has already suffered more than anyone should have to suffer," says Joona. "I don't want to put him through anything that might harm him. But at the same time I have to find his sister before the killer does. And that boy saw the attacker's face. If you won't help me find out what he knows, I'll do it myself, but obviously I prefer the better way."

"Which is?"

"Hypnosis," replies Joona.

Erik looks at him. "I don't even have permission to hypnotize—"

"I've spoken to Annika Lorentzon," says Daniella.

"What did she say?" asks Erik.

"It's hardly a popular decision, permitting an unstable patient to be hypnotized, a child in the bargain. But since I am responsible for the patient, she has left the final judgment to me," Daniella tells him.

Erik exhales, then rubs his eyes with his fingers. "I really want to get out of this."

"If you don't mind my saying so, your reluctance to use hypnosis seems to go beyond your prudent concern for the patient's well-being," says Joona.

"I have no intention of discussing the matter, but I promised ten years ago never to use hypnosis again. It was a decision on my part that I still think was the right one."

"Is it right in this case?" asks Joona.

"To be honest, I don't know."

"Make an exception," implores Daniella.

"Hypnosis, then." Erik sighs.

"I'd like you to make an attempt as soon as you feel the patient is in any way receptive to hypnosis," says Daniella.

"It would be good if you were here," says Erik.

"I've made the decision with regard to hypnosis," she explains, "on condition that you then take over responsibility for the patient."

"So I'm on my own now?"

Daniella looks at him, exhausted. "I've worked all night," she says. "I'd promised to take my daughter to school, I blew that off, and I'm going to have to deal with that tonight. But right now I have to go home and sleep."

16

Erik watches Daniella Richards walk down the corridor, red coat flapping behind her. Joona looks in at the patient. Erik goes to the washroom, locks the door, washes and dries his face. He takes out his phone and calls Simone, but there is no reply. He tries his home number and listens to the phone ringing, but when the answering machine kicks in, he no longer knows what to say: "Sixan, I . . . you have to listen to me, I don't know what you're thinking, but nothing's happened, maybe you don't care, but I promise I'm going to find a way to prove to you that I'm—"

Erik stops speaking. What's the point? He knows his assurances no longer have any meaning. He lied to her ten years ago, and he still hasn't managed to prove his love, not sufficiently, not enough for her to begin to trust him again. He ends the call, leaves the washroom, and walks over to where the detective is gazing into the patient's room.

"What is hypnosis, actually?" Joona asks, after a while.

"It's just an altered state of consciousness, coupled with suggestion and meditation," Erik replies. "From a purely neurophysiological point of view, the brain functions in a particular way under hypnosis. Parts of the brain that we rarely use are suddenly activated. People under hypnosis are very deeply relaxed. It almost looks as if they're asleep, but if you do an EEG the brain activity shows a person who is awake and alert."

"I see," Joona says hesitantly.

"When people think of hypnosis, they usually mean heterohypnosis," where one person hypnotizes another with some purpose in mind."

"Such as?"

"Such as evoking negative hallucinations, for example."

"What's that?"

"The most common is that you inhibit the conscious registration of pain."

"But the pain is still there."

"That depends on how you define it," Erik replies. "Of course the patient responds to pain with physiological reactions, but he experiences no feeling; it's even possible to carry out surgery under clinical hypnosis."

Joona writes something down in his notebook. "The boy opens his eyes from time to time," he says, looking through the window again.

"I've noticed."

"What's going to happen now?"

"To the patient?"

"Yes, when you hypnotize him."

"During dynamic hypnosis, in a therapeutic context, the patient almost always splits himself into an observing self and one or more experiencing and acting selves."

"He's watching himself, like in a theatre?"

"Yes."

"What are you going to say to him?"

"Well, he's experienced terrible things, so first of all I have to make him feel secure. I begin by explaining what I'm going to do, and then I move on to relaxation. I talk in a very calm voice about his eyelids feeling heavier, about wanting to close his eyes, about breathing deeply through his nose. I go through the body from head to toe; then I work my way back up again."

Erik waits while Joona takes notes.

"After that comes what's called the induction," says Erik. "I insert a kind of hidden command into what I say and get the patient to imagine places and simple events. I suggest a walk in his thoughts, farther and farther away, until his need to control the situation almost disappears. It's a little bit like when you're reading a book and it gets so exciting that you're no longer aware of the fact that you're sitting reading."

"I understand."

"If you lift the patient's hand like this and then let go, the hand should stay where it is, in the air, cataleptic, when the induction is over," Erik explains. "After the induction I count backwards and deepen the hypnosis further. I usually count, but others have the patient visualize a grey scale, in order to dissolve the boundaries in his mind. What is actually taking place on a practical level is that the fear, or the critical way of thinking that is blocking certain memories, is put out of action."

"Will you be able to hypnotize him?"

"If he doesn't resist."

"What happens then?" asks Joona. "What happens if he does resist?"

Erik studies the boy through the window in the door, trying to read the boy's face, his receptiveness.

"It's difficult to say what I'll get out of him. It could be of very variable relevance," he says.

"I'm not after a witness statement. I just want a hint, a clue, something to go on."

"So all you want me to look for is the person who did this to them?"

"A name or a place would be good, some kind of connection."

"I have no idea how this is going to go," says Erik, taking a deep breath.

17

Joona goes into the recovery room with Erik, sits on a chair in the corner, slips off his shoes, and leans back. Erik dims the light, pulls up a metal stool, and sits down next to the bed. Carefully he begins to explain to the boy that he wants to hypnotize him in order to help him understand what happened yesterday.

"Josef, I'm going to be sitting here the whole time," says Erik calmly. "There is absolutely nothing to be afraid of. You can feel completely safe. I'm here for your sake. You don't have to say anything you don't want to say, and you can bring the hypnosis to an end whenever you want to."

Only now, his heart pounding, does Erik begin to realize how much he has longed to do this. He must try to curb his enthusiasm. The pace of events must not be forced or hurried along. It must be filled with stillness; it must be allowed to slow down and be experienced at its own gentle tempo.

He immediately feels how receptive Josef is; his injured face grows heavier, the features fill out, and his mouth relaxes. It's as if the boy intuitively clings to the security Erik conveys. It's easy to get the boy into a state of deep relaxation; the body has already been at rest and seems to long for more.

When Erik begins the induction, it is as if he never stopped practising hypnosis; his voice is close, calm, and matter-of-fact, and the words come so easily they pour out, suffused with monotonous warmth and a somnolent, falling cadence.

"Josef, if you'd like to . . . think of a summer's day," says Erik. "Everything is pleasant and wonderful. You are lying in the bottom of a little wooden boat, bobbing gently. You can hear the lapping of the water, and you are gazing up at little white clouds drifting across the blue sky."

The boy responds so well that Erik wonders if he ought to slow things down a little bit. Difficult events can increase sensitivity when it comes to hypnosis. Inner stress can function like an engine in reverse: the braking action happens unexpectedly fast and the rev count very quickly drops to zero.

"I'm going to start counting backwards now, and with each number you hear you will relax a little more. You will feel yourself being filled with great calm; you will be aware of how pleasant everything around you is. Relax from your toes, your ankles, your calves. Nothing bothers you; everything is peaceful. The only thing you need to listen to is my voice, the numbers counting down. Now you are relaxing even more, you feel even heavier, your knees relax, along your thighs to your groin. Feel yourself sinking downwards at the same time, gently and pleasantly. Everything is calm and still and relaxed."

Erik rests a hand on Josef's shoulder. He keeps his gaze fixed on the boy's stomach, and with every exhalation he counts backwards. Erik had almost forgotten the feeling of dreamlike lightness and physical strength that fills him as the process runs its course. As he counts he can see himself sinking through bright, oxygen-rich water. Smiling, he drifts down past a vast rock formation, a continental fissure that continues down towards immense depths, the water glittering with tiny bubbles. Filled with happiness, he descends along the rough wall of rock. As Erik falls through the bright water, he reaches out an arm, grazing the rock with his fingers as he passes. The bright water shifts slowly into shades of pink.

The boy is showing clear signs of hypnotic rest. An expression of great relaxation has settled over his cheeks and mouth. Erik has always thought that a patient's face becomes broader, somehow flatter. Less attractive but more fragile, and without any trace of pretence.

"Now you are deeply relaxed," says Erik calmly. "Everything is very, very pleasant."

The boy's eyes gleam behind the half-closed lids.

"Josef, I want you to try and remember what happened yesterday. It started just like an ordinary Monday, but in the evening someone comes to the house."

The boy is silent.

"Now you're going to tell me what's happening," says Erik.

The boy responds with the faintest of nods.

"You're sitting in your room? Is that what you're doing? Are you listening to music?"

There is no reply. His mouth moves, asking, seeking.

"Your mum was at home when you got back from school," says Erik.

He nods.

"Do you know why? Is it because Lisa has a temperature?"

The boy nods and moistens his lips.

"What do you do when you get home from school, Josef?"

The boy whispers something.

"I can't hear," Erik urges gently. "I want you to speak so I can hear you."

The boy's lips move again, and Erik leans forward.

"Like fire, just like fire," Josef mumbles. "I'm trying to blink. I go into the kitchen, but it isn't right; there's a crackling noise between the chairs and a bright red fire is spreading across the floor."

"Where is the fire coming from?" asks Erik.

"I don't remember. Something happened before . . ." He falls silent again.

"Go back a little, before the fire in the kitchen," says Erik.

"There's someone there," says the boy. "I can hear someone knocking at the door."

"The outside door?"

"I don't know." The boy's face suddenly grows tense, he whimpers anxiously, and his lower teeth are exposed in a strange grimace.

"There's no danger now," Erik says. "There's no danger, Josef, you're safe here, you're calm, you feel no anxiety. You are simply watching what is happening; you are not there. You can see it all from a safe distance, and it isn't dangerous at all."

"The feet are pale blue," the boy whispers.

"What did you say?"

"Someone's knocking at the door," the boy says, slurring his words. "I open it but there's no one there; I can't see anyone there. But the knocking keeps coming. Someone's playing a trick on me." The patient is breathing more rapidly, his stomach moving jerkily.

"What happens now?" asks Erik.

"I go into the kitchen to get a sandwich."

"You eat a sandwich?"

"But now the knocking starts again, the noise is coming from Lisa's room. The door is open a little. I can see that her lamp is on. I carefully push the door open with the knife and look in. She's on her bed. She has her glasses on, but her eyes are shut and she's panting. Her face is white. Her arms and legs are totally stiff. Then she throws her head back so her throat is stretched right out, and she starts to kick the bottom of the bed with her feet. She just keeps kicking, faster and faster. I tell her to stop, but she keeps kicking, harder. I yell at her but the knife has already started to stab and Mum rushes in and pulls at me and I spin around and the knife moves forward; it just pours out of me; I need to get more knives, I'm afraid to stop, I have to keep going, it's impossible to stop. Mum is crawling across the kitchen floor, it's all red, I have to try the knives on everything, on me, on the furniture, on the walls; I hit and stab and then suddenly I'm really tired and I lie down. I don't know what's happening, my body hurts inside and I'm thirsty, but I just can't move."

Erik stays with the boy, down there in the bright water, their legs moving gently. He follows the wall of rock with his eyes, farther and farther down, endlessly, the water gradually turning darker, blue fading to blue-grey and then, temptingly, to black.

"You had seen," asks Erik, hearing his own voice tremble, "you had seen your father earlier?"

"Yes, down at the soccer field," Josef replies.

He falls silent, looks unsure, stares straight ahead with his sleeping eyes.

Erik sees that the boy's pulse rate is increasing and realizes that his blood pressure is dropping at the same time.

"I want you to sink deeper now," Erik says softly. "You're sinking, you're feeling calmer, better, and—"

"Not Mum?" asks the boy, in a feeble voice.

Erik risks a guess. "Josef, tell me, did you see your older sister, Evelyn, as well?"

65

He observes the boy's face, aware that, if he's wrong, the conjecture can create a rift in the hypnosis. But he feels he must take the leap, because if the patient's condition begins to deteriorate again he will have to stop completely.

"What happened when you saw Evelyn?" he asks.

"I should never have gone out there."

"Was that yesterday?"

"She was hiding in the cottage," the boy whispers, smiling.

"What cottage?"

"Auntie Sonja's," he says.

"Tell me what happens at the cottage."

"I just stand there. Evelyn isn't pleased. I know what she's thinking," he mumbles. "I'm just a dog to her. I'm not worth anything . . ."

The smile is gone. Tears stream from Josef's eyes, and his mouth is trembling.

"Is that what Evelyn says to you?"

"I don't want to, I don't have to, I don't want to," whimpers Josef.

"What is it you don't want to do?"

His eyelids begin to twitch spasmodically.

"What's happening, Josef?"

"She says I have to bite and bite to get my reward."

"Who? Who do you have to bite?"

"There's a picture in the cottage, a picture in a frame that looks like a toadstool. It's Dad, Mum, and Lisa, but—"

His body suddenly tenses, his legs move quickly and limply, he is rising out of the depths of hypnosis. Carefully, Erik slows his ascent, calming him before raising him a few levels. Meticulously, he closes the door on all memory of the day and all memory of the hypnosis. Nothing must be left open, once he begins the careful process of waking him up.

Josef is lying there smiling when Erik finally moves away from his bedside and leaves the room. He goes over to the coffee machine. A feeling of desolation overwhelms him, a sense that something is irrevocably wrong. He glances up when the door to the boy's room opens. The detective strolls over to join him.

"I'm impressed," says Joona quietly, getting out his cell phone.

"Before you make any calls, I just want to stress one thing," says Erik. "The patient always speaks the truth under hypnosis. But it's only a matter of what he himself perceives as the truth. His memory is as subjective as ever, and—"

"I understand that."

"I've hypnotized people suffering from schizophrenia," Erik goes on, "and they were just as deeply detached from reality under hypnosis as they were in a conscious state."

"What is it you're trying to say?"

"Josef talked about his sister."

"Yes, she wanted him to bite like a dog and so on," says Joona. He dials a number and puts the phone to his ear.

"There's no proof his sister told him to do that," Erik explains.

"But she might have," says Joona, raising a hand to silence Erik. "Anja, my little treasure."

A soft voice can be heard at the other end of the phone.

"Can you check on something for me? . . . Yes, exactly. Josef Ek has an aunt called Sonja, and she has a house or a cottage somewhere . . . Yes, that's—you're a star." Joona looks up at Erik. "Sorry. You wanted to say something else?"

"Just that it's by no means certain it was Josef who murdered the family."

"But is it possible that his wounds are self-inflicted? Could he have cut himself like this in your opinion?"

"Not likely."

"But is it possible?" Joona persists.

"Theoretically, yes," Erik replies.

"Then I think our killer's lying in there," says Joona.

"I think so too."

"Is he in any condition to run away from the hospital?"

"No." Erik smiles weakly in surprise.

Joona heads for the door.

"Are you going to the aunt's cottage?" asks Erik.

"Yes."

"I could come with you," says Erik. "The sister could be injured, or she could be in a state of shock."

18

Simone is already awake before the telephone on Erik's bedside table starts to ring.

Erik mumbles something about balloons and streamers, picks up the phone, and hurries out of the room, closing the door behind him.

The voice she hears through the door sounds sympathetic, almost tender. After a while, Erik creeps back into the bedroom and she asks who called.

"Police . . . a detective . . . I didn't catch his name," he says, and explains that he has to go to Karolinska University Hospital.

She looks at the alarm clock and closes her eyes.

"Sleep now, Sixan," he whispers, and leaves the room.

Her nightgown has twisted itself awkwardly around her. Unwinding and yanking it into place, she turns onto her side and lies still, listening to Erik's movements.

He dresses quickly, then goes rummaging for something in the wardrobe. Next, she hears a metallic *ping* when he tosses the shoehorn back into the drawer. After a little while she hears the faint sound of the street door closing.

She tries for a long time to get back to sleep, but without success. She doesn't think it sounded as if Erik was talking to a police officer. He sounded too relaxed. Maybe, she tells herself, he was just tired.

She gets up to pee, has a yoghurt drink, and goes back to bed. Then she starts to think about what happened ten years ago, and all chance of sleep is gone. She lies there for half an hour, and then, unable to resist her suspicions, switches on the bedside light, picks up the phone, and thumbs through the display to find the last incoming call. She stares at the number for a moment, knowing she ought to turn off the light and go back to sleep, but finally she calls the number anyway. It rings three times, there is a click, and she hears a woman laughing a short distance away from the phone.

"Stop it, Erik," says the woman happily, and then the voice is very close. "Daniella Richards. Hello?"

Simone says nothing. The woman waits a bit, then says *aloha* in a wearily sarcastic voice before ending the call. Simone remains sitting there, telephone in hand. She tries to understand why Erik said it was a police officer, a male police officer, who rang. She wants to find a reasonable explanation, but she can't stop her thoughts from finding their way back to that time ten years ago when she suddenly realized that Erik was deceiving her.

It just happened to have been the same day Erik informed her that he was finished with hypnosis forever.

Simone remembers that she hadn't been at her newly opened gallery that day, a rare occasion; maybe Benjamin wasn't in school, maybe she'd taken the day off, but at any rate she was sitting at the kitchen table in the terrace house in Järfälla going through the mail when she caught sight of a pale blue envelope addressed to Erik. The sender's name on the back simply said: Maja.

There are times when you know with every fibre of your being that something is wrong.

Simone had been married to Erik for eight years when, fingers trembling, she opened the envelope from Maja. Ten colour photographs fell out onto the kitchen table. The pictures had not been taken by a professional photographer. Blurred close-ups: a woman's breast, a mouth and a naked throat, pale green underwear, black hair in tight curls. Erik was in one of the pictures. He looked surprised and happy.

Maja was a pretty, very young woman with dark, strong eyebrows and a large, serious mouth. In the only photo that showed her completely, she was lying on a narrow bed dressed in just her underwear, strands of black hair falling over her broad white breasts. She looked happy, too, a faint blush high on her cheeks.

It is difficult to recall the feeling of being deceived. For a long time everything was just a sense of sorrow, a strange, empty craving in her stomach, a desire to avoid painful thoughts. And yet she remembers that the first thing she felt was surprise, a gaping, stupid surprise at being so comprehensively taken in by someone she had trusted completely. And then came the embarrassment, followed by a despairing sense of inadequacy, burning rage, and loneliness.

Simone lies in bed as these thoughts go round and round in her head, spinning off in various painful directions. She remembers the way Erik looked into her eyes and promised he hadn't had an affair with Maja—that he didn't even know anyone named Maja. She had asked him three times, and each time he had sworn he didn't know a Maja. Then she had pulled out the photos and thrown them at him, one by one.

Slowly the sky grows light above the city. She falls asleep a few minutes before Erik returns. He tries to be quiet, but when he sits on the bed she wakes up. Erik says he's going for a shower. Looking up at him, she can tell he's taken a lot of pills again. Heart pounding, she asks him the name of the policeman who called during the night. When he doesn't answer, she realizes that he's passed out in the middle of the conversation. Simone tells him she called the number, and did a policeman answer? No, it was some giggling woman called Daniella. But Erik just can't keep awake; it's infuriating. Then she yells at him, demands to know, accuses him of having destroyed everything, just when she had begun to trust him again.

She's sitting up in bed now, staring at him. He doesn't seem to understand her agitation. She says the words that, no matter how many times she has thought them, seem no less painful, sad, or distant from her hopes.

"It might be best if we separate."

That seems to get his attention momentarily. But Simone is already gathering her pillow and the duvet. Entering the guest room, she lies on the sofa and cries for a long time, then blows her nose. Now it's really morning. She hasn't the strength to deal with her family right now. She goes to the bathroom, washes up, then creeps back to the bedroom. Erik is out like a light, so she collects an outfit and dresses in the guest room.

She hastily puts on her makeup and leaves the apartment to have breakfast somewhere before she goes to the gallery.

She reads in a café in Kungsträdgården for a long time before she can manage to get down the sandwich she ordered with her coffee. She puts her newspaper down for a moment and looks through the café's big window, which overlooks a large stage. A dozen or so men are preparing for some kind of event. Pink tents have been erected. A barrier is placed around a small ramp. Suddenly something happens. The men stumble backwards, yelling at one another. There is a crackling noise and a rocket shoots up into the air. Simone leans forward to follow its flight. It rises into the bright morning sky, then bursts in a transparent blue glow, and the explosion reverberates between the buildings.

19

Simone sits in the office of the gallery, taking in the large self-portrait of the artist Sim Shulman posing in a black ninja costume, a sword raised high above his head, when the phone in her bag begins to buzz.

"Simone Bark," she answers, forcing the sadness out of her voice.

"Hello, it's Siv Sturesson from Edsberg School," says an older woman.

"Oh," says Simone hesitantly. "Yes?"

"I'm just calling to see how Benjamin is."

"I'm sorry, I don't understand."

"He's not in school today," says the woman, "and he hasn't called in sick. We always get in touch with the parents in cases like this."

"Right," says Simone. "I'll call home and check. Both Benjamin and his father were still there this morning when I left. I'll get back to you."

She rings off and immediately calls the apartment. It isn't like Benjamin to oversleep or flout the rules.

Nobody picks up at home. Erik is supposed to have the morning off. A fresh fear sinks its claws into her, before it occurs to her that Erik is probably lying there snoring with his mouth open, knocked out by his beloved pills, while Benjamin is listening to loud music. She tries Benjamin's phone; no reply. She leaves a short message, then tries Erik's mobile, but of course it's switched off.

She calls out to her assistant at the art gallery. "Yiva, I have to go home. I'll be back soon."

Her assistant peers out of the office, a thick file in her hand, and calls out, with a smile, "Kiss-kiss!"

But Simone is too stressed to return their running joke. Throwing her coat around her shoulders, she picks up her bag and almost runs to the underground station.

There is a particular silence outside the door of an empty house. As soon as Simone puts her key in the lock, she knows no one is in.

The skates lie forgotten on the floor, but Benjamin's backpack, shoes, and jacket are gone, as are Erik's overcoat and scarf. The Puma bag containing Benjamin's medication is in his room. She hopes this means Erik has given Benjamin his injection.

Simone glances around the room, thinking it is a bit sad that he has taken down his Harry Potter poster and put almost all his toys in a box in the cupboard. He was suddenly in a hurry to grow up when he met Aida.

It occurs to Simone that perhaps Benjamin is with her now.

Benjamin is only fourteen, Aida is seventeen; he claims they're just friends, but it's obvious that she's his girlfriend. Has he even told her he has a blood disorder? Does she know that the slightest blow could cost him his life if he hasn't taken his medication properly?

She sits down and buries her face in her hands, trying to stop all the terrifying thoughts. Simone can't help worrying about her son. In her mind's eye she has always seen Benjamin being hit in the face by a basketball during break time or imagined a spontaneous bleed suddenly starting inside his head: a dark bead expanding like a star, trickling along all the convolutions of his brain.

She is overcome by an almost unbearable feeling of shame when she remembers the way she lost patience with Benjamin because he wouldn't walk. He was two years old and still crawling everywhere. She would scold him and then tease him when he cried. Said he looked like a baby. Benjamin would try to walk, take a few steps, but then the terrible pain would force him to lie down again.

They didn't know then that he had a blood disorder, that the blood vessels in his joints burst when he stood up.

Once Benjamin had been diagnosed with von Willebrand's disease, it was Erik who took over the care the condition demanded, not Simone. It was Erik who gently moved Benjamin's joints back and forth after the night's immobility, in order to reduce the risk of internal bleeding; Erik who carried out the complex injections, where the needle absolutely must not penetrate the muscle but must be emptied carefully and slowly beneath the skin. The technique was far more painful than a normal injection. For the first few years, Benjamin would sit with his face pressed against his father's stomach, weeping silently as the needle went in. These days he went on eating his breakfast without looking, just offering his arm to Erik, who swabbed it, administered the injection, and put on a dressing.

The factor preparation that helped Benjamin's blood to coagulate was called Haemate. Simone thought it sounded like a Greek goddess of revenge. It was a horrible and unsatisfactory drug that was delivered in the form of a yellow, freeze-dried, granular powder, which had to be measured, dissolved, mixed, and warmed into the correct dosage before it could be administered. Haemate greatly increased the risk of blood clots, and they lived in constant hope that something better would come along. But with the Haemate, a high dose of desmopressin, and Cyklokapron in a nasal spray to prevent bleeds in the mucous membrane, Benjamin was relatively safe.

She could still remember when they had received his laminated alert card from the Emergency Blood Service, adorned with Benjamin's birthday photo: his laughing four-year-old face beneath the message:

I have von Willebrand's disease. If anything happens to me, please call the Emergency Blood Service immediately: 040-33-10-10.

Since meeting Aida, Benjamin always wears his mobile phone hanging around his neck from a black strap with skulls on it. They text each other far into the night, and Benjamin still has the phone around his neck when Erik or Simone wakes him up in the morning.

Simone searches carefully among all the papers and magazines on

Benjamin's desk. Then she opens a drawer and moves aside a book about World War II, unearthing a scrap of paper with the imprint of a pair of lips pressed upon it in black lipstick and a telephone number below. She hurries into the kitchen and punches in the number, waits while the line rings, and is throwing a stinking sponge into the waste bin when someone finally picks up.

A faint, croaking voice, breathing heavily.

"Hello," says Simone. "I'm sorry to disturb you. My name is Simone Bark. I'm Benjamin's mother. I was wondering if—"

The voice, which seems to belong to a woman, hisses that she doesn't know any Benjamin and this must be a wrong number.

"Wait, please," says Simone, trying to sound calm. "Aida and my son usually hang out together. I was hoping you might know where they could be. I really need to get hold of Benjamin."

"Ten . . . ten—"

"I'm sorry, I can't make out what you're saying."

"Ten . . . sta."

"Tensta? Aida's in Tensta?"

"Yes. That bloody . . . tattoo."

Simone thinks she can hear an oxygen machine working slowly, a rhythmic hissing noise in the background.

"I'm sorry, I don't understand. Tattoo?" she pleads.

The woman snaps something and ends the call. Simone sits there staring at the telephone, decides to ring the woman back, then suddenly understands what she meant. She quickly calls information and gets the address of a tattoo parlour in the shopping centre in Tensta. Simone's entire body shudders as she pictures Benjamin at this very moment succumbing to temptation, allowing his skin to be pierced for a tattoo; the blood begins to flow and cannot coagulate.

20

Simone stares out the window of the underground train. She is still sweating after leaving the empty flat and running to the station.

She ought to have taken a cab, but she tells herself that nothing has happened; she always worries unnecessarily.

A man opposite her fusses with a newspaper. From the reflection in the window she can see that he glances at her from time to time.

"Hey," says the man. His voice is irritatingly insistent.

She ignores him, looking out the window.

"*Hello-o?*" says the man.

She realizes he has no intention of giving up until he has her attention.

"Hey, don't you hear me? I'm talking to you!" the man persists.

Simone turns to him. "I can hear you perfectly well," she says calmly.

"Why don't you answer me, then?" he asks.

"I'm answering you now."

He blinks a couple of times, and here it comes. "You're a woman, aren't you?"

"Is that all you want to know?" she asks, turning back to the window.

He moves across to sit beside her. "Wait, listen to this. I had a woman, and my woman, my woman—"

Simone feels a few drops of spittle spatter her cheek.

"She was like Elizabeth Taylor," he goes on. "You know who she was?" He lays two fingers on her arm, confidentially. "Do you know who Elizabeth Taylor was?"

"Yes," says Simone impatiently. "Of course I do."

He leans back, satisfied with her answer. "She was always finding some new man," he whines. "Wanting better and better all the time, diamond rings and presents and necklaces."

The train slows down and Simone sees that they've arrived in Tensta.

"This is my stop. I need to get off," she says. She stands up.

"I bet you do," the man says, placing himself in her way. "Come on, give me a little hug. I just want a little hug."

Stiffly, through clenched teeth, she excuses herself and moves his arm away. She feels his hand on her butt, but at the same moment the train stops and the man loses his balance and falls back against the seat.

"Whore," he says calmly, as she moves away.

She steps off the train, runs out of the station, over a Plexiglas-covered bridge, and down the steps. In the middle of the square, inside the shopping centre, there's a huge board, a directory, and a floor plan that lists all the different shops. Breathing heavily, Simone goes through it until she finds Tensta Tattoos. It's at the far end of the mall. Simone heads in the direction of the escalator.

In her mind's eye, she imagines a circle of kids surrounding a boy lying on the ground. She pushes her way through the crowd and realizes that it's Benjamin, bleeding endlessly from some tacky unfinished tattoo.

She takes the escalator two steps at a time, reaching the top quickly. Stepping off, she catches sight of an odd movement at the other end of the centre, in a deserted area where the shops are all vacant. It looks as if someone is hanging over the barrier.

She sets off in that direction, and as she gets closer she can see clearly what is happening: two boys are holding another child, a little girl, over the second-floor barrier. It's a fall to the lower level of at least thirty feet. A tall figure is walking nearby, flapping his arms as if he were warming himself at a grill.

The girl is clearly terrified, but the other children appear calm as they dangle her over the edge.

"What are you doing?" Simone yells as she walks towards them. She wants to break into a run, but she's afraid if she startles them they will lose their grip.

The boys have spotted Simone and pretend to let the girl go. Both the girl and Simone scream, but the boys hold on and pull her up slowly. One of them gives Simone a strange smile before they run away. Only the taller boy remains behind. The girl curls up into a ball next to the barrier, sobbing. Simone stops, her heart racing, and crouches beside her.

"Are you all right?"

The girl just shakes her head.

"We need to go and find a security guard," Simone says.

The girl shakes her head again. Her whole body is trembling. The tall, plump boy is just standing there watching them. He is dressed in a dark padded jacket and black sunglasses.

"Who are you?" Simone asks him.

Instead of replying, he takes a pack of cards out of his pocket and begins to flick through them, cutting and shuffling.

"Who are you?" Simone repeats, more loudly this time. "Are those boys your friends?"

His expression doesn't change.

"Why didn't you do something? They could have killed her."

Simone can feel the adrenaline still surging through her system, the rapid pulse at her temples, the pounding in her chest. "I asked you a question. Why didn't you do something?" She stares hard at him.

He still doesn't reply.

"Idiot!" she screams.

The boy begins to move away slowly, but when she takes a step towards him as if to prevent his escape he stumbles, dropping his cards on the floor. He mutters something to himself and slinks toward the escalator.

Simone turns to take care of the little girl, but she has disappeared. Simone runs back along the upper walkway, past the dark and empty shops, but she doesn't spot the girl or either of the boys. Suddenly she realizes she's come to a stop outside the tattoo shop; the windows are covered in an opaque laminated film, with a picture of Fenrir the wolf, applied so sloppily it is creased and buckled.

She pushes open the door and enters, but the place seems to be empty. The walls are covered with pictures of tattoos. She looks around and is just about to leave when she hears a high, anxious voice. "Nicky? Where are you? Say something."

A black curtain opens and a girl comes out with a cell phone pressed to her ear. Her upper body is naked. A few small drops of blood are trickling down her throat. Her expression is concentrated, worried.

"Nicky," the girl says into the phone. "What's happened?"

Her breasts are covered in goose bumps, but she doesn't seem aware that she's half naked.

"Can I ask you something?" Simone says.

The girl leaves the shop and starts to run. Simone is following her toward the door when she hears a familiar voice come from behind.

"Aida?"

She turns to see that it's Benjamin.

"Mum, what are you doing here? Where's Nicky?" he asks.

"Who?"

"Aida's little brother. He's retarded. Did you see him out there?"

"No, I—"

"He's big, and he's wearing black sunglasses."

Simone walks slowly back inside the tattoo shop and sits down.

Aida comes back with the boy Simone chased. They stop outside the door, and Simone can see him nodding at everything Aida says, then wiping his nose. The girl comes in, shielding her breasts with one hand, walks past Simone and Benjamin without looking at them, and disappears behind the curtain. Simone just manages to see that her neck is red because she has had a dark red rose tattooed next to a small Star of David.

"What's going on?" asks Benjamin.

"I was looking for you. Then I saw some boys—they must have been sick; they were holding a little girl over the barrier. Aida's brother was just standing there and—"

"Did you say anything to them?"

"They stopped when I got to them, but they seemed to find the whole thing funny."

Benjamin looks very upset; his cheeks flush red, and his eyes dart all over the place, searching, as if he wants to run away.

"I don't like you hanging around here," says Simone.

"I can do what I want," he replies.

"You're too young to—"

"Just leave it," he says, his voice low.

"Why? Were you thinking of getting a tattoo as well?"

"No."

"They're horrible, these tattoos on necks and faces—"

"Mum."

"They're ugly."

"Aida can hear what you're saying."

"I don't care what—"

"Would you go outside, please?" Benjamin says sharply.

She looks at him. The tone doesn't sound right coming from him, but she knows that she and Erik sound exactly like that more and more these days.

"You're coming home with me," she says calmly.

"I'll come if you go outside first," he says.

Simone leaves the shop and sees Nicky standing by the dark window, his arms folded over his chest. She goes over to him, tries to look pleasant, and points to his Pokémon cards.

"Everybody likes Pikachu best," she says.

He nods to himself.

"Although I prefer Mew," she goes on.

"Mew learns things," he says carefully.

"Sorry I yelled at you."

"They can't do anything about Wailord, nobody can deal with him, he's the biggest," he goes on.

"Is he the biggest of all?"

"Yes," the boy says seriously.

She picks up a card he's dropped. "Who's this?"

Benjamin comes out, his eyes shining.

"Arceus," replies Nicky, placing the card on top of the pack.

"He looks nice," says Simone.

Nicky beams at her.

"Let's go," Benjamin says, his voice muted.

"'Bye then," says Simone, with a smile.

"Byebyetakecare," Nicky replies mechanically.

Benjamin walks alongside his mother in silence.

"We'll take a taxi," she announces as they approach the underground station. "I'm sick of the underground."

"OK," says Benjamin, turning away.

"Hang on," she says.

She's spotted one of the boys who threatened the girl. He's standing by the barrier in the station, and he seems to be waiting for something. She can feel Benjamin trying to pull her away.

"What's the matter?" she asks.

"Come on, let's go, you said we were going to take a taxi."

"I just need to have a word with him."

"Mum, just leave it," begs Benjamin.

His face is pale and anxious and he remains where he is as she resolutely goes over to the boy.

She sticks her hand out and turns the boy to face her. He is only about thirteen years old, but instead of being afraid or surprised, he smiles scornfully at her, as if she's just fallen into his trap.

"You're coming with me to the security guard," she says firmly.

"What did you say, you old cow?"

"I saw you—"

"Shut it!" the boy hisses. "Unless you shut your mouth, we'll fuck you as a punishment."

Simone is so stunned she doesn't know what to say. The boy spits on the ground in front of her, jumps over the barrier, and disappears down the passageway.

Simone is shaken; she goes back outside to Benjamin.

"What did he say?" he asks.

"Nothing," she says.

They walk to the taxi stand and settle in the back seat of a cab. As they pull away from the shopping centre, Simone tells him about the call from his school.

"Aida wanted me to be with her when she got her tattoo altered," says Benjamin quietly.

"That was kind of you."

They travel in silence.

"Did you call Nicky an idiot?" asks Benjamin.

"I said the wrong thing. I'm the one who's an idiot."

"But how could you?"

"I do the wrong thing sometimes, Benjamin," she says, subdued.

From the Tranberg bridge, Simone looks down at Stora Essingen. The ice has not formed, but the water looks slow and pale.

"It looks as if Dad and I are going to separate," she says.

"What? But why?"

"It's not because of you."

"I asked you why."

"There's no real answer," she begins. "Your dad . . . it's hard to explain. Even when you really love someone—and I really love your father—it can all just come to an end." Her voice falters. "You don't think that when you first meet, when you have a child . . . But after a while, if the lies pile up . . . I'm sorry, I shouldn't be talking about this."

"I don't want to get involved."

"Sorry I—"

"Just leave it!" he snaps.

21

Although he knew he wouldn't be able to sleep in the car, Erik has made an attempt. But he remains wide-awake as they drive toward the cottage where they hope to find Evelyn Ek, despite the fact that Detective Joona Linna has driven very smoothly toward Värmdö.

Now, though, off the main road, loose gravel begins to rattle against the bottom of the chassis as they pass an old sawmill.

Erik peers out the windscreen, waiting while Joona speaks quietly over the police radio with his colleagues, who are also on their way to Värmdö.

"I was thinking," says Erik, after Joona has replaced the transmitter.

"Yes?"

"I said Josef Ek couldn't run away from the hospital, but if he could inflict all those knife wounds on himself, maybe we can't be too sure."

"I was thinking the same thing," Joona replies, "so I've got somebody outside the room."

"It's probably completely unnecessary," says Erik.

"Yes."

They pull to the side of the road where three cars have stopped next to a telephone pole, one behind the other. Joona momentarily joins four police officers who stand talking in the white light, putting on their bullet-proof vests and pointing at a map. The sunlight flashes on the glass of an old greenhouse nearby.

Joona gets back in the car, carrying the cold air on his clothes. He drums the fingers of one hand pensively on the steering wheel as he waits for the others to return to their cars.

Suddenly a rapid sequence of notes comes from the police radio, then a loud crackling that stops abruptly. Joona switches to another channel and checks that everyone in the team is in contact, exchanging a few words with each one before turning the key in the ignition.

The cars continue alongside a ploughed field, past a grove of birch trees and a large, rusty silo.

"Stay in the car when we get there," says Joona quietly.

"Fine," says Erik.

A flock of crows struts across the surface of the road, suddenly taking flight and flapping away as the cars approach.

"Are there any negative aspects to hypnosis?" Joona asks abruptly.

"What do you mean?"

"You were one of the best in the world, but you stopped."

"People sometimes have good reasons for keeping things hidden," Erik says.

"Of course, but—"

"And those reasons are very difficult to judge when it comes to hypnosis."

Joona gives him a sceptical look. "Why do I think that's not why you gave it up?"

"I don't want to talk about it," says Erik.

Tree trunks flash by at the side of the road. As they drive deeper into the forest, it grows darker. Gravel clatters against the undercarriage of the car. Turning off onto a narrow forest track, they pass a number of summer cottages and finally come to a stop. Far away among the fir trees, Joona can see a small brown wooden house in a shady glade.

"I'm trusting you to stay put," he tells Erik before he leaves the car.

As Joona walks towards the house where the other police officers are already waiting, he thinks once again about Josef under hypnosis. The words that just poured out between his flaccid lips. A little boy describing bestial aggression with remote clarity. The memory must have been perfectly clear to him: his little sister's feverish cramps, the surge of rage, the choice of knives, the euphoria at crossing the line. But towards the end of the session, Josef's account had become confused, and it was more difficult to understand what he meant, what he was really perceiving, whether his older sister, Evelyn, had actually forced him to carry out the murders.

Gathering the four officers around him, Joona outlines the gravity of the situation and provides guidelines for the use of firearms. Any shots that might be fired must be directed at the legs, whatever the circumstances.

"I want all of you to proceed with caution so as not to frighten the girl," he says. "She may be afraid, she may be injured, but at the same time don't forget for one second that we may be dealing with a dangerous person."

They all study the house for a moment. Its chocolate-brown façade is made up of overlapping shingles; the window and doorframes are white, the front door is black. The windows are covered with pink curtains. No smoke comes from the chimney. On the porch there is a broom and a yellow plastic bucket full of pine cones. Joona sends one patrol of three officers around the house and away from the garden so they can approach the back of the house from a safe distance.

They set off along the forest track; one of them stops and inserts a plug of snuff under his top lip.

22

Joona watches the patrol spread out around the house at a reasonable distance, weapons drawn. A twig snaps. In the distance he can hear the tapping of a woodpecker echoing through the forest. Joona slowly approaches the house, trying to see something through the pink curtain fabric. He signals to Police Constable Kristina Andersson, a young woman with a pointed chin, to stop on the path. Her cheeks are red, and she nods without taking her eyes off the house. With an air of total calm, she draws her service pistol and moves a few steps to the side.

The house is empty, Joona thinks. Gingerly, he places one foot on the porch steps. They creak under his weight. He watches the curtains for sudden movements as he knocks on the door. Nothing happens. He waits for a while and then stiffens, thinking he's heard something, and scans the forest, beyond the brush and the tree trunks. He draws his pistol, a heavy Smith & Wesson that he prefers to the standard-issue Sig Sauer, removes the safety catch, and checks the cartridges. Suddenly there is a loud rustling at the edge of the forest and a deer dashes between the trees. Kristina Andersson gives Joona a strained smile when he glances over at her. He points at the window, moves cautiously forward, and looks in through a gap to one side of a curtain.

In the dim interior he can see a cane table with a scratched glass surface and a tan corduroy couch. On the back of a red wooden chair, two pairs of white pants have been hung up to dry. In the pantry there are several packets of instant macaroni, jars of pesto, canned foods, and a bag of apples. He catches the glint of various pieces of cutlery on the floor in front of the sink and under the kitchen table. He signals to Kristina that he's going in, then tries the door. The knob turns in his hand; he pushes it open and steps quickly out of the firing line, looking to Kristina for the all-clear. She nods, gesturing for him to enter. He looks inside and steps over the threshold.

From the car, Erik has only a vague sense of what is happening. He sees Joona Linna disappear into the little brown house, followed by another officer. Erik's eyes are dry and sensitive—a side effect of his codeine capsules. He peers out at the brown house and the policemen, with their careful movements and the dark glimmer of their drawn guns. It is quiet. The trees are bare in the sterile December chill. The light and the colours make Erik think of school trips when he was a child: the smell of rotting tree trunks, the funkiness of mushrooms in the wet earth.

His mother had worked part-time as a school nurse at the high school in Sollentuna and was convinced of the benefits of fresh air. It was Erik's mother who had wanted him to be called Erik Maria; she had once taken a language course in Vienna and had gone to the Burgtheater to see Strindberg's *The Father* with Klaus Maria Brandauer in the lead. She'd been so taken with the performance that she'd carried the actor's name with her for years. As a kid, Erik always tried to hide his middle name; as a teenager, he saw himself in the Johnny Cash song "A Boy Named Sue."

Some gal would giggle and I'd get red,
And some guy'd laugh and I'd bust his head,
I tell ya, life ain't easy for a boy named Sue.

Erik's father had worked for the National Insurance Office. But he'd really had only one genuine interest in life. In his spare time, he was a magician and would dress up in a homemade cape and a second-hand formal suit, crowning the outfit with a collapsible top hat, and make Erik and his friends sit on wooden chairs in the garage, where he'd built a little stage with secret trapdoors. Most of his tricks came from the Bernando catalogue: magic wands that would suddenly extend with a clatter, billiard balls that multiplied with the help of a shell, a velvet bag with secret compartments, and the glittering hand guillotine. These days Erik remembers his father with joy and tenderness: the way he would start the tape recorder with his foot, playing Jean Michel Jarre as he made magical movements over a skull floating in the air.

Erik hopes with all his heart that his father never noticed how embarrassed he became as he grew older, rolling his eyes at his friends behind his father's back.

Erik had always wanted to become a doctor. He had never really wanted to do anything else, hadn't imagined another kind of life. He remembers sitting there on the sofa in Sollentuna as an eighteen-year-old, staring at his top grades, then letting his gaze roam over his parents' prototypically middle-class living room, the bookshelves empty of books but adorned with knick-knacks and souvenirs: silver-framed photographs of his parents' confirmations, wedding, and fiftieth-birthday celebrations, followed by a dozen or more shots of Erik, from a chubby baby in a christening gown to a grinning teenager in stovepipe trousers.

His mother came into the room that day and handed him the application forms for medical school. His mother often said the Swedes were spoiled, taking their welfare society for granted when it was most probably nothing more than a small historical parenthesis. She meant that the system of free health care and dental care, free child care and primary education, free secondary schools and free university education, could simply disappear at any time. But right now there was an opportunity for a perfectly ordinary boy or girl to study to become a doctor, or an architect, or a top economist, at any university in the country without the need for a private fortune, grants, or charity hand-outs. As soon as Erik set foot in the medical school at Karolinska Institute, it was as if he had found his true home.

When he decided to specialize in psychiatry, he realized that the medical profession was going to suit him even better than he'd imagined. A trainee doctor has to perform eighteen months of general service before he is fully qualified to practise; Erik spent this period working for Médecins sans Frontières. He had wound up at a field hospital in Kismayo, south of Mogadisho, in Somalia. The equipment consisted of material discarded by Swedish hospitals: X-ray machines from the sixties, drugs well past their best-before date, and rusty, stained beds from old wards that had been closed down or rebuilt. In Somalia he encountered severely traumatized people for the first time: young people who would tonelessly relate how they had been forced to carry out horrific crimes; women who had been so severely abused they were no longer able to speak. Working with them—with children who had become completely apathetic and had lost the desire to play; with women who were unable to look up and meet another's eyes—Erik discovered that he wanted to devote himself to helping people who were held prisoner by the terrible things that had been done to them, who were still suffering despite the fact that the perpetrators were long gone.

Upon returning home, Erik trained in psychotherapy in Stockholm. But it was not until he specialized in psychotraumatology and disaster psychiatry that he came into contact with the various theories regarding hypnosis. What he found most attractive about hypnosis was its speed, the fact that a psychiatrist could get to the root of trauma straight away. When it came to working with war victims and the victims of natural disasters, speed could prove immensely important.

He pursued his training with the European Society of Clinical Hypnosis and soon became a member of the Society for Clinical and Experimental Hypnosis, the European Board of Medical Hypnosis, and the Swedish Society for Clinical Hypnosis; he became awed by the groundbreaking work of Karen Olness, the American paediatrician who turned to hypnosis to alleviate the suffering of those in chronic pain and chronically ill children, and he struck up a correspondence with her that lasted several years.

Next, Erik was with the Red Cross in Uganda. In his five years there, the situations he encountered were acute, overwhelming. There was little time to try out and develop his experience of hypnosis; he used it perhaps fewer than a dozen times, and then only in the most straightforward contexts: to block the perception of pain or to ease phobic fixations. And then, one day in his final year, he came across a young girl who was locked in a room because she wouldn't stop screaming. The Catholic nuns working as nurses explained that the girl had been found crawling along the road from the shanty town north of Mbale. They thought she was a Bagisu, because she spoke Lugisu. She hadn't slept one single night and, instead, kept shouting that she was a terrible demon with fire in her eyes. Erik asked to see her. As soon as he did, he realized she was suffering from acute dehydration, but when he tried to get her to drink, she bellowed as if the mere sight of water burned her like flames. She rolled on the floor, screaming. He decided to try hypnosis to calm her down. A nun translated his words into Bukusu, which they suspected the girl could understand, and after a while, once she began to listen, it proved very easy to hypnotize her. In one hour the girl recounted her entire psychic trauma.

A tanker truck from Jinja had run off the road just north of the shanty town on the Mbale-Soroti road. The heavy vehicle had overturned, gouging out a deep ditch along the side of the road and puncturing a hole in the huge tank. Gasoline gushed out onto the ground. The girl had raced home and told her uncle about the gasoline just disappearing into the earth. Her uncle had run to the spot with two empty plastic containers. By the time the girl caught up with him, a dozen or so people were already by the tanker, filling buckets with gasoline from the ditch. The smell was appalling, the sun was shining, and the air was hot. The girl's uncle waved to her. She took the first container and started hauling it homeward. It was very heavy. She stopped to lift it onto her head, and saw a woman in a blue head scarf standing up to her knees in gasoline by the tanker, filling small glass bottles. Farther down the road in the direction of the town, the girl caught sight of a man wearing a yellow camouflage shirt. He was walking along with a cigarette in his mouth, and when he inhaled, the tip of the cigarette glowed red.

Erik vividly remembers how the girl had looked when she was speaking. The tears poured down her cheeks as she told him in a thick, dull voice that she had caught the fire from the cigarette with her eyes and carried it to the woman in the blue head scarf. Because when she turned back and looked at the woman, she caught fire. First the blue head scarf, then her entire body was enveloped in huge flames. *The fire was in my eyes*, she said. Suddenly it was like a fire storm around the tanker. The girl began to run, hearing nothing but screams behind her.

Later, Erik and the nun talked to the girl at length about what she had revealed under hypnosis. They explained over and over again that it was the vapour from the gasoline, the fumes with the powerful smell, that had begun to burn. The man's cigarette had set fire to the tanker through the air; it had had nothing to do with her.

A month or so after this event, Erik returned to Stockholm and applied for research funding from the Swedish Medical Research Council in order to immerse himself seriously in the treatment of trauma with hypnosis at the Karolinska Institute. And not long after his return to Sweden he met Simone at a big party at the university. He had noticed her curly, strawberry-blonde hair first of all. Then he had seen her face, the curve of her pale forehead, her fair skin scattered with light brown freckles. She was excited, rosy-cheeked and sparkling, and looked like a bookmark angel, small and slender. He can still remember what she was wearing that evening: a green silk fitted blouse that set off her bright green eyes.

Erik blinks hard, leans closer to the windscreen, and tries to see between the trees, but he can only sense movement inside the brown cabin. Most likely, Evelyn is not there. The curtains shift; the front door swings open; Joona Linna steps out on the porch, and three policemen come around the house and join him. They point to the road and the other cottages. One unfolds a map, and they gather around him to consult it. Then Joona seems to want to show them something inside the house. They all go in, the last one closing the door quietly.

Suddenly Erik spots someone standing in the trees where the ground slopes down toward the bog. It's a slender woman with a double-barrelled shotgun, which she drags along the ground, letting it bounce gently against the blueberry bushes and moss.

The police have not spotted her, and she has had no opportunity to see them. Erik keys in the number of Joona's mobile phone, which begins to ring in the car. It's lying next to him on the driver's seat.

Without any urgency, the woman wanders between the trees, shotgun in hand. Erik realizes a dangerous situation could arise if the woman and the police take each other by surprise. Despite his promise to Joona, he has no choice. He gets out of the car. "Hi, there," he calls.

The woman stops and turns to look at him.

"Chilly today," he says quietly.

"What?"

"It's cold in the shade," he says, a little louder this time.

"Yes," she replies.

"Are you new here?" he asks, walking towards her.

"No, I borrow the house from my aunt."

"Is Sonja your aunt?"

"Yes," she says, with a smile.

Erik goes up to her. "What are you hunting?"

"Hare," she replies.

"Can I have a look at your gun?"

Obligingly, she breaks it and hands it over. The tip of her nose is red. Dry pine needles are caught in her sandy-coloured hair.

"Evelyn," he says calmly, "there are some police officers here who would like to talk to you."

She looks anxious and takes a step backwards.

"If you have time," he says, with a smile.

She gives a faint nod and Erik shouts in the direction of the house. Joona emerges with an irritated look on his face, ready to order Erik back to the car. When he sees the woman he stiffens.

"This is Evelyn," says Erik, handing him the shotgun.

"Hello."

The colour suddenly drains from her face, and she looks as if she's going to faint.

"I need to talk to you," Joona explains, in a serious voice.

"No," she whispers.

"Come inside."

"I don't want to."

"You don't want to go inside?"

Evelyn turns to Erik. "Do I have to?" she asks, trembling.

"No," he replies. "You decide."

"Please come in," says Joona.

She shakes her head but begins to head for the house anyway.

"I'll wait outside," says Erik.

He walks a little way up the drive. The gravel is covered in pine needles and brown cones. He hears Evelyn scream through the walls of the house. Just one scream. It sounds lonely and despairing, an expression of incomprehensible loss. He recognizes that scream well from his time in Uganda.

Evelyn is sitting on the sofa with both hands clamped between her thighs, her face ashen. On the floor by her feet is a photograph in a frame that looks like a toadstool. It's a mother and father—her mother and father—sitting in something that looks like a hammock, with her little sister between them. Her parents squint into the bright sunlight, while the little girl's glasses shine as if they were white.

"I'm sorry for your loss," says Joona.

Her chin quivers.

"Do you think you might be able to help us understand what's happened?" he asks. The wooden chair creaks under his weight. He waits for a while, then continues. "Where were you on Monday, December seventh?"

She shakes her head.

"Yesterday," he clarifies.

"I was here," she says faintly.

"In the cottage?"

She meets his gaze. "Yes."

"You didn't go out all day?"

"No."

"You just sat here?"

She makes a gesture toward the bed and the textbooks on political science.

"You were studying?"

"Yes."

"So you didn't leave the house yesterday?"

"No."

"Is there anyone who can confirm that?"

"What?"

"Was anyone here with you?" asks Joona.

"No."

"Have you any idea who could have done this to your family?"

She shakes her head.

"Has anyone threatened you?" She doesn't seem to hear him. "Evelyn?"

"What? What did you say?" Her fingers are still tightly clamped between her legs.

"Has anyone threatened your family? Do you have any enemies?"

"No."

"Did you know that your father was heavily in debt?"

She shakes her head.

"He was," says Joona. "He owed money to criminals."

"Right."

"Could it be one of them who—"

"No."

"Why not?"

"You don't understand anything," she says, raising her voice.

"What is it we don't understand?"

"You don't understand anything."

"Tell us what—"

"I can't!" she screams.

She is so distraught that she begins to cry, straight out, without covering her face. Kristina Andersson goes over and hugs her, and after a while she grows calmer. She sits there motionless, the policewoman's arms around her, as occasional sobs shudder through her body.

"There, there," Kristina whispers reassuringly. She holds the girl close and strokes her head—and then suddenly screams and pushes Evelyn away, straight onto the floor. "Goddammit, she bit me . . . she fucking bit me!"

Kristina looks in amazement at her fingers, covered in blood seeping from a wound in the middle of her throat.

On the floor, Evelyn hides a bewildered smile behind her hand. Then her eyes roll back in her head and she slumps into unconsciousness.

23

Benjamin has locked himself in his room. Simone is sitting at the kitchen table with her eyes closed, listening to the radio; it's a live broadcast from Berwald Concert Hall. She tries to imagine life as a single person. It wouldn't be all that different from what I have now, she thinks ironically. I might go to concerts, galleries, and the theatre, as all lonely women do.

She finds a bottle of single-malt Scotch in the cupboard and pours herself a drop, adding a little water: a weak yellow liquid in a heavy glass. The front door opens as the warm notes of a Bach cello concerto fill the kitchen; it is a gentle, sorrowful melody. Erik stands in the doorway looking at her, his face grey with exhaustion.

"That looks good," he says.

"Whisky," she says, handing him the glass.

She pours herself a fresh drink; they stand opposite each other and raise their glasses in a toast, their expressions serious.

"Difficult day?" she asks quietly.

"Pretty difficult," he replies, with a pale smile.

He suddenly looks so worn out. There is a lack of clarity to his features, like a thin layer of dust on his face.

"What are you listening to?" he asks.

"Shall I turn it off?"

95

"Not on my account—it's beautiful." Erik empties the glass, holds it out to her, and she pours him another. "So Benjamin didn't get a tattoo, then," he says.

"You've been following the drama on voicemail."

"Just now, on the way home. I didn't have time before—"

"No." She breaks in, thinking about the woman who answered when she called the number last night.

"I'm glad you went and picked him up," says Erik.

She nods, thinking about how all emotions are interconnected, how no relationship is autonomous and separate, how everything is affected by everything else.

They drink again, and suddenly she notices that Erik is smiling at her. His smile, with those crooked teeth, has always made her go weak at the knees. She thinks how she would love to go to bed with him now, without any discussion, any complications. One day we will all be alone anyway, she says to herself.

"I don't know what to think," she says tersely. "Or rather . . . I know I don't trust you."

"Why do you say—"

"It feels as if we've lost everything. You just sleep or else you're at work, or wherever it is you are. I wanted to do things, travel, spend time together."

He puts down the glass and takes a step towards her. "Why can't we do that?"

"Don't say it," she whispers.

"Why not?" He smiles and strokes her cheek; then his expression grows serious again. Suddenly they are kissing each other. Simone can feel how her whole body has longed for this, longed for kisses.

"Hey, Dad, do you know where—" Benjamin falls silent as he walks into the kitchen and sees them. "You're crazy." He sighs, and goes out again.

Simone calls after him. "Benjamin." He comes back. "You promised to go and pick up the food."

"Have you called?"

"It'll be ready in fifteen minutes," she says, giving him her purse. "You know where the Thai place is, don't you?"

"Mum!" He sighs.

"Go straight there and back," she says.

"Oh, please."

"Listen to your mother," says Erik.

"I'm just going to the corner to pick up a take-away; nothing's going to happen," he says, going into the hallway.

Simone and Erik smile at each other as they hear the front door close and their son's rapid footsteps on the stairs.

Erik gets three glasses out of the cupboard, stops, takes Simone's hand, and holds it against his cheek.

"Bedroom?" she asks.

He looks embarrassingly pleased, just as the telephone rings. "Leave it," he says.

"It could be Benjamin," she says, picking up the phone. "Hello?" She hears nothing, just a faint ticking sound, perhaps from a zipper being undone. "Hello?" She puts the telephone down.

"Nobody there?" asks Erik, uneasily.

Simone watches as he goes over to the window and looks down at the street. Once again she hears the voice of the woman who answered her earlier call. *Stop it, Erik.* She had laughed. Stop what? Fumbling inside her clothes, sucking at her nipple, pushing up her skirt?

"Call Benjamin," says Erik, his voice strained.

"Why do I need to—" She picks up the phone just as it rings again. "Hello?"

When no one speaks she cuts the connection and dials Benjamin's number.

"Voice mail."

"I can't see him," says Erik.

"Should I go after him?"

"Maybe."

"He'll be furious with me," she says with a smile.

"I'll go," says Erik, moving into the hallway.

He is just taking his jacket off the hanger when the door opens and Benjamin walks in with a plastic bag stacked with cartons of steaming food.

They sit down in front of the TV to watch a movie, eating straight out of the containers. Benjamin laughs at the snappy dialogue, and Erik and Simone glance happily at each other as they did when he was a child, laughing out loud at some children's programme. Erik puts his hand on Simone's knee, and she puts her hand on top of his, squeezing it.

Bruce Willis is on his back, wiping blood from his mouth. The telephone rings again and Erik puts down his food and gets up. He goes out into the hallway and answers as calmly as he can.

"Erik Maria Bark." There is no sound, just a faint clicking. "Right, that's enough," he says angrily.

"Erik?" It's Daniella's voice. "Is that you, Erik?" she asks.

"We're just in the middle of eating." He can hear her rapid breathing.

"What did he want?" she asks.

"Who?"

"Josef," she replies.

"Josef Ek?"

"Didn't he say anything?" asks Daniella.

"When?"

"Just now . . . on the phone."

Erik can see Simone and Benjamin watching the film in the living room. He thinks about the family out in Tumba. The little girl, the mother and father. The horrendous rage behind the crime.

"What makes you think he called me?" asks Erik.

Daniella clears her throat. "He must have talked the nurse into bringing him a phone. I've spoken to the exchange; they put him through to you."

"Are you sure about this?"

"Josef was screaming when I went in; he'd ripped out the catheter. I gave him alprazolam, but he said a lot of things about you before he fell asleep."

"Like what? What did he say?"

Erik hears Daniella swallow hard, and her voice sounds very tired when she replies.

"That you'd been fucking with his head and you should leave his fucking sister alone if you don't want to be eliminated. He said it several times. You can expect to be eliminated."

24

It has been three hours since Joona took Evelyn to the Kronoberg custody centre. She was placed in a small cell with bare walls and horizontal bars over the steamed-up window. A stainless steel sink reeked of vomit. Evelyn stood next to the bunk with its green plastic mattress and stared at Joona inquiringly as he left her there.

Once a suspect has been brought in, the prosecutor has up to twelve hours to decide whether the person should be arrested or released. If he decides not to release, he then has until twelve o'clock on the third day to submit an application to the court asking for the suspect to be arrested. If he fails to do this, the person is free to go. The basis for requesting an arrest can be either probable grounds for suspicion or, more seriously, reasonable grounds for suspicion.

Now Joona is back. Striding toward the women's unit along the corridor with its shiny white vinyl floor, past monotonous rows of pea-green cell doors, he catches his own reflection in door handles and locks.

Jens Svanehjälm, Chief Prosecutor for the Stockholm district, waits for him outside one of the five interview rooms. Although Svanehjälm is forty years old, he looks no more than twenty, his boyish expression and round, smooth cheeks lending a false impression of innocence and naïveté.

"So," he says, "did Evelyn force her younger brother to murder their family?"

"According to Josef."

"Nothing Josef Ek says under hypnosis is admissible. It goes against his right to remain silent and his right to avoid incriminating himself."

"I realize that," says Joona. "It wasn't an interrogation. He wasn't a suspect. I thought the boy had information that would prevent another murder from taking place."

Jens says nothing. He scrolls through e-mails on his phone.

"I'll know soon enough what actually happened," says Joona.

Jens looks back up, with a smile. "I'm sure you will," he says. "Because when I took over this job, my predecessor told me that if Joona Linna says he's going to find out the truth, that's exactly what he'll do."

"We had one or two disagreements."

"Yes, she said that, too," says Jens.

Joona nods. Motioning towards one of the interview rooms, he asks, "Ready?"

"We're questioning Evelyn Ek purely in pursuit of information," Jens stresses.

"Do you want me to tell her that she's suspected of a crime?"

"That's up to you; you're the lead interrogator. But the clock's ticking. You haven't got a lot of time."

Joona knocks twice before entering the dreary interview room, where the blinds are pulled down over the barred windows. Evelyn Ek sits, her eyes downcast. Her arms are folded across her chest; her shoulders are tense and hunched, her jaw clenched.

"Hi, Evelyn."

She looks up quickly, her soft brown eyes frightened. He sits down opposite her. Like her brother, she is attractive; her features are not striking, but they are symmetrical. She has light brown hair and an intelligent expression. Joona realizes she has a face that at first glance might appear plain but that becomes more and more beautiful the longer you look at it.

"I thought we should have a little talk," he says. "What do you think?"

She shrugs her shoulders.

"When did you last see Josef?"

"Don't remember."

"Was it yesterday?"

"No," she says, sounding surprised.

"How many days ago was it?"

"What?"

"I asked when you last saw Josef," says Joona.

"Oh, a long time ago."

"Has he been to see you at the cottage?"

"No."

"Never? He's never been to see you out there?"

A slight shrug. "No."

"But he knows the place, doesn't he?"

She nods. "We went there when he was a little kid," she replies.

"When was that?"

"I don't know . . . I was fifteen. We borrowed the cottage from Auntie Sonja one summer when she was in Greece."

"And Josef hasn't been there since?"

Evelyn's gaze suddenly flickers across the wall behind Joona. "I don't think so," she says.

"How long have you been staying there?"

"I moved there just after term started."

"In August."

"Yes."

"You've been living in a little cottage in Värmdö for four months. Why?"

Once again her gaze flutters away, moving behind Joona's head. "So I could have peace and quiet to study," she says.

"For four months?"

She shifts in the chair, crossing her legs and scratching her forehead. "I need to be left in peace," she says with a sigh.

"Has somebody been bothering you?"

"No."

"When you say that you want to be left in peace, it sounds as if someone's been bothering you."

She gives a faint, joyless smile. "I just like the forest."

"What are you studying?"

"Political science."

"And you're supporting yourself on a student loan?"

"Yes."

"Where do you buy food?"

"I bike to Saltarö."

"Isn't that a long way?"

Evelyn shrugs her shoulders. "I suppose so."

"Have you seen anyone you know there?"

"No."

He contemplates Evelyn's smooth young forehead. "You haven't seen Josef there?"

"No."

"Evelyn, listen to me," says Joona, in a new, more serious tone. "Your brother told us that he was the one who murdered your father, your mother, and your little sister."

Evelyn stares at the table. Her eyelids tremble; a faint flush rises on her pale face.

"He's only fifteen years old," Joona goes on.

He looks at her thin hands and the shining, brushed hair lying over her frail shoulders.

"Why do you think he's saying he murdered his family?"

"What?" she asks, looking up.

"It seems as if you think he's telling the truth," he says.

"It does?"

"You didn't look surprised when I said he'd confessed," says Joona. "*Were* you surprised?"

"Yes."

She sits motionless on the chair. A thin furrow of anxiety has appeared between her eyebrows. She looks very tired, and her lips are moving slightly, as if she is praying or whispering to herself. "Is he locked up?" she asks suddenly.

"Who?"

She doesn't look up at him when she replies but speaks tonelessly down at the table. "Josef. Have you locked him up?"

"Are you afraid of him?"

"No."

"I thought perhaps you were carrying the gun because you were afraid of him."

"I hunt," she replies, meeting his gaze.

There's something peculiar about her, something he doesn't yet understand. It's not the usual things: guilt, rage, or hatred. It's more like something reminiscent of an enormous resistance. He can't get a fix on it. A defense mechanism or a protective barrier unlike anything he has yet encountered.

"Hare?" he asks.

"Yes."

"Is it good, hare?"

"Not particularly."

"What does it taste like?"

"Sweet."

Joona thinks about her standing in the cold air outside the cottage. He tries to visualize the chain of events.

Erik Maria Bark had taken her gun. He was holding it over his arm and it was broken open, the brass of the cartridges visible. Evelyn was squinting at him in the sunlight. Tall and slim, with her sandy brown hair in a high, tight ponytail. A silvery padded vest and low-cut jeans, damp running shoes. Pine trees behind her, moss on the ground, low-growing lingonberry and trampled toadstools.

Suddenly Joona discovers a crack in Evelyn's story. He has already nudged at the thought, but it slipped away. Now the crack is absolutely clear. When he spoke to Evelyn in her aunt's cottage, she sat completely still on the corduroy couch with her hands clamped between her thighs. On the floor at her feet lay a photograph in a frame that looked like a toadstool. Evelyn's little sister was in the picture, sitting between her parents with the sun glinting off her big glasses.

The little girl must have been four, perhaps even five years old in the picture. In other words, the photograph can be no more than a year or two old. Evelyn claimed that Josef hadn't been to the cottage for years, but he accurately described the photo and the frame under hypnosis.

Of course, there could be several copies of the picture in other toadstool frames, thinks Joona. There's also the possibility that this particular one has been moved around. And Josef could have been in the cottage without Evelyn's knowledge.

But it could also be a crack in Evelyn's story.

"Evelyn," says Joona, "I'm just wondering about something you said a little while ago."

Jens Svanehjälm gets to his feet. The sudden movement startles Evelyn, and her body jerks. "Would you come with me for a minute, detective?" Outside, he turns to Joona. "I'm letting her go," he says, in a low voice. "This is bullshit. We don't have a thing, just an invalid interrogation with her comatose fifteen-year-old brother, who suggests that she—"

Jens stops speaking as soon as he sees the look on Joona's face.

"You've found something, haven't you?" he says.

"I think so, yes," Joona replies quietly.

"Is she lying?"

"I don't know. She might be."

Jens runs his hand over his chin, considering. "Give her a sandwich and a cup of tea," he says eventually. "Then you can have one more hour before I decide whether we're going to arrest her or not."

"There's no guarantee this will lead to anything."

"But you'll give it a go?"

Four minutes later, Joona places a Styrofoam cup of English breakfast tea and a sandwich on a paper plate in front of Evelyn and sits down on his chair. "I thought you might be hungry," he says.

"Thanks," she says, and a more cheerful expression momentarily sweeps across her features. Joona watches her carefully. Her hand shakes as she eats the sandwich and lifts the cup from the table to her lips.

"Evelyn, in your aunt's cottage there's a photograph in a frame that looks like a toadstool."

Evelyn nods. "Aunt Sonja bought it up in Mora; she thought it would look nice in the cottage . . ." She stops and blows on her tea.

"Did she buy any more like that? For gifts, say?"

"Not that I know of." She smiles. "I've never seen another like it."

"And has the photograph always been in the cottage?"

"What do you mean?" she asks faintly.

"Well, I'm not sure. Maybe nothing. But Josef talked about this picture, so he must have seen it sometime. I thought perhaps you'd forgotten something."

"No."

"Well, that clears that up," says Joona, getting up.

"Are you going?"

"Yes, I think we're done here," says Joona. He looks at her face, filled with anxiety, and acts on a hunch.

"Chances are you'll be out of here—oh, in an hour or two."

"Out of here?"

"Well, I don't think we can hold you for anything." He smiles.

She wraps her arms around herself. "You never answered my question."

"Question?"

"Is Josef locked up?"

Joona looks her square in the eye. "No, Evelyn. Josef is in the hospital. We haven't arrested him. I don't know that we can."

She begins to tremble, and her eyes fill with tears.

"What is it, Evelyn?"

She wipes the tears from her cheeks with the heel of her hand. "Josef did come to the cottage once. He took a taxi and he brought a cake," she says, her voice breaking.

"On your birthday?"

"He . . . it was *his* birthday."

"When was that?"

"On the first of November."

"Just over a month ago," says Joona. "What happened?"

"Nothing," she says. "It was a surprise."

"He hadn't told you he was coming?"

"We weren't in touch."

"Why not?"

"I need to be on my own."

"Who knew you were staying there?"

"Nobody, apart from Sorab, my boyfriend . . . well, actually, he broke up with me, and we're just friends, but he helps me, tells everybody I'm staying with him, answers when Mum calls."

"Why?"

"I need to be left in peace."

"So you've said. Did Josef go out there again?"

"No."

"This is important, Evelyn."

"He didn't come again," she replies.

"You're certain?"

"Yes."

"Why did you lie about this?"

"I don't know," she whispers.

"What else have you lied about?"

25

Erik is walking between the brightly lit display cases in the NK department store's jewellery department. A sleek saleswoman dressed in black murmurs persuasively to a customer. She slides open a drawer and places a few pieces on a velvet-covered tray. Erik pauses to study a Georg Jensen necklace: heavy, softly polished triangles, linked together like petals to form a closed circle. The sterling silver has the rich lustre of platinum. Erik thinks how beautifully it would lie around Simone's slender neck and decides to buy it for her for Christmas.

As the assistant is wrapping his purchase in dark-red shiny paper, the cell phone in Erik's pocket begins to vibrate, resonating against the little wooden box with the parrot and the native. He answers without checking the number on the display.

"Erik Maria Bark."

There's a strange crackling noise, and he can hear the distant sound of Christmas carols. "Hello?" he says.

A very faint voice can be heard. "Is that Erik?"

"Yes," he replies.

"I was wondering . . ."

Suddenly Erik thinks it sounds as if someone is giggling in the background. "Who is this?" he asks sharply.

"Hang on, doctor. I need your expert advice," says the voice, dripping

107

with contempt. Erik is about to end the call when the voice on the phone suddenly bellows, "Hypnotize me! I want to be—"

Erik snatches the phone away from his ear. He presses the button to end the conversation and tries to see who called, but it's a withheld number. A beep tells him he has received a text message, also from a withheld number. He opens it and reads: CAN YOU HYPNOTIZE A CORPSE?

Bewildered, Erik takes his purchase in its red and gold bag and leaves the jewellery department. In the lobby he catches the eye of a woman in a bulky, black coat. She is standing underneath a suspended Christmas tree, three storeys high, and she is staring at him with a hostile expression. He has never seen her before.

With one hand he flips open the lid of the wooden box in his coat pocket, tips a codeine capsule into his hand, puts it in his mouth, and swallows it.

He goes outside into the cold air. People are crowded before a shop-window where Christmas elves are dancing around in a landscape made of candy. A toffee with a big mouth sings a Christmas song. Pre-schoolers dressed in yellow vests over thick snowsuits gaze in open-mouthed silence at the scene.

The mobile phone rings again, but this time he checks the number before answering. It's a Stockholm number.

"Erik Maria Bark," he says cautiously.

"Hi, there. My name is Britt Sundström. I work for Amnesty International."

"Hi," Erik says, puzzled.

"I'd like to know whether your patient had the opportunity to say no to the hypnosis."

"What did you say?" asks Erik, as a huge snail drags a sledge full of Christmas presents across the window display. His heart begins to pound, and a burning acidity surges up through his gut.

"The CIA handbook for torture that leaves no trace does actually mention hypnosis as one of the—"

"The doctor responsible for the patient made the judgment."

"So you're saying you bear no responsibility?"

"I have no comment," he says.

"You've already been reported to the police," she says curtly.

"I see," he says feebly, and ends the call.

He begins to walk slowly toward Sergels Torg, with its shining glass tower and Culture House, sees the Christmas market, and hears a trumpeter playing "Silent Night." He turns onto Sveavägen. Outside the 7-Eleven he stops and reads the display boards showing the headlines from the evening papers:

"I KILLED MUM AND DAD"
Hypnotist Dupes Boy into Confession

IN YOUR HEAD
Doctor Risks Boy's Life to Coerce Admission

BARK WORSE THAN BITE
New Hypnosis Scandal for Tarnished Doc

OUTRAGE!
Stumped Cops Enlist Hypnodoc, Scapegoat Victim

Erik can feel his pulse begin to pound in his temples and hurries on, avoiding looking directly at those around him. He passes the spot where Prime Minister Olof Palme was assassinated back in 1986, walking home with his wife from the movies. Three red roses are lying on the grubby memorial plaque. Erik hears someone calling after him and slips into an exclusive electronics shop. Although just a few minutes ago he'd been so tired he felt almost drunk, that feeling has been replaced by a feverish mixture of nervousness and despair. His hands shake as he takes yet another strong painkiller. He feels a stabbing pain in his stomach as the capsule dissolves and the powder goes into the mucous membranes.

The radio in the shop is broadcasting a debate about the extent to which hypnosis should be banned as a form of treatment. A caller is telling the story of how he was once hypnotized into thinking he was Bob Dylan.

"I mean, like, I knew it wasn't true," he drawls, "but it was like I was kind of forced to say what I said, you know? I knew I was, like, being hypnotized. I could see my buddy was, like, sitting right there, like, waiting for me? But I still thought, like, I'm Dylan! I was even speaking English. Like, I couldn't help it; I would've admitted just about anything."

The Minister for Justice says in his Småland accent, "There is absolutely no doubt that using hypnosis as a method of interrogation is a violation of the rights of the individual."

"So Erik Maria Bark has broken the law?" the journalist asks sharply.

"We expect the Prosecutor's Office to conduct a thorough investigation of the legality of his actions."

26

By the time Erik reaches Luntmakargatan 73, sweat is pouring down his back. He punches in the code to open the door. With fumbling hands he finds his keys as the lift hums its way upwards. Once inside the apartment, he staggers into the living room and tries to take off his coat, but the pills have made him dizzy. He topples onto the couch and switches on the television.

There is the Chairman of the Swedish Society for Clinical Hypnosis sitting in a TV studio. Erik knows him very well; he has seen many colleagues affected by his arrogance and his ruthless ambition.

"We expelled Bark ten years ago and we won't be welcoming him back," the chairman says, with a tight smile.

"Does an incident like this affect the reputation of serious hypnosis?"

"All our members adhere to strict ethical rules," he says superciliously. "Moreover, Sweden has laws against charlatans."

Erik finally takes his outdoor clothes off with clumsy movements, piling them on the sofa beside him. He closes his eyes for a moment to rest but opens them immediately when he hears a familiar voice coming from the television. Benjamin is standing in a sunlit school playground. His brow is furrowed, the tip of his nose and his ears are red, his shoulders are hunched, and he looks very cold.

"So," asks the reporter. "What's it like living with the hypnodoc?"

"I don't know," says Benjamin.

"Has your dad ever hypnotized you?"

"What? No way."

"How do you know?" the reporter persists. "If he had hypnotized you, there's no guarantee that you'd be aware of it, is there?"

"I guess not," replies Benjamin with a grin, surprised by the reporter's pushy approach.

"How would you feel if it turned out he had hypnotized you?"

"I don't know."

"Pretty mad, I bet," suggests the reporter.

"Yeah," agrees Benjamin. His cheeks are flushed.

Erik turns off the television and goes into the bedroom, where he takes off his trousers and sits on the bed, placing the wooden box with the parrot on it in the drawer of the bedside table. He doesn't want to think about the longing that was aroused in him when he hypnotized Josef Ek and followed him down into that deep blue sea. He lies down, reaches out for the glass of water by the bed, but falls asleep before he has time to drink.

Still half asleep, Erik thinks dreamily about his father when he used to appear at children's parties, wearing his specially prepared suit, the sweat pouring down his cheeks. He would twist balloons into the shapes of animals and pull brightly coloured feather flowers out of a hollow walking cane. When he had moved from the house in Sollentuna to a nursing home, he would talk of putting an act together with Erik. He would be the gentleman thief and Erik would be the stage hypnotist, making people sing like Elvis and Zarah Leander.

Suddenly Erik is wide awake. He sees Benjamin in his mind's eye, shivering under the scrutiny of the TV camera and the reporter, there in the school playground in front of his classmates and teachers. He sits up, feeling the searing pain in his stomach, reaches for the telephone, and calls Simone.

"Simone Bark's gallery," she replies.

"Hi, it's me."

"Just a minute."

He hears her walk across the wooden floor and close the office door behind her.

"What the hell's going on?" she asks. "Benjamin called and—"

"The media circus is in full swing."

"The *media circus*? What are we, rock stars? Erik, what have you done? Why are reporters grilling our kid on television?"

"I haven't done anything. I was asked to hypnotize the patient by the doctor who was responsible for his care."

"I know that part. The whole world knows; it's all over the news. You hypnotized some poor victimized kid and coerced a confession—"

"Can you listen to me for a second?" he broke in. "Can you do that?"

"All right. Talk."

"It wasn't an interrogation," Erik begins.

"It doesn't matter what you call it." She falls silent. He can hear her breathing. "Sorry," she says quietly. "Please finish."

"It wasn't an interrogation. We thought he was a victim. And the police needed a description, anything they could go on, because they thought a girl's life depended on it."

"But—"

"The doctor who was responsible for the patient at the time judged that the risk was low. I wouldn't've done it otherwise." He pauses. "We were just trying to save his sister." He stops speaking and listens to Simone breathing.

"What have you done?" she says shakily. "You . . . you promised me you wouldn't practise hypnosis any more."

"It'll sort itself out. No harm done, Simone."

"No harm done?" she snaps. "You broke your promise, but you don't think any harm has been done? Erik, all you do is lie and lie and lie."

Simone stops herself, and falls silent.

Erik stands rock-still for a moment, hangs up the phone, then turns and enters the kitchen, where he mixes a soluble analgesic with antacid and swills the sweet liquid down.

27

Joona looks out into the dark, empty corridor. It's evening, almost eight o'clock, and he's the only one left in the whole department. Advent star lamps shine from every window, and the electric Christmas candles create a soft, round, double glow, reflected in the black glass. Anja has placed a bowl of Christmas sweets on his desk, and he eats more than his fill as he writes up his notes on the interview with Evelyn.

On the basis of her having lied about Josef visiting the cottage, the prosecutor made the decision to arrest her. Joona knows perfectly well that Evelyn's lie does not mean she is guilty of any crime, but it gives him three days to investigate what she is hiding and why.

He writes up the report, addresses it to the prosecutor, places it in the outgoing mail, checks that his pistol is safely locked away, and leaves the police headquarters in his car.

When he reaches Fridhemsplan, Joona hears his cell phone ringing, but it's slipped through a hole in the lining of his pocket and he has to pull over in front of the Hare Krishna restaurant to shake it loose.

"Joona Linna."

"Oh, good," says police officer Ronny Alfredsson. "We have a problem. We don't really know what to do."

"Did you speak to Evelyn's boyfriend?"

"Sorab Ramadani. That's the problem."

"Did you check where he works?"

"It's not that," says Ronny. "We located him easy. He's right here in his apartment, but he won't open the door. He doesn't want to talk to us. He keeps shouting at us to clear off, that we're disturbing the neighbours, and we're harassing him because he's a Muslim."

"What have you said to him?"

"Fuck all, just that we needed his help on a particular matter. We did exactly what you told us to do."

"Good," says Joona.

"Is it all right if we force the door?"

"Just leave him alone for the time being. I'll come over."

"Should we wait?"

"Yes, please. Outside in the car."

Joona signals, swings the car around in a U-turn, and makes his way onto Västerbron. All the windows and lights of the city are shining in the night, the sky a grey, misty dome up above.

He thinks once again about the crime scene investigation. There's something odd about the pattern that is emerging. Certain elements are simply irreconcilable. While waiting for a light to change, Joona opens the folder on the passenger seat and flips through the photographs from the soccer field. Three showers, with no partitions between them. The reflection of the flash from the camera shines on the white tiles; in one picture he can see the shower scraper and the large pool of blood, water, and dirt, strands of hair, plasters, and a bottle of shower gel.

Next to the drain in the floor is the father's arm; the white ball joint is surrounded by ligaments and severed muscle tissue. The hunting knife with its broken point lies on the floor.

Nils Åhlén found the point with the help of computer tomography; it was embedded in Anders Ek's pelvic bone.

The mutilated body is on the floor between the wooden benches and the battered metal lockers. A red tracksuit top hangs on a hook. Blood is everywhere: on the floor, on the doors, the ceiling, the benches.

Joona drums his fingers on the wheel. A locker room, of all places. The technicians have obtained hundreds of partial and complete fingerprints, thousands of fibres and strands of hair. They are dealing with DNA from hundreds of different people, much of it contaminated, but so far nothing can be linked to Josef Ek.

Joona asked the forensic technicians to concentrate on looking for blood from Anders Ek on Josef. The large amounts of blood covering his entire body from the other crime scene mean nothing. Everyone in the house was smeared with everyone else's blood. The fact that Josef had his little sister's blood on him was no stranger than the fact that she had his blood on her. But if they can find the father's blood on his son, or traces of Josef in the locker room, then he can be linked to both crime scenes. If they can just link him to the locker room, they can begin proceedings.

When Josef was initially taken to the hospital in Huddinge, a specialist was instructed by the National Forensic Lab in Linköping (which carries out DNA analysis in Sweden) to ensure that all biological traces on Josef's body were secured.

When he reaches Högalid Park, Joona calls Erixon, a very fat man who is the crime-scene investigator responsible for the investigation in Tumba.

A tired voice answers. "Go away."

"Erixon? Still alive?" jokes Joona.

"I'm asleep," comes the weary response.

"Sorry."

"No, it's fine, I'm actually on my way home. If they still recognize me there."

"I'll make it quick. Did you find any trace of Josef in the locker room?" asks Joona.

"No."

"You must have."

"No," replies Erixon. "Really. Not a trace of him."

"Have you put any pressure on our friends in Linköping?"

"I've leaned on them with my considerable weight," he replies.

"And?"

"They didn't find any of the father's DNA on Josef."

"I don't believe them either," says Joona. "I mean, he was fucking covered in—"

"Not a drop," Erixon interrupts.

"That can't be right."

"They sounded very pleased with themselves when they told me."

"LCN?"

"No, not even a microdrop. Nothing."

"But . . . we just can't be that unlucky."

"I think you're going to have to give in on this one," says Erixon.

"We'll see."

They end the conversation. Joona thinks that what can seem like a mystery is sometimes simply a matter of coincidence. The perpetrator's method appears to be identical in both places: the frenzied blows with the knife and the aggressive attempts to chop up the bodies. It is therefore very strange that the father's blood has not been found on Josef, if he is the attacker. He should have been covered in so much blood he would have attracted attention, thinks Joona, and calls Erixon back.

"I just thought of something."

"In twenty seconds?"

"Did you examine the women's locker room?"

"Nobody had been in there; the door was locked."

"Presumably the victim had the keys on him."

"But—"

"Check the drain in the *women's* shower," says Joona.

28

After following the road around Tantolunden, Joona turns onto a path and parks in front of an apartment block facing the park. He wonders where the police car is, checks the address, and considers the possibility that Ronny and his partner have knocked on the wrong door. He grimaces. That would explain Sorab's reluctance to let them in, since in that case his name probably wasn't Sorab.

The evening air is chilly, and Joona walks briskly toward the door. If Josef's account matches with what really happened, he did nothing to hide the crime at the time; did not protect himself. He had no thought for the consequences, he simply allowed himself to become covered in blood.

Joona thinks it's possible that under hypnosis Josef Ek was merely describing how he felt, a confused, enraged tumult, while in fact his behaviour at the time was much more controlled. Perhaps he acted methodically, wore a waterproof covering, and showered in the women's locker room before he went to the house.

He needs to speak to Daniella Richards, to find out when she thinks Josef will be strong enough to cope with an interview.

Joona walks in through the door. The lobby walls are tiled in black and white like a chessboard, and he sees his reflection in the black tiles: pale, frosty face, serious expression, blond, tousled hair. He takes out his cell and calls Ronny again, jabbing at the button for the lift. No reply.

Perhaps they gave it one last try, and Sorab let them in. Joona heads up to the sixth floor, waits for a mother with a buggy to take the lift down, then rings Sorab's doorbell.

He waits for a while, knocks, waits for a few more seconds, then pushes the letter box open. "Sorab? My name is Joona Linna. I'm a detective. I need to talk to you."

He hears a sound from inside, as if someone has been leaning heavily against the door but is now quickly moving away.

"You're the only one who knew where Evelyn was."

"I haven't done anything," says a deep voice from inside the apartment.

"But you said—"

"I don't know anything!" the man yells.

"All right," says Joona. "But I want you to open the door, look me in the eye, and say that to me."

"Go away."

"Open the door."

"What the fuck. Can't you just leave me alone? This has nothing to do with me. I don't want to get involved."

His voice is full of fear. He falls silent, breathing heavily, and slams his hand against something inside.

"Evelyn's fine," says Joona.

The letter box rattles slightly. "I thought—" He breaks off.

"We need to talk to you."

"Is Evelyn really fine? Nothing's happened to her?"

"Open the door."

"I don't want to."

"It would be helpful if you could come to the station."

There is a brief silence.

"Has he been here more than once?" Joona asks, all of a sudden.

"Who?"

"Josef."

"Who's Josef?"

"Evelyn's brother."

"He's never been here," says Sorab.

"So who *did* come here?"

"Why can't you understand? I'm not going to talk to you!"

"Who came here?"

"I didn't say anyone came here, did I? You're just trying to trap me."

"No, I'm not."

Silence once again. Then Joona hears the sound of a tearing sob behind the door.

"Is she dead?" asks Sorab. "Is Evelyn dead?"

"Why do you ask?"

"I don't want to talk to you."

Joona hears footsteps moving away, down the hallway, then the sound of a door closing. Loud music starts up. As Joona is walking down the stairs, he thinks someone must have frightened Sorab into telling him where Evelyn was hiding.

Joona emerges into the chilly air and sees two men wearing Pro Gym jackets waiting by his car. When they hear him coming, they turn around. One sits on the hood, his cell phone to his ear. Joona assesses them rapidly. They're both in their thirties; the one sitting on the hood has a shaved head, while the other has a schoolboy haircut. Joona guesses that the man with the boyish hair weighs over 220 pounds. Perhaps he practises aikido, karate, or kick-boxing. Probably on steroids, thinks Joona. The other one might be carrying a knife, but probably not a firearm.

There is a thin layer of snow on the grass.

Joona turns away, as if he hasn't noticed the men, and heads for the well-lit path.

"Hey, you!" shouts one of them.

Joona ignores them and heads towards the steps by a streetlamp with a green waste bin.

"Aren't you taking your car?"

Joona stops and glances quickly up at the building. He realizes that the man sitting on the hood is talking to Sorab on his mobile, and that Sorab is watching them from his window.

The man with the boyish haircut is approaching cautiously, and Joona turns and walks back toward him.

"I'm a police officer," he says.

"And I'm a fucking monkey," says the man.

Joona takes out his mobile and calls Ronny again. "Sweet Home Alabama" begins to play in the man with the boyish hair's pocket; he smiles, takes out Ronny's phone, and answers.

"Officer Pig here."

"What's this all about?" says Joona.

"You need to leave Sorab alone. He don't want to talk."

"Do you really think you're helping him by—"

"This is a warning. I don't give a fuck who you are, you just keep away from Sorab."

Joona realizes the situation could become dangerous, remembers that he locked his pistol away in the gun cupboard back at the station, and looks around for something he can use as a weapon.

"Where are my colleagues?" he asks in a calm voice.

"You hear me? Leave Sorab alone."

The man with the boyish hair runs one hand rapidly through it, begins to breathe more quickly, turns sideways, moves a little closer, and lifts the heel of his back foot an inch or two from the ground.

"I used to train when I was younger," says Joona. "If you attack me I will defend myself and I will take you."

"We're shitting our pants," says the one leaning against the car.

Joona doesn't take his eyes off the man facing him. "You're intending to kick my legs," he says. "Since you know you can't manage high kicks."

"Asshole," mumbles the man.

Joona moves to the right to open up the line.

"If you decide to kick," Joona continues, "I will not move back, which is what you are used to; instead, I will move in, against the back of your other knee, and when you fall backwards, this elbow will be waiting for the back of your neck."

"Fuck me, he talks bullshit," says the one leaning on the car.

"He does." The other grins. "And what an accent."

"If your tongue is sticking out, you'll bite it off," says Joona.

The man with the boyish hair sways slightly, and when the kick comes it is slower than expected. Joona has already taken a first step when the man's hip begins to twist. And before the leg extends and meets its target, Joona kicks as hard as he can at the back of the knee of the other leg, the one on which the man is resting all his weight. He is already off balance and falls backwards just as Joona swings around and hits the back of his neck with his elbow.

29

friday, december 11: morning

It is just 5:30 a.m. when the knocking begins somewhere in the apartment. Simone perceives the noise as part of a frustrating dream, in which she has to pick up different shells and porcelain lids. She understands the rules but still does the wrong thing. A boy knocks on the table and points out the wrong choices she has made. Simone twists and turns in her sleep, whimpering; she opens her eyes and is immediately wide awake.

Someone or something is knocking inside the apartment. She tries to locate the noise in the darkness, lying perfectly still and listening, but the knocking has stopped.

She can hear Erik snoring beside her. There is a tapping sound in the pipes. The wind blows against the windowpanes. The sound of a car outside roars through the window.

Simone just has time to think that she must have exaggerated the noise in her sleep when the knocking suddenly begins again. Someone is in the apartment! Erik has taken a pill and is out cold. His snoring quiets as she lays a hand on his arm, but he doesn't wake up, only turns over, puffing. As quietly as possible, she creeps out of bed and slips through the bedroom door, which is ajar.

A light comes from the kitchen. As she moves through the hallway she sees a glow hanging in the air like a blue cloud of gas. It's the fridge light. The fridge and the freezer are standing wide open. The freezer has begun to defrost and water is running onto the floor. Drops of water from the thawing packs of food are landing on the plastic edging with a gentle tapping noise.

Simone becomes aware of how cold it is in the kitchen. There is a smell of cigarette smoke. She looks out into the hallway.

Then she sees that the front door is wide open.

She rushes to Benjamin's room. Fast asleep. For a little while she just stands there, listening to his regular breathing.

As she walks towards the front door to close it, her heart almost stops. There is someone standing in the doorway. He nods to her and holds out an object. It takes a few seconds before she realizes this is the paperboy and he's handing her the morning paper. She says thank you and takes the paper from him; when she finally closes the door, she notices that her entire body is shaking.

She switches on all the lights and searches the entire apartment. Nothing seems to be missing.

Simone is on her knees mopping the water from the floor when Erik walks into the kitchen. He fetches a dish cloth, throws it on the floor, and starts to push it around with his foot.

"Someone leave the fridge door open? I must have done it sleepwalking," he says.

"No," she says wearily.

"The fridge is a classic, after all. I must have been hungry."

"I'd know. I'm such a light sleeper, I wake up every time you turn over in bed or stop snoring. I wake up if Benjamin goes to the toilet. I can hear when—"

"Then *you* must have been sleepwalking."

"Erik, this isn't funny. Something woke me up and the front door was open."

She falls silent, not sure she should have told him this.

"I could definitely smell cigarette smoke in the kitchen," she says eventually.

Erik laughs.

Simone's cheeks are stained with an angry flush. "Why are you laughing?"

"Come on, Sixan. One of the neighbours probably smoked a cigarette standing by the exhaust fan in their kitchen. I mean, the whole

building shares a ventilation system. Or some terrible person had a cigarette on the stairs without thinking—"

"Can you be a little more patronizing?" Simone interrupts.

He tries to reassure her. "Simone—"

"Why don't you believe someone was here?" she asks angrily. "After
all that crap about you that was in the papers? The prank calls? It's hardly
surprising if some lunatic tries to get in here and—"

"Just stop. This is not logical. Who on earth would come into our
apartment, open the fridge and the freezer, smoke a cigarette, and then
just leave?"

He tosses the wrung-out dish cloth back on the floor and begins
swabbing with his foot again.

"I don't know, Erik! I don't know, but that's what somebody has
done!"

"Calm down," says Erik irritably.

"Calm down?"

"Stop making such a fuss. I'm sure we'll find a simple explanation."

"I could feel there was someone in the apartment when I woke up,"
she says, in a subdued voice.

He sighs and leaves the kitchen. Simone looks at the dirty grey cloth
he was using.

Benjamin comes in and sits down in his usual place.

"Good morning," says Simone.

He sighs and sits there with his head in his hands. "Why do you and
Dad always lie about everything?"

"We don't," she says.

"Yeah, right."

"What makes you think we do?"

He doesn't reply.

"Are you thinking about what I said in the taxi from—"

"I'm thinking about a whole load of things," he says loudly.

"There's no need to shout at me."

He sighs. "Forget I said anything."

"I don't know what's going to happen between me and Dad. It's not
that simple," she says. "Maybe we're only fooling ourselves, but that's not
the same as lying."

"According to you," he says quietly.

"Is something else bothering you?"

"How come there aren't any pictures of me when I was little?"

"Of course there are," she answers with a smile.

"Not when I was first born," he says.

"Well, you know I had had a miscarriage . . . it's just that we were so happy when you were born, we forgot to take photographs. I know exactly what you looked like. You had wrinkled ears and—"

"Stop it!" yells Benjamin, and storms off to his room.

Erik comes into the kitchen and drops an analgesic into a glass of water. "What's up with Benjamin?" he asks.

"I have no idea."

Erik drinks from the glass over the sink.

"He says we lie about everything," says Simone.

"All teenagers feel that way. Comes with the territory." Erik burps silently.

"I did mention to him that we were going to separate," she tells him.

"How the hell could you do something so stupid?"

"I . . . I just said what I was feeling at the time."

"For fuck's sake, you can't just think about yourself!"

"Me? I'm not the one who's screwing students. I'm not the one taking a shitload of pills because—"

"Shut the fuck up!" he yells. "You don't know anything!"

"I know you're on serious painkillers."

"And what's that got to do with you?"

"Tell me, Erik: are you *in pain*?"

"I'm a doctor. I think I'm in a slightly better position to evaluate—"

"Oh, stop trying to fool me."

"What do you mean?" he says.

"You're an addict, Erik. We never have sex any more because you're always zonked."

"Maybe I don't want to have sex with you," he breaks in. "Why would I, when you're so god-damn miserable with me all the time?"

The acrimony hangs in the air between them, nearly palpable. Is this really what saying the unsayable feels like? It should be more liberating, more profound; it should boil down to something more substantial.

"Then it is best if we separate," she says.

"Fine."

She can't look at him; she just walks slowly out of the kitchen, feeling the tension and the pain in her throat, the tears springing to her eyes.

Benjamin has closed his bedroom door, and his music is so loud that the walls and doors are rattling. Simone locks herself in the bathroom, switches off the light, and weeps.

"Fucking hell!" she hears Erik yell from the hallway before the front door opens and shuts again.

30

It isn't quite 7:00 a.m. when Joona Linna gets a call from Dr. Daniella Richards. She explains that in her opinion Josef is now able to cope with a short interview.

As Joona gets into his car to drive to the hospital, he feels a dull ache in his elbow. He thinks back to the previous evening, how the blue light from the radio cars had swept over the façade of Sorab Ramadani's apartment block near Tantolunden. The man with the boyish hair had been spitting blood and muttering thickly about his tongue as he was guided into the backseat of the patrol car. Ronny Alfredsson and his partner had been discovered in the shelter down in the basement of the apartment block. They had been threatened with knives and locked in and then the men had driven their patrol car to another building and left it in the visitors' car park.

Joona had gone back inside, rung Sorab's doorbell, and, speaking once again through the letter box, told him that his bodyguards had been arrested and that the door to his apartment would be broken down unless he opened it immediately.

After a moment, Sorab had let him in. He was a pale man, wearing his hair in a ponytail. He was anxious, his eyes darting around the room, but he asked Joona to take a seat on the blue leather sofa, offered him a cup of camomile tea, and apologized for his friends.

"I'm sorry about all this, really. I've been having some problems lately. Worried about my safety. That's why I got myself some bodyguards."

"What makes you worry about your safety?" asked Joona, sipping at the hot tea.

"Someone's out to get me." He stood up and peered out the window.

"Who?" asked Joona.

Sorab kept his back to Joona, and said tonelessly that he didn't want to talk about it. "Do I have to?" he asked. "Don't I have the right to remain silent?"

"You have the right to remain silent," admitted Joona.

Sorab shrugged his shoulders. "There you go, then."

"I might be able to help you if you talk to me," Joona had ventured. "Has that occurred to you?"

"Thank you very much," said Sorab, still facing the window.

"Is it Evelyn's brother who—"

"No."

"Wasn't it Josef Ek who came here?"

"He's not her brother."

"Not her brother? Who is he, then?"

"How should I know? But he's not her brother. He's something else."

After that, Sorab became cagey and nervous again, giving only the most evasive answers to Joona's questions. When he left, Joona wondered what Josef had said to Sorab. What had he done? How had he managed to frighten him into revealing where Evelyn was?

Joona parks in front of the neurosurgical unit, walks through the main entrance, takes the lift to the fifth floor, continues through the corridor, greets the policeman on duty, and proceeds into Josef's room. An attractive woman sits in the chair beside the bed. She looks at Joona with an expression he finds appealing as she rises to introduce herself:

"Lisbet Carlén," she says. "I'm a social worker. I'll be Josef's advocate during the interview."

"Excellent," says Joona, shaking her hand.

"Are you leading the interrogation?" she asks with interest.

"Yes. Forgive me. My name is Joona Linna, and I'm from the National CID. We spoke on the telephone."

At regular intervals there is a loud bubbling noise from the Bülow drainage tube connected to Josef's punctured pleura. The drain replaces the pressure that is no longer naturally present, enabling his lung to function.

Lisbet Carlén says quietly that the doctor has explained that Josef must lie absolutely still, because of the risk of new bleeds in the liver.

"I have no intention of putting his health at risk," says Joona, placing the tape recorder on the table next to Josef's face.

He gestures inquiringly at the recorder and Lisbet nods. He starts the machine and begins by describing the situation: It is Friday, December 11, at 8:15 in the morning, and Josef Ek is being questioned to try to elicit information. He then lists the people present in the room.

"Hi," says Joona.

Josef looks at him with heavy eyes.

"My name is Joona. I'm a detective."

Josef closes his eyes.

"How are you feeling?"

The social worker looks out the window.

"Can you sleep with that thing bubbling away?" he asks.

Josef nods slowly.

"Do you know why I'm here?"

Josef opens his eyes. Joona waits, observing his face.

"There's been an accident," says Josef. "My whole family was in an accident."

"Hasn't anybody told you what's happened?" asks Joona.

"Maybe a little," he says faintly.

"He refuses to see a psychologist or a counsellor," says the social worker.

Joona thinks about how different Josef's voice was under hypnosis. Now it is suddenly fragile, almost non-existent, yet pensive.

"I think you know what's happened."

"You don't have to answer that," Lisbet Carlén says quickly.

"You're fifteen years old now," Joona goes on.

"Yes."

"What did you do on your birthday?"

"Can't remember," says Josef.

"Did you get any presents?"

"I watched TV," Josef replies.

"Did you go to see Evelyn?" Joona asks in a neutral tone.

"Yes."

"At her apartment?"

"Yes."

"Was she there?"

"Yes." Silence. "No, she wasn't," says Josef hesitantly, changing his mind.

"Where was she, then?"

"At the cottage," he replies.

"Is it nice there?"

"Not really . . . It's cosy, I guess."

"Was she happy to see you?"

"Who?"

"Evelyn." Silence. "Did you take anything with you?"

"A cake."

"A cake? Was it good?"

He nods.

"Did Evelyn like it?" Joona goes on.

"Only the best for Evelyn," he says.

"Did she give you a present?"

"No."

"But maybe she sang to you."

"She didn't want to give me my present," he says, in an injured tone.

"Is that what she said?"

"Yes, she did," he answers quickly.

"Why?" Silence. "Was she angry with you?" asks Joona.

He nods.

"Was she trying to get you to do something you didn't want to do?" asks Joona calmly.

"No, she—" Josef whispers the rest.

"I can't hear you, Josef."

He continues to whisper, and Joona leans close, trying to hear the words. "That fucking bastard!" Josef yells in his ear.

Joona jumps back and rubs his ear as he walks around the bed. He tries to smile.

Josef's face is ash-grey. "I'm going to find that fucking hypnotist and bite his throat; I'm going to hunt him down, him and his—"

The social worker moves over to the bed quickly and tries to switch off the tape recorder. "Josef! You have the right to remain silent—"

"Keep out of this," Joona interrupts.

She looks at him with an agitated expression and says in a trembling voice, "Before the interview began, you should have informed—"

"Wrong. There are no laws governing this kind of interrogation," says Joona, raising his voice. "He has the right to remain silent, that's true, but I am not obliged to inform him of that right."

"In that case, I apologize."

"No problem," mumbles Joona, turning back to Josef. "Why are you angry with the hypnotist?"

"I don't have to answer your questions," says Josef, attempting to point at the social worker.

31

Erik runs down the stairs and through the door. He stops outside and feels the sweat cooling on his back. A chill is in the air; not far away, a man sleeps under a thick mound of blankets. After a moment of indecisiveness, he walks slowly up toward Odenplan and sits down on a bench outside the library. He feels sick with fear. How can he be so stupid, pushing Simone away because he feels hurt?

After a while, Erik gets up and sets off for home, stopping to buy bread at the stone oven bakery and a *caffè macchiato* for Simone. He hurries back and, not wanting to wait for the lift, jogs up the stairs, but as soon as he unlocks the door he realizes the apartment is empty. With effort, Erik pushes aside the feeling of desolation the empty apartment fills him with. No matter what, he intends to prove to Simone that she can trust him. However long it takes, he will convince her once again. He thinks this, then drinks her coffee standing up in the kitchen; no sense letting it go to waste. It upsets his stomach, and he takes a Prilosec.

It is still only nine o'clock in the morning, and his shift at the hospital doesn't start for several hours. He takes a book to the bedroom with him and lies on top of the unmade bed in his stockinged feet. But instead of reading, he starts to think about Josef Ek; he wonders if Joona Linna will be able to get anything out of him.

The apartment is silent, deserted. A gentle calm spreads through his stomach from the medication.

Nothing that is said under hypnosis can be used as evidence, but Erik knows Josef was telling the truth about having killed his family, even if the actual motive is invisible. He closes his eyes. Evelyn must have known her brother was dangerous from an early age. Over the years she learned to live with his inability to control his impulses, gauging the risk of inciting his violent rage against her desire to live normally and independently. The family as a whole would have dealt with his violence, gradually making hundreds of infinitesimal adjustments and compromises in an effort to live with his hostility and keep it at bay. But nothing discouraged his impulses: not discipline, not punishment, not appeasement. They never really appreciated the seriousness of the situation. His mother and father might have thought that his aggressive behaviour was simply because he was a boy. Possibly they blamed themselves for letting him play brutal video games or watch slasher films.

Evelyn had escaped as soon as she could, found a job and a place of her own, but she'd sensed the increasing threat and was suddenly so afraid that she hid herself away in her aunt's cottage, carrying a gun to protect herself.

Had Josef threatened her?

Erik tries to imagine Evelyn's fear in the darkness at night in the cottage, with the loaded gun by her bed. He thinks about what Joona Linna told him after interviewing her. What happened when Josef turned up with a cake? What did he want from her? How did she feel? Was it only then that she became afraid and got the gun? Was it after his visit that she began to live with the fear that he would kill her?

Erik pictures Evelyn as she appeared on the day he met her at the cottage: a young woman in a silver-coloured down vest, a grey knitted sweater, scruffy jeans, and running shoes. She is walking through the trees, her ponytail swinging; her face is open, childlike. She carries the shotgun lazily, dragging it along the ground, bouncing it gently over the blueberry bushes and moss as the sun filters down through the branches of the pine trees.

Suddenly Erik realizes something crucial. If Evelyn had been afraid, if the gun had been to defend herself against Josef, she would have carried it differently. Erik recalls that her knees were wet, and dark patches of earth clung to her jeans.

She went out into the forest with the gun to kill herself, he thinks. She knelt on the moss and placed the barrel in her mouth, but she changed her mind; she couldn't bring herself to do it.

When he'd spied her on the edge of the trees, she was on her way back to the cottage, on her way back to the alternative from which she had wanted to escape.

Erik picks up the phone and calls Joona.

"Erik? I was going to call you, but there's been so much—"

"It doesn't matter," says Erik. "Listen, I've got—"

"I just want to say how sorry I am about all this business with the media. I promise to track down the leak when things calm down."

"It doesn't matter."

"I feel guilty, because I was the one who persuaded you to do it."

"I made my own decision. I don't blame anyone else."

"Personally, even though we're not allowed to say so at the moment, I still think hypnotizing Josef was the right thing to do. It could well have saved Evelyn's life."

"That's what I'm calling about," says Erik. "A thought occurred to me. Have you got a minute?"

Erik can hear the sound of a chair scraping against the floor and then an exhalation as Joona sits. "OK," he says. "Go on."

"When we were out at Värmdö and I spotted Evelyn from the car, I saw her walking among the trees, heading for the cabin, dragging her shotgun in the bushes."

"Yes?"

"Is that the way to carry a gun if you're afraid someone might surprise you, might be coming to kill you?"

"No," replies Joona.

"I think she'd gone out into the forest to kill herself," says Erik. "The knees of her jeans were wet. She'd probably been kneeling on the damp moss with the gun pointing at her forehead or her chest, but then she changed her mind and couldn't go through with it. That's what I think."

Erik stops speaking. He can hear Joona breathing heavily at the other end of the line. A car alarm starts screeching down on the street.

"Thank you," says Joona. "I'll go and have a chat with her."

32

The interview with Evelyn is to be conducted in one of the offices in the custody suite. In order to make the dreary room slightly more inviting, someone has placed a red tin of Christmas gingerbread cookies on the table, and electric holiday candles from IKEA glow in the windows. Evelyn and her advocate are already seated when Joona begins the recording.

"I know these questions may be difficult for you, Evelyn," he says quietly, "but I would be grateful if you would answer them anyway, as best you can."

Evelyn does not reply but looks down at her knees.

"Because I don't think it's in your best interests to remain silent," he adds gently.

She does not react but keeps her eyes firmly fixed on her knees. The advocate, a middle-aged man with shadows of stubble on his face, gazes expressionlessly at Joona.

"Are you ready to begin, Evelyn?" Joona asks.

She shakes her head. He waits. After a while she raises her chin and meets his eyes.

"You went out into the forest with the gun to kill yourself, didn't you?"

"Yes," she whispers.

"I'm glad you didn't go through with it."

"I'm not."

"Is this the first time you've tried to commit suicide?"

"No."

"Before this occasion?"

She nods.

"But not before Josef turned up with the cake?"

"No."

"What did he say to you, when he came?"

"I don't want to think about it."

"About what? About what he said?"

Evelyn straightens up in the chair, and her mouth narrows. "I don't remember," she says, almost inaudibly. "I'm sure it wasn't anything special."

"You were going to shoot yourself, Evelyn," Joona reminds her.

She stands up, goes over to the window, switches the electric candles off and on absently, walks back to her chair, and sits down with her arms folded over her stomach.

"Can't you just leave me in peace?"

"Is that what you really want?"

She nods without looking at him.

"Do you need a break?" asks her advocate.

"I don't know what's the matter with Josef," Evelyn says quietly. "There's something wrong inside his head. When he used to fight, when he was little, he would hit too hard. He wasn't just angry, like little boys get. He was trying to hurt you. He was dangerous. He destroyed all my things. I couldn't keep anything."

Her mouth trembles.

"When he was eight . . . When he was eight, he came on to me. He wanted us to kiss each other. Maybe that doesn't sound so bad, but I didn't want to, and he kept insisting. I was scared of him. He did weird things. He would sneak into my room at night when I was sleeping and bite me and make me bleed. I started to hit back. I was still stronger than he was."

She wipes away the tears rolling down her cheeks.

"It got worse. He wanted to see my breasts. He tried to get in the bath with me. He said he'd—if I didn't do what he said—he said he'd hurt Buster." She pauses for a moment to wipe away more tears. "He killed my dog and threw it off an overpass!" She leaps to her feet and moves to the window again. "He must have been about twelve when he—"

Her voice breaks and she whimpers quietly to herself before continuing.

"When he asked if he could put his cock in my mouth. I said he was disgusting. So he went into my little sister's room and began to hit her. She was only two years old."

Evelyn weeps and then composes herself.

"He made me watch while he jerked off, several times every day. If I said no, he hit my sister, told me he'd kill her. Maybe a few months later, he started demanding sex from me. Every day. He threatened me. But I came up with an answer. I don't know why it worked, but I told him he was below the age of consent and it was against the law. I wouldn't do something illegal."

She wipes the tears away again.

"He seemed to buy it; I don't know why. I thought his demands would go away. I thought—if you can believe it—that he'd *outgrow* them, like it was a *phase*. So I moved out. A year passed, but then he started calling me, reminding me he would be fifteen soon. That's when I hid. I . . . I don't know how he found out I was at the cottage." She is sobbing with her mouth open now. "Oh God!"

"So he threatened you," says Joona. "He threatened to kill the whole family if you didn't—"

"He didn't say that!" she screams. "He said he would start with Dad. It's all my fault. I just want to die . . ."

She sinks down on the floor and cowers against the wall.

33

Joona sits in his office and stares at his hands. One hand still holds the telephone. When he informed Jens Svanehjälm of Evelyn's sudden change of heart, Jens had listened in silence, sighing heavily as Joona went over the cruel motive behind the crime.

"To be perfectly honest, Joona," he had said eventually, "this is all a little bit thin, bearing in mind that Josef Ek accused his sister of being behind the whole thing. What we really need is a confession or some kind of forensic evidence."

Joona glances around the room, rubs his hand over his face, then calls Daniella Richards to arrange a suitable time to continue questioning Josef, when the suspect will have a lower level of analgesics in his body.

"His head must be clear," says Joona.

"You could come in at five o'clock," says Daniella.

"This afternoon?"

"His next dose of morphine isn't due until six. It levels out around teatime."

Joona looks at the clock. It's 2:30 p.m.

"That would suit me very well," he says.

After the conversation with Daniella Richards, he calls Lisbet Carlén and informs her of the time.

In the staff room he takes an apple from the fruit bowl; when he returns to his office, his seat is occupied by Erixon, the crime-scene technician. His entire body is wedged against the desk. His face is bright red, and he is puffing and panting as he waves a weary hand at Joona.

"If you shove that apple in my mouth, you'll have a suckling pig all ready for Christmas," he says.

"Oh, shut up," says Joona, taking a bite.

"I deserve it," says Erixon. "Since that Thai place opened on the corner, I've put on twenty-five pounds."

Joona shrugs. "The food's really good."

"Fuckin' A."

"So what did you find in the women's locker room?" asks Joona.

Erixon holds up a chubby hand in a defensive gesture. "Don't say, *What did I tell you?*"

Joona grins. "We'll see," he says diplomatically.

"All right," says Erixon, wiping the sweat from his cheeks. "There was hair belonging to Josef Ek in the drain, and there was blood from his father between the tiles on the floor."

"What did I tell you?" Joona beams.

In the lift down to the foyer, Joona calls Jens Svanehjälm again.

"I'm glad you called," says Jens. "I'm getting a lot of shit about this hypnosis business. They're saying we ought to scrap the preliminary investigation into Josef, that it's just going to cost money and—"

"Hold on."

"But I've decided to—"

"Jens?"

"What?" he replies irritably.

"We've got forensic evidence," he says seriously. "We can link Josef Ek to the first crime scene and to his father's blood."

Chief Prosecutor Jens Svanehjälm breathes heavily on the other end of the phone. "Joona, you know you've called at the last possible minute."

"But I'm in time."

"Yes."

They are just about to hang up when Joona says, "What did I tell you?"

"What?"

"I was right, wasn't I?"

There is silence at the other end of the line. Then Jens says, slowly and deliberately, "Yes, Joona, you were right."

They end the conversation, and the smile fades from the detective's face. He walks along the glass wall facing the courtyard and checks the time once again. In half an hour he wants to be at the Nordic Museum.

34

Joona walks up the staircase in the museum and down the long, empty corridors, passing hundreds of illuminated display cases without even glancing at them. He does not see the tools, the treasures, or the fine examples of handicrafts; he does not notice the exhibitions, the folk costumes, or the large photographs.

The guard has already drawn up a chair next to the faintly illuminated display case. Without saying a word, Joona sits down as usual and contemplates the Sami bridal headdress, sewn by descendents of indigenous people from the Scandinavian peninsula. Fragile and delicate, it widens out into a perfect circle. The pieces of lace are reminiscent of the cup of a flower, or a pair of hands brought together with the fingers stretching upward. Slowly Joona moves his head, so that the light gradually moves. The headdress is woven from roots, tied by hand. The material was dug from the ground, but it shines like gold.

The present is gone, but the memory lingers mercilessly.

He is driving a car, the rain has stopped, but the puddles of water glow like fire in the sunset. Everything is so wonderfully beautiful, and then gone forever.

This time, Joona sits in front of the display case for an hour before he gets to his feet, nods to the guard, and slowly leaves the museum. The slush on the ground is dirty, and he can smell diesel from a boat beneath the bridge, Djurgårdsbron. He is ambling toward Strandvägen when his cell phone rings. It's Nils Åhlén, the Chief Medical Officer.

"I'm glad I got hold of you," The Needle says when Joona answers.

"Have you finished the postmortem?"

"More or less."

Joona sees a young father on the pavement, tipping a buggy up over and over again to make his child laugh. A woman is standing motionless at a window, gazing out into the street; when he catches her eye, she immediately takes a step backwards into her apartment.

"Did you find anything unexpected?" asks Joona.

"Well, I don't know . . ."

"But?"

"Joona, these bodies were subjected to a great deal of violence. Particularly the little girl."

"I realize that," says Joona.

"Many of the wounds were inflicted purely for pleasure. It's appalling."

"Yes," says Joona, thinking about how things looked when he arrived at the scenes of the crimes: the shocked police officers, the feeling of chaos in the air, the bodies inside. He remembers Lillemor Blom's ashen cheeks as she stood outside smoking, her hands shaking. He recalls how the blood had splashed on the windowpanes, run down the inside of the patio doors at the back of the house.

"And then there's this business with the rather surgical cut to the stomach," says The Needle.

"Have you come to any conclusion about that?"

The Needle sighs. "Well, it's just as we thought. The cut was inflicted some two hours after death. Someone turned her body over and used a sharp knife to cut open the old C-section scar." He leafs through his papers. "However, our perpetrator doesn't know much about *section caesarea*. Katja Ek had an emergency C-section scar running down from the navel in a vertical line."

"And?"

The Needle puffs loudly. "Well, the thing is, the cut in the womb is always horizontal, even if the cut in the stomach is vertical."

"But Josef didn't know that," says Joona.

"No," replies The Needle. "He simply opened the stomach without realizing that a C-section always involves two incisions, one through the stomach and one through the womb."

"Is there anything else I ought to know straight away?"

"Maybe the fact that he attacked the bodies for an unusually long time; he just kept on and on. They were long dead by the time he was done with them. He must have been getting more and more tired. That kind of violence would take a lot out of you. But he couldn't get enough; his rage showed no sign of subsiding."

Silence falls between them. Joona continues along Strandvägen. He starts to think about his most recent interview with Evelyn again.

"Anyway, I just wanted to confirm this business with the C-section," says The Needle, after a while. "The fact that the cut was made some two hours after death."

"Thanks, Nils," says Joona.

"You'll have my full report in the morning."

Joona tries to remember what Evelyn had said about her mother's C-section while slumped on the floor against the wall in the interview room, talking about Josef's pathological jealousy of his little sister.

"There's something wrong inside Josef's head," she had whispered. "There always has been. I remember when he was born, Mum was really sick. I don't know what it was, but they had to do an emergency C-section." Evelyn shook her head and sucked in her lips before continuing. "Do you know what an emergency C-section is?"

"More or less," Joona replied.

"Sometimes . . . sometimes there can be complications when you give birth that way." Evelyn looked at him shyly.

"You mean the baby can be starved for oxygen, that kind of thing?" Joona asked.

She shook her head and wiped the tears from her cheeks. "I mean, not with the baby. The mother can have psychological problems. I read about it. A woman who's gone through a difficult labour and is then suddenly anaesthetized for a C-section sometimes has problems later."

"Post-natal depression?"

"Not exactly," said Evelyn, her voice thick and heavy. "My mother developed a psychosis after she gave birth to Josef. They didn't realize on the maternity ward; they just let her take him home. I was only eight, but I noticed right away. Everything was wrong. She didn't pay any attention to him at all, she didn't touch him, she just lay in bed and cried and cried and cried. I was the one who took care of him."

Evelyn looked at Joona and whispered the rest.

"Mum would say he wasn't hers. She'd say her real child was dead. In the end, she had to be hospitalized."

Evelyn smiled wryly when she mentioned the vast psychiatric unit.

"Mum came home after about a year. She pretended everything was back to normal, but in reality she continued to deny his existence."

"So you don't think your mother had really recovered?" Joona asked tentatively.

"She was fine, because when she had Lisa, everything was different. She was so happy about Lisa; she did everything for her."

"And you did everything for Josef."

"I took care of him—someone had to—but he started saying that Mum should have given birth to him properly. For him, what explained the unfairness of it all was that Lisa had been born *through her cunt* and he hadn't. That's what he said all the time: Mum should have given birth to him through her cunt . . ."

Evelyn's voice died away. She turned her face to the wall, and Joona looked at her tense, hunched shoulders without daring to touch her.

35

For once it is not totally silent in the intensive care unit at Karolinska University Hospital when Joona arrives. Someone has switched the television on in the common room, and Joona can hear the clink of tableware on dinner plates. The aroma of institutional food permeates the ward.

He thinks about Josef cutting open the old C-section scar on his mother's stomach: his passage into life, one that had condemned him to a motherless existence.

The boy must have realized from an early age that he was not like the other children. Joona considers the endless loneliness of a boy rejected by his mother. A person who has been the indisputable favourite of his mother keeps for life the feeling of the conqueror, but the opposite results not only in an absence of this feeling but also the presence of an active darkness. The only one who gave Josef love and care was Evelyn, and he couldn't cope with being rejected by her; the slightest indication that she was distancing herself from him plunged him into despair and rage, his fury directed increasingly at the beloved younger sister.

Joona nods at Sunesson, the cop on guard, who is standing outside the door of Josef Ek's room, then glances in at the boy. A heavy drip stand right next to the bed is supplying him with both fluid and blood plasma. The boy's feet protrude from beneath the pale blue blanket; the soles are dirty, hairs and bits of grit and rubbish are stuck to the surgical tape covering the stitches. The television is on, but he doesn't appear to be watching it.

The social worker, Lisbet Carlén, is already in the room. She hasn't noticed Joona yet; she is standing by the window adjusting a barrette in her hair.

Josef is bleeding anew from one of his cuts; the blood runs along his arm and drips to the floor. An older nurse leans over the boy, tending to his dressings. She loosens the compress, tapes the edges of the wound together once again, wipes the blood away, and leaves the room.

"Excuse me," says Joona, catching up with her in the hallway.

"Yes?"

"How is he? How is Josef getting on?"

"You'll have to speak to the doctor in charge," the nurse replies, setting off once again.

"I will," says Joona with a smile, hurrying after her. "But there's something I'd like to show him. Would it be possible for me to take him there—in a wheelchair, I mean?"

The nurse stops dead and shakes her head. "Under no circumstances is the patient to be moved," she says sternly. "What a ridiculous idea. He's in a great deal of pain, he can't move, there could be new bleeds, and he could begin to haemorrhage if he were to sit up."

Joona returns to Josef's room, walking in without knocking, and turns off the TV. He switches on the tape recorder, mutters the date and time and those present, and sits down. Josef opens his heavy eyes and looks at him with a mild lack of interest. The chest drain emits a pleasant, low-pitched, bubbling noise.

"You'll be discharged soon," says Joona.

"Good," says Josef faintly.

"Although you'll immediately be transferred to police custody."

"What do you mean? Lisbet said the prosecutor isn't prepared to take any action," says Josef, glancing over at the social worker.

"That was before we had a witness."

Josef closes his eyes gently. "Who?"

"We've talked quite a bit, you and I," says Joona. "But you might want to change something you've already said or add something you haven't said."

"Evelyn," he whispers.

"You're going to be inside for a very long time."

"You're lying."

"No, Josef, I'm telling the truth. Trust me. You'll be arrested, and you now have the right to legal representation."

Josef attempts to raise his hand but doesn't have the strength. "You hypnotized her," he says with a smile.

Joona shakes his head.

"It's her word against mine," he says.

"Not exactly," says Joona, contemplating the boy's clean, pale face. "We also have forensic evidence."

Josef clamps his jaws tightly together.

"I haven't got a lot of time, but if there's anything you want to tell me, I can stay for a little while longer," says Joona pleasantly.

He allows half a minute to pass, drumming his fingers on the arm of his chair, and then gets to his feet, picks up the tape recorder, and leaves the room with a brief nod to the social worker.

In the car outside the hospital, Joona considers whether he should have confronted Josef with Evelyn's story, just to see the boy's reaction. There is a simmering arrogance in Josef Ek that might lead him to incriminate himself if he were sufficiently provoked.

He considers going back inside for a moment, but he doesn't want to be late for dinner with his girlfriend. Josef Ek will keep until next time.

36

It is dark and misty when he parks the car outside Disa's cream-coloured building on Lützengatan. He feels frozen as he makes his way to the front door, glancing at the frosty grass, the black branches of the trees.

He tries to recall Josef, lying there in his bed, but all he can remember is the chest drain, bubbling and rattling away. Yet he has the feeling he saw something important without comprehending it. The sense that something isn't right continues to nag at him as he takes the lift up to Disa's apartment and rings the bell. While he waits, Joona can hear someone on the landing up above, sighing spasmodically or weeping quietly.

Disa opens the door looking stressed, wearing only her bra and pantyhose.

"I assumed you'd be late," she explains.

"Well, I'm slightly early instead," says Joona, kissing her lightly on the cheek.

"Perhaps you could come inside and shut the door before all the neighbours see my ass."

The welcoming hall smells of food. The fringe of a pink lampshade tickles the top of Joona's head.

"I'm doing sole with almonds and new potatoes," says Disa.

"With melted butter?"

"And mushrooms, and parsley."

148

"Delicious."

The one-bedroom apartment is rather shabby, but with an inherent elegance; high ceilings with varnished wood panelling, a beautifully varnished parquet floor, and graceful windows framed in teak.

Joona follows Disa into her bedroom, still trying to remember what it was that he saw in Josef's room. Disa's laptop is in the middle of her unmade bed, with books and sheets of paper strewn around.

He settles into an armchair and waits for her to finish dressing. Without a word she turns her back to him so he can zip up a close-fitting, simply cut dress.

Joona glances at one of Disa's open books and spies a large, black-and-white photo of a graveyard. A group of men, archaeologists, dressed in clothing from the 1940s, are walking along toward the back of the picture, peering at the photographer. It looks as if the site has just begun to be excavated; the surface of the ground is marked with dozens of small flags.

"Those are graves," she says quietly. "The flags show the location of the graves. The man who conducted the dig on this site was called Hannes Müller; he died a while ago, but he was at least a hundred years old. Stayed on at the institute until the end. He looked like a sweet old tortoise."

She stands in front of the long mirror, weaves her straight hair into two thin braids, and turns to face him.

"How do I look?"

"Lovely," says Joona.

"Yes," she replies sadly. "How's your mum?"

Joona catches hold of her hand. "She's fine," he whispers. "She sends you her love."

"That's nice. What else did she say?"

"She said you shouldn't have anything to do with me."

"No," says Disa gloomily. "She's right, of course."

Slowly she runs her fingers through his thick, tousled hair. She smiles at him suddenly, then goes over to the laptop, switches it off, and stashes it on the chest of drawers.

"Did you know that, according to pre-Christian law, newborn babies were not regarded as fully valid individuals until they had been put to the breast? It was permissible to place a newborn child out in the forest during the period between birth and the first feed."

"So you became a person through the choice of others," says Joona slowly.

Disa opens her wardrobe, lifts out a shoebox, and takes out a pair of dark brown sandals with soft straps and beautiful heels, made up of strips of different kinds of wood.

"New?" asks Joona.

"Sergio Rossi. They were a present to myself, because I have such an unglamorous job," she says. "I spend entire days crawling around in a muddy field."

"Are you still out in Sigtuna?"

"Yes."

"What have you actually found?"

"I'll tell you while we're eating."

He points to her shoes. "Very nice," he says, getting up from the armchair.

Disa turns away with a wry smile. "I'm sorry, Joona," she says over her shoulder, "but I don't think they make them in your size."

He suddenly stops dead. "Hang on," he says, reaching out to the wall to support himself.

Disa is looking at him inquiringly. "It was just a joke," she explains.

"No, no, it's his feet!"

Joona pushes past her into the hallway, pulls his phone out of his overcoat pocket, calls Central Control, and calmly informs them that Sunesson needs immediate backup at the hospital.

"What's happening?" asks Disa.

"His feet were really dirty," Joona tells her. "They told me he can't move, but he's been out of bed. He's been out of bed, walking around."

Joona calls Sunesson, and when no one answers he pulls on his jacket, whispers an apology, and races down the stairs.

37

At approximately the same time as Joona is ringing Disa's doorbell, Josef Ek sits up in bed in his room at the hospital.

Last night he checked to see if he could walk: he eased his feet to the floor and stood still for a long time with his hands resting on the bed-frame, as the pain from his many wounds washed over him like boiling oil and the agonizing stab from his damaged liver made everything go black. But he could walk. He had stretched out the tubes from the drip and the chest drain, checked what was in the store cupboard, and climbed back into bed.

It is now thirty minutes since the nurse on the night shift came in to see him. The hall is almost silent. Josef slowly pulls out the IV in his wrist, feels the sucking of the tube as it leaves his body. A small amount of blood trickles down onto his knee.

It doesn't hurt as much when he gets out of bed this time. He moves stiffly over to the cupboard with the scalpels and syringes he'd seen amid the compresses and rolls of gauze bandage. He pushes a few syringes into the wide, loose pocket of his hospital gown. With trembling hands he breaks open the packaging of a scalpel and slices through the chest drain tube. Slimy blood runs out, and his left lung slowly deflates. He can feel the ache behind one shoulder blade and coughs

151

slightly, but he isn't really aware of the difference, the reduced lung capacity.

Suddenly he hears footsteps out in the corridor, rubber soles against the vinyl flooring. With the scalpel in his hand, Josef positions himself behind the door, peers through the pane of glass, and waits.

The nurse stops to chat with the police officer on guard. Josef can hear them laughing about something.

"But I've quit smoking," she says.

"If you've got a nicotine patch I wouldn't say no," the police officer goes on.

"I quit those too," she replies. "But go outside if you need to, I'll be in here for a while."

"Five minutes," says the cop eagerly.

He goes away, there is the rattle of keys, and the nurse enters the room leafing through some papers. She looks up, startled. The laughter lines around the corners of her eyes become more prominent as the blade of the scalpel slices into her throat. He is weaker than he thought and has to stab at her several times. The sudden violence of his movements pulls at the scabs on his body, sending a fiery sensation shooting through him. The nurse does not fall down immediately but tries to hold on to him. They slide down to the floor together. Her body is all sweaty; steaming hot. He tries to stand up but slips on her hair, which has spread out in a wide, blonde sheaf. When he wrenches the scalpel out of her throat, she makes a whistling sound and her legs begin to jerk. Josef stands gazing at her for a while before making his way out into the corridor. Her dress has worked its way up, and he can clearly see her pink panties beneath her tights.

He makes his way down the corridor. He heads to the right, finds some clean clothes on a cart, and changes. Some distance away, a short, stocky woman is moving a mop back and forth across the shining vinyl floor. She is listening to music through headphones. Coming closer, Josef stands behind her and takes out a disposable syringe, stabbing at the air behind her back several times, stopping short of touching her. She continues mopping, oblivious. Josef can hear a tinny beat coming from the headphones. He pushes the syringe back in his pocket, and shoves the woman aside as he walks past. She almost falls over and swears in Spanish. Josef stops dead and turns to face her.

"What did you say?" he asks.

She takes off the headphones and gapes at him.

"Did you say something?" he asks.

She shakes her head quickly and goes on cleaning. He stares at her for a while and then continues on his way toward the lift.

38

Joona Linna drives along Valhallavägen at high speed, past the stadium where the summer Olympics were held in 1912, and changes lanes to overtake a big Mercedes. Out of the corner of his eye he can see the lighted redbrick façade of Sophiahemmet flickering through the trees. The tyres thunder over a large metal plate. Stomping on the gas, he passes a bus that is just about to pull out from the stop. The driver sounds his horn angrily and for a long time as Joona cuts in ahead of him. The water from a grey puddle splashes up over the parked cars and pavements just past the University of Technology.

Joona runs a red light at Norrtull, passes Stallmästaregården, and hits almost 110 miles per hour on the short stretch along Uppsalavägen before slowing when he reaches the exit ramp that dips steeply beneath the motorway and up toward Karolinska Hospital.

As he parks next to the main entrance, he sees several police cars with blue lights flashing, sweeping across the brown façade of the hospital like terrible wing beats. Reporters and camera crews surround a group of nurses who shiver outside the big doors, fear etched on their faces. A couple of them weep openly in front of the cameras.

Joona tries to go inside but is immediately stopped by a young police officer who is stamping his feet up and down, either with shock or agitation.

"Out," says the cop, giving him a shove.

Joona looks into a pair of dumb pale-blue eyes. He removes the hand from his chest and says calmly, "National CID."

There is a stab of suspicion in the pale blue eyes. "ID, please."

"Joona, get a move on, over here."

Carlos Eliasson, Head of the National CID, is waving to him in the pale yellow light by the reception desk. Through the window he can see Sunesson sitting on a bench weeping, his face crumpled. A younger colleague sits down beside him and puts an arm around his shoulders.

Joona shows his ID and the officer moves to one side, his expression surly. Large parts of the entrance have been cordoned off with police tape. The journalists' cameras flash outside the glass walls, while inside the crime team is busy taking their photographs.

Carlos is leading the investigation and is responsible for both the overall strategic approach and the immediate tactical detail. He issues rapid instructions to the scene-of-crime coordinator and then turns to Joona.

"Have you got him?" asks Joona.

"We have eyewitnesses who saw him making his way outside using a wheeled walker," says Carlos. "It's down at the bus stop." He glances at his notes. "Two buses have left since then, plus seven taxis and patient transport vehicles . . . and probably a dozen or so private cars, and just one ambulance."

"Have you sealed off the exits?"

"Too late for that."

A uniformed officer is waved through.

"We've traced the buses—no luck," he says.

"What about the taxis?" asks Carlos.

"We've finished with Taxi Stockholm and Taxi Kurir, but . . ." The officer waves a hand helplessly as if he can no longer remember what he was going to say.

"Have you contacted Erik Maria Bark?" asks Joona.

"We called him straight away. There was no answer, but we're trying to get hold of him."

"He needs protection."

"Rolle!" yells Carlos. "Did you get hold of Bark?"

"I just called," replies Roland Svensson.

"Try again," says Joona.

"I need to speak to Omar in Central Control," says Carlos, looking around. "We need to put out a national alert."

"What do you want me to do?"

"Stay here, check if I've missed anything," says Carlos. He calls over Mikael Verner, one of the technicians from the murder squad.

"Tell Detective Linna what you've found so far," Carlos orders.

Verner looks at Joona, his face expressionless, and says in a nasal voice, "A dead nurse . . . Several witnesses saw the suspect making his way out with a wheeled walker."

"Show me," says Joona.

They go up the fire escape together, since the lifts are still being examined.

Joona contemplates the red footprints left by the barefoot Josef Ek on his way down to the exit. There is a smell of electricity and death. A bloody handprint on the wall suggests that he stumbled or had to support himself. Joona sees blood on the metal lift door and something that looks like the greasy imprint of a forehead and the tip of a nose.

They continue along the corridor and stop in the doorway of the room where he spoke to Josef only an hour or so ago. A pool of almost black blood surrounds a body on the floor.

"She was a nurse," says Verner tersely. "Ann-Katrin Eriksson."

Joona looks at the dead woman's pale blonde hair and lifeless eyes. Her uniform is bunched up around her hips. It looks as if the murderer tried to pull up her dress, he thinks.

"It seems likely the murder weapon was a scalpel," says Verner.

Joona mutters something, takes out his phone, and rings the holding cells at Kronoberg. A sleepy male voice replies, saying something Joona doesn't hear.

"Joona Linna here," he says quickly. "I need to know if Evelyn Ek is still with you."

"What?"

Joona repeats his question. "Is Evelyn Ek still there?"

"You'll need to ask the duty officer," the voice responds sourly.

"Put him on, please."

"Just a minute," says the man, putting the phone down.

Joona hears him walk away, followed by the squeak of a door. Then there is an exchange of words, and something bangs. Joona looks at his watch. He's already been at the hospital for ten minutes.

He heads down to the main door, keeping the phone to his ear.

"Kronoberg," says a genial voice.

"Joona Linna, National CID. I need to know the status of one of your detainees: Evelyn Ek," he says briefly.

"Evelyn Ek," says the voice thoughtfully. "Right, yes. We let her go; it wasn't easy. She wanted to stay here."

"And you just put her on the street?"

"No, no, the prosecutor was here; she's in"—Joona can hear pages turning—"she's in one of our safe apartments."

"Good," he says. "Put some officers outside her door. Do you hear me?"

"We're not idiots."

Joona finds Carlos, who is intently studying something on the screen of his laptop. He tries to get his attention but when he fails he just keeps going, out through the glass doors.

On Joona's police radio, Omar at Central Control is repeating the code word Echo, the designation for the deployment of dog units. Joona guesses that they have traced most of the cars by this time, with no results.

He wanders over to the abandoned walker, left at the bus stop, and looks around. He blots out the people who are watching from the other side of the police cordon, he blots out the flashing blue lights and the agitated movements of the police officers, he blots out the flashing cameras of the journalists, and instead he allows his gaze to roam over the car park and in between the various buildings of the hospital complex.

Joona sets off, stepping over the fluttering tape cordoning off the area. He pushes his way through the group of curious onlookers and heads for Northern Cemetery, following the fence and peering among the black silhouettes of trees and gravestones. A network of paths, some better lit than others, extends over an area of roughly 150 acres, containing memorial groves, a crematorium, and 30,000 graves.

39

Joona passes the lodge by the gate to the large cemetery, increases his speed, glances over at Alfred Nobel's pale obelisk, and moves on past the enormous crypt.

In the quiet here, the wind rustles through the bare branches of the trees and his own footsteps echo faintly between gravestones and crosses. Some kind of heavy vehicle thunders along in the distance on the motorway. Something rustles among the dry leaves beneath a bush. Here and there, candles are burning by the graves in misty glass containers.

Joona makes for the eastern edge of the cemetery, the area facing the on-ramp for the motorway. Suddenly, he sees a pale form moving in the darkness among the tall gravestones, heading for the cemetery's office, perhaps 400 yards away. He stops and tries to focus his eyes. The figure has an angular, stooping shape. Joona begins to run between monuments and plantings, flickering candle flames and carved angels. He sees the slender figure hurry across the frosty grass, his white clothes flapping around him.

"Josef!" Joona shouts. "Stop!"

The boy keeps going, disappearing behind a huge family plot with a wrought-iron fence and neatly raked gravel. Joona draws his gun, removes the safety catch, and runs laterally, catching sight of the boy. Taking aim at his right thigh, Joona shouts to him to stop. Suddenly an old

158

woman is standing in his way, her face directly in the line of fire. She had been bending over a grave, and now she has straightened up. Joona feels a stab of fear in his stomach and lowers his gun.

"I just want to light a candle on Ingrid Bergman's grave," wails the woman.

Josef disappears behind a cypress hedge and Joona takes off after him. He gazes into the darkness, searching. Josef has disappeared among the trees and the gravestones. The few streetlamps illuminate only small areas, a green park bench or a few yards of gravel path. Joona takes out his mobile, calls Central Control, and demands immediate back-up, at least five teams and a helicopter. He hurries up the slope, jumps over a low fence, and stops. He can hear dogs barking in the distance and the crunch of gravel not far away; he begins to run in that direction. Sensing movement among the gravestones, he keeps his gaze fixed on the area, trying to get closer, to find a line of fire if he manages to spot the boy. There's an uproar, and blackbirds rise into the air. A dustbin falls over, its lid rolling along the path before clattering to a stop.

Suddenly Joona sees Josef running behind a brown frost-covered hedge. He is bent as if with pain but moves quickly. Joona pivots to follow and slips, sliding down a knoll and crashing at the bottom into a stand of watering cans and vases. By the time he gets to his feet, he has lost sight of the boy. His pulse pounds in his temples. His lower back throbs where he fell on it, and his hands are cold and numb.

Joona sprints across the gravel path and looks around. The office building where Josef had seemed to be heading is some distance away. Behind it, Joona spots an official city car. It slowly swings around in a U-turn, red tail-lights fading and the harsh beam of the headlights flickering over the trees, suddenly illuminating Josef. He is standing on the narrow track, swaying. His head is drooping heavily, but he takes a couple of stumbling steps. The car stops, and a man with a beard climbs out.

Running as fast as he can, Joona yells, "Police!" But they don't hear him.

He fires a shot into the air and, startled, the man with the beard jerks his head in Joona's direction. Josef is undeterred and moves closer to the man; something—a scalpel—in his hand gleams in the headlights. It's a matter of just a few seconds. Joona has no chance of reaching them. Kneeling, he uses a gravestone for support. The distance is over 300 yards, six times as far as the gallery in the precision shooting range. The sight wobbles in front of his eyes. It's difficult to see; he blinks and fixes his gaze. The greyish-white figure narrows and darkens. The branch of a tree keeps moving in the wind across his line of fire.

The bearded man has turned to face Josef and takes a step backwards. Joona tries to hold his aim and squeezes the trigger. The shot is fired and the recoil travels through his elbow and shoulder. The powder sears his frozen hand, but the bullet merely disappears among the trees without a trace. As Joona takes aim once again, he sees Josef stab the bearded man in the stomach. The man drops to the ground. Joona fires, the bullet whips through Josef's clothes, he wobbles and drops the scalpel, fumbles at his back, then gets into the city car. Joona begins to run, heading for the track, but Josef has put the car in gear and drives straight over the bearded man's legs and floors the accelerator.

Joona stops and aims at the front tyre; he fires and hits his target. The car swerves but keeps on going; it speeds up and disappears in the direction of the motorway. Joona holsters his gun, takes out his mobile, and reports on the situation to Central Control; he asks to speak to Omar, repeating that he needs a helicopter and adding that he needs an ambulance, too.

The bearded man is still alive; a stream of dark blood pours out of the wound in his stomach, welling between his fingers, and it looks as if both his legs are broken.

"But he was just a boy," the man repeats in a shocked voice. "But he was just a boy."

"The ambulance is on its way," says Joona; at last he hears the sound of a helicopter above the cemetery, the clattering of its rotor blades.

It is very late when Joona picks up the phone in his office, dials Disa's number, and waits for her to answer.

"Leave me alone," she responds, slurring slightly.

"Did I wake you up?" asks Joona.

"What do you think?" There is a short silence.

"Was the food good?"

"Yes, it was."

"You do understand, I really had to leave." He stops speaking; he can hear her yawning and sitting up in bed.

"Are you all right?" she asks.

Joona looks at his hands. Despite the fact that he has washed them carefully, he thinks there is a faint smell of blood on his fingers. He had knelt beside the man whose car Josef Ek had stolen, holding together the wound in the man's stomach. The man had been fully conscious the whole time, talking excitedly and almost eagerly about his son, who had just passed his final school exams and was about to go travelling alone for the first time, visiting his grandparents in northern Turkey. The man had looked at Joona, seen his hands on his stomach, and commented with amazement that it didn't hurt at all.

"Isn't that strange," he had said, gazing at Joona with the clear, shining eyes of a child.

Joona had tried to speak calmly; he explained to the man that the endorphins meant he was free of pain for the time being. His body was in deep shock and had chosen to spare the nervous system any further stress.

The man had fallen silent, then asked quietly, "Is this what it feels like to die?" He had almost tried to smile at Joona. "Doesn't it hurt at all?"

Joona opened his mouth to reply, but at that moment the ambulance arrived, and Joona felt someone gently remove his hands from the man's stomach and lead him to one side while the paramedics lifted the man onto a stretcher.

"Joona?" Disa asks again. "Are you all right?"

"I'm fine," he says. He hears her moving; it sounds as if she's drinking water.

"Would you like another chance?" she asks eventually.

"Of course I would."

"Despite the fact that you don't give a toss about me."

"You know that's not true," he replies, suddenly aware of how unutterably weary his voice sounds.

"Sorry," says Disa. "I'm glad you're all right."

They end the call.

Joona remains seated for a moment, listening to the murmuring silence in the police station; then he stands up, removes his gun from its holster, takes it apart, and slowly begins to clean and oil each part. He reassembles the pistol, goes over to the gun cupboard, and locks it away. The smell of blood has gone. Instead, his hands smell strongly of gun oil. He sits down to write a report to Petter Näslund, his immediate supervisor, explaining why he found it necessary and justified to fire his service weapon.

40

Erik watches as the three pizzas are baked and asks for more pepperoni for Simone. His mobile rings and he checks the display. When he doesn't recognize the number, he slips the phone back in his pocket: probably another reporter. He can't cope with any more questions right now. As he walks home with the large, warm boxes, he tries to plan the conversation he wants to have with Simone, explaining that he got angry because he was innocent, that he hasn't done what she thinks he's done, that he hasn't let her down again, that he loves her. He stops outside the florist's, hesitates, then goes in. There is a heavy sweetness in the air inside the shop, and the window is covered in condensation. He has just decided to buy a bunch of roses when his phone rings again. It's Simone.

"Hello?"

"Where the hell are you?" she asks.

"On my way."

"We're starving."

"Good."

He hurries home, enters the building, and waits for the lift. Through the yellow polished window set in the door, the world outside looks magical and enchanted. He puts the boxes down on the floor, opens the door of the rubbish chute, and throws away the roses.

In the lift he has second thoughts. It's possible she would have been pleased. It's possible she wouldn't have interpreted it as an attempt to bribe her, to avoid a confrontation.

He rings the bell. Benjamin opens the door and takes the pizzas from him. Erik hangs up his coat, goes to the bathroom, and washes his hands. He takes out a box containing small lemon-coloured tablets, quickly removes three of them from their blister pack, swallows them without water, and returns to the kitchen.

"We went ahead and started," says Simone.

Erik shrugs and looks at the water glasses on the table.

"When did we become a family of teetotallers?" He goes to the cabinet and gets out two wineglasses.

"Good move," says Simone, as he opens a bottle of wine.

Erik's phone rings. They look at each other.

"Aren't you going to answer that?" asks Simone.

"I'm not talking to any more journalists tonight," Erik says firmly.

"So let it ring." She cuts a slice of pizza, takes a bite, and waits expectantly. Erik pours them both a glass of wine. Simone nods and smiles.

"Oh, I forgot," she says suddenly. "It's almost gone now, but I could smell cigarette smoke when I got home."

"Do any of your friends smoke?" Erik asks, turning to Benjamin.

"No," Benjamin replies automatically.

"What about Aida?"

Benjamin doesn't respond. He just keeps eating. Suddenly he stops, puts down his knife and fork, and stares at the table.

"Hey, what's the matter?" Erik asks tentatively. "Something on your mind?"

"Nothing's on my mind, Dad."

"You know you can tell us anything."

"Yeah, right."

"Don't you think—"

"You don't get it."

"All right. Explain it to me, then," Erik ventures.

"No."

They eat in silence. Benjamin stares at the wall.

"The pepperoni's delicious," says Simone quietly. She wipes a lipstick mark off her glass. "It's a pity we've stopped cooking together," she says to Erik.

"When would we find the time to do that?"

"Stop arguing!" yells Benjamin.

He drinks his water and gazes out the window at the dark city. Erik eats almost nothing but refills his glass twice.

"Did you have your injection on Tuesday?" Simone asks Benjamin.

"Has Dad ever missed one?" He gets up and puts his plate in the sink. "Thanks."

"I went and had a look at that leather jacket you're saving up for," says Simone. "I was thinking I could pay the rest."

Suddenly, Benjamin's whole face breaks into a smile, and he goes over and hugs her. She holds him tight but lets him go the instant she senses him begin to pull away. He goes to his room.

Erik breaks off a piece of crust and pushes it in his mouth. His phone rings again. It moves across the table, vibrating, but he looks at the display and once more shakes his head. "No friend of mine," he says.

"Have you gotten tired of being a celebrity?" Simone asks gently.

"I've only talked to two journalists today," he says, with a wan smile, "but that was enough for me."

"What did they want?"

"It was that magazine called *Café*, or something like that."

"The one that has tits on the cover?"

"Usually some girl who looks amazed at being photographed in nothing but a pair of panties with a Union Jack on them."

She smiles at him. "What did they want?"

Erik clears his throat and says dryly, "They asked me if it was possible to hypnotize women to make them horny."

"Seriously? How professional."

"Totally."

"And the second conversation," she asks. "Was that a journalist from *Ritz* or *Slitz*?"

"*Radio News*," he replies. "They wondered what my views were on being reported to the Parliamentary Ombudsman."

"I'm sorry for your sake."

Erik rubs his eyes and sighs. To Simone it looks as if he's grown smaller, shrunk by several inches.

"Without the hypnosis," he says slowly, "Josef Ek might have murdered his sister as soon as he was discharged from the hospital."

"You still shouldn't have done it," says Simone softly.

"No, I know," he replies, running his finger around his glass. "I wish . . ."

He falls silent, and Simone is overcome by a sudden desire to touch him, to put her arms around him. But instead she stays where she is and just asks, "What are we going to do?"

"Do?"

"About us. We've said things, said we were going to separate. I don't know where I am with you anymore, Erik."

He rubs his hand over his eyes. "I realize you don't trust me," he says, then falls silent.

She meets his eyes, sees the worn face, the straggling hair, and thinks that there was a time when they almost always had fun together.

"I'm not the person you want," he goes on.

"Stop it," she says.

"Stop what?"

"You say I'm not happy with you, but you're the one who's deceiving me; you're the one who thinks I'm not enough."

"Simone, I—"

He touches her hand, but she moves it away. His eyes are dark; she can see that he has taken pills.

"I need to sleep," says Simone, getting up.

Erik follows her, his face grey and his eyes glazed. On the way to the bathroom, she checks the front door carefully to make sure it's locked.

"You can sleep in the spare room," she says.

He nods indifferently, seeming almost anaesthetized. She watches as he enters their bedroom, emerging a moment later with his duvet and pillow.

In the middle of the night, Simone is woken by a sudden jab in her upper arm. She is lying on her stomach; she rolls over onto her side and feels at her arm. The muscle is tense and itchy. The bedroom is in darkness.

"Erik?" she whispers, but remembers he's sleeping in the spare room.

She turns to face the door and sees a shadow slip out. The parquet floor creaks. She thinks that perhaps Erik has got up for some reason but realizes he should be in a deep sleep, thanks to his pills. Suddenly, she's frightened.

She switches on the bedside lamp, turns her arm toward the light, and sees a bead of blood coming from a small pink dot on the skin.

She can hear soft thuds coming from the hallway. Turning off the light, she slips out of bed, her legs weak. She rubs her sore arm as she eases past the threshold. Her mouth is dry, her legs warm but numb. Someone is whispering and laughing in the hallway, a muted, cooing laugh. It doesn't sound anything like Erik. Then Simone shudders: once again, the front door is wide open. The stairwell is in darkness. Cold air is pouring in. She can hear something from Benjamin's room, a faint whimpering.

"Mum?" Benjamin seems scared. "Ouch!" she hears him say. He begins to cry.

In the mirror in the corridor, Simone can see someone bending over Benjamin's bed holding a syringe. Thoughts whirl around in her head. She tries to comprehend what is happening, what she is seeing.

"Benjamin?" she says, her voice high with anxiety. "What's going on?"

She clears her throat and takes a step closer, but suddenly her legs give way; her hands grope for support, but she is unable to hold herself up. She collapses on the floor, bangs her head against the wall, and feels the pain searing her skull.

She tries again to get up, but she can no longer move; it's as if she has no connection with her legs, no sensation at all in her lower body. There is a strange fluttering sensation in her chest, and she feels short of breath. Her vision disappears for a few seconds, and when it returns it is cloudy.

Someone is dragging Benjamin along the floor by his legs. His pyjama top has worked its way up, and his arms are windmilling slowly, in confusion. He tries to hold on to the doorframe but is too weak. His head bangs against the threshold. He looks Simone in the eye. He is terrified; his mouth is moving but no words come out. She reaches sluggishly for his hand but misses it. She tries to crawl after him but hasn't the strength; her eyes roll back in her head; she can see nothing and blinks and perceives only brief fragments as Benjamin is dragged through the hallway and out onto the landing. The door is closed carefully. Simone tries to call for help, but no sound comes; her eyes close, she is breathing slowly, heavily, she can't get enough air.

Everything goes black.

41

Simone's mouth feels as if it is full of glass fragments. It hurts to breathe. Her tongue, when she tries to move it, feels monstrously large and clumsy. She tries to open her eyes, but her eyelids resist her efforts. Slowly lights appear, sliding past her, metal and curtains, a hospital bed.

Then Erik is sitting on a chair next to her, holding her hand. It's impossible to tell how much time has passed. His eyes are sunken and exhausted; he stares dully into the middle distance. Simone tries to speak, but her throat feels completely raw.

"Where's Benjamin?"

Erik gives a start. "Simone," he says. "How do you feel?"

"Benjamin," she whispers. "Where's Benjamin?"

Erik closes his eyes, his lips pressed tightly together. He swallows and meets her gaze. "What have you done?" he asks quietly. "I found you on the floor, Sixan. You had almost no pulse, and if I hadn't found you—" He runs his hand over his mouth, speaking through his fingers. "What have you done?"

Breathing is hard work. She swallows several times. She understands that she has had her stomach pumped, but she doesn't know what to say. She doesn't have time to explain that she didn't try to take her own life. It's not important what he thinks. Not right now.

"Where's our son?" she whispers. "Is he missing?"

"What do you mean?"

Tears pour down her cheeks. "Is he missing?" she repeats.

"You were lying in the hallway, darling. Benjamin had already left when I got up. Did you have an argument?"

She tries to shake her head, but the movement makes nausea sweep through her. "Someone was in our apartment . . . and took him," she says weakly.

"What?"

She is crying and whimpering at the same time.

"Benjamin?" asks Erik. "What about Benjamin?"

"Oh God," she mumbles.

"What's happened?" Erik is almost screaming.

"Someone's taken him," she replies. "I saw someone dragging Benjamin through the hall."

"Dragging? What do you mean, dragging?" A wild expression has taken over Erik's face but he stops himself, runs a trembling hand over his mouth, and then kneels on the floor at her bedside. "Simone, what happened last night?"

"I was woken during the night by a jab in my arm. I'd been injected. Somebody had given me—"

"Where? Where were you injected?"

She tries to push up the sleeve of her hospital gown; he helps her and finds a small red mark on her upper arm. When he feels the swelling around the dot with his fingertips, his face loses all its colour.

"Somebody took Benjamin," she says. "I couldn't help him."

"We need to find out what you've been given," he says, pressing the call button.

"To hell with that, I don't care. You have to find Benjamin."

"I will," he says.

A nurse comes in, is given brief instructions to run blood tests, then hurries out.

Erik turns back to Simone. "Are you sure you saw someone dragging Benjamin down the hall?"

"*Yes*," she answers, in despair.

"But you didn't see who it was?"

"He dragged Benjamin by the legs through the hall and out the door. I was lying on the floor . . . I couldn't move."

The tears begin to flow once more. He wraps his arms around her, and she sobs against his chest, exhausted and desperate, her body shaking. When she has calmed down a little, she pushes him gently away.

"Erik," she says. "You have to find Benjamin."

"Yes," he says, and stumbles from the room.

A nurse takes his place. Simone closes her eyes so she doesn't have to watch as four small containers fill with her blood.

42

Erik heads for his office in the hospital, thinking about the journey in the ambulance that morning, after he had found Simone on the floor with virtually no pulse. The rapid trip through the bright city, the rush-hour traffic giving way to the blaring siren of the ambulance. Simone's stomach being pumped, the efficiency of the female doctor, her calm, speedy actions. The oxygen, the dark screen showing the irregular rhythm of the heart.

In the corridor, Erik checks his mobile phone and realizes it is turned off. He stops and listens to all his messages. Yesterday a police officer named Roland Svensson called four times to offer police protection. There is no message from Benjamin or from anyone who had anything to do with his disappearance.

He calls Aida, and feels a chilling wave of panic as her high voice, suffused with fear, tells him she has absolutely no idea where Benjamin might be.

"Could he have gone to that place in Tensta?"

"No," she replies.

Erik calls David, Benjamin's oldest friend from childhood. David's mother answers. When she says she hasn't seen Benjamin for several days, he simply cuts off the conversation in the middle of her flow of words.

He calls the path lab to check on their analysis, but they can't tell him anything yet; Simone's blood samples have only just arrived.

"I'll hang on," he says.

He can hear them working, and after a while they report that Simone was injected with "something containing alfentanil."

"Alfentanil? The anaesthetic?"

"Somebody must have got hold of it, either from a hospital or a veterinary surgery. We don't use it here much, it's so bloody addictive. But it looks as if your wife was incredibly lucky."

"What do you mean?" asks Erik.

"She's still alive."

Erik returns to Simone's room to go through everything one more time but sees that she has fallen asleep. Her lips are cracked and sore after having her stomach pumped.

His phone rings in his pocket, and he moves into the corridor before answering. "Yes?"

"It's Linnea at reception, Dr. Bark. You've got a visitor."

It takes a few seconds for Erik to realize that the woman means reception here at the hospital, in the neurosurgical unit, and that she is the Linnea who has worked at the reception desk for four years.

"Dr. Bark?" she asks tentatively.

"A visitor? Who is it?"

"Joona Linna," she replies.

Erik stands in the corridor, waiting for Joona, his mind racing. He thinks about his voicemail messages; Roland Svensson called over and over to offer him police protection. Has somebody threatened me? Erik asks himself; a chill runs through him as he realizes how unusual it is for a detective from the National CID to come and see him in person rather than contacting him by phone.

He wanders into the cafeteria, where a platter of cold cuts and bread has been left for the taking. A feeling of nausea twists and turns inside his body. His hands shake as he pours water into a scratched glass.

Joona has come to tell me they've found Benjamin's body, he thinks. That's why he's here in person. He's going to ask me to sit down; then he's going to tell me Benjamin is dead.

Terrifying images flash through his mind with increasing speed: Benjamin's body in a ditch beside the motorway, or in a black rubbish bag in some forest, washed up on a muddy shore.

"Coffee?"

"What?"

"Would you like some coffee?"

A young woman with shining blonde hair is standing next to the coffee machine, holding up a steaming pot. She looks inquiringly at him, and he realizes he holds an empty cup in his hand. As he shakes his head, Joona Linna walks into the room.

"Let's sit down," says Joona. He wears a troubled expression.

Erik nods, and they sit down at a table by the wall. Joona fidgets with the salt shaker and whispers something.

"What?" asks Erik.

"We've been trying to reach you."

"I didn't answer my phone yesterday," says Erik faintly.

"Erik, I'm sorry to inform you that Josef Ek has run away from the hospital."

"*What?*"

"You're entitled to police protection."

Erik's mouth begins to tremble, and his eyes fill with tears.

"Was that what you came to tell me? That Josef has run away?"

"Yes."

Erik is so relieved that he would like to lie down on the floor and simply sleep. He quickly wipes the tears from his eyes. "When did this happen?"

"Last night. He killed a nurse, stole a car, and seriously injured its driver," Joona says heavily.

Erik nods several times as his thoughts rapidly make new connections. Absolute terror overwhelms the relief of a moment ago. "He came to our house in the middle of the night and took our son," he says.

"What are you saying?"

"Josef has taken my son, Benjamin."

"You mean Benjamin was abducted? Did you see it happen?"

"I didn't, but Simone—"

"What happened?"

"Simone was injected with a powerful drug," Erik says slowly. "I just got the results of her blood test; it's an anaesthetic called alfentanil, used in major surgery."

"But she's all right?"

"She will be."

Joona nods and writes down the name of the drug. "And Simone said she saw Josef take Benjamin?"

"She didn't see the person's face."

"OK."

"Are you going to find Josef?" asks Erik.

"Trust me, we'll find him. There's a national alert out for him. He's badly injured. He's going nowhere."

"But you haven't got any leads?"

Joona gives him a hard stare. "I don't think it will be long before we find him."

"Good."

"Where were you when he came to your apartment?"

"I was sleeping in the spare room," explains Erik. "I'd taken a pill, and I didn't hear a thing."

"So when he came into the bedroom, he only found Simone."

"Yes."

"This doesn't make sense," says Joona.

"It's easy to miss the spare room. It looks more like a closet, hidden when the bathroom door is open. He probably thought I wasn't home."

"I don't mean that," says Joona. "I mean this doesn't sound like Josef. He doesn't give people injections; his behaviour is far more aggressive."

"Perhaps it just looks aggressive to us," says Erik.

"What do you mean?"

"Perhaps he knows what he's doing all the time. I mean, you didn't find any of his father's blood on him back at home. That suggests he works systematically, coldly. What if he decided to get his revenge on me by taking Benjamin?"

There is silence. From the corner of his eye, Erik can see the blonde woman by the coffee machine sipping from her cup as she gazes out over the hospital complex.

Joona looks down at the table; then he meets Erik's eyes and says gently, "I am really very sorry, Erik."

43

After parting with Joona outside the cafeteria, Erik returns to his office. The notion that Benjamin has been kidnapped hasn't yet sunk in. It's simply too incredible to believe that a stranger could break into their apartment and drag his son away.

And yet that's what Simone saw.

It can't be Josef Ek who has taken his son. Yes, he just made the case for it, but it's impossible.

With a feeling that everything around him is becoming completely unmanageable, he sits down at his battered desk and calls the same people over and over and over again, as if he can tell from some nuance in their voices whether they might have overlooked some detail, whether they are lying or keeping information from him. He calls Aida three times in succession, asking first if she knows if Benjamin had any particular plans for the weekend, then if she has the phone numbers of his friends, the third time if she and Benjamin have had a fight. Her voice quavers on the other end of the phone when she answers, and Erik suddenly realizes she's just a kid, overwhelmed by the fierceness of his questioning and, in her own way, by Benjamin's absence. Protectively, he gives her all the numbers where he can be reached and establishes that she hasn't seen Benjamin since school yesterday. Then he begins calling the police. He asks what's happening, whether they're making any progress. He calls every hospital in the Stockholm area. He hears himself saying, in his most authoritative doctorly voice, "He has von Willebrand's disease, but he may not be carrying his alert card from the emergency blood service. I'd recommend screening all unidentified adolescent male admittees for the disease." He calls Benjamin's mobile, which is switched off, for the tenth time. He calls Joona's phone, demanding loudly that the police intensify the search. Joona must insist on more resources. Finally, he begs him to do his utmost.

Erik returns to Simone's room but stops outside. He places a hand on the wall to steady himself; things have begun to spin, and he can feel something tightening around him. His brain is struggling to comprehend what is happening. Within, he can hear a constant refrain: *I'm going to find Benjamin, I'm going to find Benjamin.*

When he feels steadier, Erik looks at his wife through the pane of glass in the door. She is awake, but her face is tired and confused, her lips are pale, and the dark circles around her eyes have deepened. Her strawberry-blonde hair is messy with sweat. She is turning her wedding ring around, twisting it and pressing it against the knuckle. Erik runs a hand over his face and feels the rough stubble. Simone looks back at him, but her expression doesn't change.

Erik goes in and sits heavily by her side. She glances at him, then lowers her eyes. He sees her lips draw back in a painful grimace. A few fat tears well up in her eyes, and her nose reddens with weeping.

"Benjamin tried to grab hold of me; he reached out for my hand," she whispers. "But I just lay there. I couldn't move."

"I've just found out that Josef Ek ran away last night." Erik's voice is weak.

"I'm so cold," she whispers, but she knocks his hand away when he tries to tuck the pale blue hospital blanket around her. "Don't," she says. "It's your fault. You were so fucking desperate to hypnotize him—"

"Simone, I was trying to save someone's life. This is not my fault. It's my job."

"But what about your son? Doesn't he count?" Erik reaches for her, but she pushes him away. "I'm going to call my father," she says, her voice unsteady. "He'll help me find Benjamin."

"I really don't want you to do that," says Erik.

"To be honest, I don't give a shit about what you want. I want my son back."

"I'll find him, Sixan."

"Why don't I believe you?"

"The police are doing what they can, and your father—"

"The police? It was the police who let that lunatic get away," she says angrily. "They're not going to do anything to find Benjamin."

"Josef is a serial killer. The police want to find him, and they will. But I'm not stupid. I know Benjamin isn't important, they don't care about him, not really, not like us, not like—"

"That's exactly what I'm saying."

"Joona Linna explained—"

"But it's his fault! He's the one who got you to carry out the hypnosis."

Erik shakes his head, then swallows hard. "It was my decision."

"My father will do everything he can," she says quietly.

"I understand that you're angry with me. But right now we need to put that aside. I want us to go through every little detail together. We need to think carefully, and we need to be calm."

"What the fuck can you and I do?" she cries.

Silence. Erik hears someone switch on the television in the room next door. "We need to think," he says cautiously. "I'm not sure it was Josef Ek who actually—"

"You're not right in the head," Simone snaps. She tries to get out of bed but hasn't the strength.

"Can I just say one thing?"

"I'm going to get myself a gun, and I'm going to find him," she says.

"The front door was open two nights in a row, but—"

"That's what I said!" she screams. "I said that someone was in the apartment, but you didn't believe me, you never do! If only you had believed me then—"

Erik cuts her off. "Listen to me," he says. "The front door may have been open two nights in a row, but Josef Ek was in his hospital bed the first night, so he can't have been in our apartment then."

Simone is not listening; she is still trying to get up. Groaning angrily, she manages to make it as far as the narrow closet containing her clothes. Erik stands there without helping her, watches her tremble as she gets dressed, hears her swear quietly to herself.

44

It is evening by the time Erik finally manages to get Simone discharged from the hospital. When they return home, the apartment is a complete mess. Bedclothes lie in the hallway, the lights are on, the bathroom tap is running, shoes are heaped on the hall rug, and the telephone has been thrown on the parquet floor, its batteries beside it.

Erik and Simone look around with the horrible feeling that something in their home is lost to them forever. These objects have become alien, meaningless.

Simone picks up an overturned chair, sits down, and begins to pull off her boots. Erik turns off the bathroom tap, goes into Benjamin's room, and looks at the red-painted surface of the desk. Textbooks lie next to the computer, covered in grey paper to protect them. On the bulletin board is a photograph of Erik from his time in Uganda, smiling and sunburned, his hands in the pockets of his lab coat. Erik brushes his hand over Benjamin's jeans, hanging on the back of a chair with his black sweater.

In the living room he finds Simone standing with the telephone in her hand. She pushes the batteries back in and begins to dial a number.

"Who are you calling?"

"Dad," she replies.

"Can you please leave it for now?"

She allows him to take the telephone from her. "What is it you want to say?" she asks wearily.

"I can't cope with seeing Kennet, not now." He places the telephone on the table, and runs his hands over his face before he begins again. "Can't you respect the fact that I don't want to leave everything I have in your father's hands?"

"Can't you respect the fact that—"

"Stop it."

She glares angrily at him.

"Sixan, I'm finding it difficult to think clearly right now. Please let's not play the game where we match each other, grievance for grievance. I don't have the energy. I only want to say that I can't cope with having your father around."

"Are you finished?" she says, holding out her hand for the phone.

"This is about our child," he says.

She nods.

"Can't it be that way? Can't it be about him?" he goes on. "I want you and me to look for Benjamin—along with the police—the way it should be."

"I need my father," she says.

"I need you."

"I don't really believe that," she replies.

"Why not?"

"Because you just want to tell me what to do," she says.

Erik stops pacing the room and carefully composes his features into a reasonable expression. "Sixan, your father's retired. There's nothing he can do."

"He has contacts," she says.

"He thinks he has contacts, he thinks he's still a detective, but he's only an ordinary pensioner."

"You don't know anything about it."

"Benjamin isn't some kind of hobby for old men with too much time on their hands."

"That's it. I'm not interested in what you have to say." She looks at the phone.

"I can't stay here if he's coming. You just want him to tell you I've done the wrong thing again, like he did when we found out about

179

Benjamin's illness; it's all Erik's fault, always Erik. I know that lets you off the hook—it's always been very comfortable whenever you've needed someone to blame in a crisis—but for me it's—"

"Bullshit."

"If he comes here, I'm leaving."

"That's your choice," she says quietly.

His shoulders droop. She is half turned away from him as she punches in the number.

"Don't do this," Erik begs. It's impossible for him to be here when Kennet arrives. He looks around. There's nothing he wants to take with him. He hears the phone ringing at the other end of the line and sees the shadow of Simone's eyelashes trembling on her cheeks.

"Fuck you," he says, and goes out into the hallway.

He hears Simone talking to her father. With her voice full of tears she begs him to come as quickly as he can. Erik takes his jacket from the hanger, leaves the apartment, closes the door, and locks it behind him. Halfway down the stairs, he stops. Maybe he ought to go back and say something. It isn't fair. This is his home, his son, his life.

"Fuck it," he says quietly, and continues down to the door and out into the dark street.

45

Simone stands at the window, perceiving her face as a transparent shadow in the evening darkness. When she sees her father's old Nissan Primera double-parked outside the door, she has to force back the tears. She is already standing in the hallway when he knocks on the door; she opens it with the security chain on, closes it again, unhooks the chain, and tries to smile.

"Dad," she says, as the tears begin to flow.

Kennet puts his arms around her, and when she smells the familiar aroma of leather and tobacco from his jacket she is transported back to her childhood for a few seconds.

"I'm here now, darling," says Kennet. He sits down on the chair in the hallway and perches Simone on his knee. "Isn't Erik home?"

"We've separated."

"Oh, my," says Kennet.

He fishes out a handkerchief, and she slides off his knee and blows her nose several times. Then he hangs up his jacket, noticing that Benjamin's outdoor clothes are untouched, his shoes are in the shoe rack, and his backpack is leaning against the wall by the front door.

He puts his arm around his daughter's shoulders, wipes the tears from beneath her eyes with his thumb, and leads her into the kitchen. He sits her down on a chair, gets out a filter and the tin of coffee, and switches on the machine.

"Tell me everything," he says calmly, as he gets out the mugs. "Start from the beginning."

So Simone tells him in detail about the first night when she woke up and was convinced there was someone in the apartment. She tells him about the smell of cigarette smoke in the kitchen, about the open front door, about the misty light flooding out of the fridge and freezer.

"And Erik?" asks Kennet, his tone challenging. "What did Erik do?"

She hesitates before she looks her father in the eye. "He didn't believe me. He said one of us must have been sleepwalking."

"For God's sake," says Kennet.

Simone feels her face beginning to crumple again. Kennet pours them both a cup of coffee, makes a note of something on a piece of paper, and asks her to continue.

She tells him about the jab in her arm that woke her up the following night, how she got up and heard strange noises coming from Benjamin's room.

"What kind of noises?" asks Kennet.

"Cooing," she says hesitantly. "Whispering. I don't know."

"And then?"

"I asked what was happening, and that's when I saw someone was there, someone leaning over Benjamin and—"

"Yes?"

"Then my legs gave way, I couldn't move; I just fell over. All I could do was lie there on the floor. I watched Benjamin being dragged out . . . Oh God, his face; he was so scared! He called out to me and tried to reach me with his hand, but I was completely incapable of moving by then." She sits in silence, staring straight ahead.

"Do you remember anything else?"

"What?"

"What did he look like? The man who got in?"

"I don't know."

"Did you notice anything distinguishing about him?"

"He moved in a peculiar way, kind of stooping, as if he were in pain."

Kennet makes a note. "Think," he encourages her.

"It was dark, Dad."

"And Erik?" Kennet asks. "What was he doing?"

"He was asleep."

"Asleep?"

She nods. "He's been taking a lot of pills over the past few years," she says. "He was in the spare room, and he didn't hear a thing."

Kennet's expression is full of contempt, and Simone suddenly understands, at least in part, why Erik has left.

"Pills?" says Kennet thoughtfully. "What kind? Do you know the name? Or names?"

She takes her father's hands. "Dad, it's not Erik who's the suspect here."

He pulls his hands away. "Violence against children is almost exclusively perpetrated by someone within the family."

"I know that, but—"

Kennet calmly interrupts her. "Let's look at the facts. The perpetrator clearly has medical knowledge and access to drugs."

She nods.

"You didn't see Erik asleep in the spare room?"

"The door was closed."

"But you didn't see him, did you? And you aren't certain that he took sleeping pills that night, are you?"

"No," she has to admit.

"All we can do is look at the facts and try to ascertain a kind of truth from them. I'm just looking at what we know, Sixan," he says. "We know that you didn't see him asleep. He might have been, but we don't know that."

Kennet gets up, pulls out a loaf of bread, and takes butter and cheese from the fridge. He makes a sandwich and hands it to Simone. After a while he clears his throat. "Why would Erik open the door for Josef Ek?"

She stares at him. "What do you mean?"

"If he did it, what would his reasons be?"

"I think this is a stupid conversation."

"Why?"

"Erik loves Benjamin."

"Yes, but maybe something went wrong. Perhaps Erik just wanted to talk to Josef, get him to call the police or—"

"Stop it, Dad."

"We have to ask these questions if we're going to find Benjamin."

She nods, feeling that her face is torn to shreds; then she says, almost inaudibly, "Perhaps Erik thought it was someone else at the door."

"Who?"

"I think he's seeing a woman called Daniella," she says, without meeting her father's gaze.

46

Simone wakes at five o'clock. Kennet must have carried her to bed and tucked her in. She goes straight to Benjamin's room with a flicker of hope in her chest, but the feeling is swept away as she stands in the doorway, gazing at the empty bed.

She doesn't cry, but she thinks that the taste of tears and fear has permeated everything, as a single drop of milk turns clear water cloudy. She tries to take control of her thoughts, to not think about Benjamin, not properly, to not let the fear in.

The light is on in the kitchen. Kennet has covered the table with bits of paper. On the counter, the police radio is making a murmuring, buzzing noise. Kennet stands completely still, staring into thin air; then he runs his hand over his chin a couple of times.

"I'm glad you managed to get some sleep," he says.

She shakes her head.

"Sixan?"

"Yes," she mumbles; she goes over to the sink and splashes her face with cold water. As she dries herself with the kitchen towel she sees her reflection in the window. It is still dark outside, but soon the dawn will come with its net of winter cold and December darkness.

Kennet scribbles on a scrap of paper, moves another sheet, and makes a note of something on a pad. She sits down opposite her father and tries to analyze how Josef Ek got into their apartment and where he might have taken Benjamin.

"Son of the Right Hand," she whispers.

"What, dear?" asks Kennet, still writing.

"Nothing."

She was thinking that Son of the Right Hand is the Hebrew meaning of Benjamin. In the Old Testament, Rachel was the wife of Jacob. He worked for fourteen years so he could marry her. She bore him two sons: Joseph, who interpreted the dreams of the pharaoh, and Benjamin, the Son of the Right Hand.

Simone's face contracts with suppressed tears. Without a word, Kennet leans over and squeezes her shoulder. "We'll find him," he says.

She nods.

"I got this just before you woke up," he says, tapping a folder that is lying on the table.

"What is it?"

"You know, the house in Tumba where Josef Ek . . . This is the crime-scene investigator's report."

"I thought you'd retired?"

"I have my ways." He smiles and pushes the folder over to her; she opens it and reads the systematic analysis of fingerprints, handprints, marks showing where bodies have been dragged, strands of hair, traces of skin under fingernails, damage to the blade of a knife, marrow from a spinal cord on a pair of slippers, blood on the television, blood on the lamp, on the rag rug, on the curtains.

Photographs fall out of a plastic pocket. Simone tries not to look, but her brain still manages to capture the image of a horrific room: everyday objects, bookshelves, a music system, all black with blood.

On the floor there are mutilated bodies and body parts.

She stands up abruptly and leans over the sink, retching.

"Sorry," says Kennet. "I wasn't thinking . . . Sometimes I forget that not everyone is a policeman."

She closes her eyes and thinks of Benjamin's terrified face and a dark room with cold, cold blood on the floor. She leans forward and throws up. Slimy strings of mucus and bile land among the coffee cups and spoons. She clings to the counter and breathes steadily, calming herself. Above all, she fears losing control of her emotions, lapsing into a state of helpless hysteria. She rinses her mouth, her pulse beating loudly in her ears, and turns to look at Kennet.

"I'm fine," she says faintly. "I just can't connect all this with Benjamin."

Kennet gets a blanket and wraps it around her, gently guiding her back to her chair.

"I'm not sure if I can do this," she says.

"You're doing fine. Now, I need you to listen to me. If Josef Ek has taken Benjamin, he must want something. He hasn't done anything like this before. It's not an escalation, which is what we might typically expect from a serial killer when he changes his MO. No, I think Josef Ek was looking for Erik, but when he didn't find him, he took Benjamin instead. Perhaps to do an exchange."

"In that case, he must be alive, mustn't he?"

"Absolutely," says Kennet. "We just have to figure out where Ek's hidden him, where Benjamin is."

"Anywhere. He could be anywhere."

"On the contrary," says Kennet.

She looks at him.

"It's almost exclusively a question of his home or a summer cottage."

"But *this* is his home," she says, raising her voice and tapping the plastic pocket of photographs with her finger.

47

Kennet repeats to himself the words "his home," takes the file with the photos and the write-up from the forensic investigation of the house, hides them underneath his notepad, and turns around to face his daughter.

"Dutroux," he says.

"What?" asks Simone.

"Do you remember the case of Marc Dutroux?"

"No."

In his matter-of-fact fashion, Kennet tells her about Dutroux, who kidnapped and tortured six girls in Belgium. Julie Lejeune and Melissa Russo starved to death while Dutroux was serving a short prison sentence for stealing a car. Eefje Lambrecks and An Marchal were buried alive in the garden.

"Dutroux had a house in Charleroi," he goes on. "In the cellar he had built a storeroom with a secret door weighing over four hundred pounds. It was impossible to detect the room by knocking to find a hollow space. The only way to find it was to measure the house; the measurements inside and outside didn't match. Sabine Dardenne and Laetitia Delhez were found alive."

Simone tries to get to her feet. Her heart is beating peculiarly, hammering her chest from inside. She cannot believe there are men driven by a need to wall people in, men calmed by the fear of their victims down in the darkness, behind silent walls.

"Benjamin needs his medication," she whispers.

Simone watches her father go over to the telephone. He dials a number, waits for a moment, then says quickly, "Charley? Listen, there's something I need to know about Josef Ek . . . No, it's about his house, the house in Tumba."

There is silence for a while; then Simone can hear someone speaking in a rough, deep voice.

"Yes," says Kennet. "I realize you've checked it out. I've had a look at the report."

The other person continues talking. Simone closes her eyes and listens to the hum of the police radio, which becomes part of the muted bumblebee buzz of the voice on the phone.

"But you haven't measured the house?" she hears her father ask. "No, of course not . . ."

She opens her eyes and suddenly feels a brief adrenaline rush chase away the tiredness.

"Yes, that would be good . . . Can you send the plans over here by messenger?" says Kennet. "And any planning applications . . . Yes, the same address . . . Thanks a lot." He ends the call.

"Could Benjamin really be in that house? Could he, Dad?"

"That's what we're going to find out."

"Well, come on then," she says impatiently.

"Charley's sending the plans over."

"Plans? I don't give a shit about the plans. What are you waiting for? We need to get over there. I can smash down every little—"

"That's not a good idea. I mean, it's urgent, but I don't think we'll gain any time by going over there and starting to knock down walls."

"But we have to do *something*."

"That house has been crawling with police for the past few days," he explains. "If there was anything obvious they would have found it, even if they weren't looking for Benjamin."

"But—"

"I need to look at the plans to see where it might be possible to build a secret room, get some measurements so I can compare them with the actual measurements when we're in the house."

"But what if there *is* no room? Then where can he be?"

"The Ek family shared a summer cottage outside Bollnäs with the father's brothers. I have a friend there who promised to drive over. He knows the area very well. It's in the older part of a development." Kennet looks at his watch and dials a number. "Svante? Kennet here, I was just wondering—"

"I'm there now," his friend says.

"Where?"

"Inside the house," says Svante.

"But you were only supposed to take a look."

"The new owners let me in; they're called Sjölin." Someone says something in the background. "Sorry, Sjödin." He corrects himself. "They've owned the house for over a year."

"I see. Well, thanks for your help." Kennet ends the call. A deep furrow appears in his forehead.

"What about the cottage where his sister was?" asks Simone.

"We've had people there several times. But you and I could drive out and take a look anyway."

They fall silent, their expressions thoughtful, introverted. The letter box rattles; the morning paper is pushed through and thuds onto the hall floor. Neither of them moves. They hear the rattle of more letter boxes on the next floor down; then the outside door opens.

Kennet suddenly turns up the volume of the police radio. A call has gone out. Someone answers, demanding information. In the brief exchange, Simone picks up something about a woman hearing screams from a neighbouring apartment. A car is dispatched. In the background, someone laughs and launches into a long explanation about why his younger brother still lives at home and has his sandwiches made for him every morning. Kennet turns the volume down again.

"I'll make some more coffee," says Simone.

From his khaki bag, Kennet removes a pocket atlas of Greater Stockholm. He takes the candlesticks from the table and places them in the window before opening it. Simone stands behind him, contemplating the tangled network of roads, rail, and bus links crisscrossing one another in shades of red, blue, green, and yellow. Forests and geometric suburban systems.

Kennet's finger follows a yellow road south of Stockholm, passing

Älvsjö, Huddinge, Tullinge, and down to Tumba. Together they stare at Tumba and Salem. It is a pale map showing an old and once-isolated community that was saved from decay and irrelevance when a commuter train station was built there, creating a new town centre. The detailed map indicates a post-war boom: new construction of high-rise apartments and shops, a church, a bank, and a state-owned liquor store has brought suburban convenience and comfort to the old town. Terrace houses and residential areas branch out from a central core. There are a few fields the colour of yellow straw just north of the community; after a few miles these give way to forests and lakes.

Kennet traces the street names and circles a point among the narrow rectangles that lie parallel to one another like ribs.

"Where the hell is that messenger?" he mutters.

Simone pours two mugs of coffee and pushes the box of sugar cubes over to her father. "How did he get in?" she asks.

"Josef Ek? Well, presumably he had a key, or else somebody opened the door to him."

"Couldn't he have broken in?"

"Not with this kind of lock, it's too difficult; much easier to bust down the door."

She nods, trying to think methodically. "Should we take a look at Benjamin's computer?"

"We should have done that before. I did think about it, but then I forgot. I must be getting tired," says Kennet.

Simone notices that he's looking old. She's never thought about his age before. He looks at her, his mouth sad. "Try and get some sleep while I check the computer," she says.

"Forget it."

When Simone walks into Benjamin's room with Kennet, it feels desolate. Benjamin seems so terrifyingly far away. Another wave of nausea sweeps over her. She swallows and swallows, wanting to return to the lighted kitchen where the police radio murmurs and hums. Death waits here in the darkness, a final emptiness from which she will never recover.

She switches on the computer and the screen flashes; the lights come on with a click, the fans begin to whir, and the hard drive issues its command. When she hears the welcome melody from the operating system, it feels as if something of Benjamin has come back.

Father and daughter each pull out a chair and sit down. Simone clicks on the miniature picture of Benjamin's face to log in.

"We need to take this slowly and methodically," says Kennet. "Let's start with his e-mails." But the computer demands a password. "Try his name," says Kennet. She types BENJAMIN, but is denied access. She tries AIDA, turns the names around, puts them together. She tries BARK, BENJAMIN BARK, blushes as she tries SIMONE and SIXAN, tries ERIK, tries the names of the artists Benjamin listens to: SEXSMITH, ANE BRUN, RORY GALLAGHER, JOHN LENNON, TOWNES VAN ZANDT, BOB DYLAN.

"This is no good," says Kennet. "We need to get someone over here who can hack in for us."

She tries a few film titles and directors that Benjamin talks about, but she gives up after a while; it's impossible.

"We should have gotten the plans by now," says Kennet. "I'll call Charley and see what's happening."

They both jump at the knock on the front door. Simone stays at the computer and watches, her heart pounding, as Kennet goes into the hallway and turns the latch.

48

The December sky is as pale as sand; the temperature is a few degrees above zero as Kennet and Simone drive into the part of Tumba where Josef Ek was born and grew up and where, at the age of fifteen, he slaughtered his family. The house looks just like the other houses on the street: neatly kept, unremarkable. If not for the black-and-yellow police tape, nobody would suspect that a week ago this house was the scene of two of the country's most long-drawn-out and merciless murders.

A bicycle with training wheels sits near a sandbox at the front of the house. One end of the police tape has come loose and blown about, finally getting stuck in the letter box opposite. Kennet doesn't stop but drives past slowly. Simone peers in the windows. The curtains are drawn and the place looks completely deserted. The whole row of houses seems to have been abandoned. Could she live on a street where something like this had happened? She shudders. They roll to the end of the cul-de-sac, swing around, and are approaching the scene of the crime once more when Simone's phone suddenly rings.

She answers quickly—"Hello?"—and listens for a moment. "Has something happened?"

Kennet stops the car, turns off the engine, and gets out. From the capacious boot he takes a crowbar, a tape measure, and a torch. He hears Simone say that she has to go before he slams the boot shut.

193

"What do *you* think?" Simone yells into the phone.

Kennet can hear her through the car windows and carefully gauges her distressed expression as she gets out of the passenger seat with the house plans in her hand. Without speaking they walk together towards the white gate in the low fence. It squeaks slightly as it opens. Kennet tips a key out of an envelope, continues to the door, and unlocks it. Before he goes in he turns back to look at Simone and he nods briefly, noting the resolute look on her face.

As soon as they walk into the hallway they are hit by the sickening smell of rancid blood. For a brief moment Simone feels panic rising in her chest: the stench is rotten, sweet, not unlike excrement. She glances at Kennet. He doesn't seem troubled, just focused, his movements carefully considered. They go past the living room. From the corner of her eye Simone has an impression of the bloodstained walls and soapstone fireplace, the overwhelming chaos, the fear lifting from the floor.

They can hear a strange creaking noise from somewhere inside the house. Kennet stops dead, calmly takes out his former service pistol, removes the safety catch, and checks that it is loaded.

They hear something else: a swaying, heavy, dragging noise. It doesn't sound like footsteps. It sounds more like someone slowly crawling.

49

Erik wakes in the narrow bed in his office at the hospital. It's the middle of the night. Glancing at the clock on his mobile, he sees it's almost three. He takes another pill and lies shivering under the covers until the tingling spreads through his body and the darkness comes sweeping back in.

When he wakes up several hours later, he has a splitting headache. He takes a painkiller, goes over to the window, and lets his eyes roam over the gloomy façade with its hundreds of windows. The sky is white, but every window is still in darkness.

He puts his phone down on the desk and gets undressed. The small shower stall smells of disinfectant. The warm water flows over his head and the back of his neck, and thunders against the Plexiglas.

When he has dried himself he wipes off the mirror, moistens his face, and covers it with shaving foam. He is thinking about the fact that Simone said the front door of the apartment had been open the night *before* Josef Ek ran away from the hospital. She was awake, and she went and closed it. But it couldn't have been Josef Ek on that occasion. Erik tries to understand what happened during the night, but there are too many unanswered questions. How did Josef get in? Did he simply knock on the door until Benjamin woke up and opened it?

Erik imagines the two boys standing there regarding each other in the faint light from the stairwell. Benjamin is barefoot, his hair on end; he is wearing his childish pyjamas and blinking with tired eyes at the taller boy. You could say they are not unlike each other, except that Josef has murdered his parents and his younger sister, has just killed a nurse at the hospital with a scalpel, and seriously injured a man at Northern Cemetery.

"No," Erik says to himself. "I don't believe this. It doesn't make sense."

Who would be able to get in, who would Benjamin open the door to, who would Simone or Benjamin trust with a key? Perhaps Benjamin was expecting a nocturnal visit from Aida. Not unheard-of; Erik has to think of everything. Perhaps Josef was working with someone who helped him with the door, perhaps Josef had actually intended to come on the first night but couldn't manage to get away, and his partner had left the door open for him in accordance with their plans.

Erik finishes shaving and brushes his teeth, picks up the phone, checks the time, and calls Joona.

"Good morning, Erik," says the hoarse voice that's distinctively Joona's. He must have recognized Erik's number from the display.

"Did I wake you?"

"No."

"Sorry to call again." Erik coughs.

"Has something happened?" asks Joona.

"You haven't found Josef?"

"We need to speak to Simone, go through everything properly."

"But you don't believe it was Josef who took Benjamin?"

"No, I don't," Joona replies. "But I'd like to take a look at the apartment, make door-to-door inquiries, try to find some witnesses."

"Shall I ask Simone to call you?"

"That won't be necessary."

A drop of water falls from the tap, landing in the basin with a brief, truncated *ping*.

"I still think you should accept police protection," says Joona.

"I'm staying at Karolinska Hospital. I don't think Josef will come back here of his own free will."

"And what about Simone?"

"Ask her. It's possible she might have changed her mind," says Erik. "Even though she already has a protector."

"Oh, yes, so I hear," says Joona dryly. "Can't imagine what it must be like to have Kennet Sträng as a father-in-law."

"Neither can I," replies Erik.

Joona laughs.

"Did Josef try to run away the day before yesterday?" asks Erik.

"There's nothing to suggest that," replies Joona. "Why do you ask?"

"Somebody opened our front door the previous night, just like last night."

"I didn't know that. But I'm pretty sure Josef ran because he found out he was going to be arrested, and he was given that information only yesterday," Joona says slowly.

Erik shakes his head and runs his thumb over his mouth. "This doesn't make sense." He sighs.

"Did you see the open door?" asks Joona.

"No, it was Sixan—Simone—who got up."

"Would she have any reason to lie?"

"It hadn't occurred to me."

"You don't need to answer now."

50

Erik looks into his own eyes in the mirror. He no longer knows what to think. What if Josef had someone helping him? Someone to lay the groundwork the night before the kidnapping? Perhaps the accomplice described everything to Josef: the layout, what the rooms looked like, who slept where. That would explain why Josef didn't find me, thinks Erik, because on the first night I was sleeping in my usual place, in bed next to Simone.

Or maybe this second person was sent just to see if the copied key worked, but then overstepped the mark and went into the apartment, unable to resist sneaking in and looking at the sleeping family. The situation would have given him a pleasurable feeling of control, and he might have decided to play a joke on the family by leaving the fridge and freezer open.

"Was Evelyn at the police station last Wednesday?" asks Erik.

"Yes."

"All day and all night?"

"Yes."

"Is she still there?"

"She's moved into one of our safe apartments. But she's got a double guard."

"Has she been in touch with anyone?"

"You have to let the police do their job," says Joona.

"I'm just doing *my* job," says Erik quietly. "I need to talk to Evelyn."

"What are you going to ask her?"

"Whether Josef has any friends, someone who might be able to help him."

"I can ask her that."

"What their names are."

"I can ask her that, too."

"Where they live, who he might be able to work with."

Joona sighs. "You know perfectly well I can't allow you to carry out a private investigation, Erik. Even if I personally might think it's in order."

"Can't I be there when you talk to her?" asks Erik. "I've worked with traumatized people for many years."

There is silence between them for a few seconds.

"Meet me in an hour in the National Police Headquarters lobby," says Joona eventually.

"I'll be there in twenty minutes."

"Fine, twenty minutes," says Joona, ending the call.

Empty of thoughts, Erik goes over to his desk and opens the top drawer. Among pens, erasers, and paper clips are assorted boxes of pills. He presses three different ones into his hand and swallows them.

He thinks about telling Daniella he hasn't time to attend the morning briefing but forgets to do it. He leaves his office and hurries to the cafeteria, where he drinks a cup of coffee standing in front of the aquarium, following a shoal of neon tetras with his eyes as they search around a shipwreck made of plastic. Then he wraps a sandwich in several paper napkins and stuffs it in his pocket.

In the lift to the ground floor he catches sight of himself in the mirror, meets the blank eyes. His face is sorrowful, almost absent. He thinks about the sensation in your stomach when you fall from a great height: the helpless, dizzying feeling coupled with a heady, almost sexual rush. He has hardly any strength left, but the pills lift him up onto a bright plane where all the contours are sharply defined. He can keep going a little longer, he thinks. All he needs to do is hold it together long enough to find his son again. Then everything can fall apart.

As he drives to the meeting with Joona and Evelyn, he tries to retrace his steps over the past week. His keys could have been copied on several occasions. Last Thursday his jacket was hanging up in a restaurant in Södermalm, keys in the pocket, with nobody to keep an eye on it. It has been over the back of the chair in his office at the hospital, on a hook in the staff cafeteria, and in plenty of other places. The same is doubtless true of Simone and Benjamin's keys.

While manoeuvring through the chaos caused by the redevelopment around Fridhemsplan, he gets out his phone and calls Simone's number.

"Hello?" she answers, sounding stressed.

"It's me."

"Has something happened?" she asks anxiously.

There is a roaring noise in the background, as if from a machine, then a sudden silence.

"No, no. I was just thinking that you ought to check the computer, not just e-mails but everything: what he's downloaded, what sites he's visited, any temporary folders, if he's been visiting chat rooms —"

"Obviously."

"I'm sorry. I just wasn't sure if you'd thought of it."

"We haven't started on the computer yet," she says.

"The password is Dumbledore."

"I know," she says. "I have to go."

Erik drives past police headquarters and sees its changing appearance: the smooth copper façade, the concrete extension, and finally the tall, original building in yellow plaster.

"Simone," he says, "have you told me the truth?"

"What do you mean?"

"About what happened. About the door being open the first time, about seeing someone dragging Benjamin through —"

"What do *you* think?" she yells, ending the call.

Erik hasn't the energy to look for an empty parking space. A parking ticket has no meaning; it will be due in a completely different life. Without a second thought, he pulls up right in front of the police station. The tyres rumble and he stops at the foot of the enormous flight of steps facing the town hall.

He hurries around the building and up the slope, heading toward the park and the entrance to National Police Headquarters. A father walks along with three little girls, all wearing Lucia costumes over their snowsuits. The white dresses strain over the thick winter clothing. Perched on top of their hats, the children are wearing crowns with candles in them, and one of them holds a candle in a gloved hand. Erik suddenly remembers how Benjamin loved to be carried when he was little; he would cling tightly with his arms and legs and say, *Carry me, you're big and strong, Daddy.*

Erik is out of breath by the time he reaches the entrance, a tall, glowing glass cube. He crosses the white marble floor of the lobby to the reception area on the left, where a man sits behind the open wooden desk, speaking on the phone.

Erik explains why he is there; the receptionist nods briefly, taps away on his computer, and picks up the phone. "Reception here," he says, in a subdued tone. "Erik Maria Bark to see you . . ."

Erik sits on a long bench of black creaking leather and gazes around him: at a work of art made of green glass, at the motionless revolving doors. Beyond the huge glass wall is another hallway made of glass leading through an open inner courtyard to the next building. Erik sees Joona Linna pass the waiting area to the right; he presses a button on the wall and walks through the revolving doors. He throws a banana peel into an aluminum waste bin, waves to the man on reception, and comes straight over to Erik.

As they walk to Evelyn's safe house, Joona summarizes what has emerged during his interviews with her: the confirmation that she had intended to take her own life in the forest, the years of sexual abuse she suffered at Josef's hands, his violence toward their younger sister if Evelyn refused him, his eventual demands for full sexual intercourse, Evelyn's withdrawal to the summer cottage, Josef's intimidation of her boyfriend, Sorab, to obtain her whereabouts.

"When Josef showed up at Sonja's cottage on his birthday, she refused once again to have intercourse with him, and he told her she knew what would happen and it would be her fault," Joona explains. "It looks as if Josef planned to murder his father, at least. We don't know why he chose that particular day. It may have been a matter of opportunity, the fact that his father was going to be alone somewhere away from home.

In any event, last Monday, Josef Ek packed a change of clothing, two pairs of overshoes, a towel, his father's hunting knife, a bottle of gasoline, and a box of matches in his gym bag and cycled over to the Rödstuhage playing field. After he'd killed his father and mutilated the body, he took the keys from his father's pocket, went to the women's locker room, showered and changed, locked up after himself, set fire to the bag containing the bloodstained clothes in a children's playground, then bicycled home."

"And what happened next, at home, was more or less the way he described it under hypnosis?" asks Erik.

"Not more or less—exactly, or so it seems," says Joona, clearing his throat. "But the motive—what suddenly made him attack his little sister and his mother—that's something we don't know." He looks at Erik, his expression troubled. "Perhaps he just had a feeling that he wasn't finished, that Evelyn hadn't been punished enough."

Joona stops outside an unremarkable house and calls to say that they've arrived. He taps in the code, opens the door, and lets Erik into the simple entrance hall.

51

Two police officers are waiting outside the lift when they reach the third floor. Joona shakes hands with them and then unlocks an unmarked security door. Before he pushes the door open completely, he knocks.

"Is it all right if we come in?" he asks, through the gap.

"You haven't found him, have you?"

The light is behind Evelyn, so it is impossible to make out her features clearly, only a dark oval surrounded by sunlit hair.

"No," replies Joona.

She comes to the door to usher them in and locks it quickly behind them, checking the lock; when she turns around, Erik sees she is breathing heavily.

"This is a safe apartment; you've got a police guard," says Joona reassuringly. "No one is allowed to give out information about you or search for information about you; the prosecutor has made that decision. You're safe now, Evelyn."

"As long as I stay in here, maybe," she says. "But I'm going to have to come out sometime. And Josef is good at waiting."

She goes over to the window, looks out, and sits down on the sofa.

"Where could Josef be hiding?" asks Joona.

"You think I know something."

"Do you?" asks Erik.

"Are you going to hypnotize me?"

"No." He smiles in surprise.

She is not wearing make-up, and her eyes look vulnerable and unprotected as she scrutinizes him.

"You can if you want to," she says, looking down quickly.

The apartment consists of nothing more than a bedroom with a wide bed, two armchairs, and a television set, a bathroom with a shower cubicle, and a kitchen with an eating area. The windows are made of bulletproof glass, and the walls are painted throughout in a calm yellow colour.

Erik looks around and follows her into the kitchen. "Nice little place," he says.

Evelyn shrugs her shoulders. She is wearing a red sweater and a pair of faded jeans. Her hair is carelessly caught up in a ponytail. "They're bringing a few of my things today," she says.

"That's good," says Erik. "People usually feel better when—"

"Better? What do you know about what would make me feel better?"

"I've worked with—"

"I'm sorry, but I don't give a shit about that, I don't want to talk to psychologists and counsellors."

"I'm not here in that capacity."

"So why are you here?"

"To try to find Josef."

She turns to him and says curtly, "He isn't here."

Without knowing why, Erik decides not to say anything about Benjamin. "Listen to me, Evelyn," he says quietly. "I need your help to map out Josef's circle of acquaintances."

Her eyes are shiny, almost feverish. "All right," she replies, with something resembling a small smile.

"Does he have a girlfriend?"

Her eyes darken and her mouth tenses. "Apart from me, you mean?"

"Yes."

She shakes her head.

"Who does he hang out with?"

"He doesn't hang out with anybody," she says.

"Classmates?"

She shrugs her shoulders. "He's never had any friends, as far as I know."

"If he needed help with something, who would he turn to?"

"I don't know . . . Sometimes he talks to the drunks behind the liquor store."

"Do you know their names, who they are?"

"One of them has a tattoo on his hand."

"What does it look like?"

"I can't remember . . . A fish, I think." She stands up and goes over to the window again.

Erik looks at her. The daylight strikes her young face; he can see a blue vein beating in her slender throat. "Could he be staying with one of them?"

She shrugs her shoulders vaguely. "Maybe."

"Do you think he is?"

"No."

"So what do you think, then?"

"I think he's going to find me before you find him."

Erik looks at her, as she stands with her forehead resting against the window-pane, and wonders if he should press her any further. There is something about her toneless voice, her lack of trust, that tells him she has long had a unique insight into her brother and has abandoned any hope of finding someone to share it with.

"Evelyn? What does Josef want?"

"I can't talk about that."

"Does he want to kill *me*?"

"I don't know."

"But what do you think?"

She takes a deep breath, and her voice is hoarse and tired when she answers. "If he thinks you've come between him and me, if he's jealous, then yes."

"Yes what?"

"Kill you."

"Try, you mean?"

Evelyn licks her lips, turns to face him, then looks down. Erik wants to repeat his question, but nothing comes out. Suddenly there is a knock on the door. Evelyn looks at Joona and Erik, a terrified expression on her face, and backs into the kitchen.

The knocking comes again. Joona walks over, looks through the peephole, and admits two police officers. One of them is carrying a cardboard box.

"I think we found everything on the list," he says. "Where do you want this?"

"Anywhere," says Evelyn faintly, emerging from the kitchen.

"Would you sign here?"

He holds out a delivery receipt, and Evelyn signs it. Joona locks the door behind them when they leave. Evelyn hurries over to the door, checks that he's locked up properly, and turns to face them.

"I asked if I could have some things from home."

"Yes, you told us."

Evelyn crouches down, pulls off the brown sticky tape, and opens the box. She takes out a silver money box in the shape of a rabbit and a framed picture of a guardian angel, but suddenly stops.

"My photo album," she says, and Erik sees that her mouth has begun to tremble.

"Evelyn?"

"I didn't ask for it. I didn't say anything about it."

She opens the album to the first page, revealing a large school photo of herself at about fourteen. She is wearing braces on her teeth and smiling shyly. Her skin glows; her hair is cut very short.

Evelyn turns the page, and a folded piece of paper falls out and lands on the floor. She picks it up, turns it over, and her face flushes deep red. "He's at home," she whispers, passing it to Erik.

He smooths out the paper, and he and Joona read it together:

I own you, you belong only to me, I'm going to kill the others, it's your fault, I'm going to kill that fucking hypnotist and you will help me to do it, you will, you are going to show me where he lives, you are going to show me where you fuck and party, and then I will kill him and you will watch while I do it, then you will wash your cunt with plenty of soap and I will fuck you a hundred times, because then we will be even and we will start again just the two of us.

Evelyn pulls down the blinds and stands with her arms tightly wrapped around her body. Erik places the letter on the table and gets to his feet.

Josef is back home, he thinks quickly. He must be. If he could put the photo album and the letter in the box, he must be there.

"Where else would he go?" she replies quietly.

Joona is already on his cell phone in the kitchen, speaking to the duty officer at Central Control.

"Evelyn, the police have been conducting an exhaustive investigation at the house for almost a week now. Do you know how Josef could hide from them there?"

"The cellar," replies Evelyn, looking up.

"What about the cellar?"

"There's a . . . special room down there."

"He's down in the cellar," Erik shouts in the direction of the kitchen.

On the other end of the phone, Joona can hear the slow rattle of a keyboard.

"The suspect is presumed to be in the cellar," says Joona.

"Just hang on," says the duty officer. "I have to—"

"This is extremely urgent."

After a pause, the duty officer says calmly, "We sent a car to the same address two minutes ago."

"What? To Gärdesvägen eight in Tumba?"

"Yes. The neighbours called to say there was someone inside the house."

52

Kennet Sträng stops and listens before slowly moving over to the staircase. He points his pistol at the floor, holding it close to his body. Daylight comes into the passageway from the kitchen. Simone follows her father, thinking that the murdered family's house reminds her of the house where she and Erik lived when Benjamin was little.

There is a creaking sound from somewhere, the floor or deep inside the walls.

"Is it Josef?" whispers Simone.

The torch, house plans, and crowbar she balances are heavy and awkward. Her hands feel numb.

The house is completely silent now. The creaking and the muted banging have stopped.

Kennet jerks his head at her. He wants them to go down into the cellar. Every muscle in her body is telling her it's a mistake, but she nods.

According to the plans, the best area for a hiding place is definitely the cellar. Kennet marked the drawings with a pen, showing how the wall of the section that houses the old boiler could be extended, creating a virtually invisible room. The other space Kennet marked on the plans was the innermost attic.

The cellar entrance is next to the staircase leading upstairs; it's a narrow opening in the wall, with no door. There are still small hinges on the wall where a child safety gate has been attached. The iron steps leading down into the cellar look almost home-made; the welds are large and untidy, and the steps are covered in thick grey felt.

When Kennet clicks the light switch, nothing happens; he tries again, but the bulb has blown out.

"Stay here," he says, in a low voice.

Simone feels a stab of pure terror. A heavy, dusty smell that makes her think of the stifling air inside a highway tunnel surges up from below.

"Give me the torch," he says, holding out his hand.

Slowly Simone passes it over to her father. He smiles, takes the torch, switches it on, and sets off cautiously down the steps.

"Hello?" Kennet calls gruffly. "Josef? I need to speak to you."

Not a sound comes from the cellar. Not a clatter, not a breath.

Simone clutches the crowbar and waits.

The beam of the torch illuminates little more than the walls and the ceiling of the staircase. The dense darkness below is untouched. Kennet continues down the stairs, the beam picking out individual objects: a white plastic bag, the reflector strip on an old buggy, the glass of a framed movie poster.

"I think I can help you," calls Kennet, more quietly this time.

He reaches the bottom, sweeping the torch around to make sure no one is rushing out of a hiding place. The slanting beam moves across the floor and walls, jumping over objects close by and casting sloping, swinging shadows. Kennet begins again, searching the room calmly and systematically with the shaft of light.

Simone sets off down the steps, the metal construction clanging dully beneath her feet.

"There's no one here," says Kennet matter-of-factly.

"So what did we hear, then? It was definitely something," she says.

Daylight seeps in through a dirty window just below the ceiling. Their eyes are growing accustomed to the dim light. The cellar is full of bicycles of various sizes, a buggy, sledges, skis, and a bread machine, Christmas decorations, rolls of wallpaper, and a stepladder spattered with white paint. On a box someone has written in a thick black felt-tip pen, *Josef's comics*.

A tapping noise comes from the ceiling, and Simone looks over at the stairs and then at her father. He doesn't seem to hear the sound. He walks slowly toward a door at the far end of the room. Simone bumps into a rocking horse. Kennet opens the door and glances into a utility room containing a battered washing machine and dryer and an old-fashioned wringer. Next to a geothermal pump, a grubby curtain hangs in front of a large cupboard.

"Nobody here," he says, turning to Simone.

She looks at him, seeing the grubby curtain behind him at the same time. It is completely motionless yet at the same time somehow alive.

"Simone?"

There is a damp mark on the fabric, a small oval, as if made by a mouth.

"Open up the plans," says Kennet.

It seems to Simone that the damp oval suddenly caves inward. "Dad," she whispers.

"What?" he replies, leaning against the door post as he puts his pistol back in his shoulder holster and scratches his head.

There is a sudden creaking noise. She wheels and sees that the rocking horse is still moving.

"What is it, Sixan?"

Kennet takes the plans from her and lays them on a rolled-up mattress; he shines the torch on the drawing and turns it around. He looks up, glances back at the plans, and goes over to a brick wall where an old dismantled bunk bed stands beside a wardrobe containing bright yellow life jackets. A chisel, various saws, and clamps hang from hooks on a precisely marked tool board. The space next to the hammer is empty; there's an outline for a big axe, but the axe itself is gone.

Kennet measures the wall and the ceiling with his eyes, leans over, and taps on the wall behind the bed.

"What is it?" asks Simone.

"This wall must be at least ten years old."

"Is there anything behind it?"

"Yes, quite a big space," he replies.

"How do you get in?"

Kennet shines the light on the wall again, then on the floor next to the dismantled bed. Shadows slide around the cellar.

"Shine it there again," says Simone.

When Kennet aims the beam at the floor next to the wardrobe, she can see that something scraping countless times along the floor has worn an arc into the concrete.

"Behind the wardrobe," she says.

"Hold the torch," says Kennet, drawing his pistol again.

Suddenly, from behind the wardrobe, they clearly hear the sound of someone moving slowly and carefully. Simone's pulse increases to a violent throbbing. There's someone there, she thinks. Oh my God! She wants to call out *Benjamin!* but doesn't dare.

Kennet gestures to her to move back. She is just about to speak when a loud bang explodes on the floor above. Wood is shattering, splintering. Simone drops the torch and they are plunged back into darkness. Rapid steps thunder across the floor, there is a clattering across the ceiling, and dazzling beams of light sweep down the iron staircase and flood the cellar like high waves.

"Get down on the floor," a man yells hysterically. "Down on the floor!"

Simone is frozen to the spot.

"Lie down," rasps Kennet.

"Shut your mouth!" someone yells.

"Down, down!"

Simone doesn't realize the men are talking to her until she feels a powerful blow in the stomach that forces her to her knees.

"Down on the floor, I said!"

She tries to get air, coughing and gasping for breath. The intense beams of light continue to sweep through the cellar. Black figures pull at her, drag her up the narrow staircase. Her hands are locked behind her back. Struggling to walk, she slips and hits her cheek on the sharp metal handrail.

She tries to turn her head but someone is holding her firmly, breathing fast and pushing her roughly against the wall next to the cellar door.

53

Simone blinks blindly in the daylight, but it's difficult to focus. A number of figures seem to be staring at her. Fragments of a conversation farther away reach her, and she recognizes her father's terse, stringent tone. It's his voice that makes her think of the smell of coffee when she was getting ready for school, with the morning news on the radio.

Only now does she realize that it is the police who have stormed the house. A neighbour must have seen the light from Kennet's flashlight and called them.

A cop, about twenty-five, yet with lines and blue circles beneath his eyes, is looking at her with a strained expression. His head is shaved, revealing a bumpy skull. He rubs the back of his neck with his hand.

"Name?" he demands coldly.

"Simone Bark," she says, her voice still unsteady. "I'm here with my father—"

"I want your name, not your life story," the man says rudely.

"Take it easy, Ragnar," says one of his colleagues.

"You're a fucking parasite," he goes on, turning to Simone. "But that's just my opinion of people who get off looking at blood."

He snorts and turns away. Her father is speaking in an even tone, and he sounds very tired. She sees one of the officers walking away with his wallet.

"Excuse me," says Simone to a female officer. "We heard someone down in the—"

"Shut up," says the woman.

"My son is—"

"Shut up, I said. Tape her mouth. I want her mouth taped."

The officer with the shaved head takes out a roll of broad tape, but he stops when the front door opens and a tall blond man with sharp grey eyes walks in.

"Joona Linna, National CID," he says, in his singsong lilt. "What have you got?"

"Two suspects," replies the female officer.

Joona looks at Kennet and Simone. "I'll take it from here," he says. "This is a mistake."

Two dimples suddenly appear in Joona's cheeks as he tells them to release the suspects. The female officer goes over to Kennet and removes the handcuffs, apologizes, and exchanges a few words with him, her ears bright red. The officer with the shaved head stands in front of Simone, rocking back on his heels and staring at her.

"Let her go," says Joona.

"They resisted violently and I injured my thumb," he says.

"Are you intending to arrest them?" asks Joona.

"Yes."

"Kennet Sträng and his daughter?"

"I don't give a shit who they are," the officer says aggressively.

"Ragnar," his colleague says again, in an attempt to quiet him, "take it easy. He's one of us."

"It's illegal to enter the scene of a crime—"

"Just calm down," says Joona firmly.

"But am I wrong?" he asks.

Kennet has come over, but says nothing.

"Am I wrong?" asks Ragnar again.

"We'll talk about this later," replies Joona.

"Why not now?"

"For your own sake."

The female officer comes over to Kennet again, clears her throat, and says, "We're very sorry about all this."

"It's OK," says Kennet, helping Simone up from the floor.

"The cellar," she says, almost inaudibly.

"I'll take care of it," says Kennet, turning to Joona. "There are one or more persons in a hidden room in the cellar, behind the wardrobe with life jackets in it."

"Listen carefully," Joona calls to the others. "We have reason to believe that the suspect is in the cellar. I will be leading this operation throughout. Be careful. It is possible that a hostage situation could arise, and in that case I will be the negotiator. The suspect is a dangerous individual, but fire is to be directed at the legs in the first instance."

Joona borrows a bullet-proof vest and quickly shrugs it on. Then he sends two officers around to the back of the house and gathers a team around him. They listen to his rapid instructions and then disappear with him through the doorway leading to the cellar. The metal staircase clangs loudly beneath their weight.

Simone is afraid that her whole body is shaking, so Kennet wraps his arms around her. He whispers to her that everything will be fine, but the only thing Simone wants to hear is her son's voice from the cellar; she prays that she will hear him calling to her any second.

After only a short while Joona returns, the bullet-proof vest in his hand. "He got away," he says tersely.

"Benjamin, where's Benjamin?" asks Simone.

"Not here," replies Joona.

"But the room—"

She moves toward the cellar doorway. Kennet tries to hold her back, but she yanks her hand away and pushes past Joona and down the iron steps. With three spotlights on stands filling the space with light, the cellar is now as bright as a summer's day. The stepladder has been moved and is now under the small open window. The wardrobe has been pushed to one side and a police officer guards the entrance to the secret room. Simone walks slowly toward him. She can hear her father behind her, but she doesn't understand what he is saying.

"I have to," she says faintly.

The officer raises a hand and shakes his head.

"I'm afraid I can't let you in," he says.

"It's my son."

She feels her father's arms around her, but tries to break free.

"He isn't here, Simone."

"Let go of me!"

She lurches forward and looks into a room with a mattress on the floor, piles of old comics, empty bags of crisps, cans and cereal boxes, pale blue overshoes, and a large, shiny axe.

54

In the car on the way back from Tumba, Simone listens to Kennet rant about the police and their lack of coordination. She says nothing, gazing out the window as he complains. The streets are filled with families on their way somewhere. Mothers and their toddlers dressed in snowsuits, children trying to make their way through the slush on sledges. They wear the same backpacks. A group of girls with Lucia tinsel in their hair woven into shiny headbands eat something out of a small bag and laugh with delight.

More than twenty-four hours have passed since Benjamin was taken away from us, pulled out of his own bed and dragged out of his home, she thinks. She looks down at her hands. Ugly red marks from the hand-cuffs are still clearly visible.

There is nothing to indicate that Josef Ek is involved in Benjamin's disappearance. There were no traces of Benjamin in the hidden room, only of Josef. It is more than likely that Josef was sitting in there when she and her father went down into the cellar. Realizing they had discovered his hiding place, he must have reached for the axe as quietly as possible. And when the tumult erupted, when the police came storming down to the cellar and dragged her and Kennet upstairs, Josef had taken the opportunity to push the wardrobe aside, move the ladder over to the window, and climb out. He got away, he deceived the police, and he is still at large. A national alert has gone out.

216

But Josef Ek can't have kidnapped Benjamin. They were simply two things that happened at approximately the same time, just as Erik has been trying to tell her.

"Are you coming?" asks Kennet.

She looks up and realizes that they are parked outside their apartment block on Luntmakargatan and Kennet is repeating his question.

She unlocks the door and sees Benjamin's coat hung in the hall. Her heart leaps and she just has time to think that he must be home before she remembers that he was dragged out in his pyjamas.

Her father's face is grey; again she registers how old he seems to have become. He says he's going for a shower and disappears into the bathroom.

Simone leans against the wall and closes her eyes. If I can just have Benjamin back, she thinks, I will forget everything that has happened, that is happening, that will happen; I won't talk about it, I won't think about it, I won't be angry with anyone, I'll just be grateful.

She hears the water begin to run in the bathroom.

With a sigh she slides off her shoes, lets her jacket drop to the floor, and eases down onto the bed. Suddenly she cannot remember what she's doing in the bedroom. Did she come in to get something or just to lie down and rest for a while? She feels the coolness of the sheets against the palm of her hand and sees Erik's creased pyjama bottoms sticking out from under the pillow.

Just as the shower stops running she remembers what she was going to do. She was going to get a clean towel for her father and then try to find something on Benjamin's computer that could be linked to his abduction. She takes a bath towel out of the cupboard and goes back into the hall just as the bathroom door opens and Kennet emerges, fully dressed.

"Towel," she says.

"I used the small one."

His hair is damp and smells of lavender. She realizes he must have used the cheap soap in the pump dispenser by the washbasin.

"Did you wash your hair with soap?" she asks.

"It smelled nice," he replies.

"There is shampoo, Dad."

"Same thing."

217

"Fine," she says with a smile, deciding not to tell him what the small hand towel is used for.

"I'll make some coffee," says Kennet, heading for the kitchen.

Simone drops the bath towel on the sideboard and goes into Benjamin's room, where she sits at the desk and switches on the computer. She needs to clean up in here. The bedclothes on the floor and the water glass lying on its side remind her, stabbingly, of the abduction.

The welcome melody from the computer's operating system rings out, Simone places her hand on the mouse, waits a few seconds, then clicks on the miniature picture of Benjamin's face to log in.

The computer requests a user name and password. Simone types in BENJAMIN, takes a deep breath, and writes DUMBLEDORE.

55

Benjamin's computer screen flickers, like an eye closing and then opening. She's in.

A photograph of a deer in a forest glade fills the desktop screen. The greenery is bathed in a magical dewy light. The shy animal seems totally calm at this particular moment. Despite the fact that Simone knows she is intruding into Benjamin's private space, it's as if something of him is suddenly close to her again.

"You're a genius," she hears her father say behind her.

"I'm not," she replies.

Kennet places one hand on her shoulder, and she launches the e-mail program.

"How far back should we go?" she asks.

"We'll go through everything."

She scrolls through the inbox, opening message after message. A classmate has a question about a portfolio. A school group project is discussed. Someone claims Benjamin has won four million euros in a Spanish lottery.

Kennet disappears and returns with two mugs of coffee. "Best drink in the world, coffee," he says, sitting down. "How the hell did you manage to crack the computer?"

She shrugs diffidently and takes a sip of coffee. But she can't bring herself to tell him that Erik provided her with the password.

"I'll have to call my computer friend and tell him we don't need his help. He's too slow!"

She moves through the list, opening a message from Aida, who tells him all about a bad film in an amusing way, saying that Arnold Schwarzenegger is a lobotomized Shrek.

The weekly bulletin from school. A warning from the bank about the importance of not revealing details of your account to anyone. Facebook, Facebook, Facebook, Facebook, Facebook.

Simone logs onto Benjamin's Facebook page. There are hundreds of inquiries featuring the group *hypno monkey*. Every comment has to do with Erik, various sneering theories that Benjamin has been hypnotized into being a nerd, evidence that Erik has hypnotized the entire Swedish nation, one person demanding compensation because Erik has hypnotized his cock.

There is a link to a clip on YouTube. Simone follows it and finds a short film titled *Asshole*. The sound track features a researcher describing how serious hypnosis works, while the film shows Erik pushing past a number of people. He happens to bump into an elderly woman using a wheeled walker, and she gives him the finger behind his back.

Simone goes back to Benjamin's e-mail inbox and finds a short note from Aida that makes the hair on the back of her neck stand on end. There is something about these few words that make a formless fear begin to rise up in her stomach. Her palms are suddenly sweaty. She turns the screen toward Kennet.

"Read this, Dad."

Nicky says Wailord is angry and has opened his mouth against you. I think this could be really dangerous, Benjamin.

"Nicky is Aida's younger brother," says Simone.

"And Wailord?" asks Kennet, taking a deep breath. "Do you know about this?"

Simone shakes her head. The fear inside her is so dark, so dense, it feels as if it's made of marble. What does she actually know about Benjamin's life?

"I think Wailord is the name of a Pokémon character," she says.

Simone clicks on the SENT folder and finds Benjamin's agitated response:

Nicky has to stay indoors. Don't let him go down to the sea. If Wailord is really angry, one of us is in trouble. We should have gone to the police straight away. I think it's too dangerous to do it now.

"Fuck," says Kennet.

"I don't know if this is genuine or if it's part of a game."

"It doesn't sound like a game."

"No."

Kennet lets out a long breath and scratches his stomach. "Aida and Nicky," he says slowly. "What kind of people are they, then?"

Simone looks at her father and wonders how to answer him. He would never understand a person like Aida: a girl who always dresses in black, wears lots of make-up, has piercings and tattoos, and whose home circumstances are peculiar to say the least.

"Aida is Benjamin's girlfriend," says Simone. "And Nicky is her younger brother. There's a picture of her and Benjamin somewhere."

She finds Benjamin's wallet and digs out the picture of Aida. Benjamin has his arm around her shoulders. Aida looks slightly uncomfortable, but Benjamin is laughing into the camera, his expression relaxed.

"But what kind of people are they?" asks Kennet stubbornly, looking at Aida's face with its harsh make-up.

"What kind of people?" she says slowly. "I don't really know. I just know that Benjamin is extremely fond of her. And she seems to take good care of her brother. I think he's got some kind of learning disability."

"Aggressive?"

"I don't think so."

"Benjamin writes about a real threat," Kennet says, "but Wailord doesn't really exist."

56

Kennet folds his arms. He leans back and looks up at the ceiling. Then he straightens up and says in a serious tone, "So Wailord is a cartoon character?"

"A Pokémon," she replies.

"Am I supposed to know what that means?"

"If you have children of a certain age, you know about it whether you want to or not," she says.

Kennet is looking blankly at her.

"Pokémon," Simone repeats. "It's a kind of game."

"A game?"

"It was something Benjamin loved when he was younger. He used to collect the cards and talk about the different powers, about how the characters transformed themselves."

Kennet shakes his head.

"He must have been into it for about two years," she says.

"But not any more?"

"He's a bit too old now."

"I used to see you playing with dolls when you came home from riding camp."

"Well, who knows, maybe he plays in secret," she replies.

"So what's it all about, this Pokémon?"

"How can I explain? It's Japanese, originally. It became really popular in the nineties. A whole industry, really. The characters are pocket monsters. They're animals but not real animals. They're invented; they can look like insects or robots, something along those lines. Some of them are cute, others are just revolting. The person playing keeps them in his pocket; they can be rolled up and placed in little balls. The whole thing is really stupid. You compete against other players by arranging fights between your different Pokémons. Very violently, of course. Anyway, the goal is to beat as many as possible, because then you get money—the player gets money, the Pokémon character gets points."

"And the one with the most points is the winner?" says Kennet.

"I don't actually know. It never seems to end."

"So this is a computer game?"

"It's everything, Dad. Computer game, Nintendo, a TV show, a movie, stuffed toys, sweets, trading cards."

"I don't know if I'm really any the wiser," he says.

"No," she says hesitantly.

He studies her. "What are you thinking?"

"I've just realized that's exactly the point: adults are to be excluded," she says. "The kids are ignored, left to their own devices, because we can't understand. We dismiss it, call it stupid, but really the Pokémon world is too big, too complex for us."

"Do you think Benjamin has started playing again?" asks Kennet.

"Not in the same way. This must be something else," she says, pointing at the screen.

"You think this Wailord is a real person," he says.

"Yes."

"Who has nothing to do with Pokémon?"

"I don't know . . . Aida's brother talked to me about Wailord as if he was talking about a Pokémon. Perhaps that's just his way of talking. As I said, he's a little . . . off. But everything is cast in a different light when Benjamin writes *Don't let Nicky go down to the sea*."

"It does sound as if Benjamin's taking the threat seriously," says Kennet.

"But the sea," she says. "What sea? There is no sea here, it only exists in the game. The sea is pretend, but the threat is genuine," she says thoughtfully.

"We have to find this Wailord."

"It could be a Lunar," she says hesitantly. "Or an Avatar, or something."

He looks at her with a small smile. "I'm beginning to understand why it was time for me to retire."

"Lunar is an identity on a chat page," Simone explains, moving closer to the screen. "I'll do a search for Wailord."

The result gives 85,000 hits. Kennet goes into the kitchen, and she hears the sound of the police radio being turned up. Crackling and hissing is mixed with human voices.

She skims through page after page of Japanese Pokémon material.

Wailord is the largest of all identified Pokémon up to now. This giant Pokémon swims in the open sea, eating massive amounts of food at once with its enormous mouth.

"There's your sea," says Kennet quietly, reading over her shoulder. She didn't hear him come back.

The text describes how Wailord chases its prey and herds them by making a gigantic leap and landing in the middle of the shoal. It is terrible, Simone reads, to see Wailord swallow its prey in one gulp.

She refines the search by requesting only pages written in Swedish and enters a forum where she finds a conversation:

Hi, how do you get a Wailord?
    If you want to get a Wailord, the easiest thing is to catch a Wailmer somewhere out at sea.
    OK, but where?
    Almost anywhere, as long as you use Super Rod.

"Anything useful?" asks Kennet.

"This could take a while."

"Go through all his messages, check the trash, and try to track down this Wailord."

She looks up and sees that Kennet has his leather jacket on.

"I'm off," he says briefly.

"Off where? Home?"

"I need to talk to Nicky and Aida."

"Shall I come with you?" she asks.

Kennet shakes his head. "It's better if you're the one who goes through the computer."

Kennet tries to summon up a smile as she walks to the door with him. He looks very tired. She gives him a hug before he goes, locks up behind him, and hears him press the button for the lift.

She walks into the kitchen and sees a brioche sitting on the flattened paper bag it came in, a slice cut from it. The coffee machine is still on, but there is only a dark sediment in the bottom of the pot.

The smell of burnt coffee mingles with a sense of panic over the feeling that her life has been divided into two acts and that the first act, the happy one, has just ended. She can't bring herself to think about Act Two. Outside the window lies the December darkness. It looks windy. The traffic signals, suspended over the junctions, swing back and forth, and wet snowflakes are falling through the light.

She finds a deleted message from Aida: *I feel sorry for you, living in a house of lies.* The message has a large attachment. Simone feels the pulse at her temples beating faster. Just as she is about to click open the file, there is a tentative knock at the front door. It is almost a scraping sound. She holds her breath, hears another knock, and stands up. Her legs feel weak as she begins to walk down the long passage leading to the hall and the outside door.

57

Kennet sits in his car outside the entrance to Aida's apartment in Sund-byberg, pondering the strange threat on Benjamin's computer:

Nicky says Wailord is angry, and that he has opened his mouth against you.

And Benjamin's response:

Don't let him go down to the sea.

Kennet thinks about the number of times in his life when he has both seen and heard fear. He himself knows how fear feels, because none of us walks without it.

The building where Aida lives is quite small, only three storeys. It looks unexpectedly idyllic, old-fashioned and authentic. He looks at the photo Simone gave him. A girl with piercings, her eyes heavily made up with black. He wonders why he finds it difficult to imagine her living in this building, eating at a kitchen table, sleeping in a room where posters of ponies have been replaced by Marilyn Manson.

Kennet gets out of the car and is about to creep over to the balcony he thinks belongs to Aida's family, but he stops when he catches sight of a tall, shambling figure moving back and forth along the path behind the building.

Suddenly the door opens and Aida comes out. She seems to be in a hurry. She glances over her shoulder, takes a pack of cigarettes out of her bag and shakes one out, tucks it between her lips, and lights it without ever slowing down. Kennet follows her towards the underground station. He will approach her once he figures out where she's headed. A bus thunders past, and somewhere a dog starts barking. Kennet suddenly sees the tall figure from behind the building rush towards Aida. She turns around to face him, but rather than frightened she's happy; her whole face is smiling, and the pale, powdered cheeks and kohl-rimmed eyes are suddenly childlike. The figure jumps up and down in front of her. She pats him on the cheek, and he responds with a hug. They kiss the tips of each other's noses, and then Aida waves goodbye. Kennet moves closer, thinking that the tall figure must be her brother. He is standing motionless, watching Aida as she walks away; then he gives a little wave and turns. Kennet sees the boy's face, soft and open. One eye has a significant squint. Kennet stops beneath a streetlamp and waits. The boy heads toward him with long, heavy strides.

"Hi, Nicky," says Kennet.

Nicky stops and looks at him with an expression of terror. There is a blob of saliva at both corners of his mouth. "Not allowed," he says, slowly and uncertainly.

"Sure you are. My name is Kennet, and I'm a police officer. Or, to be more accurate, I'm getting on a bit now and I've retired, but that doesn't change anything, I'm still a police officer."

The boy smiles in surprise. "Have you got a gun, then?"

Kennet shakes his head. "No," he lies. "And I haven't got a police car either."

The boy's expression grows serious. "Did they take it away when you got old?"

Kennet nods. "Yep."

"Are you here to catch the thiefs?" asks Nicky.

"What thieves?"

Nicky tugs at the zip of his jacket. "Sometimes they take things from me," he says, kicking at the ground.

"Who does?"

Nicky looks at him impatiently. "The thiefs."

"Right."

"My hat, my watch, my special stone with the glittery edge."

"Are you scared of anyone?"

He shakes his head.

"Everybody here is pretty nice, huh?" Kennet asks hesitantly.

The boy puffs out his cheeks, hums, and gazes after Aida.

"My sister is searching for the worst monster."

Kennet nods in the direction of the newspaper kiosk by the underground station. "Would you like a Coke?"

The boy walks alongside him, chatting away. "I work in the library on Saturdays. I take people's coats and hang them up in the cloakroom, and they get a ticket with a number on it, thousands of different numbers."

"Good for you," says Kennet. He buys two bottles of Coca-Cola.

Nicky looks pleased and asks for an extra straw. Then he drinks, burps, drinks, and burps again.

"What did you mean when you mentioned your sister and a monster?" Kennet asks casually.

Nicky frowns. "It's that boy. Aida's boyfriend. Benjamin. She hasn't seen him today. But before he was really mad, really really mad. Aida cried."

"Why was Benjamin angry?"

Nicky looks at Kennet in surprise. "Benjamin isn't angry, he's nice. He makes Aida happy and she laughs."

Kennet looks at the tall boy. "So who was angry, Nicky? Who was it that was angry?"

Nicky suddenly looks uneasy. He stares at his drink, searching for something. "I'm not allowed to accept things from—"

"This is different, remember? I'm a policeman. It'll be fine this time, I promise," says Kennet. "Who was angry, Nicky?"

Nicky scratches his throat and wipes the foam from the corners of his mouth. "It's Wailord—his mouth is this big." He demonstrates with his arms.

"Wailord?"

"He's evil."

"Where's Aida gone, Nicky?"

The boy's cheeks quiver as he replies. "She can't find Benjamin; it's not good."

"But where did she go just now?"

Nicky looks as if he's about to burst into tears as he shakes his head. "No, no, no, I'm not allowed to talk to men I don't know."

"Of course you're not. But, look, Nicky, I'm no ordinary man," says Kennet, taking out his wallet and finding a photograph of himself in his police uniform.

Nicky looks closely at the picture. Then he says seriously, "Aida is going to see Wailord. She's afraid he's bitten Benjamin. Wailord opens his mouth this wide."

Nicky demonstrates with his arms again, and Kennet tries to keep his voice completely calm as he says, "Do you know where Wailord lives?"

"At the sea."

"The sea. And how do you get there?"

"I'm not allowed to go to the sea, not even close."

"I understand that, Nicky. But I can go. How do you get there?"

"On the bus."

58

Nicky fishes for something in his pocket, whispering to himself, then looks up at Kennet. "Wailord played a trick on me once when I had to pay," he says, trying to smile. "He was just joking. They tricked me into eating something you're not supposed to eat."

Kennet waits. Nicky blushes and fiddles with his zipper. His fingernails are dirty.

"What did you eat?" asks Kennet.

The boy's cheeks quiver violently again. "I didn't want to," he replies, and a few tears trickle down his face.

Kennet pats Nicky on the shoulder and tries to keep his voice calm and steady. "You know what it sounds like? It sounds like Wailord is really stupid."

"Stupid."

Kennet wonders what Nicky keeps fiddling with in his pocket. "I'm a police officer, you know that, and I say that nobody is allowed to do stupid things to you."

"You're too old."

"But I'm strong."

Nicky looks more cheerful. "Can I have another Coke?"

"If you want."

"Yes, please."

"What have you got in your pocket?" asks Kennet, feigning indifference.

Nicky smiles. "It's a secret."

"I see," says Kennet, and refrains from asking any further.

Nicky takes the bait. "Don't you want to know what it is?"

"Oh, no. I understand secrets. You couldn't be a policeman for as long as I have without being able to keep a secret. You don't have to tell me if you don't want to, Nicky."

"You'll never guess what it is."

"I'm sure I couldn't."

Nicky takes his hand out of his pocket. "I'll tell you what it is." He opens his fist. "It's my power."

In Nicky's hand lies a small lump of soil. Kennet looks inquiringly at the boy who simply smiles.

"I am a ground-type Pokémon," he says contentedly.

"A ground-type Pokémon," Kennet repeats.

Nicky closes his fist and pushes it back in his pocket. "Do you know what my powers are?"

Kennet shakes his head. Across the street, a man with a pointed head slowly passes the dark, damp façades of the buildings. He seems to be searching for something; he has a cane in his hand and is poking at the ground with it. Kennet automatically thinks that the man is trying to look in through the windows on the ground floor. He thinks he ought to go over and ask him what he's doing. But Nicky has placed a hand on his arm.

"Do you know what my powers are?" the boy says again.

Kennet drags his gaze reluctantly away from the man. Nicky begins to count on his fingers.

"I'm good against all electric Pokémons, fire Pokémons, poison Pokémons, rock Pokémons, and steel Pokémons. They can't beat me; I'm safe when it comes to all of those. But I can't fight flying Pokémons or grass-and-insect Pokémons."

"Really?" says Kennet distractedly. The man has stopped at one of the windows. Tucking his cane under his arm, he busily goes through his pockets, as if looking for a key or a match, but Kennet can see he's actually leaning into the glass.

"Are you listening?" Nicky asks anxiously.

Kennet tries to smile encouragingly at him, but when he turns back to look, the man has disappeared. Kennet can't make out whether the ground-floor window is open.

"I can't fight water," Nicky explains sadly. "Water's the worst. I can't fight it. I'm scared of water."

Kennet carefully loosens Nicky's grip on his arm. "Just hang on a minute," he says, taking a few steps toward the curb.

"Hey, what time is it?" asks Nicky suddenly.

"The time? It's quarter to six."

"I better go. He'll be mad if I'm late."

"Who'll be mad, your dad?"

Nicky laughs. "I haven't got a dad, silly!"

"Your mum, I mean."

"No, Ariados will be mad. He's coming to pick up some things." Nicky looks uncertainly at Kennet, then down at the ground. "Can you give me some money? Because if I haven't got enough, he has to punish me."

"Wait a minute," says Kennet, who is beginning to pay attention to what Nicky is saying. "Is it Wailord who wants money from you?" Nicky has begun to wander away from the newspaper stand, and Kennet follows, asking again. "Is it Wailord who wants money?"

"Are you crazy? Wailord? He'd swallow me up. But the others, they . . . they can swim to him."

Nicky looks back over his shoulder. Kennet tries again. "Who wants money from you?"

"Ariados, I told you," the boy says impatiently. "Have you got any money? I can do something if I get the money. I can give you a little bit of power."

"There's no need," says Kennet, taking out his wallet. "Will twenty kronor be enough?"

Nicky laughs delightedly, pushes the note in his pocket, and runs off down the road without even saying goodbye.

Kennet sets off after him, trying to make sense of what he's heard. When he turns the corner, he sees Nicky waiting at the crossing for the light to change. It looks as if he's heading for the library in the square. Kennet follows him across the road, stopping by a cash machine when Nicky stops. Now the big boy is stomping around impatiently by the fountain outside the library. The lighting is poor, but Kennet can see he's fingering the soil in his pocket all the time.

Suddenly a younger boy walks straight through the shrubbery next to the dental centre and out into the square. He approaches Nicky, stops in front of him, and says something. Nicky immediately lies down on the ground and holds out the money. The boy counts it and pats Nicky on the head, then suddenly grabs hold of his collar, urging him to the edge of the fountain. Nicky crawls over and allows his face to be pushed down into the water. Kennet's instinct is to go to him, but he forces himself to stay where he is. He's here to find Benjamin. He must not scare off the boy who might be Wailord or who might lead him to Wailord. He stands, tensing his jaws, counting the seconds before he has to rush over. Nicky's legs jerk and kick and Kennet sees the inexplicable calm on the other boy's face as he lets go. Nicky slumps on the ground next to the fountain, wheezing and coughing. The boy gives Nicky a last pat on the shoulder and walks away.

Finally Kennet can hurry after the boy, through the bushes and down a muddy grass slope to a path. He follows him past several apartment blocks, until the boy goes inside one. Kennet speeds up and grabs the door before it closes, following the boy onto the lift, where he manages to see that he has pressed the button for the sixth floor. Kennet gets off at the sixth floor as well, hesitates, pretends to search through his pockets, and watches the boy go over to one of the doors and pull out a key.

"Hey, son, got a moment?" says Kennet casually.

The boy does not react, so Kennet goes over, grabs hold of his jacket, and spins him around.

"Let go of me, Pops," says the boy, looking him straight in the eye.

"Don't you know it's against the law to demand money from people?"

Kennet is looking into a pair of slippery, surprisingly calm eyes.

"Your surname is Johansson," says Kennet, glancing at the door.

"That's right." The boy smiles. "What's your name?"

"Detective Inspector Kennet Sträng."

The boy simply stands there looking at him, showing no sign of fear.

"How much money have you taken from Nicky?"

"I don't take any money. If people want to give it to me, that's their business. I don't take it. Everybody's happy, nobody's upset."

"I'm going to have a word with your parents."

"Whatever."

"Shall I do that?"

"Oh, no, please don't," says the boy mockingly.

Kennet rings the bell, and he and the boy wait until the door is opened by a fat sunburned woman.

"Good afternoon," says Kennet. "I'm a detective inspector, and I'm afraid your son is in a bit of trouble."

"My son? I haven't got any children," she says.

Kennet notices that the boy is gazing at the floor, smiling.

"You don't know this boy?"

"Could I see your police ID, please?" the fat woman says.

"This boy is—"

The boy interrupts. "He hasn't got any ID."

"Oh, yes, I have," Kennet lies.

"He's not a cop," says the boy, taking out his wallet. "Here's my bus pass, I'm more of a cop than—"

Kennet grabs the boy's wallet.

"Give that back."

"I just want to take a look," says Kennet.

"He said he wanted to suck my dick," says the boy.

"I'm calling the police," says the woman, sounding scared.

Kennet pushes the lift button. The woman looks around, hurries out, and starts banging on the doors of the other apartments.

"He gave me money," the boy tells her, "but I didn't want to go with him."

The lift doors glide open. A neighbour opens the door with the security chain on.

"You damn well better leave Nicky alone in future," says Kennet quietly.

"He's mine," the boy replies.

The woman is shouting for the police. Kennet gets in the lift, presses the green button, and the doors close. Sweat is pouring down his back. The boy must have noticed he was tailing him from the fountain, and tricked him into following him all the way to a strange apartment. The lift moves slowly downward, the light flashes, the steel cables above bang loudly. Kennet looks inside the boy's wallet: almost a thousand kronor, a membership card for a video shop, a bus pass, and a creased blue card with THE SEA, LOUDDSVÄGEN 18 on it.

59

A giant smiling sausage has been erected on top of the diner; with one hand it gives a thumbs-up, with the other it covers itself with ketchup. Erik orders a burger with fries, sits down on one of the high stools at the narrow counter by the window, and looks out through the misty glass. There is a locksmith on the opposite side of the street; his Christmas decorations consist of knee-high elves frolicking among an assortment of safes, locks, and keys.

Four hours ago, Joona called to tell him they had missed Josef again. He had been in the cellar but had escaped. There was nothing to suggest that Benjamin had been there. On the contrary, preliminary DNA results indicated that Josef had been alone in the room the whole time.

A bone-deep fatigue comes over him. Josef Ek wants to harm me. He's jealous, he hates me, he's got it into his head that Evelyn and I have a sexual relationship, and now he's determined to take his revenge on me. But he doesn't know where I live. In the letter he demands that Evelyn tell him. *You are going to show me where he lives*, he wrote. If Josef doesn't know where I live, he wasn't the one who got into our apartment and dragged Benjamin out.

Erik opens his bottle of mineral water, takes a sip, and calls home. He hears his own voice on the answering machine, exhorting himself to leave a message. He cuts the connection and calls Simone's mobile instead. She doesn't answer.

"Hi, Simone," he says to her voicemail. "Look, I do think you ought to accept police protection. Apparently, Josef Ek is very angry with me. But that's it, as far as we know. He didn't take Benjamin."

He gulps down a bite of the hamburger, aware suddenly of the gnawing emptiness in his stomach. He spears the crisply fried potatoes on his plastic fork, thinking about Joona's face when he read Josef's letter to Evelyn. It was as if the temperature in the room had fallen. The pale grey eyes became like ice, but with an uncompromising sharpness. Erik tries to recall Evelyn's face, her exact words when she suddenly realized Josef had returned to the house. Mulling it over, Erik decides she didn't deliberately fail to mention the secret room but had simply forgotten about it.

He eats some more of the burger, wipes his hands on the paper napkin, and makes another attempt to get hold of Simone. Not only does she need to be told that it wasn't Josef Ek who took Benjamin, but he also wants to ask what else she can recall from the night Benjamin was abducted. Despite his relief at finding that his son is not in Josef Ek's hands, he knows they have to start all over, think the whole thing through from the beginning. He opens a notebook, writes Aida's name on it, then changes his mind and tears out the sheet. It's Simone he needs to talk to. She must remember more, he says to himself, she must have seen something. Joona had interviewed her, but she hadn't remembered anything else. Of course, they'd been concentrating on Josef then.

His cell phone rings and he puts down the burger, wipes his hands again, and answers without looking at the display.

"Erik Maria Bark."

There is a dull crackling, roaring noise.

"Hello?" says Erik, more loudly this time.

Suddenly he hears a faint voice. "Dad?"

The hot oil hisses as the basket of potatoes is lowered in.

"Benjamin?" A half-dozen burgers are slapped on the grill. The telephone roars. "Hang on, I can't hear you."

Erik pushes his way past the customers lined up to order and out into the car park.

"Benjamin?"

Snow is whirling around the yellow streetlamps. "Can you hear me now?" asks Benjamin, sounding close.

"Where are you? Tell me where you are!"

"I don't know, Dad. I don't get it, I'm lying in the boot of a car and we've just been driving forever."

"Who's taken you?"

"I woke up here. I can't see anything, I'm thirsty—"

"Are you hurt?"

"Dad!" He sobs.

"I'm here, Benjamin."

"What's going on?" He sounds small and afraid.

"I'll find you," says Erik. "Do you know where you're going?"

"I heard a voice just when I woke up; it was all mushy, like, he was talking through a blanket. What was it again? It was something about . . . a house . . ."

"Tell me more! What kind of house?"

"No, not just a house, a haunted house."

"Where?"

"We're stopping now, Dad, the car's stopped, they're coming," says Benjamin, sounding terrified. "I can't talk any more."

Erik hears strange rummaging noises, followed by a creaking sound and then Benjamin's sudden scream. His voice is shrill and unsteady; he sounds terribly frightened:

"Leave me alone, I don't want to, please, I promise—"

Then silence; the connection has been broken.

Erik stares at his phone but does not use it; he doesn't want to risk blocking another call from his son. He waits by the car, praying Benjamin will call again, tries to go over the conversation but keeps losing the thread. Benjamin's fear stabs through his head, over and over again. He realizes he has to tell Simone.

60

Erik gets into the car, his hands shaking so fiercely he can't slide the key into the ignition. He knows he's left his hat and gloves next to his burger in the diner, but he can't be bothered to go back inside. The surface of the road shimmers in shades of grey from the wet snow as he reverses into the darkness and drives home. He parks on Döbelnsgatan and strides down to Luntmakargatan, feeling a strange sense of alienation as he walks in the door and hurries up the stairs. He rings the doorbell, waits, hears footsteps, the small click as the metal cover of the peephole is pushed to one side. He hears the door being unlocked from the inside, but it doesn't open to admit him, so he opens it himself. Simone has moved back down the dark hallway. In her jeans and blue knitted sweater, arms folded over her chest, she looks resolute.

"You're not answering your phone," says Erik.

"I saw you'd called," she says in a subdued voice. "Was it something important?"

"Yes."

Her face cracks, revealing all the anxiety she's been struggling to hide. She puts her hand over her mouth and stares at him.

"Benjamin called me half an hour ago."

"Oh my God!" She moves closer. "Where is he?" she asks, raising her voice.

"I don't know. He didn't know himself, he didn't know anything."

"What did he say?"

"He told me he was in the boot of a car."

"Was he hurt?"

"I don't think so."

"But what—"

"Hang on," Erik interrupts. "I need to borrow a phone. It might be possible to trace the call."

"Who are you going to call?"

"The police. I've got a contact who—"

"I'll talk to Dad—it'll be quicker."

Erik briefly considers protesting but thinks better of it. She takes the phone and he sits on the low hall seat in the darkness, feeling his face growing hot in the warmth.

"Were you asleep?" Simone asks. "Dad, I have to . . . Erik's here; he's spoken to Benjamin; you have to trace the call . . . I don't know . . . No, I haven't . . . You'd better speak to him."

Erik takes the phone and holds it to his ear. "Hi."

"Tell me what happened, Erik," says Kennet.

"I wanted to call the police, but Simone said you could trace the call more quickly."

"She could well be right."

"Benjamin called me half an hour ago. He had no idea where he was or who had taken him; all he really knew was that he was lying in the boot of a car. While we were talking the car stopped, Benjamin said he could hear someone coming, he started shouting, and then everything went quiet."

Erik can hear the sound of suppressed sobs from Simone.

"Did he call from his own phone?" asks Kennet.

"Yes."

"Because it's been switched off. I tried to trace it the day before yesterday; mobile phones send signals to the nearest base station even when they're not being used."

Erik listens in silence as Kennet quickly explains that mobile phone operators are obliged to assist the police in accordance with paragraphs 25 to 27 of the law governing telecommunications, if the minimum punishment for the crime under investigation is at least two years' imprisonment.

"What can they find out?" asks Erik.

"The precision varies—it depends on the station and the exchanges—but with a bit of luck we'll soon have a location within a radius of a hundred yards."

"Hurry up, please hurry."

Erik ends the call, stands with the phone in his hand, and then passes it to Simone. "What happened to your cheek?" he asks.

"What? Oh, it's nothing." They look at each other, tired and fragile. "Do you want to come in, Erik?"

He nods, remains where he is for a moment, then kicks off his shoes and moves along the passageway; he sees that the computer is on in Benjamin's room and goes in. "Found anything?"

Simone stops in the doorway. "Some messages between Benjamin and Aida," she says. "It seems as if they felt threatened."

"By whom?"

"We don't know. Dad's working on it."

Erik sits down at the computer. "Benjamin's alive," he says quietly, giving her a long look.

"Yes."

"It doesn't look as if Josef Ek was involved."

"You said that in your message; you said he doesn't know where we live. But he did call here, didn't he, so he could have—"

"That's a different matter."

"Is it?"

"The switchboard put the call through," he explains. "I've asked them to do that if something sounds important. He hasn't got our telephone number or our address."

"But someone's taken Benjamin and put him in a car." She falls silent.

Erik reads the message from Aida in which she says she feels sorry for him, living in a house of lies. Then he opens the picture she attached: a colour photo taken with a flash at night, showing an overgrown patch of grass, bleached yellow in the harsh xenon light of the flash, curving outward toward a low hedge. Behind the dry hedge it is just possible to make out a brown wooden fence. At the edge of the grass, there is a green plastic leaf basket and something that might be a potato patch.

Erik looks closely at the picture, trying to understand what the subject is, whether there might be a hedgehog or a shrew somewhere that he hasn't spotted yet. He tries to peer into the darkness beyond the camera flash to see if there is a person there, a face, but he finds nothing.

"What a strange photo," whispers Simone.

"Maybe Aida attached the wrong picture," says Erik.

"That would explain why Benjamin deleted the message."

"We need to talk to Aida about this as well."

Simone suddenly whimpers. "Benjamin's medication."

"I know."

"Did you give him the factor concentrate last Tuesday?"

Before he has time to reply, she leaves the room and heads for the kitchen. He follows her. By the time he gets there she is standing by the window, blowing her nose on a piece of paper towel. Erik reaches out to her, but she pulls away. Without the injection, the drug that helps Benjamin's blood to coagulate and protects him from spontaneous bleeds, he can haemorrhage to death from something as simple as a rapid movement.

"I gave the injection to him last Tuesday morning, at twenty past eight. He was going to go skating, but he went to Tensta with Aida instead."

She nods and calculates. "It's Sunday today. He ought to have another injection soon," she whispers.

"There's no real danger for a few more days," Erik says reassuringly.

He looks at her: tired face, lovely features, freckles. The low-cut jeans, her yellow briefs just visible at the waistband. He'd like to stay here; he would like them to sleep together; actually, he would like to make love to her, but he knows it's too soon for all that, too soon even to start wanting her.

"I'd better go," he mumbles. She nods. They look at each other. "Call me when Kennet's traced the call."

"Where are you going?" she asks.

"I have to work."

"Are you sleeping in your office?"

"It's a practical solution."

"You can sleep here," she says.

He's surprised; suddenly he doesn't know what to say. But the brief moment of silence is enough for her to misinterpret his reaction as hesitation.

"That wasn't meant as an invitation," she says quickly. "Don't go getting any ideas."

"I wasn't."

"Have you moved in with Daniella?"

"No."

"We've already separated," she says, raising her voice, "so you don't need to lie to me."

"OK."

"What? OK what?"

"I've moved in with Daniella," he lies.

"Good," she whispers.

"Yes."

"I'm not going to ask if she's young and pretty and—"

"She is."

Erik puts on his shoes in the hallway, leaves the apartment, and closes the door. He waits until he hears her lock up and slide the security chain in place before he sets off down the stairs.

61

Simone is awakened by the ringing of the telephone. The curtains are open and the bedroom is filled with wintry sunlight. Could it be Erik? She wants to cry when she realizes he isn't going to call. He'll be waking up next to Daniella this morning. She is completely alone now.

She picks up the phone from the bedside table.

"Simone? It's Yiva. I've been trying to get hold of you for days."

Yiva sounds stressed out. Simone glances at the clock. It's already ten. "I've had other things on my mind," she says tersely.

"They haven't found him?"

"No."

Silence. A few shadows drift past outside the window. Simone can see flakes of paint falling from the metal roof opposite; men in bright yellow overalls are scraping it.

"Sorry," Yiva says. "I won't disturb you."

"What's happened?"

"The auditor is coming tomorrow."

Simone stands up and glances at the tinted mirror on the wardrobe. She looks thin and tired. It feels as if her face has been smashed into tiny pieces and then put back together again.

"What about Sim Shulman?" she asks. "How's his exhibition coming along?"

Yiva sounds excited. "He says he needs to speak to you."

"I'll give him a call."

"He wants to show you something to do with the light." She lowers her voice. "I have no idea how things are between you and Erik, but—"

"We've separated," Simone replies tersely.

"Well, I really think—"

"What do you think?" Simone asks patiently.

"I think Shulman has a serious thing for you."

Simone meets her own eyes in the mirror and feels a sudden tingle in her stomach. "I'd better come in," she says.

"Could you?"

"I just need to make a call first."

Simone hangs up but remains sitting on the edge of the bed for a little while. Benjamin is alive, that's the most important thing. The person who took him doesn't seem interested in killing him; he has something else in mind. Ransom? She runs quickly through her assets. What does she actually own? The apartment, the car, a few works of art. The gallery, of course. She could borrow money. Everything will work out. She isn't rich, but her father could sell the summer cottage and his apartment. They could move in, everyone in a rented apartment, anywhere. Just so long as she gets back Benjamin; as long as she can have her boy again.

Simone calls her father, but he doesn't answer. She leaves a short message telling him she's going to the gallery, then takes a quick shower, brushes her teeth, puts on clean clothes, and leaves the apartment without bothering to switch off the lights.

It's cold and windy outside, a few degrees below freezing. The gloom of the mid-December morning is filled with oppressive quietness, somnolence, a graveyard atmosphere. A dog runs past with its leash trailing in the puddles. No sign of the owner.

As soon as she arrives at the gallery, she meets Yiva's gaze through the glass door. She walks in and Yiva rushes over and gives her a hug. Simone notices that Yiva has forgotten to touch up her roots; the grey forms a straight line down the centre of her black hair. But her face is smooth and perfectly made-up, her mouth dark red as always. She is wearing grey culottes over black-and-white striped tights and clumpy brown shoes.

Simone looks around. A greenish light shimmers from a series of paintings by Sim Shulman, glowing, aquarium-green oils.

"Fantastic," says Simone. "You've done a brilliant job."

"Thank you," says Yiva.

Simone goes over to the paintings. "I hadn't seen them like this, grouped together, the way they were intended. I'd only seen them individually." She takes a step closer. "It's as if they're flowing sideways."

She moves into the second room. The block of stone with Shulman's cave paintings is on a wooden stand.

"Sim Shulman wants oil lamps in here," says Yiva. "I've told him it's impossible; people want to see what they're buying."

"No, they don't."

Yiva laughs. "So Shulman gets what he wants?"

"Yes," Simone replies. "He gets what he wants."

"Well, you can tell him yourself."

"What?"

"He's in the office."

"Shulman?"

"He said he needed to make a few calls."

Simone looks over toward the office, and Yiva clears her throat. "I'm going out to get a sandwich for lunch."

"What, at this hour?"

"I just thought," says Yiva, her eyes downcast.

"Go on then."

Simone knocks on the office door and goes in. Shulman is sitting behind the desk sucking a pencil.

"How are you?" he asks, beginning to rise.

"Not so good."

"That's what I thought."

There is silence between them, and he moves closer. She lowers her head. A feeling of exposure, of having been worn down to the most fragile part of herself fills her. Her voice trembles as she blurts out:

"Benjamin is alive. We don't know where he is or who's taken him, but he's alive."

"That's good news," Shulman says quietly.

"Fuck," she whispers, turning away and wiping the tears from her face with a trembling hand.

Shulman gently touches her hair. She moves away without knowing why. She really doesn't want him to stop. His hand drops. They look at each other. He's wearing his soft black suit, with a hood sticking up above the collar of his jacket.

"You're wearing the ninja suit," she says, smiling in spite of herself.

"Shinobi, the correct word for ninja, has two meanings," he says. "It means 'a hidden person,' but it also means 'one who endures.'"

"Endures?"

"Perhaps the most difficult art of all."

"It's impossible alone, at least it is for me."

"No one is alone."

"I can't cope with this," Simone whispers. "I'm falling apart. I have to stop thinking about it all the time. I have nowhere to go. I walk around thinking I just want something to happen. I could hit myself over the head or jump into bed with you just to stop this panic inside of me—" She stops abruptly. "What I just said. It sounded completely . . . I'm really sorry, Sim."

"So which would you choose, in that case?" he asks with a smile. "Would you jump into bed with me or hit yourself over the head?"

"Neither," she answers quickly. Then she realizes that doesn't sound right and tries to smooth things over again. "I don't mean . . . I'd really like—" She stops again, feeling her heart pounding in her chest.

"What would you like to do?" he asks.

She meets his gaze. "I'm not myself. That's why I'm behaving like this," she says simply. "I feel incredibly stupid." She lowers her eyes; her cheeks are burning, and she clears her throat.

They gaze at each other, no longer focusing on the conversation.

"Simone," he says; he leans forward and kisses her on the mouth, just briefly.

Her legs feel weak, her knees are trembling. His silky voice, the warmth of his body. The smell from his soft jacket, a mixture of sleep and fine herbs. As his hand moves gently over her cheek and around to the back of her neck, it feels as if she has forgotten the wonderful silkiness of a caress; as his grip tightens slightly to draw her face nearer to his, she realizes how long it has been since she has felt truly desired. Shulman gazes at her intently. She is no longer thinking about running away from the gallery. Maybe this is just a way of escaping for a little while from the terror thudding in her chest, but that's all right. Let me escape, she thinks. Let me forget all the terrible things.

This time she responds to his kiss. She is breathing rapidly, feeling his hands on her back, at the base of her spine, on her hips. Her emotions overwhelm her; she feels a burning sensation, a sudden blind urge to have him inside her. The force of her desire startles her; she pulls away, hoping he can't see how excited she is. She wipes her mouth and clears her throat again as she turns away, hastily trying to adjust her clothing.

"Somebody . . . someone . . . might . . ."

"What should we do?" Shulman asks, and she can hear the tremor in his voice.

62

Without replying, Simone takes a step toward Shulman and kisses him again. She no longer has any thoughts. She fumbles for his skin beneath his clothes and feels his warm hands on her body. His hands search inside her clothes, and when he makes it down to her panties and feels how wet she is, he groans. She wants them to fuck right here, up against the wall, on the desk, on the floor, as if nothing else matters, just as long as she can divert the panic for a few minutes. Her heart is beating fast, her legs are shaking. She pulls him toward the wall, and as he moves her legs to thrust inside her, she whispers to him, telling him to do it, to hurry up but do it. At that moment they hear the cool tone signalling that someone has entered the gallery. The parquet floor creaks, and they let go of each other.

"We'll go to my place," he whispers.

She nods, aware that her cheeks are flushed. He wipes his mouth and leaves the office. She stays behind, waits for a while, leaning on the desk for support, her whole body trembling. She tidies herself up, and when she walks out into the gallery Shulman is already standing by the door.

"Have a nice lunch," says Yiva.

In the taxi on the way to Sim's apartment, Simone changes her mind. I'll call Dad, she thinks; then I'll explain to Sim that I have to go. The very thought of what she is about to do makes her feel sick with guilt, panic, and agitation.

They walk up the narrow staircase to the fifth floor, and as he is unlocking the door she begins to rummage in her bag for her phone. "I just need to call my father," she says evasively.

He doesn't reply, simply walks ahead of her into the terracotta hall and disappears down the passageway.

She stands there with her coat on, looking around. Photographs cover the walls, and a recess containing stuffed birds runs along just below the ceiling. Shulman returns before she has time to dial Kennet's number.

"Simone," he whispers. "Don't you want to come in?"

She shakes her head.

"Just for a little while?"

"OK." She keeps her coat on as she follows him into the living room.

"We're adults," he announces. "We can do what we like." He pours two glasses of cognac, and they toast each other and drink.

"That was good," she says quietly.

One wall is made entirely of glass. She moves across and looks out over the copper roofs of Södermalm and the dark reverse side of a neon advertising sign depicting a tube of toothpaste.

Shulman comes over, stands behind her, and puts his arms around her.

"Do you realize I'm crazy about you?" he whispers. "I have been right from the start."

"Sim, I just don't know . . . I don't know what I'm doing," Simone says.

"Do you always have to know what you're doing?" asks Shulman, drawing her towards the bedroom.

She goes with him as if she has known all along that this would happen. She has wanted this to happen, and the only thing that held her back was the fact that she didn't want to be like her mother. No, like Erik: a liar furtively dealing with phone calls and text messages. She has always thought of herself as having a natural barrier against infidelity. But now she has no sense of betrayal whatsoever. Shulman's bedroom is dark. The walls are covered in something that looks like deep blue silk, the same fabric that has been used for long curtains covering the windows, and the spare, slanting midwinter light penetrates the fibres of the material like a fainter darkness.

With a trembling hand she unbuttons her coat and tosses it on the floor. Shulman removes all his clothes, and Simone's eyes travel over his muscular shoulders and down the line of thick, curly dark hair that runs along his navel.

He studies her calmly. She begins to undress but is overwhelmed by a dizzying feeling of loneliness as she stands there before him. He lowers his eyes, moves closer, and kneels, his hair spreading over his shoulders. He traces a line over her hipbone with his finger.

He gently pushes her down onto the edge of the bed and begins to pull down her panties; she raises herself up, keeping her legs together, and feels them slip down and get stuck for a moment around one ankle. She leans back, closes her eyes, allows him to part her thighs, and feels his warm kisses on her stomach, over her hipbone and groin. She is panting, running her fingers through his long, thick hair. She wants Shulman inside her; the desire roars through her body like a storm, waves of darkness surging through her blood, pools of liquid heat flooding her, sucking and tickling, down towards her sex. He moves on top, and she hears herself sigh as he pushes inside her. He whispers something she cannot hear. When she pulls him towards her, she does so in a hunger for escape, for just one brief moment of calm.

She feels the weight of Sim's toned body on top of her, she feels the physical pleasure, but the possibility of escape is gone, and she knows it. It is not attainable. She cannot stop thinking. She has to get home. She has to keep looking for Benjamin. She has to find him.

63

The day is bitterly cold, the sky open and blue. People are moving silently, lost in their own worlds. Tired children are on their way home from school. Kennet stops outside the 7-Eleven on the corner. There's a special offer on coffee and a saffron Lucia bun. He goes inside, and as he joins the queue his cell phone rings. It's Simone.

"Have you been out, Sixan?"

"I had to go to the gallery. Then I had a job to do." She stops abruptly. "I just got your message, Dad."

"Have you been asleep? You sound—"

"Yes. Yes, I slept for a little while."

"Good," says Kennet.

He meets the assistant's tired eyes and points to the sign advertising the special offer.

"Have they traced Benjamin's call?" asks Simone.

"I haven't had a reply yet. This evening at the earliest, they said. I was just going to give them a ring now."

The assistant is waiting for Kennet to choose which Lucia bun he would like, and he quickly points to the biggest one. She puts it in a bag, takes his crumpled twenty-kronor note, and waves in the direction of the coffee machine and cups. He nods, walks past the grill where the sausages are turning, and manages to extricate a cup from the dispenser while continuing his conversation with Simone.

"You spoke to Nicky yesterday?" she says.

"He's a very nice kid," he says.

"Did you find out anything about Wailord?"

"Quite a lot."

"Like what?"

"Hang on a minute."

Kennet removes the steaming coffee cup from the machine, snaps on a lid, and takes it and the bag containing the bun over to one of the small round plastic tables.

"Are you still there?" he asks, sitting down on a wobbly chair.

"Yes."

"I think this is about a group of kids who are shaking Nicky down for his money and telling him they're Pokémon characters."

Kennet notices a man with tousled hair pushing an oversize buggy. A big girl in a pink snowsuit—too old to be pushed, Kennet thinks—reclines inside, sucking on a dummy with a tired smile on her face.

"Does this have anything to do with Benjamin?"

"The Pokémon boys? I don't know. Maybe he tried to stop them," says Kennet.

"We need to talk to Aida," Simone says resolutely.

"After school, I thought."

"What do we do now?"

"I've actually got an address," says Kennet.

"For what?"

"The sea."

"The sea?"

"That's all I know." He takes a sip of the coffee, breaks off a piece of the Lucia bun, and pops it in his mouth.

"Where is the sea?"

"Close to the Frihamnen," says Kennet as he chews, "out on Loudden."

"Can I come with you?"

"Are you ready?"

"Give me ten minutes."

Gathering up his coffee and the rest of his bun, Kennet heads out into the very cold afternoon to pick up his car by the hospital. A cyclist darts through traffic, slaloming in between the cars. As he stops at the crossing, Kennet feels as if he has overlooked something important, as if he has seen something crucial but failed to interpret it. The traffic thunders past. He can hear a rescue vehicle somewhere in the distance. He takes a sip of coffee and watches a woman waiting on the other side of the road, her dog trembling on the end of a short leash. A truck passes just in front of him, and the ground shakes with its considerable weight. He hears someone giggling and has just registered that it doesn't sound genuine when he feels a hard shove in his back. He takes several steps out into the road to avoid losing his balance, turns, and sees a ten-year-old girl looking at him, her eyes open wide. She must be the one who pushed me, he just has time to think. There's no one else there. At the same moment, he hears the screech of brakes and feels an incomprehensible force hurl itself at him. Something like a gigantic hammer knocks his legs out from under him. There is a cracking sound at the back of his neck. All at once his body is soft and faraway, in free fall, and then there is darkness.

64

Erik Maria Bark is sitting at the desk in his office. A pale light finds its way in through the window that faces the empty inner courtyard. A take-away container holds the remains of a salad, and a warm two-litre bottle of Coca-Cola sits next to the desk lamp with its pink shade. Erik is studying a printout of the photo Aida sent to Benjamin. Despite having looked at it dozens of times, he cannot grasp what the subject of the picture really is.

He considers calling Simone and having her read out Aida's message and Benjamin's reply word for word, but then tells himself that Simone doesn't need to hear from him at this point. He can't understand why he was so nasty, why he told her he was having an affair with Daniella. Perhaps it was only because he longed to be forgiven by Simone while she found it so easy to distrust him.

Suddenly he hears Benjamin's voice in his mind once again, calling from the boot of the car. Erik takes a pink capsule out of the wooden box and washes it down with the Coke. His hand has started to shake so much that he has difficulty replacing the bottle on the desk.

Benjamin was trying so hard to be grown up, not to sound afraid. But the boy must be terrified, thinks Erik, shut in the boot of a car in the dark.

How long can it take for Kennet to trace the call? Erik is irritated

254

with himself for handing the job over to the old man, but if his father-in-law can find Benjamin, nothing else is of any importance.

He picks up the phone. He needs to call the police and get them to hurry it up. He must find out if they've traced the call, if they have any suspects yet. When he calls and explains why he's calling, he's put through to the wrong extension. He has to call again. He's hoping to speak to Joona Linna but is put through to a detective named Fredrik Stensund, who confirms that he is involved in the preliminary investigation into the disappearance of Benjamin Bark. He is very understanding and says he has teenage children himself.

"You worry all night when they're out, you know you have to let go, but—"

"Benjamin is not out partying," Erik says firmly.

"No, we have had certain information which contradicts—"

"He's been kidnapped."

"I understand how you must be feeling—"

"But the search for my son is obviously not a priority," Erik retorts.

There is a silence; Stensund takes several deep breaths before continuing. "I am taking what you say very seriously, and I can promise you that we are doing our best."

"Make sure you trace the call, then," says Erik.

"We're working on that right now," replies Stensund, sounding less amenable.

"Please," Erik begs, a weak conclusion.

He sits there with the phone in his hand. They have to trace the call, he thinks. We have to have a location, a circle on a map, a direction; that's all we have to go on. The only thing Benjamin could say was that he heard a voice.

As if it were coming from under a blanket, thinks Erik, but he isn't sure if he's remembering correctly. Did Benjamin really say he'd heard a voice, a mushy voice? Perhaps it was just a murmur, a sound that reminded him of a voice, without words, without meaning. Erik rubs a hand over his mouth, looks at the photograph, his eyes sweeping across the overgrown grass, the hedge, the back of the fence, the plastic basket, all enhanced, distorted by the photographer's powerful flash. He can't see anything new. What's in that basket? When he leans back and closes his eyes, the image remains: the hedge and the brown fence flash in shades of pink and the yellowish-green hillock is dark blue, slowly drifting. Like a piece of fabric against a night sky, Erik thinks, and at the same moment he realizes that Benjamin told him that the mushy voice had said something about a house, a haunted house.

He opens his eyes and gets to his feet. How could he have forgotten? *That* was what Benjamin said before the car stopped.

As he pulls on his coat he tries to remember where he has seen haunted houses, the kind you see in horror films. There aren't that many. He recalls one north of Stockholm, over the ridge, past the collective, down to Lake Mälaren. Before you reach the ship mound at Runsa stronghold, the building is on the left-hand side, facing the water. A kind of miniature castle built of wood, with towers, verandas, and over-the-top ornamentation.

Erik leaves his office and walks quickly along the corridor, trying to remember the trip. Benjamin had been in the car with them. They had looked at the ship barrow, one of the largest Viking burial sites in Sweden. They stood in the middle of the ellipse, large grey stones in green grass. It was late summer and very hot. Erik remembers the stillness of the air and the butterflies fluttering over the gravel in the parking lot as they got into the hot car and set off for home with the windows down.

In the lift down to his car, Erik remembers that after a few miles he pulled over to the side of the road, stopped, pointed at the building, and jokingly asked Benjamin if he would like to live there.

"Where?"

"In the haunted house," he had said, but he no longer recalls Benjamin's response.

The sun is already setting; the slanting light flashes on the frozen puddles in the neurosurgical unit visitors' car park, and the gravel on the asphalt crunches under his tyres as he heads for the main exit. Erik realizes it is unlikely that Benjamin was referring to this particular haunted house, but it isn't impossible. He heads north as dwindling light blurs the contours of the world and blinks to help himself see better. Only when the shades of blue begin to dominate does his brain understand that it is actually getting dark.

Half an hour later he is approaching the haunted house. He has tried to get hold of Kennet four times to see if he has managed to trace Benjamin's call, but Kennet has not answered his phone and Erik has not left a message.

Above the vast lake the sky still retains a faint glow, while the forest is completely black. He drives slowly along the narrow road into the small community that has gradually grown up around the water. The headlights pick out spanking new homes, small summer cottages, and comfortable houses from the turn of the century. Rounding a curve, they sweep across a tricycle left behind in a driveway. He slows down and sees the silhouette of the haunted house behind a tall hedge. He drives past a few more houses and then parks on the side of the road. Getting out of the car, he sets off back down the road on foot; as quietly as possible he opens the garden gate of a house made of dark brick, padding across the lawn and around the back. A cable is whipping against a flagpole. Erik climbs over the fence into the next garden and walks past a swimming pool with a creaking plastic cover. The big windows of the low villa facing the lake are in darkness, and the stone terrace is covered with sodden leaves. Erik speeds up; he senses the haunted house on the other side of the fir hedge and pushes his way through.

This garden is better protected from prying eyes, he thinks.

A car passes by along the road, the headlights picking out a few trees, and Erik thinks about Aida's strange photograph. The yellow grass and the bushes. He moves closer to the big wooden building and notices that it looks as if a blue fire is burning in one of the rooms.

65

The building has tall, heavily barred windows and a projecting roof that looks like crocheted lace. The view over the lake must be magnificent. A taller hexagonal tower at one end and two bay windows with pointed gables make the house look like a miniature wooden castle. The walls are mainly made up of horizontal planks, but the line is broken by a false panel, creating a multidimensional impression. The door is surrounded by ornate carvings: wooden columns and a beautiful pointed roof.

When Erik reaches the window he sees that the blue light is coming from a television. Someone is watching figure skating. The cameras track sweeping leaps across the ice, and the blue light flickers across the walls of the room. A fat man in grey tracksuit bottoms sits on the sofa. He seems to be alone in the room. Only one cup sits on the table. Erik moves to the next window and peers into the adjacent room. Something is rattling faintly inside the glass. He sees into a bedroom with an unmade bed and a closed door. Crumpled tissues lie next to a glass of water on the bedside table. A map of Australia hangs on the wall. Water is dripping onto the window ledge. Erik moves along to the next window. The curtains are drawn. It is impossible to see between them, but he hears the strange rattling again, along with a kind of clicking noise.

He continues around the corner of the hexagonal tower and finds himself looking into a dining room. A table and chairs made of dark wood stand in the middle of the polished wooden floor. Something tells Erik it is very rarely used. A black object is lying on the floor in front of a display cupboard—a guitar case, he thinks. The rattling noise comes again. Erik leans into the glass and sees a huge dog racing towards him across the floor. It thuds against the window and rears up, barking and pawing at the glass. Erik jumps back, stumbles over a pot, and quickly moves to the back of the house, where he waits with a pounding heart.

The dog stops barking after a while; the outside light is switched on, then off again.

This was a bad idea, Erik thinks. He has no idea what he's doing here, peeping into strangers' windows. He realizes it's best if he returns to his office at Karolinska Hospital, so he sets off toward the front of the haunted house and the drive down which he parked.

As he turns the corner he sees someone standing in the light from the doorway. It's the fat man, wearing a padded jacket. He looks frightened when he catches sight of Erik. Perhaps he had been expecting a deer or some children messing about.

"Good evening," says Erik.

"This is private property," the man shouts in a shrill voice.

The dog begins to bark behind the closed front door. Erik keeps walking. A yellow sports car is parked in the drive. It has only two seats, and the boot is obviously too small to accommodate Benjamin.

"Is that your Porsche?"

"Yes."

"Is it your only car?"

"Why do you want to know that?"

"My son has disappeared," Erik says.

"It's my only car," the man says. "All right?"

Erik writes down the number.

"I'd like you to leave now."

"Sure," says Erik, heading for the gate.

He stands out in the road in the darkness for a while, looking at the haunted house, before returning to his car. He takes out the little wooden box with the parrot and the native, shakes a number of small tablets into the palm of his hand, counts them with his thumb, round and smooth, and then tips them into his mouth.

After a brief hesitation, he dials Simone's number. It rings and rings, each purring tone a serrated gash in the silence between them. She's probably at Kennet's, eating salami sandwiches with pickled gherkins. Erik pictures their apartment in the darkness, the hallway with their coats and winter gear, the candle sconces on the wall, the kitchen with its oak table and chairs. The mail is lying on the doormat, a pile of newspapers, bills, and advertising circulars encased in plastic. When the tone sounds, he does not leave a message but simply ends the call and begins driving toward Stockholm.

He has no one to turn to, he thinks, and at the same time he sees the irony. After spending so many years researching group dynamics and collective psychotherapy, he suddenly finds himself isolated and alone, without one single person he can rely on, no one he wants to talk to. And yet it was the power of groups that drove him on in his profession. He had tried to understand why people who had survived war together found it much easier to deal with their trauma than those who had faced the same kind of outrage alone. He wanted to discover why individuals in a group who had been tortured or raped or had seen their families killed were able to heal their wounds more easily than those who had suffered alone. What is it about community that heals us? Is it reflection, channelling, the very normalization of trauma? Or is it in fact solidarity?

Under the yellow lights of the motorway he calls Joona's cell phone.

"Joona here," a distracted voice responds.

"Hi, it's Erik. You haven't found Josef Ek?"

"No." Joona sighs.

"He seems to be following a pattern all his own."

"I've said it before and I intend to keep on saying it, Erik. You ought to accept protection."

"I have other priorities."

"I know." Silence. "Benjamin hasn't been in touch again?" Joona asks.

"No." Erik can hear a voice in the background, possibly from a television. "Kennet was going to try and trace the call."

"Yes, I heard about that. But it can take time," says Joona. "I don't know if he made you any promises."

"Not me," says Erik.

"Simone."

"More than likely."

"In any case, you have to send a technician out to those particular exchanges, that particular base station."

"But then at least they know which station it is."

"I think they can find that out straight away," Joona replies.

"Can you get that information for me? The base station?"

There is a brief silence. Then he hears Joona's neutral voice.

"Why don't you talk to Kennet?"

"I can't get hold of him."

Joona sighs faintly. "I'll check it out, but don't get your hopes up."

"What do you mean?"

"Only that it's probably a base station in Stockholm, and that won't tell us anything until a technician can pin down the position."

Erik can hear him doing something; it sounds as if he's unscrewing the lid of a jar.

"I'm making my mother a cup of green tea," Joona says. There is the sound of a tap running and then being turned off.

Erik holds his breath for a second. He knows Joona has to prioritize Josef Ek's disappearance. He knows that to the police Benjamin's case is in no way unique; a teenage boy going missing from his home is a long way from the kind of work the National CID usually does. But he has to ask; he can't simply let it go.

"Joona, I want you to take the case of Benjamin's abduction. I really want you to take it on."

He stops. His jaws are aching; he's been grinding his teeth without even realizing it.

"We both know this isn't an ordinary disappearance. He didn't run away. He hasn't simply forgotten to call. Someone injected Simone and Benjamin with an anaesthetic normally used in surgery. I know your priority is the hunt for Josef Ek, and I realize Benjamin is no longer your case, now that the link to Josef has disappeared, but something even worse might have happened."

He stops again, feeling himself growing upset, and takes a moment to collect himself.

"I've told you about Benjamin's illness," he eventually manages to say. "Tomorrow he'll need to receive an injection to help his blood coagulate. Without it, within a week the blood vessels will be under so much strain that he could be paralyzed, or have a brain haemorrhage, or a bleed in the lungs if he so much as coughs."

"He has to be found," says Joona.

"Can't you help me?"

Erik sits there with his plea hanging defencelessly in the air. It doesn't matter. He would sink to his knees and beg for help. The hand holding the phone is wet and slippery with sweat.

"I can't just take over a preliminary investigation from the Stockholm police," says Joona.

"His name is Fredrik Stensund. He seems very nice, but he's not going to leave his cosy warm office."

"I'm sure they know what they're doing."

"Don't lie to me," Erik says evenly. "As far as Stensund's concerned, Benjamin's just another runaway."

"I don't think I can take the case," Joona says heavily. "There's nothing I can do about that. But I would like to try and help you. You need to sit down and think about who could have taken Benjamin. It could be someone whose attention you got when you were in the papers. It happens. But it could also be someone you know. If you don't have a suspect, you have no case, nothing. You need to think, go through your life, over and over again, everyone you know, everyone Simone knows, everyone Benjamin knows. Neighbours, relatives, colleagues, patients, rivals, friends. Is there anyone who threatened you? Who threatened Benjamin? Try to remember. It could be an impulsive action, or it could have been planned for many years. Think very carefully, Erik. Then get back to me."

Erik opens his mouth to ask Joona once again to take the case, but before he can speak he hears a click on the other end of the line. He sits there in his car watching the traffic racing along on the motorway, his eyes burning.

66

It is cold and dark in his office at the hospital. Erik kicks off his shoes, catching the smell of damp greenery on his coat as he hangs it up. He is shivering as he boils some water on the hot plate, makes a cup of tea, takes two strong tranquillizers, and sits down at his desk. There are no lights on except the desk lamp. He stares into the deep black darkness of the windowpane, where he can glimpse an outline of himself, framed by the light. Who hates me? he wonders. Who envies me? Who wants to punish me, take everything I have away from me, take my life, take what lives within me? Who wants to crush me?

Erik switches on the main light and begins to pace back and forth. Incapable of gathering his thoughts, he reaches for the phone on his desk and knocks over a plastic cup of water. He watches without interest for a moment as a thin stream slowly heads toward one of his medical journals. Without another thought, he dials Simone's cell number, leaves a short message about wanting to look at Benjamin's computer again, and then falls silent, unable to say anything else.

"Sorry," he says quietly, and tosses the phone back on the desk.

The lift rumbles in the corridor. He hears the doors *ping* and glide open, then the sound of someone pushing a squeaking hospital trolley to his door.

The pills are beginning to work; he feels the calm rise through his body like warm milk, a memory, a movement inside him, a dip in the pit of his stomach. Like falling from a great height, first through clear cold air, then down into warm oxygen-rich water.

"Come on," he says to himself. Someone has taken Benjamin; someone has done this to me; there has to be a key to this somewhere in my memory.

"I will find you," he whispers.

Erik contemplates the sodden pages of his medical journal. In one photograph, the new director of the Karolinska Institute is leaning over a desk. The ink has run, blurring and darkening her face. When Erik peels the magazine from his desktop, the back pages stick to its surface, leaving behind random letters, so he begins to scratch off the bits of paper with his thumbnail. Suddenly he stops and stares at a combination of letters: e v A.

Up from the depths of his memory rolls a slow wave, full of reflections and facets; then comes the clear image of a woman who refuses to give back what she has stolen. Her name is Eva. Her mouth is tense, with flecks of froth on the narrow lips. She is screaming at him in outraged fury. *You're the one who takes! You take and take! What the fuck would you say if I took things from you? How do you think that would feel?* She hides her face in her hands and says she hates him; she repeats it over and over again, perhaps a hundred times, before she calms down. Her cheeks are white, her eyes red-rimmed; she looks at him, uncomprehending and exhausted.

He remembers her; he remembers her very well: Eva Blau. Right from the start, he knew he'd made a mistake in accepting her as a patient.

It was many years ago, when he was using hypnosis as a strong, effective element in therapy. Eva Blau. The name comes from the other side of time, before he swore off hypnosis. Before he promised never to use it again.

Why did Eva Blau become his patient? He can no longer remember the source of her pain. He'd met so many people, people with devastating histories, often aggressive, always afraid, compulsive, paranoid, sometimes with self-mutilation and suicide attempts in their background. Many came with only the thinnest of barriers separating them from psychosis or schizophrenia. They had been systematically abused and tortured; they had suffered mock executions; they had lost their children; they had been subjected to incest and rape; they had witnessed terrible things or been forced to participate in them.

What was it she stole? Erik asks himself. I accused her of stealing, but what was it she stole?

He can't quite pin down the memory. He takes a few steps, stops, and closes his eyes. Something else happened, but what? Did it have anything to do with Benjamin? He remembers explaining to Eva Blau that he wanted to find a different therapy group for her. Why can't he remember what happened? Had she begun to threaten him?

What comes quite clearly is an early meeting here in his office. Eva Blau had shaved off all her hair and made up only her eyes. She sat down on his sofa, unbuttoned her blouse, and showed him her breasts in a matter-of-fact manner.

"You've been to my house," said Erik.

"You've been to *my* house," she responded.

"Eva, you told me about your home," he went on. "Breaking in is another matter altogether."

"I didn't break in."

"You broke a window."

"The stone broke the window," she said.

67

Erik begins to search through the papers he keeps in his office. Somewhere in here, there will be information about Eva Blau. Because whenever his patients act differently from what he expects, Erik keeps his notes handy until he can understand the reasons for these deviations.

It could be an observation or some forgotten object. He rummages through papers, files, scraps of paper, and receipts with notes written on them. Faded photographs in a plastic wallet, an external hard drive, some diaries from the time when he believed in complete openness between doctor and patient, a drawing that a traumatized child made one night. Several cassettes and videotapes from his lectures at Karolinska Institute. A book by Hermann Broch, full of annotations. Erik's hands stop moving. Around a videotape is a piece of paper held in place by a brown rubber band. On the spine of the tape it simply says *Erik Maria Bark, Tape 14*. He removes the piece of paper, angles the lamp, and recognizes his own handwriting: THE HAUNTED HOUSE.

Ice-cold shivers run up his back and out along his arms, and the hair on the back of his neck stands up. He can suddenly hear the ticking of his watch. His head is pounding and his heart is racing. He sits down, looks at the tape again, picks up the phone with trembling hands, and calls the porters' office to ask that a videotape player be sent to his office.

With feet as heavy as lead he walks over to the window again and peers out at the covering of snow in the inner courtyard. Heavy flakes drift slowly at an angle through the air, landing on the windowpane before losing their colour and melting from the warmth of the glass. He tells himself it's probably just a coincidence, a strange coincidence, but at the same time he realizes that some of the pieces of the puzzle may fit together.

The haunted house. Those few words written on a piece of paper have the power to transport him back to the past, to the time when he was still involved with hypnosis. He knows that against his will he must walk up to a dark mirror and try to see what is hiding there, behind the reflections created by all the time that has passed.

The porter taps gently on the door. Erik opens it, confirms his request, and wheels in the stand with the television and the oddly antiquated video player. He inserts the tape, turns off the overhead light, and sits down. "I'd almost forgotten this," he says to himself, pointing the remote at the machine.

The picture flickers and the sound crackles and breaks up for a little while, and then he hears his own voice coming from the TV. He sounds as if he has a cold as he dutifully notes the place, date, time, and conclusion. "We have had a short break but are still in a post-hypnotic state."

Erik is riveted by the shaky picture on the screen. It's been ten years, he thinks, swallowing hard. The video steadies, revealing a half circle of chairs. Then Erik appears, and begins to tidy up. There is a lightness in his ten-years-younger body, a spring he no longer has. Here, his hair is not yet grey; the deep furrows in his forehead and cheeks do not yet exist.

Almost too well, Erik remembers the atmosphere in the room that day. The group was still affected by the first phase of hypnosis before the break, when they were disturbed by the arrival of the new member. They had got to know one another, had begun to identify with one another's stories. The new addition was deeply unsettling. This, Erik realizes, is what he's about to see.

The patients come into view, moving listlessly; they sit down on the chairs. A few talk in subdued tones. One laughs. Others sit in silence. The tape is grainy, and their blurred faces are difficult to make out.

Leaning forward in his chair, Erik swallows hard and hears himself explaining in a tinny voice that it is time to continue the session. He sees himself standing by the wall, making notes on a pad. Suddenly there is a knock on the door, and Eva Blau walks in. Even on the tape, across the distance of years, Erik can tell that she is under stress. He can make out patches on her throat and cheeks as he watches himself take her coat, hang it up, and lead her over to the group; he introduces her briefly and welcomes her. The others nod warily or perhaps they whisper hello; a few take no notice of her, staring down at the floor instead.

The group was usually made up of eight people, including Erik. Therapy focused on investigating each person's past under hypnosis, gradually approaching the most painful point. This hypnosis always took place in front of the group and together with the group. The idea was that this way they would all become more than witnesses to one another's experiences; via hypnotic openness, they would be able to share the pain and grieve together, as in collective disasters.

Eva Blau sits down on the one empty chair and stares straight into the camera; her face is suddenly sharp and hostile.

This is the woman who broke into his home ten years ago, he thinks. But what did she steal, and what else did she do?

On the screen, Erik introduces the second part of the session by referring back to the first and follows up with playful free associations. This was his way of lightening the mood, helping the group feel that a certain spirit was possible despite the dark, bottomless undercurrents constantly swirling inside everything they said and did. A patient named Pierre is conjuring "a hippie on a chopper" when Eva suddenly leaps to her feet with a crash, protesting the exercise.

"This is just childish nonsense," she says.

"Why do you feel that way?" asks Erik.

Eva doesn't reply but sits back down, crossing her arms tightly.

Getting no response, Erik turns to Pierre to see if he would like to carry on with his association, but Pierre shakes his head and forms a cross with his index fingers, pointing them at Eva. "They shot Dennis Hopper because he was a hippie," he murmurs.

A young, stocky woman—Sibel, her name was Sibel—giggles and glances sideways at Erik. A patient named Jussi clears his throat and raises his hand in Eva's direction. "In the haunted house you won't have to listen to our childish non . . . sense," he says, in his slow and heavy Norrland dialect.

Everyone falls silent. Eva whips around to face Jussi, but whatever she means to say, something makes her change her mind. Perhaps it's the seriousness in his voice, maybe the cool expression in his eyes.

68

The haunted house. The words reverberate in Erik's head as he stares at the old video frames. He hears himself explain to Eva the principles behind the process of hypnosis, how they always begin with group relaxation exercises before he moves on to hypnotize one or two individuals.

He watches himself pull up a chair and sit down in front of the semi-circle, getting them to close their eyes and lean back. While their eyes are closed, he stands up, talking to them about relaxation; he moves behind them, observing the degree of relaxation in each of them individually. Their faces become softer, looser, less and less aware, more and more incapable of lies, secrets, defences. Erik stops behind Eva Blau and places a hand on her shoulder.

As he watches himself begin to hypnotize her, Erik's stomach tingles. The younger Erik gently slips into a steep induction with hidden commands; he is so totally assured of his own skill, so pleasurably aware of his ability.

"You are ten years old, Eva," he says. "You are ten years old. This is a good day. You are happy. Why are you happy?"

"Because the man is dancing and splashing in the puddles," she says, her face moving almost imperceptibly.

"Who's dancing?"

"Who?" she repeats. "Gene Kelly, Mummy says."

"Oh, so you're watching *Singin' in the Rain?*"

She nods slowly.

"What happens?"

Eva closes her mouth and lowers her head. "My tummy is big," she says almost inaudibly.

"Your tummy?"

"It's huge," she says, and the tears begin to flow.

"The haunted house," whispers Jussi. "The haunted house."

"Eva, listen to me," Erik goes on. "You can hear everyone else in this room, but you must listen only to my voice. Pay no attention to what the others say, pay attention only to my voice."

"All right."

"Do you know why your tummy is big?" Erik asks.

"I want to go into the haunted house," she whispers.

In his hospital office, Erik gets up off his chair, massages his neck, and rubs his eyes, aware that he is moving closer to his own inner rooms, closer to what has been packed away.

Looking at the flickering screen, he mutters, "Open the door."

He hears himself counting down, immersing Eva more deeply in the hypnotic state. He explains that she will soon do as he says, without thinking, she will simply accept that his voice is leading her in the right direction. She shakes her head slightly and he continues counting backward, letting the numbers fall.

The picture quality suddenly deteriorates; Eva looks up with cloudy eyes, moistens her lips, and whispers, "I can see them taking someone. They just come up and take someone."

"Who's taking someone?" Erik asks.

Her breathing becomes irregular. "A man with a ponytail." She whimpers. "He's hanging the little—"

The tape crackles and the picture disappears.

Erik fast-forwards to the end of the tape, but the picture does not return: half the tape is ruined, erased. He sits in front of the blank screen. He can see himself looking back out of the deep, dark reflection. He can see the face of the man he was then, together with his face as it is now, ten years older. He looks at the video, tape 14, and he looks at the rubber band and the piece of paper with the words THE HAUNTED HOUSE.

69

Erik jabs repeatedly at the button until the doors of the lift close. He knows it won't speed things up, but he can't help himself. Benjamin's words from the darkness of the car are mixed with the strange fragments of memory stirred up by the videotape. Once again he hears Eva Blau's faint voice saying that a man with a ponytail has taken someone. But there was something insincere about her mouth as she said it, something almost like a smile.

There is a roaring sound high up in the shaft as the lift moves downwards with a whine.

"The haunted house," he repeats to himself, hoping it's just a coincidence and Benjamin's disappearance has nothing to do with his past.

The lift stops and the doors open at the underground car park. He walks quickly through it and into a narrow stairwell. Two floors down, he unlocks a steel door, continues along a white tunnel to a secure door, and leans on the buzzer, eventually receiving a response from within. He explains his errand into the microphone.

The storage facility contains all archived patient notes, all research and experiments, records of tests, and questionable investigations. On the shelves are thousands of files, including the results of secret tests on suspected HIV cases in the eighties, compulsory sterilizations, arguments concerning thalidomide, and dental experiments on those with

272

mental health issues from the time when Swedish dental health reform was due to be sanctioned and children from orphanages, the mentally ill, and the elderly were forced to sit with sugar paste in their mouths until their teeth were eaten away by decay—all meticulously archived and preserved here.

The door buzzes and Erik steps into an unexpectedly warm brightness. There is something about the lighting that makes the storeroom feel pleasant, far from the windowless cavern deep underground that it actually is.

The sound of opera is coming from the security guard's office: a rippling coloratura from a mezzo-soprano. Erik pulls himself together, tries to assume a calm expression, and searches within himself for a smile as he walks over to the sound.

A short, stocky man wearing a straw hat is standing with his back to the door, watering some plants.

"Hi, Kurt."

"Erik Maria Bark, it's been a long time. How are things?"

Erik doesn't really know what to say. "I've got a few family problems to deal with at the moment."

"Right."

"Lovely flowers," says Erik, to avoid further questions.

"Pansies. I love them. Conny kept saying nothing could flower down here. What do you mean, nothing can flower down here? I said. Look at me!"

"Exactly," Erik replies.

"I installed ultraviolet lamps all over the place. It's like a solarium down here." Kurt holds out a tube of sunscreen.

"I won't be staying that long."

"Oh, just a little bit on your nose," says Kurt, squeezing out some cream and holding it up.

"Thanks."

Kurt lowers his voice and whispers, his eyes sparkling, "Sometimes I walk around down here in just my underpants. But don't tell anybody."

Erik smiles at him, feeling the strain on his face. There is a silence. Kurt looks at him, expectantly.

"Many years ago," Erik begins, "I used to videotape my hypnosis sessions."

"How many years ago?"

"About ten. There's a series of VHS tapes—"

"VHS?"

"Yes, they were more or less out of date even then."

"All our videotapes have been digitalized."

"Good."

"They're in the computer archive."

"So how do I get access?"

Kurt smiles. Erik notices how white his teeth are in his sunburned face.

"Well, it so happens I can help you with that."

They walk over to four computers in an alcove by the shelving. Kurt rapidly keys in a password and clicks through folders containing recordings that have been transferred.

"Would the tapes have been in your name?" he asks.

"They should be," says Erik.

"Well, they're not," says Kurt slowly. "I'll try under HYPNOSIS."

He types in the word and carries out a new search. "Huh," he says. "Have a look for yourself."

None of the hits have anything to do with Erik's documentation of his therapy sessions. He tries the words HAUNTED HOUSE. He searches under Eva Blau's name, although the members of his group were not registered as patients with the hospital. "Nothing," he says wearily.

"We ran into trouble when we were transferring a lot of the material," Kurt says. "Some of it was in pretty fragile shape to begin with. Stuff got destroyed, like all the Betamax."

"Who transferred the material?"

Kurt turns to him with an apologetic shrug. "Me and Conny."

"But the original tapes must still be around somewhere, surely," Erik ventures.

"Sorry, I've no idea."

"Do you think Conny might know anything?"

"No."

"Can you call and ask him?"

"He's down in Simrishamn."

Erik turns away, trying to think calmly.

"I know a lot of stuff got erased by mistake," Kurt says.

Erik stares at him. "This was totally unique research," he says dully. "I'm sorry."

"I know, I didn't mean to criticize."

Kurt nips a brown leaf from a plant. "You gave up the hypnosis, didn't you?" he says. "I'm right, aren't I?"

"Yes. But I need to check, to look at—"

Erik stops speaking. He hasn't the energy to explain. He just wants to go back to his office, take a pill, and sleep.

"We've always had problems with technology down here," Kurt goes on. "Out of sight, out of mind, I guess. Every time we mention it, they tell us we have to do the best we can. Just chill out, they said, when we happened to erase an entire decade's lobotomy research: old films, sixteen millimetre, that had been transferred onto videotapes in the eighties but didn't make it into the computer age. It's a shame."

70

Early in the morning, the vast shadow of the town hall covers the façade of the police headquarters. Only the tallest central tower is bathed in sunlight. During those first few hours after dawn, the sun gradually moves down the building, revealing its yellow glow. The copper roof gleams, the beautiful metalwork with its built-in gutters and small castle-like funnels, also of copper, which carry rainwater down into drainpipes, are covered with shimmering drops of condensation. During the day the light remains, while the shadows of the trees below shift with the sun, moving around like the hands of a clock. It is not until a few hours before dusk that the façade once again turns grey.

Carlos Eliasson is standing by his aquarium gazing out the window when Joona knocks on his door and opens it.

Carlos jumps and turns around. When he sees Joona, his face expresses his usual conflicted feelings. He welcomes him with a mixture of shyness, pleasure, and antipathy. When he waves a hand in the direction of the visitor's chair he realizes that he is still holding the drum of fish food.

"I've just noticed it's been snowing," he says vaguely, putting the food down next to the aquarium.

Joona sits down and glances out the window. Kronoberg Park is covered in a thin, dry layer of snow.

"Perhaps we'll have a white Christmas, who knows?" Carlos smiles

276

cautiously, sitting down behind his desk. "In Skåne, where I grew up, we never had any real weather to speak of at Christmas. It always looked the same: a grey gloom hanging over the fields." Carlos stops abruptly. "But you haven't come to discuss the weather," he says.

"Not exactly." Joona looks at him calmly and leans back. "I want to take over the case of Erik Maria Bark's son, the boy who's disappeared."

"Out of the question," says Carlos, without hesitation.

"I was the one who started—"

"No, Joona, you were given permission to follow the case as long as there was a connection with Josef Ek."

"There's still a connection."

Carlos stands up and leans forward on his desk. "Our instructions are crystal clear. The resources we have are not meant—"

"I believe the kidnapping is strongly linked to the fact that Josef Ek was hypnotized."

"What are you talking about?"

"It can't be a coincidence that Benjamin Bark disappeared less than a week after his father's first hypnosis in ten years."

Carlos sits down again. Suddenly he sounds less sure of himself than he tries to come across. "Some kid who's run away has nothing to do with the National CID. It's out of the question."

"He didn't run away," Joona says tersely.

Carlos glances over at the fish, leans forward, and lowers his voice. "Just because you have a guilty conscience, Joona, I can't let you—"

"Then I'm requesting a transfer," says Joona, getting to his feet.

"A transfer?"

"To the squad that's handling the case."

"You're being stubborn again," says Carlos.

"But I'm on the right track." Joona smiles.

"Oh God," says Carlos, shaking his head anxiously. "Fine. You can't take over the case—it isn't your case—but you can have a week to investigate the boy's disappearance."

"Good."

"So now you don't need to say, 'What did I tell you?'"

"All right."

Joona rides the lift to his floor, greets Anja—who waves to him without taking her eyes off the computer screen—and passes Petter Näslund's office, where the radio is on. A sports journalist is commentating on the women's biathlon with simulated energy in his voice. Joona turns and goes back to Anja.

"Haven't got time," she says, without looking at him.

"Yes, you have," he says calmly.

"I'm in the middle of something really important."

Joona peers over her shoulder. "What exactly are you working on?" he asks.

"Nothing."

"What's that?"

She sighs. "It's an auction. I'm in with the highest bid at the moment, but another idiot keeps pushing the price up."

"An auction?"

"I collect Lisa Larson figurines," she replies tersely.

"Those little fat children made of clay?"

"It's art, but I wouldn't expect you to understand." She looks at the screen. "It'll be over soon. As long as nobody else makes a higher bid."

"I need your help," Joona persists, "with something important. That actually has something to do with your job."

"Hang on, hang on." She holds her hand up defensively. "I got them! I got them! I got Amalia and Emma!" She closes the page and turns to him. "OK, Joona, my friend. What was it you wanted help with?"

"I want you to lean on the telecom team and get me a location for the call made by Benjamin Bark on Sunday—two days ago. I want clear information on where he was calling from. Within the next five minutes."

Anja sighs. "Goodness, you're in a bad mood."

"Three minutes." Joona amends his demand. "Your shopping just cost you two minutes."

"Fuck off," she says softly, as he leaves the room.

He goes to his office, sifts through the post, and reads a postcard from Disa. She's gone to London and says she's missing him. Disa knows he can't stand pictures of chimpanzees playing golf or getting tangled up in toilet paper and always manages to find a suitably offensive card. Joona wonders whether to turn the postcard over or just throw it away, but his curiosity gets the better of him. He turns it over and shudders with distaste. A bulldog wearing a sailor's cap, with a pipe in its mouth. He smiles at the effort Disa has put in, and is just putting the card on his bulletin board when the phone rings.

"Yes?"

"I've got an answer," says Anja.

"That was quick."

"Did you give me any choice? Anyway, they said they've had technical problems, but they called Kennet Sträng an hour ago and told him the base station was in Gävle."

"In Gävle," he repeats.

"They said they haven't quite finished yet. In a day or two, or this week at any rate, they'll be able to say exactly where Benjamin was when he made the call."

"You could have come to my office to tell me, I mean, it's only four steps away."

"I am not your servant."

"No."

71

Joona writes *Gävle* on a blank page on the pad in front of him and picks up the phone again.

"Erik Maria Bark," comes the immediate answer.

"Hi, it's Joona."

"How's it going? Have you found anything out?"

"I've just been given an approximate location for the call."

"Where was he?"

"The only thing we've got so far is that the base station is in Gävle."

"Gävle?"

"Slightly north of—"

"I know where the place is. I just don't understand."

Joona can hear Erik moving around the room. "We'll get a more precise location sometime this week," he says.

"Sometime?"

"Tomorrow, hopefully."

"So will you take over the case?" Erik asks, his voice full of tension.

"I'm taking over the case, Erik," says Joona firmly. "I will find Benjamin."

"Thank you." Erik clears his throat, and goes on, once his voice is steady again. "I've been giving some thought to who could have done this, as you

280

suggested, and I have the name of a person I'd like you to trace. Eva Blau. She was a patient of mine about ten years ago."

"Blau? Like blue in German?"

"Yes."

"Had she threatened you?"

"It's hard to explain."

"I'll do a search right away." Joona writes the name on a pad. "One other thing. I'd really like to see you and Simone as soon as possible."

"All right. What's up?"

"Nobody did a reconstruction of the crime, did they?"

"No."

"To remind Simone of exactly what she saw. And there may have been witnesses. It'll help us figure out who may have had the opportunity to see the crime take place. Will you be home in half an hour?"

"I'll call Simone," says Erik. "We'll wait for you there."

"Good."

"Joona," says Erik.

"Yes?"

"I know it's usually a matter of hours if the perpetrator is caught. I know it's the first twenty-four hours that count. And now it's—"

"Don't you believe we're going to find him?"

"It's . . . I don't know," Erik whispers.

"I'm not usually wrong," Joona replies quietly, but with a sharpness in his voice. "And I believe we're going to find your son."

Joona hangs up. He takes the piece of paper with Eva Blau's name on it and goes to see Anja again. There is a strong smell of oranges in her office. A bowl of assorted citrus fruits stands next to the computer with its pink keyboard; on one wall hangs a large shiny poster showing a muscular Anja swimming the butterfly in Barcelona, at the 1992 Summer Olympics.

Joona smiles. "I was the safety officer when I was doing my military service. I could swim ten kilometres with a signal flag. But I've never been able to do butterfly."

"It's a waste of energy, that's what it is."

"Oh, not at all. I think it's beautiful—you looked like a mermaid, swimming along," says Joona.

Anja's voice reveals a certain amount of pride as she tries to explain. "The coordination technique is very demanding. It's all about a counter rhythm and—who cares?"

Anja straightens up contentedly, her large chest almost brushing Joona where he stands.

"Anyway," he says, holding out the piece of paper, "I'd like you to do a search for me."

Anja's smile stiffens. "I should have known you wanted something, Joona. It was a bit too good to be true. You come along with that sweet smile, and I was almost beginning to think you were going to ask me out to dinner or something."

"Oh, I will, Anja. All in the fullness of time."

She shakes her head and snatches the piece of paper from him. "Is it urgent?"

"It's extremely urgent, Anja."

"So why are you standing here flirting with me?"

"Thought you liked it."

Anja studies the piece of paper for a moment. "Eva Blau," she says thoughtfully.

"There's no guarantee that it's her real name."

Anja chews on her lip. "A made-up name," she says. "It's not much to go on. Haven't you got anything else? An address or something?"

"Nothing. The only thing I know is that she was a patient of Erik Maria Bark at Karolinska University Hospital ten years ago, probably for just a few months. But you can check the electoral roll and all the other databases. Is there an Eva Blau who enrolled in a university course? If she bought a car, she's registered to drive. Or has she ever applied for a visa? Does she have a library card . . . clubs, the temperance movement? I want you to look at witness protection programmes as well, victims of crimes—"

"Yes, all right, all right. Now go away," says Anja, "and let me get on with my work."

72

Joona turns off the audio book; Per Myrberg is reading Dostoyevsky's *Crime and Punishment* with his own peculiar mixture of calm and intensity. He parks the car outside Lao Wai, an Asian vegetarian restaurant that Disa keeps nagging him to try. He glances in through the window and is struck by the ascetic, simple beauty of the wooden furniture, the absence of anything unnecessary, the lack of decorative bits and pieces within the restaurant.

Erik and Simone are waiting for him in their apartment. Joona runs through what he intends to do.

"We're going to reconstruct the kidnapping as far as possible. The only one of us who was really there when it happened is you, Simone."

She nods resolutely.

"So you will play yourself. I'll be the kidnapper and you, Erik, can be Benjamin."

"All right."

Joona points to the clock. "Simone, what time do you think the break-in took place?"

She clears her throat. "I'm not sure . . . but the paper hadn't come, so it was before five. I'd got up for a drink of water at about two . . . then I lay awake for a while . . . so sometime between half past two and five o'clock."

"Good. I'll set the clock at half past three, somewhere in the middle," says Joona. "Now, I'm going to unlock the door, creep into Simone's bedroom, and pretend to give her an injection. Then I'll go into Benjamin's room and inject you, Erik, and drag you out of the room. Is Benjamin a big boy?"

"Not particularly," says Simone. "Why?"

"Erik's heavier, then. When I drag him along the hall and through the front door, I'll need to compensate by adding a minute or so to the time. Simone, try to move exactly the way you did that night. Lie down in the same position at the same time. I want to know what you could see and what you could only sense."

Simone nods, her face pale. "Thank you," she whispers. "Thank you for doing this."

Joona looks at her with ice-grey eyes. "Believe me. We are going to find Benjamin."

Simone rubs her hand rapidly over her forehead. "I'm going into the bedroom," she says hoarsely, as Joona leaves the apartment with the keys in his hand.

She is lying under the duvet when Joona comes in. He moves quickly toward her, not in haste but with purpose. She feels a tickling sensation as he lifts her arm and pretends to inject her. Just as she meets Joona's gaze as he bends over her, she remembers being woken by a distinct jab in her arm and seeing someone slip out through the doorway and into the hall. The memory alone makes her arm tingle unpleasantly where the needle went in. Joona disappears, and she sits, rubs her arm, and slowly gets up. She goes into the hallway, peers into Benjamin's room, sees Joona bending over the bed—and suddenly she simply comes out with the words, as if they have been echoing in her memory.

"Benjamin? What's going on?"

She moves hesitantly down the hallway. Her body seems to recall the sensations it felt that night; how quickly its strength faded. Her legs give way and she falls, banging her head. She remembers the feeling of sinking deeper and deeper into a black numbness, penetrated by ever briefer flashes of light. As she sits half propped up against the wall, she sees Joona dragging Erik along by his feet. Her memory replays the incomprehensible: Benjamin trying to cling to the doorframe, his head banging on the threshold, the slow windmilling of his hands growing weaker and weaker as he reaches out to her.

As Erik is dragged past Simone, it's as if a figure made of mist or steam appears there in the hallway for a fraction of a second: she is looking at Joona's face from below, and the image shifts: a glimmer of the kidnapper's face flashes through her mind: a shadowed face, a yellow hand around Benjamin's ankle. Simone's heart is pounding as she hears Joona drag Erik out onto the landing and close the door behind him.

An air of unpleasantness pervades the entire apartment. Simone cannot shake off the feeling that she has been drugged again; her limbs feel numb and slow as she gets to her feet and waits for them to come back.

As Joona drags Erik across the scratched marble floor of the landing, he looks around him the entire time, checking angles and vantage points, searching for unexpected places where an eyewitness might have had a good view of the incident. He moves toward the lift, whose doors he's propped open in advance, and drags Erik inside. From there he can see the apartment door to his right, the letter box and name-plate made of brass, but to the left there is only a wall. From deeper inside, Joona looks over at the large mirror on the landing, but even by craning his neck he can see nothing new. The window on the stairwell is hidden the whole time. Nothing seems to reveal itself when he looks back over his shoulder. Then suddenly he discovers something unexpected. From a certain vantage point, from a smaller security mirror mounted at an angle, he can see reflected in the landing's mirror the shining peephole in the door of an apartment that had seemed to be out of sight. Joona lets the lift doors shut and notes as they close that the mirror still allows him to stare straight at the door. If someone were standing inside that apartment looking out—roused, perhaps, by the commotion next door—that person would be able to see his face with absolute clarity right now. But if he moves his head just two inches in any direction, the view immediately disappears.

When they reach the ground floor, Joona helps Erik up and checks his watch. "Eight minutes."

They return to the apartment. Simone is standing in the hallway; it's obvious that she has been crying.

"He was wearing rubber gloves," she says. "Yellow rubber gloves."

"Are you sure?" asks Erik.

"Yes."

"In that case, there's no point in looking for fingerprints," says Joona.

"What now?" she asks.

"The police have already carried out door-to-door inquiries," Erik says gloomily, as Simone brushes dirt and dust off his back.

Joona takes out a sheet of paper. "Yes, I've got a list of the people they've spoken to. Needless to say, they concentrated on this floor and the apartments directly below. There are five people they haven't spoken to yet."

He checks the list and sees that the apartment diagonally behind the lift has been crossed out. That was the door he could see via the two mirrors.

"One apartment has been crossed out," he says. "The one on the far side of the lift."

"They were away," says Simone. "They still are. They've gone to Thailand for six weeks."

Joona looks at them, his expression serious. "Time for me to knock on some doors," he says.

The nameplate on the door says ROSENLUND. This was the apartment ignored by the officers carrying out door-to-door inquiries, since it was hidden from view and was empty.

Joona bends down and peers in through the letter box. He can't see any mail or advertising leaflets on the doormat. Suddenly he hears a faint noise from farther inside. A cat comes padding out of one of the rooms and into the hallway. It stops dead and stares at Joona, peering through the slot.

"Nobody leaves a cat for six weeks," Joona says slowly to himself.

The cat is listening, its whole body alert.

"You don't look as if you're starving," Joona says to the animal.

The cat gives an enormous yawn, jumps up onto a chair in the hallway, and curls itself into a ball.

Joona straightens up and glances at the paper in his hand. The apartment directly opposite the lift is occupied by a couple, but when the police called, only Alice Franzén was at home. The first person Joona wants to speak to is her husband.

Joona rings the doorbell and waits. He remembers being young, going around ringing doorbells with May Day flowers or an occasional charity collection box. The feeling of strangeness at looking into someone else's home, the expression of distaste in the eyes of those who open the door.

He rings again. A woman in her thirties answers. She looks at him with a watchful, reserved expression that makes him think of the cat in the empty apartment.

"Yes?"

"My name is Joona Linna," he says, showing her his ID. "I'd like to speak to your husband."

She glances over her shoulder. "I'd like to know what it's about first. He's actually very busy at the moment."

"It's about the early morning of Saturday, December the twelfth."

"We've already answered all your questions," the woman says irritably.

"My colleagues spoke to you but not to your husband."

The woman sighs. "I don't know if he's got time."

Joona smiles. "It'll only take a minute, I promise."

The woman shrugs her shoulders, then yells, "Tobias! It's the police!"

After a while a man appears with a towel wound around his hips. His skin looks as if it's burning; he's leathery and very tanned. "Hi. I was on the sun bed."

"Nice," says Joona.

"No, it isn't," Tobias Franzén replies. "There's an enzyme missing from my liver. I have to spend two hours a day on that thing."

"That's quite another matter, of course," Joona says dryly.

"You wanted to ask me something."

"I want to know if you saw or heard anything unusual in the early morning of Saturday, December the twelfth."

Tobias scratches his chest. His fingernails leave white marks on his sunburned skin.

"Let me think, last Friday night. I'm sorry, but I really can't remember anything in particular."

"OK, thank you very much, that's all," says Joona, inclining his head.

Tobias moves to close the door.

"Correction. One more thing. The Rosenlunds," he remembers.

"They're very nice people." Tobias smiles. "I haven't seen them for a while."

"No, I understand that they're away. Do you know if they have a cleaner or anything like that?"

Tobias shakes his head. He is now shivering and pale beneath his tan.

"Sorry, I've no idea."

73

Joona moves on to the next name on the list: Jarl Hammar, on the floor below Erik and Simone. A pensioner who wasn't at home when the police called.

Jarl Hammar is a thin man who is clearly suffering from Parkinson's disease. He is neatly dressed in a cardigan, with a handkerchief knotted around his neck.

"Police?" he repeats in a hoarse, almost inaudible voice as his eyes, cloudy with cataracts, look Joona up and down. "What do the police want with me?"

"I just want to ask a question," says Joona. "Did you by any chance see or hear anything unusual in this building or on the street in the early morning of December the twelfth?"

Jarl Hammar tilts his head to one side and closes his eyes. After a brief moment he opens them again and shakes his head. "I'm on medication," he says. "It makes me sleep very heavily."

Joona catches sight of a woman farther inside the apartment.

"And your wife?" he asks. "Could I have a word with her?"

Jarl Hammar gives a wry smile. "My wife was a wonderful woman. But unfortunately she is no longer with us; she died almost thirty years ago." He turns and waves a shaky arm at the dark figure behind him.

"This is Anabella. She helps me out with the cleaning and so on. Unfortunately she doesn't speak Swedish, but apart from that she's beyond reproach."

The shadowy figure moves into the light when she hears her name. Anabella looks as if she's from South America; she is in her twenties, with noticeable pockmarks on her face. Her hair is caught up in a loose black braid, and she is very short.

"Anabella," Joona says softly. "*Soy comisario de policía,* Joona Linna."

"*Buenos días,*" she replies in a lisping voice, looking at him with black eyes.

"*¿Tu limpias más departamentos aquí, en este edificio?*"

She nods, yes, she does clean other apartments in this building.

"*¿Qué otros?*" asks Joona.

"*Espera un momento,*" says Anabella, thinking for a moment before beginning to count on her fingertips: "*Los pisos de Lagerberg, Franzén, Gerdman, y Rosenlund, y el piso de Johansson también.*"

"Rosenlund," says Joona. "*¿Rosenlund es la familia con un gato, no es verdad?*"

Anabella smiles and nods. She cleans the apartment where the cat lives. "*Y muchas flores,*" she adds.

"Lots of flowers," says Joona, and she nods.

Joona asks in a serious tone whether she noticed anything unusual four nights earlier, when Benjamin disappeared. "*¿Notabas alguna cosa especial hace cuatros días? Por la mañana temprano.*"

Anabella's face stiffens. "*No,*" she says quickly, trying to retreat into Jarl Hammar's apartment.

"*De verdad,*" Joona says quickly. "*Espero que digas la verdad, Anabella.* I expect you to tell me the truth." He repeats that this is very important, it's about a child who has disappeared.

Jarl Hammar, who has been listening the whole time, holds up his violently trembling hands and says, in his hoarse, shaky voice, "Be nice to Anabella, she's a very good girl."

"She has to tell me what she saw," Joona explains firmly, turning back to Anabella. "*La verdad, por favor.*"

Jarl Hammar looks helpless as fat tears begin to fall from Anabella's dark, shining eyes.

"*Perdón*," she whispers. "*Perdón, señor*."

"Don't get upset, Anabella," says Jarl Hammar. He waves at Joona. "Come in. I can't have her standing here on the doorstep crying."

They go inside and sit down at a spotless dining room table; Hammar gets out a tin of Christmas biscuits as Anabella quietly explains that she has nowhere to live, she has been homeless for three months but has managed to hide in storage rooms belonging to the people she cleans for. When the Rosenlunds gave her a key to their apartment so she could look after the plants and feed the cat, she was finally able to sleep safely and take care of her personal hygiene. She repeats over and over again that she isn't a thief, she hasn't taken any food, she hasn't touched anything, she doesn't sleep in the beds, she sleeps on a rug in the kitchen.

Then Anabella looks at Joona, her expression serious, and tells him that she's been a very light sleeper ever since she was a little girl responsible for her younger siblings. Early Saturday morning she woke up when she heard a noise from the landing. It was strange enough to frighten her, so she gathered her things together, crept to the front door, and looked out through the peephole.

The lift door was open, she says, but she didn't see anything. Suddenly she heard noises and slow footsteps; it was as if an old, heavy person were moving along.

"But no voices?"

She shakes her head. "*Sombras*."

When Anabella tries to describe the shadows she saw moving across the floor, Joona nods and asks, "What did you see in the mirror? *¿Qué viste en el espejo?*"

"In the mirror?"

"You could see into the lift, Anabella."

She thinks, then says slowly that she saw a yellow hand. "And then," she adds, "after a little while I saw her face."

"Her face? It was a woman?"

"*Sí, una mujer.*" Anabella explains that the woman was wearing a hood that obscured much of her face, but for a brief moment she saw the cheek and the mouth. "*Sin duda era una mujer*," she repeats. It was definitely a woman.

"How old?"

She shakes her head. She doesn't know.

"As young as you?"

"*Tal vez.*" Perhaps.

"A little bit older?"

She nods, but then says she doesn't know; she saw the woman only for a second, and most of her face was hidden.

"*¿Y la boca de la señora?*" Joona demonstrates. What did the woman's mouth look like?

"Happy."

"She looked happy?"

"*Sí. Contenta.*"

When Joona can't get any other description out of her, he asks about details, turns his questions around, and makes suggestions, but it's obvious that Anabella has told him everything she saw. He thanks her and Jarl Hammar for their help.

On his way back upstairs, Joona calls Anja. She answers immediately. "Anja, have you found out anything about Eva Blau yet?"

"I might have, but you keep calling me up and disturbing me."

"Sorry, but it *is* urgent."

"I know, I know. But I haven't got anything yet."

"Fine, call me when you do."

"Quit nagging," she says, and hangs up.

Erik is sitting in the car next to Joona, blowing on a paper cup of coffee. They drive past the university, past the Natural History Museum. On the other side of the road, down toward Brunnsviken, the greenhouse shines out in the falling darkness.

"You're sure of the name, Eva Blau?" asks Joona.

"Yes."

"There's nothing in any telephone directory, nothing in the criminal records database, nothing in the database of suspects, or in the register of those licensed to carry a weapon, nothing in the tax office records, the electoral register, or with the vehicle licensing authority. I've had every local record checked: the county councils, the church records, the National Insurance Office, the immigration authorities. There is no Eva Blau in Sweden, and there never has been."

"She was my patient," Erik persists.

"Then she must have another name."

"Look, I damn well know what my—"

He stops as something flutters by, the faintest awareness that she might indeed have had another name, but then it simply disappears.

"What were you going to say?"

"I'll go through my papers. Perhaps she just called herself Eva Blau."

The white winter sky is dense and low; it looks as if it might start snowing at any moment.

Erik takes a sip of his coffee, sweetness followed by a lingering bitterness. Joona turns off into a residential area. They drive slowly past houses, past gardens dusted with snow, with bare fruit trees and small ponds covered for the winter, conservatories equipped with cane furniture, snow-covered trampolines, strands of coloured lights looping through cypress trees, red sledges, and parked cars.

"Where are we actually going?" asks Erik.

Small round snowflakes whirl through the air, gathering on the hood and along the windscreen wipers.

"We're almost there."

"Almost where?"

"I found some other people with the surname Blau," says Joona.

He pulls up in front of a detached garage but leaves the engine idling. In the middle of the lawn stands a plastic Winnie-the-Pooh, six feet high, with the colour flaking off its red sweater. Other toys are scattered throughout the garden. A path made up of irregular pieces of slate leads up to a large yellow wooden house.

"This is where Liselott Blau lives," says Joona.

"Who's she?"

"I've no idea, but she might know something about Eva." Joona notices Erik's dubious expression. "It's all we have to go on at the moment."

Erik shakes his head. "It's been a long time. I never think about those days now."

"Before you gave up hypnosis."

"Yes." Erik meets Joona's ice-grey eyes. "Perhaps this has nothing to do with Eva Blau."

"Have you tried to remember?"

"I think so," Erik replies hesitantly, looking at his coffee cup.

"Really tried?"

"Maybe not really."

"Do you know if she was dangerous?"

Erik looks out the window and sees that someone has taken a felt pen and drawn fangs and ugly eyebrows on Winnie-the-Pooh. He sips his coffee and suddenly remembers the day he heard the name Eva Blau for the first time.

It was half past eight in the morning. The sun was pouring in through the dusty windows. I'd been on call overnight, and I'd slept in my office, he thinks.

ten years ago

It was half past eight in the morning. The sun was pouring in through the dusty windows. I'd slept in my office after night duty, I felt tired, but I was packing my gym bag anyway. Lars Ohlson had been postponing our badminton matches for several weeks. He'd been too busy travelling between the hospital in Oslo and Karolinska and lecturing in London; he was due to take a seat on the board. But he'd called unexpectedly yesterday.

"Erik, are you ready?"

"Damn right I'm ready," I'd said.

"Ready to get beaten," he'd said, but without the usual vigour in his voice.

I poured the last of the coffee down the sink, left the cup in the pantry, ran downstairs, and biked over to the gym. Lars Ohlson was already in the chilly locker room when I got there. He looked up at me, then turned away and pulled on his shorts. Something in his expression was strange, almost afraid.

"You won't be able to hold your head up for a week when I'm done with you today," he said, looking at me. But his hand was shaking as he turned the key in his locker.

"You've been working too hard," I said.

"What? Well, yes, it's been—" He stopped and slumped down on the bench.

"Are you OK?" I asked.

"Absolutely. What about you?"

I shrugged. "I'm seeing the board on Friday."

"Of course. It's the end of your funding. Same song and dance every time, isn't it?"

"I'm not particularly worried," I said. "I think it'll be fine. My research is making good progress, after all. I've had some excellent results."

"I know Frank Paulsson," he said, getting to his feet. Paulsson was a member of the board.

"Oh? How do you know him?"

"We did our military service together; he's very much on the ball and quite open."

"Good," I said quietly.

We left the locker room and Lars took my arm. "Should I give him a call and tell him they just have to invest in you?"

"Can you do that sort of thing?"

"Well, it's not exactly accepted practice. But what the hell."

"In that case, it's probably best if you don't." I smiled.

"But you have to carry on with your research."

"I'll be fine."

"Nobody would know."

I looked at him and said hesitantly, "Maybe it wouldn't be such a bad idea."

"I'll give Paulsson a call tonight."

I nodded, and he smiled and gave me a slap on the back.

When we got into the big hall, with its echoes and squeaking shoes, Lars suddenly asked, "Would you take over a patient of mine?"

"Why?"

"I haven't really got time for her," he replied.

"I don't know that I could do much better by her. My list is pretty full at the moment."

I started stretching as we waited for a court to become free. Lars jogged on the spot but seemed distracted. He ran a hand through his hair and cleared his throat. "Actually, I think you could."

"Could what?"

"Could do better by her. I think Eva Blau would benefit from being in your group," he said. "She's completely locked around some trauma.

296

At least, that's what I think, because I just can't penetrate her shell. I haven't got through to her once."

"I'd be happy to offer my advice, if you—"

"Advice?" He lowered his voice. "To be honest, I'm through with her." Even speaking quietly, he said this with some vehemence.

"Has something happened?"

"No, no, it's just . . . I thought she was really ill. Physically, I mean."

"But she wasn't?"

He smiled, which seemed only to etch the stress on his face more deeply, and looked at me. "Can you just do me this favour?" he asked.

"I'll think about it."

"We'll talk about it later," he said quickly.

He fell silent and looked over at the court, where two young women who looked like medical students had a couple of minutes left of their session. When one of them stumbled and missed a simple drop shot, he snorted. "What a klutz."

I rolled my shoulders and pretended to be looking at the clock, but I was actually studying Lars. He stood there biting his nails. Although it was chilly and he hadn't begun to exert himself, he was sweating. And his face had definitely aged, grown thinner. Somebody yelled outside the hall, and he jumped and wheeled towards the door.

The women gathered up their things and left the court, chatting away.

"Let's play," I said, starting to move.

"Erik, wait a second." He put a hand on my shoulder to stop me. "I've never asked you to take on a patient before."

"I know. It's just that I'm pretty full right now, Lars."

"What if I cover your on-call hours?" he said, searching my face for a reaction.

"That's quite a commitment," I said, surprised.

"I know, but you've got a family and you ought to be at home."

"Is she dangerous?"

"What do you mean?" he asked with an uncertain smile, fiddling with his racquet.

"Eva Blau. Is that your assessment?"

He glanced over at the door again. "I don't know how to answer that," he said quietly.

"Has she threatened you?"

He considered his response for a moment. "Every patient of this kind can be dangerous. It's difficult to judge . . . But I'm sure you'll be able to cope with her."

"I expect I will."

"You'll take her? You will take her, won't you, Erik? Please?"

"Yes," I said.

His cheeks flushed, he turned away and moved toward the baseline. Suddenly a trickle of blood ran down the inside of his thigh; he wiped it away with his hand and looked at me. When he realized I had seen the blood, he mumbled that he was having a problem with his groin; he apologized and limped off the court.

I had just got back to my consulting room two days later when there was a knock at the door. Lars was standing in the corridor. Several feet away, a woman in a white raincoat waited. She had a sharp and narrow face and a troubled expression in her eyes, which were heavily made up with blue and pink eyeshadow.

"This is Erik Maria Bark," said Lars. "He's a very good doctor, better than I'll ever be."

"You're early," I said.

"Is that all right?" he asked anxiously.

I nodded and invited them in.

"Erik, I can't," he said quietly.

"I think it would be helpful if you were here."

"I know, but I have to run," he said, raising his voice again and clapping me on the shoulder. "Call me any time. I'll pick up, in the middle of the night, any time at all."

He hurried off and Eva Blau came into my room, closing the door behind her. "Is this yours?" she asked suddenly, holding out a porcelain elephant on the palm of her hand, which was shaking.

"No, that's not mine."

"But I saw the way you were looking at it," she said, in a sneering tone of voice. "You want it, don't you?"

I took a deep breath. "Why do you think I want it?"

"Don't you want it?"

"No."

"Do you want this, then?" she asked.

She yanked open the raincoat. She wasn't wearing anything underneath, and her pubic hair had been shaved off.

"Eva, don't do that," I said.

"All right," she said, her lips trembling with nerves.

She was standing far too close to me. She smelled strongly of vanilla.

"Shall we sit down?" I asked, keeping my voice neutral.

"On top of each other?"

"Why don't you sit on the couch?"

"The couch," she said.

"Yes."

"That would be a real treat, wouldn't it?" she said. She went over to the desk and sat down in my chair.

"Would you like to tell me something about yourself?" I asked.

"What are you interested in?"

I wondered whether she was a person who would be easy to hypnotize, despite the intense effort she was making to appear hard, or whether she would resist, trying to remain reserved and observant.

"I'm not your enemy," I explained calmly.

"No?" She pulled open one of the desk drawers.

"Please don't do that."

She ignored me and scrabbled carelessly among the papers. I went over, removed her hand, closed the drawer, and said firmly, "You are not to do that. I asked you not to."

She looked at me defiantly and opened the drawer again. Without taking her eyes off me, she took out a bundle of papers and hurled them on the floor.

"Stop that," I said harshly.

Her lips began to quiver. Her eyes filled with tears. "You hate me," she whispered. "I knew it. I knew you'd hate me. Everybody hates me." She suddenly sounded afraid.

"Eva," I said carefully, "I just want to talk to you for a bit. You can use my chair if you want or you can sit on the couch."

She nodded and got up to move. Then she suddenly turned and asked quietly, "Can I touch your tongue?"

"No. Sit down, please."

She eventually sat down but immediately started fidgeting restlessly. She seemed to be holding something in her hand.

"What have you got there?" I asked.

She quickly hid her hand behind her back. "Come and look if you dare," she challenged, her tone one of frightened hostility.

I felt a wave of impatience rush through me but forced myself to sound calm as I asked her, "Would you like to tell me why you're here?"

She shook her head.

"Why do you think you're here?"

Her face twitched. "Because I said I had cancer," she whispered.

"Were you afraid you had cancer?"

"I thought he wanted me to have it."

"Lars Ohlson?"

"They operated on my brain. They operated a couple of times. They knocked me out. They raped me while I was unconscious." Her eyes met mine, and a fleeting smile crossed her lips. "So now I'm both pregnant and lobotomized."

"What do you mean?"

"It's good, because I long to have a child, a son, a boy to suck at my breast."

"Eva," I said, "why do you think you're here?"

She brought her hand from behind her back and slowly opened her clenched fist. Despite myself, I was leaning forward with curiosity.

The hand was empty; she turned it over several times. "Do you want to examine my cunt?" she whispered. She grasped the lapels of her raincoat with both hands, as if to part them again.

I felt I had to leave the room or call someone in. But Eva Blau stood up quickly.

"Sorry," she said. "Sorry. I'm just scared you're going to hate me. Please don't hate me. I want to stay. I need help."

"Eva, I'm just trying to have a conversation with you. As you know, the plan is for you to join my hypnosis group. Dr. Ohlson said you were positive about the idea, that you wanted to give it a try."

She nodded soberly, then reached out and knocked my coffee cup to the floor. "Sorry," she said again.

When Eva Blau had gone, I gathered up my papers from the floor and sat down at the desk. A light rain was falling outside the window, and it occurred to me that Benjamin was on an outing with his nursery school today, and both Simone and I had forgotten to send his rain gear with him.

I wondered if I ought to call the school and ask them to let Benjamin stay indoors. Every outing terrified me. I didn't even like the fact that he had to go down two flights of stairs to get to the dining room. In my mind's eye, I saw other children bumping into him, someone letting a heavy door swing back in his face. I saw him tripping over the shoes stacked in grubby heaps. I give him his injections, I thought. The medication means he won't bleed to death from a little cut. But he's still far more vulnerable than the other children.

◎

I remember the sunlight the following morning, penetrating the dark grey curtains. Simone was sleeping naked next to me. Her mouth was half open, her hair a jumbled mess. I admired her shoulders and breasts, covered with small pale freckles. Goose pimples suddenly appeared on her arm, and I pulled the duvet over her.

Benjamin coughed faintly. He sometimes crept in at night and lay down on the mattress on the floor if he was having nightmares, and I would lie uncomfortably beside him, holding his hand until he went back to sleep. I hadn't noticed him come in last night, though. I saw that it was six o'clock, rolled over, closed my eyes, and thought how nice it would be to have just a few more hours of sleep.

"Daddy?" Benjamin whispered all of a sudden.

"Go back to sleep for a little while," I said quietly.

He sat up, looked at me, and said in his high, clear voice, "Daddy, you were lying on top of Mummy last night."

"Was I?" I said, and felt Simone wake up beside me.

"Yes, you were lying under the duvet rocking on top of her."

"That sounds a bit silly," I said, trying to sound casual.

"Mm."

Simone giggled and hid her head under the pillow.

"Maybe I was having a dream," I said evasively.

Simone was now shaking with laughter underneath the pillow.

"Did you dream you were rocking?"

"Well—"

Simone looked up with a big grin. "Go on, answer the question," she said, her voice perfectly controlled. "Did you dream you were rocking?"

"Daddy?"

"I must have."

"But," Simone went on with a laugh, "why were you lying on top of me when you—"

"Time for breakfast," I said.

I saw Benjamin grimace as he got up. The mornings were always the worst. His joints had been immobile for several hours, which often led to spontaneous bleeds.

"How are you feeling?"

He held on to the wall for support as he stood.

"Just a minute, little man, I'll give you a massage."

Benjamin sighed as he lay down and let me gently bend and stretch his joints. "I don't want a shot," he said dejectedly.

"Not today, Benjamin, the day after tomorrow."

"Don't want it, Daddy."

"Just think about Kalle," I said. "He's diabetic. He has to have injections every day."

"David doesn't have to," he complained.

"But maybe there's something else he finds difficult," I said.

There was a silence. "His daddy's dead," Benjamin whispered.

"See?" I finished massaging his arms and hands.

"Thanks, Daddy," Benjamin said, getting up slowly.

"Good boy."

I hugged his slender little body, but as usual I suppressed the urge to hold on until he squirmed to get free.

"Can I watch Pokémon?" he asked.

"Ask your mother," I replied, and heard Simone shout "Coward!" from the kitchen.

After breakfast I sat down in the study and called Lars Ohlson. His secretary answered, and I chatted with her for a few moments before asking if I could have a word with Lars.

"Just a moment," she said.

I was intending to ask him not to mention me to Frank Paulsson, if it wasn't already too late.

After waiting a minute or so, she came back on the line. "Lars isn't available at the moment."

"Tell him it's me."

"I already did," she said stiffly.

I hung up without a word, closed my eyes, and realized that something wasn't right. Perhaps I had been conned; presumably Eva Blau was far more troublesome than Lars Ohlson had told me.

"I can cope," I told myself.

I wasn't thinking of Eva Blau as a potentially dangerous person then, at least not primarily. My foremost concern was that she would throw my hypnosis group out of balance. I had assembled a small number of men and women whose problems and backgrounds were completely dissimilar. Some were easily hypnotized, others not. I'd wanted to achieve communication within the group, to help each of them move out of their shells and begin to develop new relationships, both with others and with themselves. The one thing most of them had in common was a feeling of guilt, a burden that had caused them to withdraw. Yet, while they blamed themselves for having been raped or tortured or otherwise abused, their burden was compounded by their having lost all trust in the world. I'd worked hard with them to forge the fragile bond that now existed among them, and I was worried that the addition of Eva Blau might separate them.

During our last session, the group had gone to a deeper level than we'd ever managed before. After our usual opening discussion, I'd made an attempt to put Marek Semiovic under deep hypnosis. All my past efforts had failed; he'd been unfocused and defensive.

In hypnosis, the practitioner may try to find a starting point, often a familiar or idealized place that the subject can imagine and from which he can proceed without fear or anxiety. I hadn't yet found that starting point with Marek.

"A house? A soccer field? A forest?" I suggested.

"I don't know," Marek replied, as usual.

"Well, we have to start somewhere."

"But where?"

"Try to imagine the place you'd have to return to in order to understand the person you are now," I suggested.

"Zenica, out in the country," said Marek, his tone neutral. "Zenica-Doboj."

"Good," I said, making a note. "Do you know what happened there?"

"Everything happened there, in a big building made of dark wood, like a castle, a landowner's house, with a steep roof and turrets and verandas."

The group was focused now; everyone was listening; they all realized that Marek had suddenly opened a number of inner doors.

"I was sitting in an armchair, I think," Marek said hesitantly. "Or on some cushions. Anyway, I was smoking a Marlboro while . . . there must have been hundreds of girls and women from my home town passing by me."

"Passing by?"

"Over the course of a few weeks . . . They would come in through the front door, and then, they were taken up the main staircase to the bedrooms."

"Was it a brothel?" asked Jussi, in his strong Norrland accent.

"I don't know what went on there. I don't know anything, really," Marek replied quietly.

"Did you ever see the upstairs?" I asked.

He rubbed his face with his hands and took a deep breath. "I have this memory," he began. "I walk into a little room and I see one of my teachers from high school, and she's tied to a bed, naked, with bruises on her hips and thighs."

"What happens?"

"I'm standing just inside the door with a kind of wooden stick in my hand—and I can't remember anything else."

"Try," I said calmly.

"It's gone."

"Are you sure?"

"I can't . . . I can't do any more."

"All right, fine, that's enough," I said.

"Wait a minute," he said, and sat without speaking for a long time. Then he sighed, rubbed his face, and stood up.

"Marek?"

"I don't remember anything!" he said, his voice shrill.

I made a few notes; I could feel Marek watching me all the time.

"I don't remember, but everything happened in that freaking house," he said, looking at me intently. I nodded.

"Everything that's me—it's in that wooden house!"

"The haunted house," said Lydia, from her seat beside him.

"Exactly," he said, "it was a haunted house," and when he laughed, his face was etched with anguish.

◎

I checked my watch again. In an hour I was to meet with the hospital board to present my research. If they didn't agree to continue my funding, I would have to start winding down both the research and the therapy. So far, I hadn't had time to start feeling nervous. I went over to the sink and rinsed my face, then stood for a while looking at myself in the mirror and trying to summon up a smile before I left the bathroom. As I was locking the door of my office, a young woman stopped in the corridor just a few steps away.

"Erik Maria Bark?"

Her dark, thick hair was caught up in a knot at the back of her neck, and when she smiled at me, deep dimples appeared in her cheeks. She looked happy and smelled of hyacinth, of tiny flowers. She was wearing a doctor's coat, and her badge indicated that she was an intern.

"Maja Swartling," she said, holding out her hand. "I'm one of your greatest admirers."

"I'm honoured," I said.

"I'd love to have the opportunity to work with you while I'm here," she said, with an uncommon directness I found appealing.

"Work with me?"

She nodded and blushed. "I find your research to be incredibly exciting."

"Frankly, I don't even know if there's going to be any more research," I explained. "I hope the board of directors is as enthusiastic as you are."

"What do you mean?"

"My funding only lasts until the end of the year." My imminent appearance before the board suddenly loomed up. "Right now I have an important meeting."

Maja jumped to one side. "I'm sorry," she said. "God, I'm so sorry."

"Don't worry about it," I said, smiling at her. "Walk me to the lift."

She blushed again and we set off together. "Do you think there'll be a problem renewing your funding?" she asked anxiously.

The usual procedure was for the applicant to talk about his or her research—results, targets, and time frame—but I always found it difficult, because no matter how meticulously I presented my case, I knew I'd inevitably run into difficulties because of the pervasive prejudice against hypnosis.

"If psychotherapy is a soft science, Maja, hypnosis is even softer. By its very nature, even the most exhaustive research in the field leads to relatively inconclusive results," I said.

"But if they read all your reports, the most amazing patterns are emerging. Even if it is too early to publish anything."

"You've read all my reports?" I asked sceptically.

"There are certainly plenty of them," she replied dryly.

We stopped at the lift.

"What do you think about my ideas relating to engrams?" I said, to test her.

"You're thinking about the patient with the injured skull?"

"Yes," I said, trying to hide my surprise.

"Interesting," she said. "The fact that you're going against conventional wisdom on the way memory is dispersed throughout the brain."

"Any thoughts of your own on the subject?"

"I think you should intensify your research into the synapses and concentrate on the amygdala."

"I'm impressed," I said, pressing the button for the lift.

"You have to get the funding."

"I know."

"What happens if they say no?"

"If I'm lucky, I'll be given enough time to wind down the therapy and help my patients into other forms of treatment."

"And your research?"

I shrugged. "I could apply to other universities, see if anyone would take me."

"Do you have enemies on the board?" she asked.

"I don't think so."

She placed her hand gently on my arm and smiled apologetically. Her cheeks flushed even more. "I know I'm speaking out of turn. But you will get the money, because your work is ground-breaking." She looked hard at me. "And if they can't see that, I'll talk to them. All of them."

Suddenly I wondered if she was flirting with me. There was something about her obsequiousness, that soft, husky voice. I glanced quickly at her badge to be sure of her name: MAJA SWARTLING, INTERN.

"Maja—"

"I'm not easily put off, you know," she said playfully. "Erik Maria Bark."

"We'll discuss this another time," I said, as the lift doors slid open.

Maja Swartling smiled, revealing dimples; she brought her hands together beneath her chin, bowed deeply and mischievously, and said softly, "*Sawadee*."

I realized I was smiling at the Thai greeting as I took the lift up to the director's office.

◎

Despite the fact that the door was open, I knocked before entering the conference room. Annika Lorentzon was there already, gazing out the picture window at the fantastic view, far out across Northern Cemetery and Haga Park.

"Just gorgeous," I said.

Annika Lorentzo smiled calmly at me. She was tanned and slim. Once, her beauty had made her runner-up in the Miss Sweden contest, but now a fine network of lines had formed beneath her eyes and on her forehead. She didn't smell of perfume but rather of cleanliness; a faint hint of exclusive soap surrounded her.

"Mineral water?" she asked, waving in the direction of several bottles.

I shook my head and noticed for the first time that we were alone in the conference room. The others ought to have gathered by now, I thought; my watch showed that the meeting should have begun five minutes earlier.

Annika stood up and explained, as if she'd read my mind, "They'll be here, Erik. They've all gone for a sauna." She gave a wry smile. "It's one way of having a meeting without me. Clever, eh?"

At that moment the door opened and five men with bright red faces came in. The collars of their suits were damp from wet hair and wet necks, and they were exuding steamy heat and aftershave.

"Although of course my research is going to be expensive," I heard Ronny Johansson say.

"Obviously," Svein Holstein replied, sounding worried.

"It's just that Bjarne was rambling on about how they were going to start cutting. The finance boys want to slash the research budget right across the board."

The conversation died away as they came into the room.

Svein Holstein gave me a firm handshake.

Ronny Johansson, the pharmaceutical representative on the board, just waved half-heartedly at me as he took his seat, while at the same time the local government politician, Peter Mälarstedt, took my hand. He smiled at me, puffing and panting, and I noticed he was still perspiring.

Frank Paulsson barely met my eye; he simply gave me the briefest of nods and then stayed on the far side of the room. Everyone chatted for a while, pouring out glasses of mineral water and admiring the view. For one crystal moment I observed them: these people who held the fate of my research in their hands. They were as sleek, well-groomed, and savvy as my patients were awkward, shabby, and inarticulate. Yet my patients were contained in this moment. Their memories, experiences, and all they had suppressed lay like curls of smoke trapped motionless inside this glass bubble.

Annika softly clapped her hands and invited everyone to take their seats around the conference table. The members of the board settled down, whispered, and fidgeted. Someone jingled coins in his pocket. Another flipped through his calendar. Annika smiled gently and said, "Over to you, Erik."

"My method," I began, "involves treating psychological trauma through group hypnosis therapy."

"So we've gathered," said Ronny Johansson.

I tried to provide an overview of what I'd done thus far. I could hear feet shuffling, chair legs scraping against the floor.

"Unfortunately, I have another commitment," Rainer Milch said after a while. He got to his feet, shook hands with the men next to him, and left the room. My audience listened without really paying attention.

"I know this material can seem dense, but I did provide a summary in advance. It's fairly comprehensive, I know, but it's necessary; I couldn't make it any shorter."

"Why not?" asked Peter Mälarstedt.

"Because it's a little too early to draw any conclusions," I said.

"But if we move forward two years?" he asked.

"Hard to say, but I am seeing patterns emerge," I said, despite the fact that I knew I shouldn't go down that path.

"Patterns? What kind of patterns?"

"Can you tell us what you're hoping to find?" asked Annika Lorentzon, with an encouraging smile.

I took a deep breath. "I'm hoping to map the mental barriers that remain during hypnosis—how the brain, in a state of deep relaxation, comes up with new ways of protecting the individual from the memory of trauma or fear. What I mean—and this is really exciting—is that when a patient is getting closer to a trauma, the core, the thing that's really dangerous, when the suppressed memory finally begins to float towards the surface during hypnosis, the mind begins to rummage around in a final attempt to protect the secret. What I have begun to realize and document is that the subject incorporates dream material into his or her memories, simply in order to avoid seeing."

"To avoid seeing the situation itself?" asked Ronny Johansson, with a sudden burst of curiosity.

"In a way. It's the perpetrator they don't want to see," I replied. "They replace the perpetrator with something else, often an animal."

There was silence around the table. I could see Annika, who had so far looked mainly embarrassed on my behalf, smiling to herself.

"Can this be true?" said Ronny Johansson, almost in a whisper.

"How clear is this pattern?" asked Mälarstedt.

"Clear, but not fully established," I replied.

"Is there any similar research going on elsewhere in the world?" Mälarstedt wondered.

"No," Ronny Johansson replied abruptly.

"But does it stop there?" said Holstein. "Or will the patient always find some new way of protecting himself under hypnosis, in your opinion?"

"Yes, is it possible to move beyond this protective mechanism?" asked Mälarstedt.

I could feel my cheeks beginning to burn; I cleared my throat. "I think it's possible to move beyond the mechanism, to find what lies beneath these images through deeper hypnosis."

"And what about the patients?"

"I was thinking about them, too," Mälarstedt said to Annika Lorentzon.

"This is all very tempting, of course," said Holstein. "But I want guarantees. No psychoses, no suicides."

"Yes, but—"

"Can you promise me that?"

Frank Paulsson was just sitting there, scraping at the label on his bottle of mineral water. Holstein looked tired and glanced openly at his watch.

"My priority is to help my patients," I said.

"And your research?"

"It's—" I cleared my throat again—"it's a by-product, when it comes down to it," I said quietly. "That's how I have to regard it. I would never develop an experimental technique if there was any indication that it was detrimental to a patient's condition."

Some of the men around the table exchanged glances.

"Good answer," said Frank Paulsson, all of a sudden. "I am giving Erik Maria Bark my full support."

"I still have some concerns about the patients," said Holstein.

"Everything is in here," Paulsson said, pointing to the folder of notes

I had provided in advance. "He's written about the development of the patients; it looks more than promising, I'd say."

"It's just that it's very unusual therapy. It's so bold we have to be certain we can defend it if something goes wrong."

"Nothing can really go wrong," I said, feeling shivers down my spine.

"Erik, it's Friday and everybody wants to go home," said Annika Lorentzon. "I think you can assume that your funding will be renewed."

The others nodded in agreement, and Ronny Johansson leaned back and began to applaud.

◎

Simone was standing in our spacious kitchen when I got home. She'd covered the table with groceries: bundles of asparagus, fresh marjoram, a chicken, a lemon, jasmine rice. When she caught sight of me she laughed.

"What?" I asked.

She shook her head and said with a broad grin, "You should see your face."

"What do you mean?"

"You look like a little kid on Christmas Eve."

"Is it so obvious?"

"Benjamin!" she shouted.

Benjamin came into the kitchen with Pokémon cards in his hand. Simone hid her merriment and pointed at me. "How does Daddy look, Benjamin?"

He studied me for a moment and began to smile. "You look happy, Daddy."

"I am happy, little man. I am happy."

"Have they found the medicine?" he asked.

"What medicine?"

"To make me better, so I won't need injections," he said.

I picked him up, hugged him, and explained that they hadn't found the medicine yet but I hoped they soon would, more than anything.

"All right," he said.

I put him down and saw Simone's pensive expression.

Benjamin tugged at my trouser leg. "So what was it, Daddy?"

I didn't understand.

"Why were you so happy, Daddy?"

"It was just money," I replied, subdued. "I've got some money for my research."

"David says you do magic."

"I don't do magic. I try to help people who are frightened and unhappy."

Simone let Benjamin run his fingers through the marjoram leaves and inhale their scent. "Tomorrow I sign the lease for the space on Arsenalsgatan."

"But why didn't you say anything? Congratulations, Sixan!"

She laughed. "I know exactly what my opening exhibition is going to be," she said. "There's a girl who's just finished at the art college in Bergen. She's absolutely fantastic; she does these huge—"

Simone broke off as the doorbell rang. She tried to see who it was through the kitchen window, before she went and opened the front door. I followed her and saw her walk through the dark hall and toward the doorway, which was filled with light. When I got there, she was standing looking out.

"Who was it?" I asked.

"Nobody. There was nobody here."

I looked out over the shrubbery toward the street.

"What's that?" she asked suddenly.

On the step in front of the door lay a rod with a handle at one end and a small round plate of wood at the other.

"Strange," I said, picking up the old tool and turning it over in my hands.

"What is it?"

"A ferrule, I think. It was used to punish children in the old days."

◎

It was time for a session with the hypnosis group. They would be here in ten minutes. The usual six plus the new woman, Eva Blau.

I picked up my pad and read through my notes from the session a week earlier, when Marek Semiovic had talked about the big wooden house in the country in the region of Zenica-Doboj.

It was Charlotte's turn to begin this time, and I thought I might then make a first attempt with Eva Blau.

I arranged the chairs in a semicircle and set up the video camera tripod as far away as possible.

I was eager that day. The stress of worrying about funding had been relieved, and I was curious as to what would emerge during the session. I was becoming increasingly convinced that this new form of therapy was better than anything I had practised in the past—that the importance of the collective was immense in the treatment of trauma. I was excited by the way the lonely isolation of individual pain could be transformed into a shared and empathetic healing process.

I inserted a new tape in the video camera, zoomed in on the back of a chair, adjusted the focus, and zoomed out again.

Charlotte Ceder entered. She was wearing a dark blue trench coat with a wide belt tightly cinched around her slender waist. As she pulled off her hat, her thick, chestnut-brown hair tumbled around her face. As always, she was beautifully, and terribly, sad.

I went over to the window, opened it, and felt the soft spring breeze blowing over my face. When I turned around, Jussi Persson had arrived.

"Doctor," he said in his calm Norrland accent.

We shook hands and he went over to say hello to Sibel, who had just come in. He patted his beer belly and said something that made her giggle and blush. They chatted quietly as the rest of the group arrived: Lydia, Pierre, and finally Marek, slightly late as usual.

I stood motionless, waiting until they felt ready. As individuals, they had one thing in common: they had each suffered traumatizing abuse of one kind or another, abuse that had created such devastation within their psyches that they had concealed what had happened from themselves in order to survive. In some cases, I had a greater command of the facts of their lives than they did. They were each, however, acutely aware that their lives had been decimated by terrible events in the past.

"The past isn't dead, it isn't even past." I would often quote William Faulkner. I meant that every little thing that happens to people remains with them throughout their lives. Every experience influences every

choice. In the case of traumatic experiences, the past occupies almost all the space available in the present.

Everyone was waiting for me to start, but Eva Blau had not yet arrived. I glanced at the clock and decided to begin without her.

Charlotte always sat farthest away. She had taken off her coat and was as usual dressed elegantly. When our eyes met, she smiled tentatively at me. Charlotte had tried to take her own life fifteen times before I accepted her into the group. The last time she had shot herself in the head with her husband's elk rifle, right in the drawing room of their villa. The gun had slipped, and she had lost one ear and a small part of her cheek. There was no trace of it now; she had undergone expensive plastic surgery and changed her hairstyle into a smooth, thick bob that concealed her prosthetic ear and hearing aid. Yet despite the fact that she was beautiful and impeccably groomed, I sensed an abyss within her, on whose edge she was constantly teetering. Whenever I saw her tilt her head to one side, favouring her good ear as she politely and respectfully listened to the others, I always went cold with anxiety.

"Are you comfortable, Charlotte?" I asked.

She nodded and replied, in her gentle, beautifully articulated voice, "I'm fine, thank you."

"Today we're going to investigate Charlotte's inner rooms," I explained.

"My own haunted house." She smiled.

"Exactly." I was always pleased and a little amazed at the way that certain meaningful phrases and expressions were commonly adopted as part of the private idiom in use within the group.

Marek grinned joylessly and impatiently at me as our eyes met. He had been training at the gym all morning, and his muscles were suffused with blood.

"Are we all ready to begin?" I asked.

Sibel spat her chewing gum into a tissue and got up quickly to throw it away. She glanced at me shyly and said, "I'm ready, doctor."

Slowly I led them into a trance, evoking the image of a wet wooden staircase down which I was leading them. A familiar special energy began to flow among us, a unique warmth we all shared. My own voice, clear and articulated at first, began to register as a series of mesmerizing, calming sounds that guided the patients. I seemed to be watching through someone else's eyes as their bodies settled more heavily into their chairs and their features flattened and relaxed, assuming the coarse, open expression shared by those under hypnosis.

I moved behind them, gently touching their shoulders, guiding them individually all the time, counting backward, step by step.

"Continue down the staircase," I said quietly.

I hadn't told the board that the hypnotist also becomes immersed in a kind of parallel trance as he puts his patients under. In my opinion this was both unavoidable and a good thing. My own trance always took place underwater. I didn't understand why, but I liked the image of water; it was clear and pleasant, and I had developed a way of using it as a visual and tactile metaphor to help me understand and interpret the course of events during sessions.

My patients were each seeing something completely different, of course; all drifting down into memories, into the past, ending up in the rooms of their childhood, the places where they had spent their youth; returning to their parents' summer cottages, or the garage of the little girl who lived next door. They didn't know that for me they were deep underwater at the same time, slowly floating down past an enormous coral formation, a deep-sea plinth, the rough wall of a continental rift, all of us sinking together through gently bubbling water.

This time I wanted to try to take them all with me into a deeper hypnosis. My voice kept on counting, speaking of pleasant relaxation as the water roared in my ears. I watched them.

Jussi hissed something to himself.

Marek's mouth was open, and a trickle of saliva ran out.

Pierre looked thinner and weaker than ever.

Lydia's hands hung loosely over the arms of her chair.

"I want you to go even deeper, even farther," I said. "Continue moving downward, but more slowly now, more slowly. Soon you will stop, very gently coming to rest . . . a little deeper, just a little more, and now we are stopping."

The whole group stood facing me in a semicircle on a sandy seabed, level and wide like a gigantic floor. The water was pale and slightly green. The sand beneath our feet moved in small, regular waves. Shimmering pink jellyfish floated above us. From time to time, a flatfish whirled up a little cloud of sand, then darted away.

"We are all deep down now," I said.

They opened their eyes and looked straight at me.

"Charlotte, it's your turn to begin," I went on. "What can you see? Where are you?"

Her mouth moved silently.

"There's nothing here that is dangerous," I reminded her. "We're right behind you all the time."

"I know," she said in a monotone.

Her eyes peered at me like those of a sleepwalker, empty and distant.

"You're standing outside the door," I said. "Would you like to go in?"

She nodded, and her hair moved with the currents of water.

"Let's go through the door now," I said.

"Yes."

"What do you see?"

"I don't know."

"Have you gone inside?" I asked, feeling distantly that I was rushing things.

"Yes."

"Can you see anything?"

"Yes, I can."

"Is it something strange?"

"I don't know. I don't think so."

"Tell me what you see," I said quickly.

She shook her head. Small air bubbles were released from her hair and rose towards the surface, glittering. The nagging sense that I was doing the wrong thing seemed closer now, more insistent, warning me that I wasn't listening, that I wasn't helping lead her forward but, instead, was pushing her. Still, I couldn't help saying, "You're in your grandfather's house."

"Yes," she replied, her voice subdued.

"You're inside the door, and you're moving forward."

"I don't want to."

"Just take one step."

"Maybe not right now," she whispered.

"Raise your head and look."

"I don't want to." Her lower lip was trembling.

"Can you see anything strange?" I persisted. "Anything that shouldn't be there?"

A deep furrow appeared in her forehead, and I suddenly realized that she would very soon let go and simply be ripped out of her hypnotic state. This could be dangerous; she could end up in a deep depression if it happened too quickly. Large bubbles were floating out of her mouth like a shining chain. Her face shimmered, and blue-green lines played across her brow.

"You don't have to look, Charlotte," I said reassuringly. "You can open the French doors and go out to the garden if you like."

But her body was shaking, and I realized it was too late.

"We are completely calm now," I whispered, reaching out to pat her gently.

Her lips were white, her eyes wide open.

"Charlotte, we are going to return to the surface together, very slowly," I said.

Her feet kicked up a dense cloud of sand as she floated upward.

"Wait," I said faintly.

Marek was looking at me, trying to shout something.

"We are already on our way up, and I am going to count to ten," I continued, as we moved quickly towards the surface. "And when I have counted to ten you will open your eyes and you will feel fine."

◎

Charlotte was gasping for breath as she got unsteadily to her feet. She adjusted her clothing and looked at me entreatingly.

"Let's take a short break," I said.

Sibel got up slowly and went out for a smoke. Pierre followed her. Jussi remained where he was, heavy and inert. None of them was completely awake. The ascent had been too steep, too quick. I remained seated; I rubbed my face and was taking some notes when Marek sauntered over.

"Well done," he said, with a wry grimace.

"It didn't quite go as planned," I replied, without looking up.

"I thought it was funny," he said.

"What?" I asked. "What was funny?" I met his eyes, which burned with an obscure hostility.

Lydia was on her way over, jewellery rattling. Her henna-dyed hair glowed like threads of copper as she walked through a sunbeam.

"The way you put that upper-class whore in her place," Marek said.

"What did you say?" asked Lydia.

"I'm not talking about you, I'm talking about—"

"You're not to call Charlotte a whore, because it isn't true," Lydia said softly. "Right, Marek?"

"Fine, whatever."

I moved away, looking at my notes, but kept on listening to their conversation.

"Do you have issues with women?" she continued.

"Things happened in the haunted house," he said quietly. "If you weren't there, you wouldn't understand."

He fell silent, clamping his teeth so tightly together I could see his jaw muscles working.

"There is actually nothing that is wrong," she said, and took his hand in both of hers.

Sibel and Pierre came back. Everyone was quiet and subdued. Charlotte looked very fragile. Her slender arms were crossed over her chest; her hands were on her shoulders.

I changed the tape in the video camera, gave the date and time, and explained that everyone was still in a post-hypnotic state. I looked through the lens, raised the tripod a fraction, and refocused the camera. Then I straightened the chairs and asked the group to sit down again.

"Let's continue," I said.

There was a sudden knock at the door and Eva Blau walked in. I could see instantly that she was under stress and went over to greet her.

"Welcome," I said.

"Am I?"

"Yes."

Eva Blau sat down on the empty chair and clamped her hands firmly between her thighs. I went back to my place and carefully introduced the second session.

"Please get comfortable. Let's keep our feet on the floor, hands on our knees. The first part didn't quite turn out as I expected."

"I'm sorry," said Charlotte.

"Nobody need apologize, least of all you; I hope you understand."

Eva Blau was staring at me the whole time.

"We're going to begin with thoughts and associations from the first session," I said. "Would anyone like to comment?"

"Confusing," said Sibel.

"Frus . . . tra . . . ting," said Jussi. "I mean, I only just had time to open my eyes and scratch my head, and it was all over."

"What did you feel?" I asked him.

"Hair," he answered, with a smile.

"Hair?" asked Sibel, giggling.

"When I scratched my noggin," Jussi explained.

Some of them laughed.

"Let's have some associations with hair," I said, with a smile. "Charlotte?"

"I don't know. Hair? Beard, maybe . . . no."

Pierre interrupted her in his high voice. "A hippie, a hippie on a chopper," he said with a smile. "He's sitting like this, chewing a piece of Juicyfruit, and—"

Suddenly Eva got up with such a violent movement that the chair banged behind her. "This is just childish nonsense," she said angrily, pointing at Pierre.

"Why do you feel that way?" I asked.

Eva didn't reply, she merely met my gaze before sulkily flopping back down on her chair.

"Pierre, would you continue, please," I said calmly.

He shook his head, forming a cross with his index fingers and pointing them at Eva, pretending to protect himself against her.

"They shot Dennis Hopper because he was a hippie," he whispered conspiratorially.

Sibel giggled even more loudly and glanced expectantly at me. Jussi raised his hand and turned to Eva.

"In the haunted house you won't have to listen to our childish nonsense," he said, in his strong accent.

The room fell completely silent. It occurred to me that Eva had no way of knowing what the haunted house meant to our group, but I left it.

Eva Blau turned to Jussi. It looked as if she were going to yell something at him, but he simply gazed back at her with such a calm, serious expression that she appeared to change her mind and settled back down.

"Eva, we begin with relaxation exercises and breathing and then I hypnotize you, one by one or in pairs," I explained. "Of course, everyone participates all the time, regardless of the level of consciousness on which you find yourself."

An ironic smile passed over Eva's face.

"And sometimes," I went on, "if I feel it will work, I try to put the whole group into a deep hypnosis."

I pulled up my chair and asked them to close their eyes and lean back. "Your feet should be on the floor, your hands should be resting on your lap," I repeated.

As I gently led them deeper into a state of relaxation, I decided to begin by investigating Eva Blau's secret rooms. It was important for her to make some contribution soon, in order to be accepted by the group. I counted backwards and listened to their breathing, immersing them in a light hypnotic state and leaving them just beneath the silvery surface of the water.

"Eva, I am speaking only to you," I said. "You should feel safe and relaxed. Just listen to my voice and follow my words. Follow my words spontaneously all the time. Do not question them. You are amid their flow, not anticipating, not analyzing, but right here in the moment the whole time."

We were sinking through grey water, falling down into the dark depths past a thick rope, a hawser festooned with swaying ribbons of seaweed. I looked up and glimpsed the rest of the group dangling there with the tops of their heads brushing the rippling mirror.

At the same time, I was actually standing behind Eva Blau's chair with one hand on her shoulder, speaking calmly, my voice growing softer. She was leaning back, her face relaxed.

In my own trance, the water around her was sometimes brown, sometimes grey. Her face lay in shadow, her mouth tightly closed. Her brow was furrowed, but her gaze was completely blank. Lars Ohlson's notes contained almost nothing about her background, so I decided to try a cautious entry strategy. Evoking a calm and happy time ironically often proves to be the quickest way into the most difficult areas.

"You are ten years old, Eva," I said, coming around so that I could observe her from the front.

Her chest was barely moving; she was breathing calmly, gently, from down in her diaphragm.

"You are ten years old, Eva. This is a good day. You are happy. Why are you happy?"

Eva pouted sweetly, smiled to herself, and said, "Because the man is dancing and splashing in the puddles."

"Who's dancing?" I asked.

"Who?" She didn't speak for a moment. "Gene Kelly, Mummy says."

"Oh, so you're watching *Singin' in the Rain?*"

A slow nod.

"What happens?"

I saw her face slowly sink towards her chest. Suddenly a strange expression flitted across her lips.

"My tummy is big," she said, almost inaudibly.

"Your tummy?"

"It's huge," she said, with tears in her voice.

Jussi was breathing heavily beside her. From the corner of my eye I could see that he was moving his lips.

"The haunted house," he whispered, in his state of light hypnosis. "The haunted house."

"Eva, listen to me," I said. "You can hear everyone else in this room, but you must listen only to my voice. Pay no attention to what the others say, pay attention only to my voice."

"OK," she said, her expression contented.

"Do you know why your tummy is big?" I asked.

"I want to go into the haunted house," she whispered.

I counted backwards, suggesting the staircase that led ever down. As I counted, I was thinking that something wasn't right. I myself was immersed in pleasantly warm water, as I slowly drifted down past the rock face, deeper and deeper.

Eva Blau lifted her chin, moistened her lips, sucked in her cheeks, and whispered, "I can see them taking someone. They just come up and take someone."

"Who's taking someone?" I asked.

Her breathing became irregular. Her face grew darker. Brown, cloudy water drifted in front of her.

"A man with a ponytail. He's hanging the little person up on the ceiling," she whimpered.

She was clutching the hawser with the billowing seaweed tightly with one hand; her legs were paddling slowly.

Something wasn't right. With an effortful thrust I pushed myself outside the hypnosis. Eva Blau was faking. I was absolutely certain that she wasn't under hypnosis. She had resisted, blocked my suggestion. *She's lying, she isn't under hypnosis at all,* my brain whispered coldly.

She was throwing herself back and forth on her chair. "The man is pulling and pulling at the little person, he's pulling too hard." Suddenly she met my gaze and stopped moving. Her lips distended in a wide, ugly grin. "Was I good?" she asked me.

I didn't reply. I just watched as she stood up, took her coat from the hook, and calmly walked out of the room.

◎

I wrote THE HAUNTED HOUSE on a piece of paper, wrapped it around tape number 14, and secured it with a rubber band. But instead of archiving the tape as usual, I took it to my office. I wanted to analyze Eva Blau's lie and my own reaction, but I was still in the hall when I realized what had been wrong all along: Eva had been aware of her face and had tried to look sweet; she had not had the listless, open face that those under hypnosis always have. A person under hypnosis can smile, but it isn't their usual smile, it's a somnolent, slack smile.

As I turned the corner leading to my office, I saw Maja Swartling waiting outside my door. I surprised myself by remembering her name. When she caught sight of me, her face lit up and she waved.

"Sorry to keep bothering you like this," she said quickly, "but since I'm basing part of my dissertation on your research, my advisor suggested that I interview you." She looked at me intently.

"I understand," I said.

"Is it all right if I ask you a few questions?" she asked.

Suddenly she looked like a little girl: wide awake but unsure of herself. Her eyes were very dark, set off against the milky glow of her fair skin. She wore her shiny hair in looped braids: an old-fashioned hairstyle, but it suited her.

"Is it all right?" she repeated softly. "You have no idea how persistent I can be."

I realized I was standing there smiling. There was something so bright and healthy about her. She laughed and gave me a lingering, satisfied look. I unlocked the door and she followed me into the office, settled down in the visitor's chair, and took out a notepad and pen.

"What would you like to ask me?"

Maja blushed deeply and sat, then began to talk.

"I've read your reports," she said, "and your hypnosis group is made up not only of victims, people who have been subjected to some kind of abuse, but also perpetrators, those who have done terrible things to others."

"You have to understand that sometimes the level of coercion is so great that a person is forced to commit terrible acts. The victim becomes the perpetrator through the very process of victimization. In any event, for patients like this, it works the same way in the subconscious, and in the context of group therapy this is in fact a resource."

"Interesting," she said, taking more notes. "I want to come back to that, but what I'd like to know now is how the perpetrator sees himself or herself during hypnosis—after all, you do put forward the idea that the victim often replaces the perpetrator with something else, like an animal."

"I haven't had time to investigate how perpetrators see themselves, and I don't want to speculate."

Maja leaned forward, lips pursed. "But you've got an idea?"

"I have a patient, for example, who—" I fell silent, thinking of Jussi Persson, the man from Norrland who carried his loneliness like a dreadful self-imposed weight.

"What were you going to say?"

"Under hypnosis this patient returns to a hunting tower. It's as if the gun is in control of him; he shoots deer and simply leaves them lying there."

We sat in silence, looking at each other.

"It's getting late," I said.

"I still have a lot of questions."

I waved my hand. "We'll have to meet again."

She looked at me. My body suddenly felt strangely hot as I noticed a faint flush rising on her pale skin. There was something mischievous between us, a mixture of seriousness and the desire to laugh.

"Can I buy you a drink to say thank you? There's a really nice Lebanese—"

She stopped abruptly as the telephone rang. I apologized and picked it up.

"Erik?" It was Simone, sounding stressed.

"What's wrong?" I asked.

"I . . . I'm out in back, on the bike path. It looks like someone's broken into our home."

An ice-cold shudder ran through me. I thought about the ferrule that had been left outside our door, the old instrument of punishment.

"What happened?"

I heard Simone swallow hard. Some children were playing in the background; they might have been up on the soccer field. I heard the sound of a whistle and screams.

"What was that?" I asked.

"Nothing, a class of schoolchildren," she said firmly. "Erik, Benjamin's veranda door is open and the window has been smashed."

Maja Swartling stood and pointed at the door, asking if she should go. I nodded briefly, with an apologetic shrug. She bumped into the chair, which scraped along the floor.

"Are you alone?" asked Simone.

"Yes," I said, without knowing why I was lying.

Maja waved and closed the door soundlessly behind her. I could still smell her perfume.

"It's just as well you didn't go inside," I went on. "Have you called the police?"

"Erik, you sound funny. Has something happened?"

"You mean apart from the fact that there might be a burglar inside our house right now? Have you called the police?"

"Yes, I called Dad."

"Good."

"He said he was on his way."

"Move farther away from the house, Simone."

"I'm standing on the bike path."

"Can you still see the house?"

"Yes."

"If you can see the house, anyone inside the house can see you."

"Stop it!" she said.

"Please, Simone, go up to the soccer field. I'm on my way home."

◎

I stopped behind Kennet's dirty Opel and got out of the car. Kennet came running toward me, his expression tense.

"Where the hell is Sixan?" he shouted.

"I told her to wait on the soccer field."

"Good, I was afraid she'd—"

"She would have gone inside otherwise, I know her; she takes after you."

He laughed and hugged me tightly. "Good to see you, kid."

We set off around the block, to get to the back. Simone was standing not far from our garden. Presumably she had been keeping an eye on the broken veranda door the whole time; it led straight to our shady patio. She looked up, left her bike, came straight over and gave me a hug, and looked over my shoulder. "Hi, Dad."

"I'm going in," he said, his tone serious.

"I'm coming with you," I said.

Simone sighed. "Women and children wait outside."

All three of us stepped over the low potentilla hedge and walked across the grass to the patio, with its white plastic table and four plastic chairs.

Shards of glass covered the step and the doorsill. On the wall-to-wall carpet in Benjamin's room, a large stone lay among fragments and shards. As we went in, I reminded myself to tell Kennet about the ferrule that we'd found outside our door.

Simone followed us and switched on the ceiling light. Her face was glowing, and her strawberry-blonde hair hung down in curls over her shoulders.

Kennet went into the hall, looked into the bedroom on the right, and into the bathroom. The reading lamp in the TV room was on. In the kitchen, a chair lay on its side on the floor. We went from room to room, but nothing seemed to be missing. In the downstairs bathroom, the toilet paper had been yanked violently off the roll and lay strewn across the floor.

Kennet looked at me with an odd expression. "Do you have any unfinished business with anyone?" he asked.

I shook my head. "Not as far as I know," I said. "Obviously, I meet a lot of damaged people in my work. Just like you."

He nodded.

"They haven't taken anything," I said.

"Is that normal, Dad?" asked Simone.

Kennet shook his head. "It isn't normal, not if they break a window. Somebody wanted you to know they'd been here."

Simone was standing in the doorway of Benjamin's room. "It looks as if someone has been lying in his bed," she said quietly. "What's the name of that fable? Goldilocks, isn't it?"

We hurried into our bedroom and saw that somebody had been lying in our bed too. The bedspread had been pulled down and the sheets were crumpled.

"This is pretty weird," said Kennet.

There was silence for a little while.

"The ferrule!" Simone exclaimed.

"Exactly. I thought about it and then I forgot," I said. I went into the hall and got it from the stand.

"My God," said Kennet. "I haven't seen one of these since I was a boy."

"It was outside our door yesterday," said Simone.

"Let me have a look," said Kennet.

"They used to use it for corporal punishment," I said.

"I know what it is," said Kennet, running his hand over it.

"I don't like this at all. The whole thing feels creepy," said Simone.

"Has anyone threatened you, or have you experienced anything that could be construed as a threat?"

"No," she replied.

"But perhaps that's how we should regard it," I said. "Perhaps someone thinks we should be punished. I thought maybe it was just a bad joke, because we coddle Benjamin so much. I mean, if you didn't know about Benjamin's illness, we'd seem pretty neurotic."

Simone went straight to the telephone and called Benjamin's pre-school to check that he was all right.

◎

That evening we put Benjamin to bed early; as usual, I lay down beside him and told him the entire plot of a children's film about an African boy. Benjamin had watched it many times and almost always wanted me to tell him the story when he settled down to go to sleep. If I forgot the smallest detail he would remind me, and if he was still awake when I got to the end, Simone got to sing lullabies.

That night, he fell asleep easily. I made a pot of tea, and Simone and I settled down to watch a video. But neither of us could focus on the movie, so I paused the machine and we talked about the break-in, re-assuring ourselves with the fact that nothing was stolen; someone had just unrolled the toilet paper and messed up our beds.

"Maybe it was some teenagers who wanted a place to screw around," said Simone.

"No, I don't think so. They would have left more of a mess if that were the case."

"But don't you think it's a bit strange that the neighbours didn't no-tice anything?" asked Simone. "I mean, Adolfsson doesn't usually miss much."

"Maybe he was the one who did it," I suggested.

"Screwed around in our bed?"

I laughed and pulled her close. How good she smelled! She was wearing my favourite scent, Aromatics Elixir, heavy, but not cloying or sweet. She pressed herself to me, and I felt her slim, boyish body against mine. I slipped my hands inside her loose shirt, running them over her silky skin. Her breasts were warm, her nipples hard. She groaned when I kissed her throat; a blast of hot breath shot into my ear.

We undressed by the glow of the television, helping each other with rapid, seeking hands, fumbling, laughing, and kissing again. She drew me to the bedroom and pushed me down onto the bed with playful severity.

"Time for the ferrule," she said.

I nodded, transfixed, and watched as she moved closer to me, bowing her head to allow her hair to trail over my legs; she smiled as she moved steadily upward. Her curls cascaded over her slender, freckled shoulders. Her arm muscles tensed as she straddled my hips. Her cheeks flushed deep red as I pushed inside her.

For a few seconds the memory of some photographs flickered through my mind. I had taken the pictures on an isolated beach in the Greek archipelago, two years before Benjamin was born. We'd taken a bus along the coast and got off at what we thought was the prettiest spot. When we realized the beach was completely deserted, we decided not to bother with swimsuits. We ate warm watermelon in the sunshine and then lay naked in clear, shallow water, kissing and caressing each other. We made love perhaps four times that day on the beach, growing ever warmer and more indolent. I recalled Simone's skin, sticky with salt water, her heavy, sun-drenched gaze, her introverted smile. Her small, taut breasts, her freckles, her pale pink nipples. Her flat stomach, her navel, her reddish-brown pubic hair.

Now Simone leaned forward, chasing her orgasm. She thrust backwards, kissed my chest, my throat. She was breathing faster, her eyes closed; she gripped my shoulders and whispered. "Don't stop, Erik, please don't stop."

She was moving faster, heavier, her back slippery with sweat. She groaned loudly, still thrusting backwards, over and over again, stopping with quivering thighs before starting again; she stopped, whimpering, gasped for air, moistened her lips, and supported herself on my chest with her hands.

◎

I parked my bike outside the neurological unit and stood for a little while, listening to the birds rustling in the trees; I could see their bright spring colours among the dense leaves. I thought about waking up next to Simone this morning and looking into her green eyes.

My office looked just as I had left it; the chair on which Maja Swartling had sat while she interviewed me was still pulled out, and my desk lamp was on. I switched it off. It was only half past eight, and I had plenty of time to go through my notes from yesterday's abortive hypnosis session with Charlotte. It was easy to understand why it had turned out as it had: I had forced the pace of events, striving only to reach the goal. I should have known better. I was far too experienced to make that kind of mistake. It's impossible to force a patient to see something she absolutely does not want to see. Charlotte had gone into her room but had not wanted to look up. That should have been enough for one session, it was courageous enough.

I changed into my white coat, disinfected my hands, and thought about the group. I wasn't completely happy with the role Pierre had assumed; it was a little unclear. He often hung around Sibel or Lydia and was talkative and mischievous, but he remained extremely passive during hypnosis. He was a hairdresser, openly homosexual, who wanted to be an actor. On the surface he lived a perfectly functioning life—except for one recurring detail. Every Easter he went on a charter holiday with his mother. They locked themselves in their hotel room, got drunk, and had sex. What his mother did not know was that Pierre sank into a deep depression after every trip and frequently tried to commit suicide.

I didn't want to force my patients. I wanted it to be their own choice to talk about issues.

There was a knock at the door. Before I had time to answer, it opened and Eva Blau walked in. She had shaved off all her hair and made up only her eyes. She made a strange face, as if she were trying to smile without using her facial muscles.

"No, thank you," she said suddenly. "There's no need to invite me to supper, I've already eaten. Charlotte is a wonderful person. She cooks for me, meals for the whole week; I put them in the freezer."

"That's kind of her," I said.

"She's buying my silence," Eva explained cryptically, moving to stand behind the chair where Maja had sat the previous day.

"Eva, would you like to tell me why you've come here?"

"Not to suck your cock—just so you know."

"You don't have to continue with the hypnosis group," I said calmly.

She looked down. "I knew you hated me," she mumbled.

"No, Eva, I'm just saying you don't have to be part of the group. Some people don't want to be hypnotized, some aren't receptive even though they really do want to try, and some—"

"You hate me."

I took a moment. "Eva, I don't hate you. I'm just saying that your participation in the group isn't meaningful or helpful to you, if you're unwilling to be hypnotized."

"That's not what I meant," she said. "But you're not to stick your cock in my mouth."

"Stop it," I said.

"Sorry," she whispered, and took something out of her bag. "Look, this is for you."

I took the object from her. It was a photograph. The picture showed Benjamin's christening. I recognized it immediately.

"Sweet, isn't he?" she said proudly.

I could feel my heart beginning to pound. "Where did you get this?" I asked her.

"That's my little secret. I look out for myself, you know. It's the only way to be in this life."

She sat down on the sofa, calmly unbuttoned her blouse, and exposed her breasts to me. "Stick your cock in then, if it makes you happy."

"You've been to my house," I said.

"You've been to *my* house," she answered defiantly.

"Eva, you told me about your home. Breaking in is another matter altogether.

"I didn't break in," she retorted quickly.

"You broke a window."

"The stone broke the window."

I felt suddenly exhausted; I was losing control and was about to turn my fury on a sick, confused woman.

"Why did you take this picture from me?"

"You're the one who takes! You take and take! What the fuck would you say if I took things from you? How do you think that would feel?"

She hid her face in her hands and said she hated me; she repeated it over and over again, perhaps a hundred times, before she calmed down.

Then she said steadily, "You have to understand that you make me angry when you claim that I take things. I *gave* you something, a lovely picture."

"Yes."

She smiled broadly and licked her lips. "Now I want you to give *me* something."

"What do you want?" I asked calmly.

"I want you to hypnotize me," she replied.

"Why did you leave a ferrule outside my door?" I asked.

She stared blankly at me. "What's a ferrule?"

"It's a flat stick that was once used to punish children," I said.

"I didn't leave anything outside your door."

"That isn't true. You left an old—"

"Don't lie!" she screamed.

"Eva, I will call the police if you don't know where the boundaries are, if you can't understand that you have to leave me and my family alone."

"What about *my* family?" she said.

"Just listen to me."

"Fascist pig!" she yelled. She leaped to her feet and left the room.

◎

My patients sat before me in the semicircle. It had been easy to hypnotize them this time, and we had drifted softly down together through lapping water. I was working with Charlotte again. Her face was relaxed yet sorrowful, with deep, dark circles under her eyes; the point of her chin was slightly crumpled.

I waited. It was clear that Charlotte was under deep hypnosis. She was breathing heavily but silently.

"You know you're safe with us, Charlotte," I said. "Nothing can harm you. You feel good. You are pleasantly relaxed."

She nodded sadly and I knew she could hear me; she was following my words and was no longer able to distinguish between actual reality and the reality of hypnosis. It was as if she were watching a film in which she herself took part. She was both audience and actor, united as one.

"Don't be cross," she whispered. "Sorry, I'm so sorry. I will console you, I promise, I will console you."

We were in the haunted house. I knew we had reached Charlotte's dangerous rooms and I wanted her to stop; I wanted her to have the strength to look up from the floor and see something, to catch a glimpse of the thing she was so afraid of. I could hear the group breathing around me. I wanted to help her, but I had no intention of forcing the pace this time; I was not about to repeat last week's mistake.

"It's cold in Grandfather's gym," Charlotte said suddenly.

"Can you see anything?"

"Long floorboards, a bucket, a cable," she said, almost inaudibly.

I could see her eyelids quivering. Fresh tears seeped through her eyelashes. Her open hands were nested in her lap, palms up, like an old woman.

"You know you can leave the room whenever you want to."

"Can I?"

"Whenever you want."

"That's probably for the best."

She fell silent, lifted her chin, then slowly turned her head, her mouth half open like a child's.

"I'll stay a little while longer," she said.

"Are you alone in there?"

She shook her head. "I can hear him," she murmured, "but I can't see him." She frowned, as if she were trying to see something that was out of focus. "There's an animal here," she said suddenly.

"What kind of animal?" I asked. The hair rose on the back of my neck.

"Daddy has a big dog . . ."

"Is your daddy there?"

"Yes, he's here, he's standing in the corner; he's upset, I can see his eyes. I've hurt Daddy, he says. Daddy is upset."

"And the dog?"

"The dog is moving about in front of his legs, sniffing. It comes closer, moves back. Now it is standing quietly beside him, panting. Daddy says the dog is to guard me. I don't want that, it shouldn't be allowed to do that; it isn't—"

Charlotte gasped for breath. A dreadful shadow passed over her face. I thought it was best to come up out of the trance, up out of the black sea. She ran the risk of wrenching herself out of the hypnosis if she moved forward too quickly. We had found the dog; she had stayed and looked at it. This was an enormous step forward. In time we would solve the riddle of who the dog actually was.

As we floated up through the water, I saw Marek part his lips and bare his teeth at Charlotte. Lydia reached out through a dark green cloud of seaweed, trying to stroke Pierre's cheek; Sibel and Jussi closed their eyes and drifted upward. We met Eva Blau hovering just beneath the surface.

We were almost awake. The dividing line where reality dissolves into the influence of hypnosis is always unclear, and the same is true during the reverse journey, back to the territory of consciousness.

"We'll take a break now," I said, and turned to Charlotte. "Good idea?"

"Thank you," she said, lowering her eyes.

Marek got up, asked Sibel for a cigarette, and went outside with her. Pierre remained in his seat next to Jussi. Lydia stood up slowly, stretched her arms languidly above her head, and yawned. I thought I would tell Charlotte I was pleased she had chosen to stay a little while longer in her haunted house, but she had left the room.

I had picked up my pad to make a few quick notes when Lydia came over to me. Her heavy jewellery clinked softly, and I could smell her perfume as she stood next to me. "Isn't it my turn soon?"

"Next time," I replied, without looking up from my notepad.

"Why not today?"

I put my pen down and met her gaze. "Because I was intending to continue with Charlotte."

"But if she doesn't come back," Lydia persisted.

"Lydia, I try to help all my patients."

She tilted her head to one side. "But you're not going to succeed, are you?"

"What makes you think that?"

She shrugged her shoulders. "Statistically, one of us will commit suicide, a couple will end up in an institution, and—"

"You can't reason like that."

"Yes, I can," she said, "because I want to be one of those who makes it." She took a step closer to me and her eyes gleamed with unexpected cruelty as she lowered her voice. "I think Charlotte will be the one who takes her own life."

Before I had time to respond, she simply sighed and said, "At least she hasn't got any children."

I watched Lydia go and sit down. When I glanced at the time, I realized more than fifteen minutes had passed. Pierre, Lydia, and Jussi had returned to their seats. I called Marek in; he was wandering around in the hall, talking to himself. Sibel was standing in the doorway, smoking, and giggled wearily when I asked her to come in.

Lydia's expression was smug when I finally had to admit that Charlotte hadn't returned.

"Right," I said, bringing my hands together. "Let's continue."

I saw their faces before me. They were ready. In fact, the sessions were always better after the break; it was as if they were all longing to return to the depths, as if the lights and the currents down there were whispering to us, inviting us to join them once again.

The effect of the induction was immediate. Lydia sank into a deep hypnosis in just ten minutes.

We were falling. I could feel lukewarm water washing over my skin. The big grey rock was covered with corals. The tentacles of their polyps were waving in the water. I could see every detail, every glowing, vibrant color.

"Lydia," I said, "where are you?"

She licked her dry lips and tipped her head back; her eyes were just closed, but she had an irritated expression around her mouth, and her brow was furrowed. "I'm taking the knife." Her voice was dry and rasping.

"What kind of knife is it?" I asked.

"The knife with the serrated edge, the one on the draining-board," she said in a surprised tone, then sat in silence for a while, her mouth half open.

"A bread knife?"

"Yes." She smiled.

"Go on."

"I cut the pack of ice cream in half. I take one half and a spoon to the sofa in front of the TV. *Oprah Winfrey*. Dr. Phil is sitting in the audience. She asks him a question and he holds up his index finger. There's a piece of red thread tied around it, and he's just about to tell us why when Kasper starts yelling. I know he doesn't want anything, he's just trying to spite me. He yells because he knows it will upset me. I won't tolerate bad behaviour in my house."

"What is he yelling?"

"He knows I want to hear what Dr. Phil says. He knows I enjoy *Oprah*; that's why he's yelling."

"And what is he yelling right now?"

"There are two closed doors between us," she goes on. "But I can hear him yelling."

"What is he saying?"

"Horrible words. He's yelling *cunt, cunt, cunt.*" Lydia's cheeks were red, and her forehead was beaded with sweat.

"What do you do?" I asked.

She licked her lips again, her breathing heavy. "I turn up the TV," she said, her voice subdued. "It thunders out, the applause makes the set rattle, but it feels wrong, it's no good any more. I'm not enjoying it. He's ruined it. That's how it is, but I ought to explain it to him."

She smiled faintly with her lips pressed together; her face had now lost all its colour. The water shimmered in metallic rolls over her forehead.

"Is that what you do?" I asked.

"What?"

"What do you do, Lydia?"

"I . . . I go past the pantry and down into the rec room in the basement. I can hear whistling and strange buzzing noises from Kasper's room . . . I don't know what he's up to. I just want to go back upstairs and watch TV, but I keep going to Kasper's room. I open the door and go in." She fell silent. The water was forced out through her half-closed lips.

"You go in," I repeated. "What do you walk in on, Lydia?"

Her lips were moving slightly. The air bubbles sparkled and disappeared upward.

"What do you see?" I asked cautiously.

"He's pretending to be asleep when I walk in," she said slowly. "He's ripped up the photo of Grandmother! He promised to be careful if I let him borrow the picture, and now he's destroyed it! It's the only one I've got. And he's just lying there, pretending to be asleep. I need to have a serious talk with Kasper on Sunday; that's when we go through how we have behaved towards each other during the past week. I wonder what advice Dr. Phil would give me. I look down and see that I still have the spoon in my hand, but when I look at it I see a teddy bear reflected in the metal. It must be hanging from the ceiling . . ."

Lydia suddenly grimaced, as if she were in pain. She tried to laugh, but only strange noises came out. She tried again, but it still didn't sound like laughter.

"What do you do?" I asked.

"I look," she said, turning her face upward.

Suddenly she slid off her chair, banging the back of her head on the seat. I rushed over. She sat on the floor, still under hypnosis, but no longer as deeply. She stared at me with terrified eyes as I spoke reassuringly to her.

I left the waiting room and walked down the hallway towards my office. The hospital lobby was empty, apart from a few elderly women waiting for transport. It was so beautiful out, I thought I ought to go for a run tonight as soon as I finished work.

Maja was waiting by my office door. Her full red lips parted in a broad smile, and a hair clasp in her coal-black hair sparkled as she bowed to me. With her usual playfulness, she said, "I hope you don't regret the fact that you've committed yourself, doctor."

"Committed myself? That's a hell of a thing to say to a psychiatrist." She laughed, but I still felt the need to reassure her. "Of course I don't regret it," I said.

I stood next to her to unlock the door, feeling a distinct tingling inside. But when our eyes met, I saw an unexpected seriousness in her expression, and I was able to dismiss the sensation. She passed me and went inside. It was hard not to be self-consciously aware of my own body; my feet, my mouth. Maja blushed as she took out a folder containing her papers, pen, and notebook.

"What's happened since we last met?" she asked.

I made her a cup of coffee and began to describe the afternoon's session.

"I think we've found Charlotte's perpetrator," I said. "The person who victimized her so badly that she attempts suicide over and over again."

Maja looked at me with a gratifyingly rapt expression. "Who is it?"

"A dog," I said seriously.

Maja didn't laugh; she was well versed in my work. The most daring and the most striking of my ideas was based on the ancient structure of the fable: to depict people in animal form, to assign forbidden acts and proscribed behaviour to beasts, is one of the oldest ways to circumvent narrative taboos or simply avoid truths that are too frightening or too tempting.

It was very easy, almost treacherously easy, for me to talk to Maja Swartling. She was familiar with the subject, she asked intelligent questions, and above all she was an excellent listener.

"And Marek Semiovic? How is he getting on?" she asked, sucking the end of her pen as she waited for my response.

"Well, you know his background. He came here as a refugee during the war in Bosnia but was given help only for his physical injuries at the time."

"Yes."

"He's . . . interesting . . . for my research, even if I don't really understand yet what's happening with him. When he's under very deep hypnosis, he always ends up in the same room, with the same memory—he's being forced to torture people, people he knows, boys he used to play with, shopkeepers he used to buy from, teachers at his school—but then something happens."

"During the hypnosis?"

"Yes. He refuses to go any further."

"He refuses?"

"Free will under hypnosis is limited only by the fact that we can't lie to ourselves."

Time passed, and it was evening. The hall outside my office was silent and deserted.

Maja put her things away in her briefcase, wound her scarf around her neck, and stood up.

"I don't know where the time went," she said apologetically.

"Thanks for listening," I said, holding out my hand.

She hesitated. "I'm the one who should thank *you*. I wonder if I could buy you a drink this evening to express my gratitude?"

I quickly ran through my plans. Simone and her friends were going to see *Tosca*, and she would be home late. Benjamin was staying with his grandfather, and as far as everyone was concerned, I'd intended to work all evening.

"One drink," I said, picking up my jacket. I tamped down the feeling that I was overstepping the mark.

"I know a little place on Roslagsgatan," said Maja, "called Peterson-Berger. It's very simple but really nice."

"Good." I turned off the light and locked the door behind us.

It was about seven-thirty, and there was hardly any traffic. We took our bikes and rode down to Norrtull. The spring quivered in the sound of birdsong in the trees.

When we were met by the restaurant's smiling proprietress, I grew doubtful. Should I really be here? What would I say if Simone rang and asked what I was doing? A wave of unease rose up, but I justified the outing to myself: Maja was a colleague. We wanted to continue our discussion. Simone, who never hesitated to go out alone with friends, was probably drinking wine right now in the restaurant at the opera house.

"I love their spit-roasted chicken with cumin," Maja said, leading the way to a table at the far side of the restaurant.

We sat down, and a waitress immediately came over with a jug of water. Maja rested her chin on her hand, gazed at her glass, and said calmly, "If we get fed up with being here, we can always go back to my place." She looked at me expectantly. For a moment I allowed myself to wonder what she was doing here with me. She was gorgeous, young, and outgoing. I must have been fifteen years older than she was, and I was married.

"Maja, are you flirting with me?"

She laughed, showing deep dimples. "My dad has always said I was born that way. An incorrigible flirt."

I realized I knew nothing about her. "Is your father a doctor too?" I asked.

She nodded. "Professor Jan E. Swartling."

"The brain surgeon," I said, impressed.

"Or whatever you call it when somebody pokes around inside another person's head," she said acidly. It was the first time the smile had left her face.

We ate. To counter my anxiety, I was drinking too quickly and ordered more wine. It was as if the looks the staff were giving us, their obvious assumption that we were a couple, were making me nervous. I got drunk and didn't even look at the bill before I signed it, crumpled up the receipt, and missed the wastepaper basket next to the cloakroom. Out on the street, in the lovely, mild spring evening, I was definitely intending to go home. But Maja pointed to a door and asked if I would like to come up, just to see what her apartment was like and to have a cup of tea.

"Maja," I said, "you are incorrigible. Your father is right."

She giggled and tucked her arm under mine.

We stood very close to each other in the lift. I couldn't help looking at her smiling mouth, her pearly white teeth, her high forehead, and her black, shiny hair.

She noticed and tentatively caressed my cheek; I leaned down to kiss her, but the lift stopped with a jerk.

"Come on," she whispered, as she unlocked her door.

Her studio apartment was small but very pleasant. The walls were painted a soft Mediterranean blue, and white linen curtains hung at the one window. The kitchen area was fresh, with a white tiled floor and a small, modern gas stove. Maja went into the kitchen, and I heard her opening a bottle of wine.

"I thought we were having tea," I said, when she emerged with the bottle and two wineglasses. I was slurring my words.

"This is better for you," she said.

"Well, in that case," I said, accepting a glass and spilling wine on my hand.

She wiped my hand with a tea towel, sat down on the narrow bed, and leaned back.

"Nice place," I said.

"It seems strange, having you here," she said with a smile. "I've admired you for such a long time."

Suddenly she leaped up.

"I have to take a picture of you," she exclaimed, giggling. "The important doctor here in my little place!" She got her camera and trained the lens on me.

"Look serious," she said, peering through the viewfinder.

She giggled some more as she snapped away, encouraging, joking, telling me I was hot, I was gorgeous, asking me to pout. Gradually, I relaxed.

"Unbelievably sexy." She laughed light-heartedly.

"Will I make the front cover of *Vogue*?"

"Unless they choose me," she said, handing me the camera.

I got to my feet unsteadily and pointed the camera at her. She had thrown herself down on the bed.

"You win," I said, and took a picture.

"My brother always called me Pudding," she said. "Do you think I'm fat?"

"You're incredibly beautiful," I murmured. She sat up and pulled her sweater over her head. She was wearing a pale green silk bra over her voluptuous breasts.

"Take a picture now," she whispered, unhooking her bra.

She was blushing furiously and smiling. I focused, looking into her dark, shimmering eyes, at her smiling mouth, her young, generous breasts with their pale pink nipples.

"I'll take a close-up," I mumbled and knelt down, feeling desire pulse through my body.

She supported one heavy breast with her hand. The camera flashed. I had a powerful erection; it was aching and pulling. I lowered the camera, leaned forward, and took one breast in my mouth. She pressed it against my face, and I licked and sucked at the hard nipple.

"God, yes," she whispered. "God, that's wonderful."

Her skin was hot, steaming. She unbuttoned her jeans, pulled them down, and kicked them off. I stood up, thinking that I mustn't go to bed with her, that I couldn't do that, but I picked up the camera and photographed her again. She was wearing only a pair of thin pale-green panties.

"Come here," she whispered.

I looked at her through the lens again as she smiled and parted her legs. I could just see the dark pubic hair curling around the crotch of her panties.

"It's fine," she said.

"I can't."

She smiled. "Oh, I think you can."

"Maja, you're dangerous, so dangerous," I said, putting down the camera.

"I know I'm a naughty girl."

"But I'm a married man, you have to understand that."

"Don't you think I'm beautiful?"

"You're amazingly beautiful, Maja."

"More beautiful than your wife?"

"Stop it."

"But I turn you on, don't I?" she whispered, then giggled before suddenly becoming serious.

I nodded, moved back, and saw her give a very satisfied smile. "I can still carry on with my interviews, can't I?"

"Absolutely," I said, moving toward the door.

She blew me a kiss, I blew one back, and then I left her studio, hurried downstairs, and headed for my bike.

◎

That night I dreamed I was looking at a stone relief depicting three nymphs. I woke myself up saying something out loud, so loud I could hear the echo of my own voice in the dark, silent bedroom. Simone had come home while I was asleep; she stirred in her sleep beside me. I was drenched with sweat from my dream, and the alcohol was still coursing through my blood. A street cleaning truck rumbled past the window, flashing its light. The building was silent. I got up to take a pill and tried not to think, but what had happened the previous evening returned, immediately and vividly: I had photographed Maja Swartling while she was practically naked. I had taken pictures of her breasts, her legs, and her transparent spring-green panties. But we didn't have sex, I kept repeating to myself. I hadn't intended to, I hadn't wanted to—I had overstepped, but I hadn't betrayed Simone. Had I? I was wide awake now, chillingly wide awake. What was the matter with me? How the hell had I let myself be persuaded to photograph Maja naked? She was beautiful and seductive, and I had been flattered by her attention. Was that all it took? I realized with surprise that I had discovered a real weak point in myself: I was vain. Nothing within me could claim I was falling in love with her. It was my vanity that enjoyed her company so much.

I rolled over and pulled the duvet over my face, and after a while I fell into a heavy sleep again.

Marek was in a state of deep hypnotic rest. He sat low in his chair, his sweater straining over his powerful upper arms and his overdeveloped back muscles. His hair was cropped very short, exposing a scalp covered with scars. His jaws were chewing slowly; he raised his head and looked at me with empty eyes.

"I can't stop laughing," he said loudly. "The shocks are making this guy from Mostar jump around like a cartoon character."

Marek looked happy, his head swaying from side to side.

"He's lying on the concrete floor, dark with blood, breathing fast, very fast. And then he curls up and starts crying. Fucking pussy. I shout at him, tell him to get on his feet, tell him I'll kill him if he doesn't get up. I lean over to give him one more shock, but his body just jerks like a dead pig. I call over to the door and tell them the fun is over, but they come in with this guy's older brother. I know him, we worked together for a couple of years at Aluminij, the factory—"

Marek stopped speaking, his chin quivering.

"What happens now?" I asked quietly.

He sat in silence for a while before he began speaking again. "The floor is covered with green grass; I can't see the guy from Mostar any more; there's just a little mound of grass."

"Isn't that strange?" I asked.

"I don't know, maybe, but I can't see the room any more. I'm outside, walking across a summer meadow; the grass is damp and cold beneath my feet."

Carefully, I brought everyone out of the hypnosis, checking to make sure each of them was all right before I started the discussion. Marek wiped the tears from his cheeks and stretched. He had big patches of sweat under his arms.

"I was forced to do it, that was their thing. They forced me to torture my old friends," he said.

"We know."

He looked at us with a shy, searching smile. "I laughed because I was frightened. I'm not like that. I'm not dangerous," he said.

"You liked hurting people," Lydia said with a soft smile. "Why can't you admit that?"

"Shut your mouth!" yelled Marek, moving over to her with his hand raised.

"Sit down," I said forcefully.

"Don't shout at me, Marek," Lydia said calmly.

He met her gaze and stopped. "Sorry," he said, with an uncertain smile; he ran his hand over his head a couple of times and sat down. I called for a break.

It was a gloomy day. Rain hung heavily in the air. The wind blowing in was cold, and carried with it a faint smell of wet leaves, a reminder of winter that made me feel glum. My patients began to return to their seats.

Eva Blau was dressed all in blue; she had even painted her narrow lips with blue lipstick and made up her eyes with blue mascara. She seemed anxious as usual, placing her cardigan around her shoulders and then taking it off, over and over again.

Lydia was talking to Pierre; as he listened, his eyes and mouth contracted in painful, repetitive tics.

Marek had turned his back on me. His body-builder's muscles twitched as he searched for something in his backpack.

I waved to Sibel; she carefully stubbed out her cigarette on her shoe and replaced it in the pack.

"Let's continue," I said, intending to make a fresh attempt with Eva Blau.

Although Eva Blau's face was tense, a teasing smile played across her blue-painted lips. I was wary of her pliancy; it was a form of manipulation. I had an idea of how I could stress the voluntary nature of hypnosis to her, though. It was obvious to me that she needed help to relax and begin to sink.

I watched Eva as I told everyone to let their chin drop to their chest. She immediately reacted with a big smile. As I counted backwards, I could feel the descent against my back, the water enveloping me, but I remained alert. Eva was sneaking a look at Pierre, trying to breathe with the same rhythm.

343

"You are sinking slowly," I said. "Deeper down into rest, into relaxation, into a pleasant heaviness."

I moved behind my patients, seeing their pale necks and rounded backs; I stopped behind Eva and placed a hand on her shoulder. Without opening her eyes she turned her face up slowly, pushing her lips out slightly.

"Now I am talking only to Eva," I said. "Eva, I want you to remain awake but relaxed the whole time. You are to listen to my voice when I speak to the group. You will feel the same calmness, the same pleasant immersion, but you will not be hypnotized; you will remain awake throughout."

I felt her shoulders relax.

"Now I am speaking to everyone again. Listen to me. I am going to count, and with each number we will sink deeper, deeper into relaxation. Eva, you will accompany us, but you will remain conscious and awake all the time."

As I returned to my place I counted backwards, and when I sat down in front of them I could see that Eva's face was limp, completely relaxed. It was almost hard to believe it was the same person. Her lower lip was drooping, the wet, pink inside a stark contrast to the blue lipstick, and her breathing was very heavy. I turned inwards, let go, and sank through the water in a dark shaft. We were inside a shipwreck or a flooded house. A stream of salt water came up to meet me from below. Air bubbles and small pieces of seaweed floated by.

"Keep going, deeper, calmer," I exhorted them gently.

After perhaps twenty minutes we were all standing deep underwater on a perfectly smooth steel floor. A few odd molluscs had managed to attach themselves to the metal. Small clumps of algae could be seen here and there. A white crab scuttled sideways across the flat surface. The group stood in a semicircle in front of me. Eva's face was pale, her expression faintly surprised. A grey, watery light billowed over her cheeks, reflecting and flowing.

Her face looked naked, almost innocent, when she was so deeply relaxed. A bubble of saliva formed at the side of her open mouth.

"Eva, tell us what you can see."

"Yes," she murmured.

"Tell the rest of us," I urged calmly. "Where are you?"

She suddenly looked strange. It was as if something had surprised her. "I've gone away. I'm walking along the soft track with the pine needles and long pine cones," she whispered. "Maybe I'll go to the canoe club and look in through the window at the back."

"Is that what you do now?"

Eva nodded and puffed out her cheeks like a sulky child.

"What can you see?"

"Nothing," she said, quickly and firmly.

"Nothing?"

"Just one little thing . . . I am writing on the road outside the post office with a piece of chalk."

"What are you writing?"

"Nothing important."

"And you can't see anything through the window?"

"No . . . just a boy. I'm looking at a boy," she slurred. "He's lovely, really sweet. He's lying on a narrow bed, a sofa bed. A man in a white terry-cloth robe lies down on top of him. It looks nice . . . I like looking at them. I like boys. I want to kiss them."

◎

Afterward, Eva sat there, her mouth twitching and her eyes darting back and forth over everyone in the group. "I wasn't hypnotized," she said.

"You were relaxed; that works just as well," I replied.

"No, it didn't work at all, because I wasn't thinking about what I was saying. I made it all up. I just said whatever came into my head. It was all just in my imagination."

"So the canoe club doesn't actually exist?"

"Nope," she replied tersely.

"The soft track?"

"I made everything up," she said, shrugging her shoulders.

Eva Blau was a person who exerted an effort never to give away anything about herself. It was obvious she was troubled by the fact that she had been hypnotized and had described events she was really involved in.

Marek spat silently into the palm of his hand when he noticed that Pierre was watching him. Pierre blushed and quickly looked away.

"I have never done anything to boys," Eva went on, raising her voice. "I'm nice. I'm a nice person. Children like me. All children like me. I'd be happy to babysit, Lydia. I went to your house yesterday, but I didn't have the nerve to ring the bell."

"Please don't do that again," said Lydia quietly.

"Do what?"

"Don't come to my house again," Lydia said.

"You can trust me," Eva went on. "Charlotte and I are already best friends. She cooks for me, and I pick flowers for her to put on the table." Eva's lips twitched as she turned to Lydia once again. "I bought a present for Kasper. It's a fan that looks like a helicopter. It's fun. You fan yourself with the rotors."

"Eva," said Lydia darkly.

"The rotors are plastic, soft plastic. It's not dangerous at all, he can't hurt himself with it, I promise."

"Don't come to my house," said Lydia. "Do you hear me?"

"Oh, not today, I can't come today. Today I'm going to Marek's. I think he could use some company."

"Eva, you heard me," Lydia persisted.

Eva responded with a smile. "I haven't got time tonight."

Lydia's face grew white and tense. She stood up quickly and left the room. Eva remained in her seat, gazing after her.

◎

Simone hadn't arrived when I was shown to our table at the K.B. restaurant. I sat down and wondered whether to order a drink while I was waiting. It was ten past seven. I had booked the table myself. It was my birthday and I was feeling happy. We rarely managed to go out in those days; she was busy with her gallery project, I with my research. When we did have a free evening together, we usually chose to spend it on the sofa with Benjamin, watching a film or playing a video game.

At twenty past seven, the waiter brought me a martini glass containing Absolut vodka, a few dashes of Noilly Prat, and a long twist of lime peel. I decided to wait a little while before calling Simone, but when the drink was half gone, I was starting to feel anxious and annoyed. Reluctantly I took out my phone, dialed Simone's number, and waited.

"Simone Bark." She sound distracted, her voice echoing in an empty space.

"Sixan, it's me. Where are you?"

"Erik? I'm at the gallery, what's . . ." Her voice died away; then I heard a loud groan. "Oh, no. No! I'm so sorry, Erik, I completely forgot. There's been so much going on today; we've had the plumber here and the electrician and—"

"You're at the gallery?" I couldn't hide the disappointment in my voice.

"Yes, and I'm covered in paint and plaster."

"We were supposed to be having dinner together," I said wearily, lowering my voice. I glanced around at the other diners, embarrassed at having been stood up.

"I know, Erik. I'm so sorry. I forgot."

"At least we have a good table," I added sarcastically.

She sighed. "There's no point in waiting for me." I could hear how upset she was and took some cold comfort in shaming her. "Erik," she whispered. "Forgive me."

"It's OK," I said. I pressed the button to end the call.

Well, there wasn't much point in going anywhere else, and I was hungry and I was in a restaurant. I quickly waved the waiter over and ordered herring with beer for an appetizer, crispy fried duck breast with diced bacon and orange sauce for my main course, along with a glass of Bordeaux, and, to finish, a Gruyère Alpage with honey.

"You can take away the other place," I said to the waiter, adding, in a mournful tone, "I'll be dining alone, it seems." He gave me a sympathetic look as he poured my Czech beer and set out the herring and crispbread.

I wished I had at least brought my notepad so I could have done something useful while I was eating.

My mobile phone suddenly rang in my inside pocket. Ah, I thought. Simone was kidding; she's on her way.

"Hi, it's Maja Swartling."

"Maja, hi."

"I was going to ask—wow, there's a lot of noise around you. Is this a bad time?"

"I'm sitting in K.B.," I said. "It's my birthday," I added morosely.

"Oh, congratulations, it sounds like a big party."

"I'm alone," I said tersely.

"Oh." She was silent for a moment. I didn't expect what she said next. "Erik, I'm sorry I tried to seduce you. I'm so ashamed." She cleared her throat and tried to adopt a neutral tone as she went on. "I was going to ask if you'd mind reading the transcripts of my first interviews with you. I've finished them, and I'm about to hand them in to my advisor, but if you'd like to read them first—"

"Just leave them in my cubbyhole."

We said goodbye. I poured the last of the beer into my glass, knocked it back, and the waiter cleared the table. He returned almost immediately with the duck breast and red wine.

I ate with a sense of gloomy emptiness, unnaturally aware of the mechanisms of chewing and swallowing, the muted scrape of my knife and fork against the plate. I drank my third glass of wine and watched the pictures on the wall metamorphose into members of my hypnosis group. The voluptuous woman gathering her dark hair sensually at the back of her neck, causing her swelling breasts to lift, was Sibel. The skinny, anxious man in the suit was Pierre. Jussi was hidden behind a strange grey shape, and Charlotte, elegantly dressed and straight-backed, was sitting at a round table with Marek, who was wearing a childish suit.

I don't know how long I had been staring at the pictures when I suddenly heard a breathless voice behind me. "Oh, you're still here! I'm so glad I caught you." It was Maja Swartling. She was beaming and gave me a big hug, to which I responded awkwardly.

"Happy birthday, Erik."

Her thick black hair smelled wonderfully clean, and a faint scent of jasmine was hiding somewhere at the nape of her neck. She pointed at the chair opposite me. "May I join you?"

I ought to have sent her away. I had promised myself I wouldn't see her again, and she should have known better than to come. But I hesitated, because in spite of everything I was glad of the company.

She was standing by the chair, waiting for my answer.

"I find it difficult to say no to you," I said, hearing the ambiguity in my words.

She sat down, summoned the waiter, and ordered a glass of wine. Then she gave me a mischievous look and placed a box beside my plate. "It's only something small," she explained, blushing furiously once again.

"A present?"

She shrugged her shoulders. "Purely symbolic. I only found out it was your birthday twenty minutes ago."

I opened the box and discovered to my surprise something that looked like miniature binoculars. My bewilderment must have shown on my face.

"They were called 'anatomical binoculars,'" Maja explained. "My great-grandfather invented them. Actually, I think he won the Nobel Prize—though not for the binoculars. It was in the days when only Swedes and Norwegians used to win," she added apologetically.

"Anatomical binoculars," I repeated wonderingly.

"Anyway, they're really quaint—sweet, even—and very old. I know it's a silly present—"

"It certainly isn't, it's wonderful." I looked into her eyes and saw how beautiful she was. "It's very, very kind of you, Maja. Thank you so much."

I placed the binoculars carefully back in their box and put them in my pocket.

"My glass is empty already," she said in surprise. "Shall we order a bottle?"

◎

It was late by the time we decided to go on to Riche, which was not far from the national theatre. We almost fell over when we were handing our coats in at the cloakroom; Maja was leaning on me and I misjudged the distance to the wall. When we regained our balance and saw the morose, deadly serious expression on the attendant's face, Maja burst out laughing and, glancing at him apologetically, I led her away to the bar.

We each ordered a gin and tonic. It was hot and crowded, and we had to stand close together, leaning in to speak directly into each other's ears in order to talk. Suddenly, we found ourselves kissing passionately. The back of her head thudded against the wall as I pressed myself against her. The music throbbed. She was speaking close to my ear, telling me we should go back to her place.

We rushed outside and into a taxi.

"We're only going to Roslagsgatan," she slurred. "Roslagsgatan seventeen."

The driver nodded and pulled out into traffic. It was something like two o'clock in the morning, and the sky was beginning to lighten. The buildings flashing by were pale grey shadows. Maja leaned against me. I thought she was going to go to sleep when I felt her hand caressing my crotch. I was hard at once, and she laughed quietly, her lips against my neck.

I'm not sure how we got up to her studio. I remember standing in the lift licking her face, aware of the taste of salt and lipstick and powder, catching sight of my own drunken face in the blotchy mirror.

Inside her place, Maja stood in the hallway, let her jacket fall to the floor, and kicked off her shoes. She drew me over to the bed, helped me undress, and pulled off her white panties.

"Come here," she whispered. "I want to feel you inside me."

I lay down heavily between her thighs; she was very wet, and I simply sank into the warmth as she wrapped herself around me, squeezing me tightly. She groaned in my ear, clung to my back, moved her hips gently.

We had sex carelessly, drunkenly. I began to feel more and more detached from myself, more and more isolated and mute. I was getting close to my orgasm; I intended to pull out, but instead simply gave in to a convulsive, rapid ejaculation. She was breathing fast. I lay there panting as my penis grew limp and slid out of her. My heart was still pounding. I saw Maja's lips part in a strange smile, which made me feel uncomfortable.

I felt ill. I no longer understood what had happened. What was I doing here? Stupid. This was so stupid.

I sat up in bed beside her.

"What's the matter?" she asked, stroking my back.

I shrugged off her hand. "Don't," I said abruptly. My heart was thudding with fear.

"Erik? I thought—"

She sounded upset. I felt I couldn't look at her, I was angry with her. What had happened was my fault, of course. But it would never have happened if she hadn't been so persistent.

"We're both tired and drunk," she whispered.

"I have to go," I said, in a choked voice; I picked up my clothes and staggered into the bathroom. It was very small and full of creams, brushes, towels. A fluffy bathrobe was hanging from a hook, along with a pink razor on a soft, thick cord. I did my best to avoid looking at myself in the mirror as I washed myself with a pale blue cake of soap shaped like a rose. As I dressed, my elbows bumped into the walls.

When I came out she was waiting anxiously. She stood with the sheet wound around her body, looking very young. "Are you angry with me?" she asked, and I could see her lips trembling as if she were about to cry.

"I'm angry with myself, Maja. I should never, ever—"

"But I wanted to, Erik. I'm in love with you, can't you see that?" She tried to smile at me, but her eyes filled with tears. "You're not allowed to treat me like shit now," she whispered, reaching out to touch me.

I moved away and said this had been a mistake, my tone somewhat more dismissive than I had wished.

She nodded and lowered her eyes. I didn't say goodbye, I simply left the studio and closed the door behind me.

I walked all the way to the hospital. Perhaps I could convince Simone that I had spent the night in my office.

◎

In the morning I took a taxi home to our house in Järfälla. It was a mistake; my body heaved with nausea every time the cab hit a bump. Worse, I felt disgust at what I'd done the night before. I couldn't possibly have been unfaithful to Simone. It couldn't be true. Maja was beautiful and amusing, but she was not someone I could ever care about in any real way. How the hell could I have let myself be flattered into going to bed with her?

I didn't know how I was going to tell Simone this, but I had to do it. I had made a mistake, people do, but people can forgive each other if they just explain, and I felt that our relationship was strong enough to withstand the explanation.

I knew I could never let Simone go. I would be hurt, badly, if she was unfaithful to me, but I would find a way to forgive her. I would never leave her because of something like that.

◎

Simone was in the kitchen pouring herself a cup of coffee when I got home. She had on her tatty, pale pink silk robe. We'd bought it in China when Benjamin was only one, and they had both gone with me to a conference.

"Coffee?" she asked.

"Please." I sat down heavily at the table.

"Erik, I'm so sorry I forgot your birthday."

"I stayed over at the hospital," I explained, thinking it must be obvious from the tone of my voice that I was lying.

She looked down at the floor for a moment—I held my breath, waiting for anger or an accusation—the strawberry-blonde hair obscuring her face. Then, without a word, she went into the bedroom, returning a moment later with a package. She extended it toward me with a shy smile on her face and I tore off the paper with playful eagerness.

It was a boxed set of CDs by Charlie Parker, containing concert recordings from each of his appearances during his only visit to Sweden: two shows at the concert hall in Stockholm, two in Gothenburg, one at Amiralen in Malmö and the subsequent jam session at the Academic Club, the show at Folkets Park in Helsingborg, at the arena in Jönköping, at Folkets Park in Gävle, and finally at the Nalen jazz club in Stockholm.

"Thank you," I said.

"What does your day look like?" she asked.

"Well, I have to go back to work."

"I was thinking," she said, "that maybe we should have a really nice meal together at home tonight."

"Sounds good," I said.

"Only it can't be too late—the painters say they are coming at seven tomorrow morning. Why the hell do they always have to come so early?"

I realized she was expecting an answer. "And you always end up waiting for them anyway," I mumbled.

"Exactly." She smiled, sipping her coffee. "So what shall we have? Perhaps that thing with tournedos in a port wine and currant sauce, do you remember?"

"That was a long time ago," I said, struggling not to sound on the verge of tears.

"Don't be pissed off with me."

"I'm not, Simone." I tried to smile at her.

Later, when I was standing in the hall with my shoes on, just about to leave, she emerged from the bathroom. She had something in her hand.

"Erik," she said.

"Yes?"

"What's this?"

They were Maja's miniature anatomical binoculars.

"Oh, that. A present," I said, hearing the elusiveness in my voice.

"It's a beautiful object. It looks antique. Who gave it to you?"

I turned away to avoid looking her in the eye. "Just a patient," I said, trying to sound absent-minded as I pretended to search for my keys. "God knows how he found out it was my birthday."

She laughed in amazement. "I thought doctors weren't allowed to accept gifts from their patients. Isn't that unethical?"

"Maybe I shouldn't have taken it," I said, opening the door.

Simone's gaze was burning into my back. I should have talked to her, but I was frightened of losing her. I didn't dare. I didn't know how to begin.

◎

As I was about to go into the therapy room, Marek stopped me. He was barring the door and smiling an empty, odd smile at me.

"We're having a bit of fun in here," he said.

"What's going on?"

"It's a private party."

I looked at him carefully. Suddenly, I heard screaming through the door.

"Let me in, Marek," I said.

He grinned. "Doctor, that's not possible at the moment."

I pushed past him. The door opened, Marek lost his balance, grabbed for the doorknob, but ended up on the floor anyway.

"I was just joking," he said. "It was only a joke, for God's sake."

All the patients were staring at us, frozen.

Marek stood up and dusted himself off.

I noted that Eva Blau had not arrived yet, and then I went over to the tripod and started adjusting the camera. I checked the wide-angle view and zoomed in; I saw Sibel wipe away tears, or so I thought. I tested the microphone through my headphones. I heard Lydia cheerfully exclaim, "Exactly! That's always the way with children! Kasper doesn't talk about anything else anymore; it's just Spider-Man, Spider-Man, all the time!"

And I heard Charlotte respond, "I've gathered they're all crazy about him at the moment."

"Kasper doesn't have a daddy. Perhaps Spider-Man acts as his male role model," said Lydia, laughing so loudly that my headphones reverberated. "But we're fine," she went on. "We laugh a lot, even if we've had a few problems lately." She dropped her voice confidentially. "It's as if he's jealous of everything I do, he wants to destroy my things, he doesn't want me to talk on the phone, he throws my favourite book down the toilet, he yells at me . . . I think something must have happened, but he just won't tell me."

Jussi began to talk about his haunted house: his parents' home up in Dorotea, in southern Lapland. They owned a lot of land close to an area where the Sami people lived in their traditional huts, even as late as the 1970s. "I live very close to a lake, Djuptjärnen," he explained. "The last part of the route is old wooden tracks. In the summer, kids come there to swim. They love the myths about Nächen, the water sprite."

"The water sprite?" I asked.

"People have seen him sitting and playing his fiddle by Djuptjärnen for over three hundred years."

"But not you?"

"No," he said, with a grin.

"But what do you do up there in the forest all year?" asked Pierre, half smiling.

"I buy old cars and buses, fix them up, and sell them; the place looks like a scrapyard."

"Is it a big house?" Lydia asked.

"No, but it's green. My dad painted the place one summer, a kind of peculiar pale green. I don't know what he was thinking; someone must have given him the paint." He laughed, then fell silent. It was time for a break.

Lydia produced a tin of saffron-scented biscuits that she offered around. "They're totally organic," she said, urging Marek to take some.

Charlotte smiled and nibbled a tiny bit from one edge.

"Did you make them yourself?" asked Jussi with an unexpected grin, which brought a gentle light to his heavy face.

"I almost didn't have time," said Lydia, shaking her head and smiling. "I almost got into a quarrel at the playground."

Sibel sniggered and ate her biscuit in a couple of fierce bites.

"It was Kasper." Lydia sighed. "We'd gone to the playground as usual this morning, and one of the mothers came over and said Kasper had hit her little girl on the back with a shovel."

"Shit," whispered Marek.

"I went completely cold when she said that," said Lydia.

"What do you do in a situation like that?" Charlotte asked politely.

Marek took another biscuit and listened to Lydia with an unusually focused expression on his face, as if he were studying her as much as listening to her. For the first time, I wondered if he had a crush on her.

"I don't know. I told the mother that I took it very seriously. I think I was quite upset, actually. Even though she said it was nothing to worry about, and she thought it had been an accident."

"Of course," said Charlotte. "Children play with such wild enthusiasm."

"But I promised to speak to Kasper. I told her I would deal with it," Lydia went on.

"Good." Jussi nodded.

"She said Kasper seemed to be a really sweet boy," Lydia added with a smile.

I sat down on my chair and flicked through my notes; I was anxious to get the second session under way as quickly as possible. It was Lydia's turn again.

She met my eyes and smiled tentatively. Everyone was silent, expectant, as I began. The room was quiet with our breathing. A dark silence, growing more and more dense, followed our heartbeats. With each exhalation, we sank more deeply. After the induction my words led them downward, and after a while I turned to Lydia.

"You are moving deeper, sinking gently; you are very relaxed. Your arms are heavy, your legs are heavy, your eyelids are heavy. You are breathing slowly and listening to my words without question; you are surrounded by my words, you feel safe and compliant. Lydia, right now you are very close to the thing you do not want to think about, the thing you never talk about, the thing you turn away from, the thing that always lies hidden to the side of the warm light."

"Yes," she answered, with a sigh.

"You are there now," I said.

"I am very close."

"Where are you at this moment?"

"At home."

"How old are you?"

"Thirty-seven."

I looked at her. Reflections and flashes of light passed across her high, smooth forehead, her neat little mouth, and her skin, so pale it was almost sickly. I knew she had turned thirty-seven two weeks ago. She hadn't gone far back in time like the others, but just a few days instead.

"What's happening? What's wrong?" I asked.

"The telephone . . ."

"What about the telephone?"

"It rings, it rings again, I pick up the receiver and put it down straight away."

"You are perfectly calm, Lydia."

She looked tired, troubled perhaps.

"The food will get cold," she said. "I've made lentil soup and I've baked bread. I was going to eat in front of the TV, but of course that won't be possible."

Her chin quivered, then stopped.

"I wait a while, look out into the street through the blinds. There's no one there. I can't hear anything. I sit down at the kitchen table and eat a little bit of warm bread with butter, but I have no appetite. I go down to the cellar, it's cold down there as usual, and I sit on the old leather sofa and close my eyes. I have to compose myself. I have to gather my strength."

She fell silent. Strips of seaweed drifted past and came between us.

"Why do you have to gather your strength?" I asked.

"So I'll be able to get up and walk past the red rice-paper lantern with the Chinese symbols and the tray of scented candles and polished stones. The floorboards sag and creak beneath the plastic mat."

"Is anyone there?" I asked Lydia quietly, but immediately regretted it.

"I pick up the stick and push down the bubble in the mat with my foot so I can open the door and go in and switch on the light," she said. "Kasper's blinking in the light, but he doesn't sit up. He's peed in the bucket. It smells very strong. He's wearing his pale blue pyjamas. He's breathing hard. I poke him with the stick through the bars. He makes pitiful noises, moves away a fraction, and sits up. I ask if he's changed his mind and he nods, so I push a plate of food into the cage. The cod's shrivelled up and turned a dark colour. He crawls over and eats it and I'm pleased, and I'm just about to tell him how happy I am that we understand each other when he throws up on the mattress."

Lydia's face contorted in a wry grimace. "And there I was"—her lips were taut, the corners of her mouth turning down—"I thought we were done." She shook her head and licked her lips. "Do you understand how this makes me feel? He says sorry. I repeat that it's Sunday tomorrow; I slap my face and scream at him to look."

Charlotte was looking at Lydia through the water with frightened eyes.

"Lydia," I said, "you are going to leave the basement now, without being frightened or angry; you are going to feel calm and collected. I am going to lift you slowly out of this deep relaxation, up to the surface, up to clarity, and together we are going to talk about what you've said, just you and I, before I bring the others out of their hypnosis."

She snarled quietly, tiredly.

"Lydia, are you listening to me?"

She nodded.

"I'm going to count backwards, and when I reach one you will open your eyes and be fully awake and aware: ten, nine, eight; you are rising gently to the surface, your body feels completely relaxed and comfortable; seven, six, five, four; soon you are going to open your eyes but remain seated on your chair; three, two, one . . . now open your eyes. You are fully awake."

Our eyes met. Lydia's face looked somehow shrivelled, dried up. This was not something I had expected. I still felt cold because of what she had told me. If the rule of confidentiality had to be weighed against the duty of disclosure, this was a case in which it was crystal clear that the obligation to remain silent no longer applied, since a third party was obviously in danger.

"Lydia," I said quietly, "you understand that I have to contact Social Services?"

"Why?"

"What you told me leaves me no choice."

"In what way?"

"Don't you see?"

Lydia drew back her lips. "I didn't say anything."

"You described how—"

"Shut your mouth," she snapped. "You don't know me, you have nothing to do with my life, and you have no right to meddle in what I do in my own home."

"I have reason to suspect that your child—"

"Shut your mouth!" she screamed, and left the room.

◎

I'd parked next to a high fir hedge three hundred feet from Lydia's large wooden house in Rotebro. The social worker had agreed to my request to accompany her on the first home visit. My report to the police had been received with a certain amount of scepticism but had, of course, led to a preliminary investigation.

A red Toyota drove past me and stopped outside the house. I got out of the car, walked over, and introduced myself to the short, stocky woman who stood outside the car.

Sodden advertising leaflets were sticking out of the letter box. The low gate stood open. We went up the path to the house. I noticed there were no toys in the neglected garden. No sandbox, no swing in the old apple tree, no bike on the path. It was a sunny day, but all the blinds were closed. The hanging baskets were full of dead plants. A flight of rough stone steps led up to the door. I thought I sensed a movement behind the yellow opaque glass. The social worker rang the bell. We waited, but there was no answer, no sound except birdsong and the intermittent noise of distant traffic. She yawned, looked at her watch, rang the bell again, and tried the handle. The door was not locked. She opened it. We were looking into a small hallway.

"Hello?" she shouted. "Lydia?"

We walked in, took off our shoes, and continued through a door into a passageway with pink wallpaper and pictures of people meditating, with bright light around their heads. There was a pink telephone on the floor next to a hall table.

"Lydia?"

I opened a door and saw a narrow staircase leading to the basement.

"It's down here," I said.

The social worker followed me down the stairs and into the rec room, which contained an old leather sofa and a table, the top of which was made up of brown tiles. On a tray stood several scented candles among polished stones and pieces of glass. A deep red rice-paper lantern with Chinese characters on it hung from the ceiling. A plastic mat lay over the floorboards. Against one wall was a door. My heart was pounding as I moved over to it. When I tried to open it, the door got stuck on a large bubble in the plastic mat. I pushed down the bubble with my foot and went inside.

There was no cage. Instead, an upturned bicycle stood in the middle of the floor with the front wheel removed. A repair kit lay beside a blue plastic box: rubber patches, glue, monkey wrenches. One of the shiny hooks had been inserted under the edge of the tyre and braced against the spokes. Suddenly there was a creaking sound from the ceiling, and we realized someone was walking across the floor of the room above. Without exchanging a word we hurried up the stairs. The kitchen door was ajar. I noticed there were slices of bread and crumbs on the yellow linoleum floor.

"Hello?" the social worker called out.

I went in and saw that the fridge door was open. Lydia was standing in the pale glow of the light, her eyes gazing at the floor. Only after a few seconds did I see the knife in her hand. It was a long bread knife with a serrated edge. Her arm was hanging loosely by her side. The knife blade glimmered beside her thigh as her hand shook.

"I don't want you here," she hissed, suddenly looking at me.

"All right," I said, moving backwards towards the doorway.

"Shall we sit down and have a little chat?" said the social worker, keeping her tone neutral.

I pushed open the door and saw that Lydia was slowly moving closer.

"Erik," she said. I started to close the door, and Lydia sprang forward. I raced down the hall, but the door at the end was locked. Lydia kept pace, making a strange wailing noise as she ran. I yanked open another door and stumbled into a TV room. Lydia followed me in. I bumped into an armchair as I made for the balcony door, but it was impossible to turn the handle. Lydia flew at me with the knife, and I took cover behind a large oval table.

"It's your fault," she said, as she chased me this way, that way, around the table.

The social worker ran into the room. She was completely out of breath. "Lydia," she said sharply. "Stop this right now."

"It's all his fault," said Lydia.

"What do you mean?" I asked. "What's my fault?"

"This," said Lydia, drawing the knife across her throat. She looked into my eyes as the blood splashed down over her dress and her bare feet. Her mouth was trembling. The knife fell to the floor. One hand groped for support, but she sank down to the floor, coming to rest, balanced on one hip, like a mermaid.

◎

Annika Lorentzon's smile was troubled. Rainer Milch leaned across the table and poured a glass of mineral water with a hiss of carbon dioxide. His cuff links flashed royal blue and gold.

"I'm sure you understand why we wanted to speak to you as soon as possible," said Peter Mälarstedt, adjusting his tie.

I opened the folder they had handed to me. Identical materials sat before each board member. The contents of the folder stated that Lydia had made a complaint against me. She claimed that I had driven her to attempt suicide by coercing her to confess to things that had not taken place. She accused me of having used her for the purposes of my experiments and implanted false memories in her mind during deep hypnosis, and she said I had persecuted her ruthlessly and cynically in front of the others until she was completely shattered and had suffered severe emotional distress.

I looked up from the papers. "Is this some kind of joke?" I said.

Annika Lorentzon looked away. Svein Holstein's face was completely expressionless as he said, "She's your patient, and these are serious accusations."

"I don't want to accuse a very disturbed patient of lying," I said angrily, "but she's either lying or she's delusional. It's impossible to implant memories during hypnosis. I can lead them to a memory, but I can't create one. I lead them up to doors, but I can't open those doors on my own."

Rainer Milch looked at me, his expression grave. "The suspicion alone could destroy all your research, Erik, so I'm sure you realize how critical this is."

I shook my head irritably. "Under hypnosis, she related events concerning herself and her son that I considered so serious I felt I had no choice but to contact Social Services. The fact that she would react in this way was—"

Ronny Johansson interrupted me sharply. "But she hasn't even got any children. It says so here." He tapped on the folder with a long finger. I snorted and got a strange look from Annika.

"Erik, being arrogant in this situation is not particularly helpful," she said quietly.

"From the very first day she walked into this hospital, her relationship with her son has been the focus of almost every remark," I said, with an irritable smile. "And not only in a therapeutic context. Whenever she chats with the others, she—"

Annika leaned over the table. "Erik," she said slowly, "she has no son. She's never had any children."

"She hasn't got any children?"

"No."

The room fell silent.

I watched the bubbles in the mineral water rising to the surface.

"I don't understand. She still lives in her childhood home." I attempted to explain as calmly as I could. "All the details matched. I can't believe—"

"You can't believe," Milch broke in, "but you were wrong."

"They can't lie like that under hypnosis."

"Are you certain she was under hypnosis?"

"I'd stake my reputation on it."

"In a way, you have, Erik. But it doesn't matter now. The damage is already done."

"I don't understand," I said, half to myself. "Perhaps she was talking about her own childhood; it's nothing I've come across, but perhaps she was working through a memory of her own."

"It could be exactly as you say," Annika interjected. "It could be a number of things. But the fact remains that your patient made a suicide attempt for which she blames you. We suggest you take a leave of absence while we investigate the matter." She smiled wanly at me. "This will all sort itself out, Erik, I'm sure of it," she said gently. "But right now you have to step aside until we've looked into everything. We simply can't afford to let the press wallow in this."

I thought about Charlotte, Marek, Jussi, Sibel, Pierre, and Eva. We'd all worked to establish trust, a rapport. All individual progress had been the hard-won result of the specific chemistry we'd achieved as a group. My abandonment of them would leave them feeling betrayed and let down.

"I haven't done anything wrong," I said.

Annika patted my hand. "It will sort itself out. Lydia Everson is obviously unstable and confused, but the most important thing now is to do things by the book. You will request a leave of absence from your activities involving hypnosis while we conduct an internal investigation into these events. I know you're a good doctor, Erik. I'm sure you'll be back with your group in no more than"—she shrugged her shoulders—"six months."

"Six months?" I leaped to my feet. "I have patients; they rely on me. I can't just leave them," I said furiously.

Annika's gentle smile disappeared like a candle flame being extinguished. Her face closed down and her voice turned brittle. "Your patient has demanded that an immediate ban be placed on your activities.

She has also made a complaint against you to the police. These are not trivial matters as far as we are concerned; we have invested in your work, and if it should transpire that your research has not been up to the required standard, we will have to take appropriate measures."

I didn't know what to say; I just wanted to laugh at the whole thing. "This is ridiculous," was all I managed to get out. I turned to leave the room.

"Erik," Peter Mälarstedt called after me, "consider this a good opportunity."

I stopped. "What?"

"To—ah—reconsider the trajectory of your work."

I wheeled to face him. "Peter, do you believe all that crap about implanting false memories?"

Annika slammed the palm of her hand down on the table. "Erik, enough. That's not the important thing. The important thing is to follow the rules. Take a leave of absence from your work with hypnosis, try to regard it as an offer of reconciliation. You can continue with your research, you can work in peace and quiet, but you will not practise hypnosis therapy while we are conducting our investigation."

"I can't admit to something that isn't true."

"That's not what I'm asking."

"Well, that's what it sounds like. If I request a leave of absence, it looks as if I'm making an admission."

"Tell me you'll request a leave of absence," she insisted stiffly.

"This is fucking idiotic," I said with a laugh, and left the room.

◎

It was late in the afternoon. The sun was sparkling in the puddles after a brief shower, and the smell of the forest—wet earth and rotten roots—rose up from the ground as I ran along the track around the lake, pondering Lydia's actions. I was certain she had been speaking the truth under hypnosis—but which truth had she actually told me? Presumably she was describing a real concrete memory, but she had placed the memory in the wrong time. During hypnosis it is even more obvious that the past is not past, I reminded myself.

I filled my lungs with the fresh, cold spring air and sprinted the last stretch home through the forest. When I got to our street I saw a big black car parked in front of our drive, with two men leaning against the bonnet, waiting. One of them was checking his reflection in the shiny paintwork as he smoked a cigarette. The other was taking pictures of our house. They hadn't seen me yet. I slowed down and was just wondering whether to turn around when they spotted me. The man with the cigarette quickly stubbed it out with his foot, while the other immediately turned the camera on me. I was still out of breath as I approached them.

"Erik Maria Bark?" asked the man who had been smoking.

"What do you want?"

"We're from the press, *Expressen*."

"The press?"

"Yes. We'd like to ask you a few questions about one of your patients."

I shook my head and waved a hand. "I can't discuss my patients."

"Right."

The man's gaze slid over my flushed face, my black track-suit top, my bulky trousers, and my woolly hat. I heard the photographer behind him cough. A bird darted through the air above us, its body describing a perfect arc, reflected in the roof of the car. Above the forest, the sky was thickening and darkening. It looked like more rain.

"There's an interview with your patient in tomorrow's paper. She makes some pretty serious accusations against you," said the journalist.

I met his gaze. He had a fairly sympathetic face: middle-aged, running slightly to fat.

"This is your chance to respond," he said quietly.

The lights weren't on in our house. No doubt Simone was still at the gallery. Benjamin was at preschool.

"Otherwise her version will be printed with no contradiction from you," the man said frankly.

"I would never dream of discussing a patient," I repeated slowly. I walked up the drive past the two men, unlocked the door, went inside and stood in the hall, and listened to them drive away.

◎

The telephone rang at seven-thirty the following morning. It was An-nika Lorentzon. "Erik," she said, sounding strained. "Have you seen the paper?"

Simone sat up in bed beside me, her expression anxious; I waved dismissively and moved into the hall.

"If this is about Lydia's accusations, I'm sure everybody realizes they're just lies."

"No," she said sharply. "Everybody doesn't realize that at all. After reading this story, many people will see her as a weak, defenceless, vul-nerable person, who has been used by a particularly manipulative doc-tor toward his own selfish ends. The man she trusted most of all, the man in whom she confided, has betrayed and exploited her. That's what's in the paper."

I could hear her breathing heavily at the other end of the line. She sounded hoarse and tired. "This compromises everything we do, as I'm sure you understand."

"I'll write a response," I said curtly.

"That won't be enough, Erik." She paused briefly, then said tone-lessly, "She's intending to sue."

I snorted. "She'll never win."

"You still don't understand how serious this is, do you?"

"So what is she saying?"

"I suggest you go out and buy a paper. Then I think you ought to sit down and think about your response. The board would like to see you at four o'clock this afternoon."

◎

When I saw my face on the front page, I felt as if my heartbeat were slow-ing down. It was a close-up of me in my woolly hat and black top. My face was flushed, I looked bilious and irritable, and I seemed to be wav-ing my hand dismissively. I bought a copy of the paper and went back home. The centre spread was adorned with a picture of Lydia, curled up with a teddy bear in her arms. The whole article focused on how I, Erik Maria Bark, had used her as a kind of lab rat, persecuting her with asser-tions of abuse. I had broken her down, taking advantage of her suggestibility during deep hypnosis to manipulate her into believing herself guilty of imaginary crimes. The culmination of my persecution had come when I stormed into her house and challenged her to commit suicide. She had simply wanted to die, she said. She compared herself to a member of a cult and me to a cult leader and asserted that, thanks to me, she had no will of her own. It was only when she was in the hospital that she finally dared to start questioning my treatment of her. According to the reporter, she had wept and explained that she wasn't interested in any kind of compensation. Money could never make up for what she had been through. All she wanted was that I never be allowed to do this to anyone else.

On the next page was a picture of Marek. The ex-torturer agreed with Lydia, saying that my activities were life-threatening, and that I was obsessed with making up sick ideas to which my patients were then forced to confess under hypnosis.

Farther down the page, a so-called "expert" furnished a comment— I'd never heard of the man—but here he was denigrating the whole of my research, equating hypnosis with a séance and hinting that I probably drugged my patients in order to get them to do what I wanted.

There was an empty silence inside my head. I sat at the kitchen table until the door opened and Simone walked in. When she had read the paper, her face was ashen.

"What's happening?" she whispered.

"I don't know," I said. My mouth was completely dry.

I sat there staring into empty space, thinking the unthinkable. What if my theories were wrong? What if hypnosis *didn't* work on deeply traumatized individuals? What if it was true that my desire to find patterns had influenced their memories? I didn't believe it was possible for Lydia to see a child that didn't exist while she was under hypnosis. I had been convinced that she was describing a genuine memory, but now I was beginning to doubt myself.

◎

It was a strange experience, walking the short distance through the lobby to the lift up to Annika Lorentzon's office. For years, the place had been like a second home to me, but now none of the staff wanted to look me in the eye. When I passed people I knew and associated with, they simply looked stressed and strained, turned away, and hurried off.

Even the smell in the lift was strange. It smelled of rotten flowers, and it made me think of rain, farewells, funerals.

As I walked out of the lift, Maja Swartling slipped quickly past, ignoring me. Rainer Milch was waiting for me in the doorway of Annika's office. He moved aside and I went in and said hello.

"Please sit down, Erik," said Rainer.

"Thank you, I'd prefer to stand," I said curtly, but regretted it at once. What the hell had Maja Swartling been doing in here? Perhaps she had come to my defence. After all, she was one of the few people who had a real, detailed knowledge of my research.

Annika Lorentzon was standing by the window on the far side of the room. I thought it was both odd and impolite of her not to welcome me. Instead she stood there with her arms wrapped around her body, staring fixedly out the window.

"We gave you a real opportunity, Erik," said Peter Mälarstedt.

Rainer Milch nodded.

"But you refused to back down," he said. "You refused to step aside voluntarily while we conducted our investigation."

"I could reconsider," I said quietly.

"It's too late now. We could have used it to defend ourselves the day before yesterday; today it would just look pathetic."

Annika opened her mouth. "I'm going to appear on TV tonight to explain how we could have allowed you to continue," she said faintly, without turning to face me.

"But I haven't done anything wrong," I said. "The fact that a patient comes along with ridiculous accusations surely can't be allowed to negate years of research, countless treatments that have always been beyond reproach—"

"It isn't just one patient." Rainer Milch interrupted me. "It's several. In addition, we have a contact who has been studying your work for several years. In her opinion, you have overreached, and almost all your theses are built on castles in the air. You have no proof, and you constantly disregard the best interests of the patients in order to ensure that you are right."

I was completely at a loss. "And the name of this expert?" I asked.

They didn't respond.

"Is her name perhaps Maja Swartling?"

Annika Lorentzon's cheeks flushed red. "Erik," she said, turning to face me at last. "You are suspended from today onwards. I don't want you in my hospital any longer."

"But what about my patients? I have to see—"

She cut in. "They will be transferred."

"That won't do them any good, they—"

"Well, whose fault is that?" she said, raising her voice.

There was total silence in the room. Frank Paulsson stood with his face averted; Ronny Johansson, Peter Mälarstedt, Rainer Milch, and Svein Holstein remained seated, their faces expressionless.

"So that's it, then," I said emptily.

Just a few weeks before I had stood in this same room and been allocated new funding. Now it was all over.

When I reached the lobby, a group of people were waiting for me. A very tall woman with blonde hair thrust a microphone in front of my face.

"Hi," she said brightly. "Do you still believe that hypnosis is a good form of treatment?" she asked.

"Yes."

"So you're going to continue practising?"

I turned away, but the television cameraman followed me, the black gleam of the lens seeking me out. I looked at the blonde woman, read the name badge on her chest, STEFANIE VON SYDOW, saw her white crocheted hat and her hand, waving the camera over.

"I wonder if you'd like to comment on the fact that another of your patients, a woman named Eva Blau, was committed last week to a secure psychiatric unit."

"What are you talking about?"

◎

The white light streaming through the tall hospital windows at the end of the corridor was reflected in the recently mopped floor of the secure psychiatric unit at Southern Hospital. I passed a long row of locked doors with flaking paint and rubber strips around their edges and stopped outside B39. Looking back down the corridor, I noticed that my shoes had left tracks in the shining film covering the floor.

From a distant room, loud thuds could be heard, then the faint sound of weeping, and then silence. I stood for a while trying to gather my thoughts before I knocked on the door, turned the key in the lock, and went in.

The waft of disinfectant I brought in with me blended with the miasma of sweat and vomit in the dark room and almost made me retch. Eva Blau was lying on the bed with her back to me. I went over to the window to pull up the roller blind and let in some light, but the mechanism was stuck. Out of the corner of my eye I could see Eva starting to turn over. I tugged at the blind but lost my grip and it flew up with a loud crack.

"Sorry," I said, "I just wanted to let in a bit of light."

In the sudden brightness, Eva Blau was sitting up and looking at me with heavily drugged eyes, the corners of her mouth curving downwards bitterly. My heart was pounding. The tip of Eva's nose had been cut off. She was hunched over, with a bloodstained bandage around her hand, just staring at me.

"Eva, I came as soon as I heard," I said.

She banged her clenched fist slowly against her stomach. The circular wound from the severed tip of her nose glowed red in her tortured face.

"I tried to help you all," I said. "But I'm beginning to understand that I was wrong about almost everything. I thought I was on to something important, that I understood how hypnosis worked. But I didn't, I didn't understand anything. I'm sorry I couldn't help you, not one of you."

She rubbed her nose with the back of her hand, and blood began to trickle from the wound above her mouth.

"Eva? Why have you done this to yourself?" I asked her.

"It was you, you, it's your fault!" she yelled. "It's all your fault. You've destroyed my life, you've taken everything I have!"

"I understand that you're angry with me because—"

"Shut the fuck up, You don't understand anything. My life has been destroyed, and I will destroy yours. I can wait, I can wait as long as it takes, but I will have my revenge."

Then she started to scream, her mouth wide open, the sound hoarse and insane. The door flew open and a doctor came in.

"You were supposed to wait outside," he said. He sounded shaken, but he was angry.

"The nurse gave me the key, so I thought—"

He pulled me into the corridor, closed the door, and locked Eva in.

"Haven't you done enough harm? This patient is suffering from persecutory delusions—"

I interrupted him with a smile. "I don't think so."

"That is my assessment of this patient," he said.

"Of course. I'm sorry."

"Hundreds of times every day she demands that we lock her door and lock the key inside the key cupboard."

"Yes, but—"

"And she keeps saying she won't testify against anyone, that we can subject her to electric shocks and rape, but she won't tell us anything. What the hell did you actually do to your patients? She's terribly frightened. I can't believe you went ahead and—"

"She's angry with me, but she isn't afraid of me."

"I heard her screaming," he said.

◎

After my visit to the hospital and my encounter with Eva Blau, I drove to Television Centre and asked to speak to Stefanie von Sydow, the TV news reporter who had tried to get a comment out of me earlier. The receptionist dialled an editorial assistant and then handed me the phone. I said I was ready to do an interview if they were interested. After a little while the assistant came downstairs. She was a young woman with short hair and an intelligent expression.

"Stefanie can see you in ten minutes," she said.

"Good."

"I'll take you to make-up."

The interview was brief. When I went home, the entire house was in darkness. I called out but there was no reply. I was surprised to find Simone upstairs sitting in front of the television, but it wasn't switched on.

"Has something happened?" I asked. "Where's Benjamin?"

"He's at David's," she answered tonelessly.

"Isn't it time he was home? What did you tell him?"

"Nothing."

"But what's the matter? Talk to me, Simone."

"Why should I? I don't even know you."

Anxiety rose sharply within me like mercury in a thermometer; I moved closer and tried to brush a strand of hair from her face.

"Don't touch me," she snapped, snatching her head away.

"What is it? Talk to me, Simone."

She nodded, and in a voice full of pain, she said, "Erik, please tell me the truth. Have you been unfaithful?"

My heart raced, but my voice stayed gruesomely steady. "What are you talking about?"

"Who is Maja?"

"Maja? I don't know . . . should I know who that is?"

"Have you been cheating on me?" Simone's lips quivered.

"Simone? What is this about?"

My thoughts swirled. How could she know? "I would never . . . I get it . . . You're talking about Maja Swartling. Yes? She hates me for some reason, she's already influenced the board, and—"

"Erik," Simone interrupted. "You get one more chance. Have you slept with another woman?"

"No."

"You have not been unfaithful. You give me your word?" Her eyes filled with tears.

"I promise," I whispered.

She opened a pale blue envelope and tipped out several photographs: I saw myself posing in Maja Swartling's apartment, then a series of pictures of her dressed only in those pale green panties. Tresses of her dark hair curled over her broad white breasts. She looked happy, blushing high on her cheeks. A number of photographs were close-ups of one breast in varying degrees of fuzziness. In one of the pictures she was lying with her thighs wide apart.

"Sixan, let me try to—"

"I can't cope with your lies," she said, and hurled the photos at me, one by one.

The evening news was on. Suddenly there was a report on a scandal brewing at Karolinska University Hospital, involving a hypnotist. Annika Lorentzon did not wish to comment on the case during the ongoing investigation, but when the reporter brought up the significant funding recently allocated by the board to the hypnotist in question, Annika Lorentzon found herself on the defensive.

"That was a mistake," she said.

"What was a mistake?"

"Erik Maria Bark has been suspended until further notice."

"Only until further notice?"

"He will not be practising hypnosis at Karolinska Hospital in the future," she said.

Then I saw my own face on the screen; I was sitting in the television studio looking frightened.

"Will you be continuing to practise hypnosis at other hospitals?" the interviewer asked me.

For a moment I looked confused, as if I didn't understand the question, and then I shook my head almost imperceptibly.

"Erik Maria Bark, do you still believe that hypnosis is a good form of treatment?" she persisted.

"I don't know," I answered feebly.

"Will you continue to practise?"

"No."

"Never?"

"I will never hypnotize anyone again," I replied.

"Is that a promise?"

"Yes."

75

Erik gives a start, and the hand holding the coffee cup jerks and spills the liquid all over his jacket and shirt cuffs.

Joona turns to him in surprise and without a word pulls a tissue from a box of Kleenex on the dashboard.

Erik looks out at the big yellow wooden house, the garden, the lawn, and the enormous Winnie-the-Pooh with the fangs drawn on it.

"Is she violent?" asks Joona.

"Who?"

"Eva Blau."

"Maybe. I mean, she's certainly capable of it."

Joona switches off the engine and they get out of the car. "Just don't expect too much," he says in a melancholy tone. "Liselott Blau might have nothing to do with Eva."

"No," Erik replies absently.

They walk up a path made of flat, dark-gray slate. A heavy white veil of little snowflakes whirls in the air.

"We have to be careful," says Joona. "Because this could actually be the haunted house." His face lights up in a faint smile.

Erik stops in the middle of the path. The wet fabric around his wrist has grown cold. He smells of stale coffee. "I should explain. The haunted house is a house in the former Yugoslavia," he says. "It's also an apartment in Jakobsberg, a gym in Stocksund, a pale green house up in Dorotea, and so on."

He can't help smiling as he meets Joona's questioning gaze.

"The haunted house isn't a specific place, it's a term my hypnosis group adopted," he explains. "One member called the place where he had been traumatized the haunted house, and it became what we called anywhere that their abuse had taken place."

"I think I understand," says Joona. "Where was Eva Blau's haunted house?"

"That's the problem. She was the only one who didn't find her way there. Unlike the rest of the group, she never described a central place."

"Well, maybe this is it," says Joona.

They stride up the path. Erik fumbles in his pocket for the box with the parrot and the native on it. He feels sick, as if his emotional responses to the events he's recalled have been suspended in his nerve centre, as powerful and confusing as ever. He wants to take one of his pills, yearns for a pill, but he knows he must remain absolutely clear-headed. He has to find Benjamin, he has to stop taking the pills, he can't go on like this, he can't keep hiding.

He pushes the doorbell, hearing the deep chime through thick wood. He waits, although he wants to pull the door open, rush inside, and shout Benjamin's name. Joona's hand is tucked inside his jacket. After a little while the door is opened by a young woman with glasses, red hair, and a patch of tiny scars on each cheek. Erik studies her carefully.

"We're looking for Liselott Blau," says Joona.

"That's me," she replies warily.

Joona looks at Erik, who shakes his head slightly. This is not Eva.

"We're actually looking for Eva," Joona says.

"Eva? I don't know any Eva. What's this about?" asks the woman.

Joona shows her his police ID and asks if they can come in for a while. She hesitates, looking back nervously into the house. "Or talk to us out here, if you prefer. You should put on a jacket, though, it's chilly," he says.

A few minutes later they are standing on the lawn, crunchy under-foot with frost, their breath forming white condensation in the air as they speak.

"I live alone," she says, hugging herself.

"Big house," Joona says, nodding at the large structure.

The woman smiles thinly. "I'm in a fortunate position."

"Is Eva Blau a relative?"

"I told you, I don't know anyone called Eva Blau."

Joona shows her three pictures of Eva that he has taken from the video recording, but the red-haired woman simply shakes her head.

"Look closely," says Joona firmly.

"Don't tell me what to do," she snaps.

"I'm asking, for now."

"I pay your salary," she says. "My taxes pay your salary."

"Please look at the pictures."

"I've never seen her."

"This is important," Erik says.

"To you, maybe, but not to me."

"She calls herself Eva Blau," Joona goes on. "Blau is quite an unusual name in Sweden."

Erik sees a curtain suddenly sway in an upstairs window. He bolts for the house as the others call after him.

76

Erik dashes through the door, spots the wide staircase and takes it two steps at a time.

"Benjamin!" he calls out, then freezes.

The hallway, lined with closed doors, stretches in both directions. Somewhere, a floorboard creaks. He tries to work out which window he was looking at when he saw the curtain move, and hurries to his right, to the last door of the corridor. He tries the handle, but it's locked.

"Benjamin?" Erik calls softly.

He bends down and peers through the keyhole. The key's in the lock, but Erik thinks he can sense movement within.

"Open the door," he barks.

He hears someone rush into the house, and then the red-haired woman is on her way up the stairs.

"I don't want you in here!" she shouts.

Ignoring her, Erik takes a step backwards, kicks the door open, and walks in. The room is empty: a large unmade bed with pink sheets, a pale pink carpet, a wardrobe with tinted mirrors on its doors. A camera on a tripod is pointing at the bed. He opens the wardrobe, but there is no one there; he turns around, studying the room. A narrow pair of men's jeans is folded neatly and draped over the back of a chair. Erik bends down and sees someone curled up in the darkness under the bed: shy, terrified eyes, narrow thighs, and bare feet.

"Come out here," he says sharply.

He reaches out, grabs hold of an ankle, and drags out a naked boy, who cowers as he speaks rapidly to Erik in a language that sounds like Arabic. He grabs the jeans and pulls them on. Then another boy peeps out and says something in a harsh tone of voice to his friend, who immediately falls silent. The red-haired woman is standing in the doorway, insisting in a trembling voice that he is to leave her friends alone.

"Are they minors?" Erik asks.

"Get out of my house," she says furiously.

The second boy has wrapped the duvet around him. He takes a cigarette from a pack on the bedside table and stares at Erik, smiling.

"Out!" screams Liselott Blau.

As Erik slowly descends the stairs, the woman follows, yelling, "Go to hell!" Erik leaves the house and walks down the slate path. Joona is waiting with his gun drawn and hidden close to his body. The woman stops in the doorway.

"You're not allowed to do this kind of thing," she shouts. "It's not legal. The cops need a warrant to enter somebody's house like that."

"I'm not a cop," Erik yells back.

"I'll be making an official complaint about this!"

"Feel free," says Joona. "You can make the complaint to me. As I said, I am a police officer."

77

Back at the wheel, Joona pulls to the side of the road and takes a piece of paper out of his pocket. A flatbed truck carrying a load of dusty crushed stone passes by.

"There are five more people named Blau in the Stockholm area, three in Västerås, two in Eskilstuna, and one in Umeå." He folds up the paper and smiles encouragingly at Erik.

"Charlotte," Erik says quietly.

"There was no Charlotte on the list," replies Joona, wiping a mark off the rearview mirror.

"Charlotte Ceder. She was kind to Eva. I think Eva had a room at her place in those days."

"Where do you think we might find Charlotte?"

"She lived in Stocksund ten years ago."

Joona dials Anja.

"I need a phone number and address for one Charlotte Ceder. I mean like right now. She lives in Stocksund, or at least she used to." He abruptly pulls the phone from his ear and stares at it, a wry expression on his face. Erik can hear a woman's agitated voice on the other end. "Same to you. Yes. Yes, *please*." There's a pause. "Sure, hang on," he says, taking out a pen and making a note. "Thanks a lot."

378

He flicks on the left-turn signal and pulls out into the traffic.

"Is she still living there?" asks Erik.

"No, but we're in luck. She lives near Rimbo."

Erik feels a stab of anxiety in his stomach. He doesn't know why he finds it frightening that Charlotte has moved from Stocksund; perhaps he ought to interpret it as a positive development.

"The Husby estate," says Joona, inserting a disk into the CD player. Turning up the volume, he turns to Erik and says apologetically, "This is my mother's music. Saija Varjus." He shakes his head sadly and joins in. "*Dam dam da da di dum.*"

The mournful music fills the whole car.

When the song is over they sit in silence for a short while. Then Joona says in a voice that sounds almost surprised, "I don't like Finnish music any more." He clears his throat a couple of times.

"I thought it was lovely," says Erik.

Joona smiles, giving him a quick sideways glance. "My mother was there when she became the tango queen of Seinäjoki."

Heavy sleet is falling when they turn off onto the 77 at Sätuna. The sky to the east is growing dark, and the farms they pass are difficult to make out in the gathering dusk.

Joona taps on the dashboard. The heat comes pouring out of the vents with a low hum. Erik can feel his feet getting damp from the peculiar warmth in the car.

"All right, let's see what we've got here," says Joona to himself as he drives through the small community and turns onto a straight but narrow road between dark fields. In the distance they can see a large white house behind a high fence. They park outside the open gates and walk the last few yards to the house. A young woman in a leather jacket is raking the gravel path. She looks scared as they approach. A golden retriever is jumping around her legs.

"Charlotte," the woman calls out. "Charlotte!"

A woman appears around the side of the enormous house, dragging a big black rubbish bag behind her. She is wearing a pink down vest, a thick grey sweater, scruffy jeans, and wellingtons.

Charlotte, thinks Erik. It really is Charlotte.

Gone is the slender, cool woman with her elegant clothes and her

379

well-cared-for short bob. The person coming toward them looks completely different. Her hair is long and grey, woven into a thick braid. Her face is full of laughter lines, and she isn't wearing a scrap of make-up. She's more beautiful than ever, thinks Erik. When she catches sight of him a deep flush spreads over her face. At first she looks totally amazed; then she begins to smile broadly.

"Erik!" she says, and her voice is just the same: deep, articulate, and warm. She lets go of the rubbish bag and grabs his hands. "Is it really you? It's wonderful to see you again."

She says hello to Joona and then stands for a little while, just looking at them. A powerfully built woman opens the front door. She has a tattoo on her neck and is wearing a black hooded jacket.

"Need any help?" she calls.

"Friends of mine," Charlotte shouts back, waving her away.

Charlotte smiles as the big woman closes the door. "I've . . . I've turned this place into a women's shelter. There's plenty of room, so I take in women who need to get away, or however you want to put it. I let them live here—we cook together, look after the stables—until they feel ready to go back, ready to do things on their own terms. The whole thing is very straightforward."

"Charlotte, it all sounds wonderful!" Erik says.

She nods and gestures toward the door, inviting them in.

"Charlotte, we need to get hold of Eva Blau," says Erik. "Do you remember her?"

"Of course I remember her. She was my first guest here. I had the rooms in the wing and—"

She breaks off but begins again. "It's strange that you should mention Eva. She called me only a week or so ago."

"What did she want?"

"She was angry."

"Yes," says Erik, with a sigh.

"Why was she angry?" asks Joona.

Charlotte takes a deep breath. Erik can hear the wind in the bare branches of the trees. Someone has tried to build a snowman with the small amount of snow that has fallen, a forlorn and crumpled-looking figure.

"She was angry with Erik."

He feels his flesh crawl as he thinks of Eva Blau's sharp face, her aggressive voice, her flashing eyes, and her nose with its cruelly severed tip.

"I think it upset a lot of people when it came out that you'd been practising hypnosis again, Erik."

"It was a special case."

She takes his hand in hers. "I never thought, never believed—" She stops. "You helped me," she whispers. "That time when I saw . . . do you remember?"

"I do remember," Erik says quietly.

Charlotte smiles at him. "It was enough. I went inside the haunted house. I looked up and saw the person who had hurt me."

"I know."

"It would never have happened without you, Erik."

"Yes, but—"

"Something inside me became whole again," she says, gesturing toward her heart.

"Where is Eva now?" asks Joona.

Charlotte frowns. "When she was discharged she moved into a apartment in the centre of Åkersberga and became a Jehovah's Witness. At first we kept in contact—I helped her out financially—but then we lost touch. She thought she was being persecuted. She kept talking about finding protection, saying that evil was after her."

Charlotte looks at Erik. "You look sad," she says.

"My son is missing. Eva is our only clue."

Charlotte's expression is troubled. "I'm sorry, Erik. I hope you find him."

"Do you know what her name is?" asks Joona.

"Her real name, you mean? She doesn't tell anyone that; perhaps she doesn't even know it herself."

"OK."

"But she called herself Veronica when she rang me."

"Veronica?"

"It comes from the story of the veil of Veronica."

They hug each other briefly, then Erik and Joona hurry back to the car. As they drive south, heading for Stockholm, Joona calls Anja to ask her to look for someone called Veronica in the centre of Åkersberga, and he requests an address for the Jehovah's Witnesses, either their office or the Kingdom Hall. Erik half listens, his mind thick with exhaustion. He feels his eyes slowly begin to close.

"Yes, Anja, I'm writing it down," he hears Joona say. "Västra Banvägen . . . hang on, Stationsvägen 5, all right, thanks."

78

Erik wakes up as they are driving down a long hill beside a golf course.

"Nearly there," says Joona.

"I fell asleep," says Erik, mainly to himself.

"Eva Blau rang Charlotte on the same day you were featured in all the newspapers," Joona muses.

"And the following day Benjamin was kidnapped," says Erik.

"Because someone spotted you."

"Or because I broke my promise never to hypnotize anyone again."

"In which case it's my fault," says Joona.

Erik doesn't really know what to say.

"I'm sorry," says Joona, his eyes fixed on the road.

They pass a discount shop with smashed windows. Joona glances in the rear-view mirror. A woman wrapped in a shawl sweeps up broken glass on the pavement.

"I don't know what happened with Eva," says Erik. "Every now and then a patient completely eludes you. It was as if my treatment aggravated her condition. She blamed me and my hypnosis for everything, she became delusional, she harmed herself, and in the end . . . I should never have accepted her into the group. I should never have hypnotized anyone."

"But you helped Charlotte," Joona says.

383

"So it seems," Erik says quietly.

Just after a traffic circle, they bump over a railroad crossing, turn off to the left at a playing field, drive across a river, and stop outside a large grey apartment building.

Joona points to the glove compartment. "Would you pass me my gun, please."

Erik opens the compartment and hands over the heavy weapon. Joona checks the barrel and the magazine and makes sure the safety catch is on before slipping the gun into his pocket.

They walk quickly across the parking lot, passing a playground with swings, a sandbox, and a jungle gym.

Erik points out the way to the main door; he looks up and sees flashing Christmas decorations and satellite dishes on virtually every balcony.

An old woman is standing inside the locked door, leaning on a wheeled walker. Joona knocks and waves cheerily. She looks at them and shakes her head. Joona shows her his ID through the glass, but she just shakes her head again. Erik rummages in his pockets and finds an envelope containing a receipt he was supposed to hand in to the finance office. He walks up to the glass, taps on it, and holds up the envelope. The woman immediately moves over to the door and presses the button to release the electrical lock.

"Is it the mail?" she asks shakily.

"Express delivery," Erik replies.

"There's so much sobbing and screaming in here," the woman whispers toward the wall.

"What did you say?" asks Joona.

Erik looks at the list of names and finds Veronica Andersson on the second floor. The narrow staircase is covered with graffiti. A rank smell comes from the rubbish chute. The fluorescent fixture overhead flickers. They locate the right door and Joona rings the bell. Muddy footprints from children's boots lead up and down the stairs.

No response.

"Try again," says Erik.

Joona pushes open the letterbox and shouts that he has a letter from The Watchtower. Erik sees the detective's head jerk back, as if he has been hit by a blast wave.

"What is it?"

"I don't know, but I want you to wait outside," says Joona, his expression strained in the flickering light.

"No."

"I'm going in alone."

Something crashes to the floor in one of the neighbouring apartments. Joona reaches out and tries the door. It isn't locked. A powerful smell surges out as the door swings open. Joona draws his gun and gestures sharply to Erik to stay where he is.

79

Erik clamps a hand to his nose and mouth. His heart pounds in his chest and the blood rushes to his ears. The stillness within is horribly ominous. Benjamin can't be here. The lights in the stairwell go out altogether, and darkness surrounds him. Suddenly Joona is standing in front of him again.

"I think you're going to have to come in, Erik," he says.

They go inside and Joona switches on the main light. The bathroom door is wide open. The smell of decay is unbearable. Eva Blau is lying in the empty shower stall. Her face is swollen, and flies are crawling around her mouth and buzzing in the air. Her blue blouse has worked its way up; her stomach is distended and bluish green. Deep black incisions run along both her arms. The fabric of her blouse and her blonde hair have stuck fast to the coagulated blood. Her skin is pale grey, and a brown network of veins is clearly visible all over her body. The stagnant blood has rotted inside the vascular system. Piles of small yellow eggs laid by flies can be seen in the corners of her eyes and around her mouth and nostrils. The blood has overflowed the drain and trickled onto the small bath mat, whose edges have darkened in colour. A blood-stained kitchen knife is lying in the bath beside the body.

"Is that her?" asks Joona.

"Yes. That's Eva."

"She's been dead for at least a week. The stomach has had time to swell up significantly."

"I realize that," Erik replies.

"So she wasn't the one who took Benjamin," Joona states.

"I need to think," says Erik. "I was so sure."

He looks out the window. There is a low brick building on the other side of the railroad tracks. Eva could see the Kingdom Hall from her window. He thinks that probably made her feel more secure.

80

Simone tastes blood. She has bitten her lower lip without noticing. She sits beside her father's bed in a dim room at St. Göran's Hospital. He has been lying here for days while the doctors try to establish how badly hurt he is. All she knows for certain is that Kennet was hit by a car, and the impact could have killed him. Her headache is a steel ball, rolling around inside her head. She has lost Erik, she may have lost Benjamin, and now it's possible she could lose her father, too.

She doesn't know how many times she's done it already, but just to be on the safe side she gets her mobile phone out, checks that it's working, and returns it to the outside pocket of her bag, where it will be easy to get hold of, on the outside chance that it should ring.

She leans over her father and straightens the covers. He is sleeping, but there isn't a sound. She's always struck by this: Kennet Sträng is probably the only man in the world who doesn't make a noise when he's asleep.

His head is bound in a chalk-white bandage, from beneath which a dark shadow creeps out, an eggplant-coloured bruise that extends down across one cheek. He looks terrible: the bruising, the pale grey complexion, the swollen nose, the mouth drooping at one corner.

But he isn't dead, she thinks. He's alive. And Benjamin is alive, too; she knows it, he has to be.

She gets up and paces back and forth. She thinks about the conversation she'd had with her father the other day, just as she'd gotten home from Sim Shulman's apartment, just before the accident. He'd told her he'd found Wailord and was going to a place called "the sea," somewhere out on Loudden.

She looks at her father again. His sleep is so deep.

"Dad?"

She immediately regrets speaking. He doesn't wake, but a troubled expression flits across his face like a cloud. Simone cautiously touches the wound on her lower lip. Her gaze falls on the Advent candles in the window. Some Christmas this year, she thinks. She looks at her shoes in their blue plastic protectors. The headache pounds against her temples. She shudders and pulls her cardigan more tightly around her, although she isn't cold. She thinks about an afternoon many years ago, when she and Kennet watched her mother wave and then disappear in her little green Fiat.

Suddenly Kennet gives a low groan.

"Daddy," she says, like a little child.

He opens his eyes. They seem unfocused, not fully awake. The white of one eye is covered in blood.

"Daddy, it's me," says Simone. "How are you feeling?"

His gaze wanders past her. She's suddenly afraid that he can't see.

"Sixan?"

"I'm here, Dad."

She sits down beside him and gently takes his hand. His eyes close again, his eyebrows contract as if he is in pain.

"Dad," she asks again, "how are you feeling?"

He tries to pat her on the hand, but he can't quite manage it. "I'll soon be on my feet," he wheezes. "Don't you worry about me."

Silence. Simone tries to keep her thoughts at bay, to ward off the anxiety hurtling toward her. She doesn't want to put any pressure on him in this state, but panic forces her to make an attempt.

"Dad?" she asks tentatively. "Do you remember what we were talking about just before the accident?"

He peers wearily at her and shakes his head.

"You said you knew where Wailord was. You talked about the sea. You said you were going to the sea."

Kennet's eyes flicker. He tries to sit up but falls back with a groan.

"Dad, tell me, I have to know where it is. Who's Wailord? Who is he?"

He opens his mouth, his chin trembling as he answers. "A . . . child . . . It's . . . a child."

"What are you saying?"

But Kennet has closed his eyes and no longer seems able to hear her. Simone goes over to the window and looks out at the hospital complex. She can feel a cold draft. There is a strip of dirt along the glass. When she breathes on it, she can see the impression of someone else's face in the mist for a brief moment. Someone else has stood in this exact spot, leaning against the windowpane.

The church on the opposite side of the street is in darkness, the streetlamps reflected in its black arched windows. She thinks about Benjamin's message to Aida, telling her not to let Nicky go to the sea.

"Aida," she says aloud. "I'll go and see Aida, and this time she's going to tell me everything."

81

It is Nicky who opens the door when Simone rings the bell. He looks at her in surprise.

"Hi, Nicky," she says.

"I've got some new cards," he tells her eagerly.

"That's great," she says.

"They're girl cards, but lots of them are really strong."

"Is your sister in?" Simone asks, patting Nicky on the arm.

"Aida! Aida!" Nicky runs off down the dark hall and disappears inside the apartment.

Simone waits in the entry-way. Then she hears a strange pumping noise, something rattles faintly, and after a while she sees an emaciated, stooping woman coming toward her. She is pulling a small trolley behind her with an oxygen tank mounted on it. A hose runs from the tank to the woman, pumping oxygen into her nostrils through thin, transparent plastic tubes.

The woman taps her chest with a tiny clenched fist. "Em . . . physema," she wheezes. Her wrinkled face contracts in a painful, debilitating bout of coughing.

When she eventually stops, she gestures to Simone to come in. They walk together through the long, dark hallway until they reach a living room full of heavy furniture. On the floor, between a stereo system with glass doors and a low television unit, Nicky is playing with his Pokémon cards. Aida is sitting on the brown sofa, which has been squeezed in between two large indoor palms.

Simone barely recognizes her. She isn't wearing a scrap of make-up. Her face is sweet and very young. Her hair has been brushed until it shines and is caught up in a neat ponytail. If not for the cigarette she holds in a trembling hand, she would look like a child.

"Hello, Aida," says Simone. "How are you doing?"

Aida shrugs her shoulders. She looks as if she's been crying. She takes a drag on her cigarette and lifts a green saucer up toward the glowing tip, as if she's afraid of dropping ash on the furniture.

"Sit . . . down," her mother wheezes to Simone, who perches on one of two wide armchairs crammed in beside the sofa, the table, and the palms.

Aida taps the ash onto the green saucer.

"I've just come from the hospital," Simone says. "My father was hit by a car. He was on his way to the sea, to Wailord."

Nicky suddenly lurches to his feet. His face is bright red. "Wailord is angry, very angry, very angry."

Simone turns to Aida, who swallows hard and then closes her eyes.

"What's all this about?" Simone asks. "Who's Wailord? What's going on?"

Aida stubs out her cigarette, then says unsteadily, "They've disappeared."

"Who?"

"A gang who used to be horrible to us. Nicky and me. They were terrible, they were going to mark me, they were going to make—" She falls silent and looks at her mother, who makes a snorting sound. "They were going to make a bonfire . . . of Mum," Aida says slowly.

"Shit . . . fuck," wheezes her mother from the other armchair.

"They use Pokémon names; they're called Azelf, Magmortar, or Lucario. Sometimes they change the names. You never know what they're doing."

"How many of them are there?"

"I don't know, maybe only five," she replies. "They're just kids; the oldest is about my age, the youngest is only about six. But they decided that everybody who lives here had to give them something," says Aida, looking Simone in the eye for the first time. Her eyes are the colour of amber, beautiful, clear, but full of fear. "The little ones had to give them sweets or pens," she goes on in her thin voice. "They gave them all their money so they wouldn't get beaten up. Others gave them their stuff: cell phones, Nintendo games. They took my jacket, they took cigarettes. And Nicky—they just used to beat Nicky up; they took everything he had, they were so horrible to him."

Her voice dies away and tears spring to her eyes.

"Did they take Benjamin?"

Aida's mother waves her hand. "That . . . boy . . . is . . . no . . . good."

"Answer me, Aida," Simone says sharply. "You're going to give me an answer!"

"Don't . . . shout . . . at . . . my . . . daughter," her mother hisses.

Simone ignores the shrunken woman and says, even more firmly this time, "You're going to tell me what you know, do you hear me?"

Aida swallows hard. "I don't know much," she says eventually. "Benjamin stepped in, told us we shouldn't give those kids anything. Wailord went crazy; he said it was a declaration of war and demanded loads of money from us."

She lights a fresh cigarette, takes a drag, carefully taps the ash onto the green saucer, then goes on.

"When Wailord found out about Benjamin's disease, he gave the others needles to scratch him with." The girl stops and shrugs her shoulders.

"What happened?" Simone asks harshly.

Aida bites her lips and removes a flake of tobacco from her tongue.

"What happened?"

"Wailord just stopped," she whispers. "Suddenly he was gone. I've seen the other kids around; they went after Nicky just the other day. Now they're following someone who calls himself Ariados, but it's not the same. They're confused and desperate since Wailord disappeared."

"When was this? When did Wailord disappear?"

Aida considers the question. "I think . . . I think it was last Wednesday. Three days before Benjamin disappeared." Her mouth begins to tremble. "Wailord's taken him," she whispers. "Wailord's done something terrible to him. And now he's hiding out."

She begins to sob, loudly and convulsively. Her mother gets to her feet with difficulty, takes the cigarette out of her hand, and slowly stubs it out on the green saucer.

"Fucking . . . monstrosity," wheezes her mother.

Simone has no idea who she's talking about. "Who is he?" she asks again. "What's Wailord's real name? You have to tell me who he is."

"I don't know," yells Aida. "*I don't know!*"

Simone takes out the photograph of the patch of grass and the bushes in front of a brown fence.

"I found this on Benjamin's computer," she says firmly.

Aida looks at the print-out, her face blank.

"Where is this?" Simone asks.

Aida shrugs her shoulders and glances briefly at her mother. "Haven't a clue," she says tonelessly, handing it back.

"But you sent it to him," Simone says angrily. "It came from you, Aida."

The girl's eyes slide away, seeking out her mother once again, sitting with the hissing oxygen tank at her feet.

Simone waves the sheet of paper in front of her face. "Look at it, Aida. Look again. Why did you send this to my son?"

"It was just a joke," she whispers.

"A joke?"

Aida nods. "Would you like to live here, Benjamin? Something like that," she says feebly.

"I don't believe you," Simone says doggedly. "Tell me the truth!"

Aida's mother struggles to her feet again and waves at Simone. "Get out of my house. You people think you can come in here and say whatever the hell you want to whoever the hell you want."

"Why are you lying?" Simone asks, as Aida finally meets her gaze.

The girl looks deeply unhappy. "Sorry," she says in a small voice. "Sorry."

On her way out, Simone meets Nicky. He's standing in the darkness in the hallway, rubbing his eyes.

"I have no power. I'm a worthless Pokémon."

"I'm sure that isn't true," Simone responds. "I'm sure you do have power."

82

When Simone gets back to Kennet's room, he's sitting up in bed. His face has a little more colour, and he wears a wry, self-satisfied expression, as if he'd known she was about to walk in.

She goes over, bends down, smiles, and gently presses her cheek against his.

"Do you know what I dreamed, Sixan?" he asks.

"No."

"I dreamed about my father."

"About Granddad?"

He laughs quietly. "Can you imagine? He was standing in his workshop with a big grin, sweating. *My boy.* That was all he said. I can still smell the diesel." Kennet shakes his head cautiously.

Simone swallows. There's a hard, painful lump in her throat. "Dad," she whispers. "Do you remember what you were telling me just before the car hit you?"

He looks at her, his expression serious, and suddenly it's as if a light has come on behind his sharp, intelligent eyes.

"Do you remember, Dad?"

"I remember everything." He tries to get up, but moves too quickly and falls back onto the bed. "Help me, Simone," he says impatiently. "We need to hurry, I can't stay here."

He runs his hand over his eyes, clears his throat, and extends his arms. "Grab hold of me," he orders, and this time, with Simone's help, he manages to sit up in bed and swing his legs over the side. He rests for a moment, breathing heavily.

"I need my clothes."

Simone quickly pulls his clothes from the wardrobe. She is helping him on with his socks when the door is opened by a young doctor.

"I'm getting out of here," Kennet says belligerently, before the man is even fully inside the room.

Simone gets to her feet. "Good afternoon," she says, shaking hands with the young doctor. "Simone Bark."

"Ola Tuvefjäll," he says, looking slightly confused as he turns to Kennet, who is busy fastening his trousers.

"Listen," says Kennet, tucking his shirt into his waistband. "I'm sorry we won't be staying, but this is an emergency."

"I can't force you to stay here," the doctor says calmly, "but I would advise against leaving. You've suffered a very severe blow to your head, and we haven't yet determined the extent and severity of your other injuries. You might feel fine at the moment, but serious complications could arise at any time."

Kennet goes over to the sink and splashes cold water over his face. "They won't be any less complicated here than out there," he says.

"It's your decision," the doctor says.

"As I said, I'm sorry," Kennet says, straightening up. "But I have to go to the sea."

The doctor looks puzzled as he watches them go down the corridor, Kennet leaning on the wall for support.

"Where are we going?" Simone asks, and for once Kennet doesn't protest as she climbs into the driver's seat. He simply gets in beside her and fastens his seatbelt. "Dad, you have to tell me where we're going," she repeats. "How do we get there?"

He gives her a strange look. "To the sea . . . I need to think." He leans back in his seat, closes his eyes, and remains silent for a while.

Mistake, she thinks, he's in no shape for this. I have to get him back upstairs. But all at once he opens his eyes and speaks clearly.

"Take Sankt Eriksgatan across the bridge and right into Odengatan. Go straight down to Östra Station, follow Valhallavägen east all the way to the Swedish Film Institute, and turn off onto Lindarängsvägen. That goes right down to the harbour."

"Who needs GPS?" says Simone with a smile as she pulls out into the heavy traffic.

As she manoeuvres her way through it, Simone tells him about her visit to see Aida.

"I wonder . . ." Kennet says thoughtfully, but then stops.

"What?"

"I wonder if the parents have any idea what their kids are up to."

Simone gives him a quick sideways glance. They are passing Gustav Adolfs Church. She catches a glimpse of a long procession of children dressed in robes. They are carrying candles and slowly making their way in through the door of the church.

"Extortion, abuse, violence, and threats," Simone replies wearily. "Mummy and Daddy's little darlings."

She thinks back to the day she went to Tensta, to the tattoo parlour. The boys holding the little girl over the railing. They hadn't been afraid at all; they had been threatening, dangerous. She remembers Benjamin trying to keep her from confronting the boy in the underground station. He must have been one of them. He was one of the ones who use Pokémon names.

"What's wrong with people?" she asks rhetorically.

"I didn't have an accident, Sixan. I was pushed in front of a car," Kennet says suddenly, a sharp edge to his voice. "And I saw who did it."

"Pushed? Who did it?"

"It was one of them. It was a child, a little girl."

Christmas decorations glow from the dark windows of the Film Institute. The temperature has risen slightly, and the surface of the road is covered in wet slush. Swollen, heavy clouds hang over the park; it looks as if a real shower of thawing rain will soon be falling on the dog owners and their happy animals.

Loudden is a promontory just to the east of Stockholm's harbour. At the end of the 1920s an oil dock with almost one hundred tanks was built here. The area is composed of low industrial buildings, a water purification plant, a container port, underground storage areas, and docks.

Kennet takes out the crumpled card he found in the child's wallet.

"Louddsvägen eighteen," he says, gesturing to Simone to stop the car. She pulls over onto a patch of asphalt surrounded by high metal fences.

"We'll walk the last bit," says Kennet, undoing his seatbelt.

They go between enormous tanks, with narrow flights of steps twisting like serpents around the cylindrical structures. Every surface is acned with rust: the hand-rails, between the curved, welded metal plates, along the fittings.

A thin, cold rain falls. Very soon it will be dusk, and then they won't be able to see a thing. There are no streetlamps anywhere. Narrow passageways have been left between the vast shipping containers, piled high: yellow, red, blue, arranged so that a series of narrow passageways runs between them. They pass among the tanks, loading docks, and low offices. Closer to the water the main building looms with its cranes, ramps, barges, and dry docks.

A low shed with a dirty Ford pick-up parked outside sits at an angle to a large warehouse made of corrugated aluminium. Self-adhesive letters, half peeling away now, have been stuck on the dark window of the shed: THE SEA. The smaller letters below have been scraped off, but it is still possible to read the words in the dust: DIVING CLUB. The heavy bar is hanging down beside the door.

83

Kennet waits for a second, listening, then cautiously pulls open the door. It is dark inside the little office, which contains nothing but a desk, a few folding chairs with plastic seats, and a couple of rusty oxygen tanks. On the wall is a crumpled poster showing exotic fish in emerald-green water. It's obvious that the diving club is no longer here; maybe it moved or went bust and ceased to exist altogether.

A fan begins to whirr and an inner door clicks. Kennet puts a finger to his lips. They can hear the distinct sound of footsteps. Moving forward, Kennet pushes open the door to reveal an expansive storage area. Someone is running away in the darkness. Kennet takes up the pursuit but suddenly cries out.

"Dad?" shouts Simone.

She can't see him, but she can hear his voice. He swears and calls to her to be careful. "They've put up barbed wire."

There's a metallic rattling sound across the concrete floor. Kennet has started to run again. Simone follows him, carefully climbing over the barbed wire and moving on into the large space. The air is cold and damp. It's dark, and she halts for a moment to get her bearings. She can hear rapid footsteps farther away.

Light from the spotlight on a container crane shines in through a dirty window, and Simone can see a figure next to a fork-lift truck. It's a boy with a mask covering his face, a grey mask made of fabric or cardboard. He's crouching slightly, and he's got a piece of iron pipe in his hand.

Kennet is getting close to him, moving quickly along rows of metal shelves.

"Behind the fork-lift," Simone shouts.

The boy in the mask rushes out and hurls the metal pipe at Kennet. It spins through the air and passes just above his head.

"Wait, we just want to talk to you," yells Kennet.

The boy slams into a metal door, which opens with a bang. Light floods in as the boy rushes out.

"He's getting away," Kennet hisses as he reaches for the door.

The slush has made the ground treacherous, and when Simone follows, she slips on the wet jetty. Getting to her feet, she sees her father running along the edge of the dock. To one side is a steep drop into black, freezing water, enormous shards of ice creaking in the darkness. She runs, following the two figures ahead of her. If she trips and slips over the edge, she knows it wouldn't take long before the ice-cold water paralyzed her; she would sink like a stone with her thick coat and her boots full of black winter water.

She thinks about the journalist who was assassinated as she drove alongside the dock with a friend. Their car sank like a weighted fishing creel, straight down into the water; it was swallowed up by the soft mud and disappeared.

When she reaches Kennet, she is out of breath, trembling with fear and exertion. Her back is soaked from the rain. Kennet is waiting for her, bent double; the bandage around his head has come loose, and a trickle of blood is running from his nose. His breathing sounds harsh and painful. On the ground lies a mask made of cardboard. It has started to disintegrate in the rain, and when the wind catches hold of it, it swirls up in the air and disappears.

"Fucking hell," says Kennet.

They move away from the water as the darkness increases around them. The rain has eased, but a strong wind has blown up, howling around the huge metal buildings. They pass a long, rectangular dry dock and Simone hears the wind singing down below. Tractor tyres on rusty chains hang along the side, acting as buffers. She looks down into the huge empty space, blasted out of the rock, a vast pit with rough walls strengthened with concrete and reinforced with steel. Fifty yards below she can see a concrete floor with huge plinth blocks.

A tarpaulin flaps in the wind and the light from a crane flickers across the perpendicular walls of the dry dock. Suddenly Simone spots someone hiding behind a concrete plinth down below.

Kennet sees her stop, and looks at her inquiringly. Without speaking, she points down into the dry dock. The crouching figure moves away from the light.

Kennet and Simone dash toward a set of narrow steps leading down the wall. The figure starts to run toward something that looks like a door down there. Kennet clings to the rail as he runs down the steep steps; he slips but regains his balance. There is a heavy, acrid smell of metal, rust, and rain. Keeping close to the wall, they continue downwards, their footsteps echoing in the depths of the dry dock.

The bottom of the dock is covered with several inches of water; Simone shivers as she feels the cold water seeping in through her boots.

"Where did he go?" she shouts.

Kennet moves among the enormous blocks big enough to hold a ship in place when the dry dock is emptied of water. He points to the spot where the boy disappeared.

"It's not a door," he says, "it's some kind of air vent." He peers inside but sees nothing. Out of breath, he runs his hand over his forehead and neck. "Out you come," he puffs. "That's enough."

They hear a rasping noise, heavy and rhythmic. Kennet begins to crawl inside the air vent.

"Careful, Dad."

There's a knocking sound, then the sluice gate begins to creak. Suddenly there's a deafening hiss, and Simone realizes what's happening.

"He's letting the water in," she yells.

"There's a ladder in here," Kennet bellows.

With terrifying pressure, thin streams of ice-cold water begin to gush into the dry dock through the tiny gap between the sluice gates. As the doors continue to move apart, the onrushing water builds into a deafening cataract. Simone races toward the steps, but the vast space fills rapidly, and soon she is struggling through knee-deep freezing water. The light from the crane flickers over the rough walls. The strong current sends the water in powerful eddies, dragging Simone backward. She bangs into a large metal mounting and feels white-hot pain. An ocean of black water is engulfing her. Weeping with terror, she reaches the steps and lunges for the hand-rail, gripping it tightly and searching for purchase with her numbed feet. Finally, step by step, she is climbing above the level of the water, outdistancing it. When the water is safely below her, she turns around. She can't see her father. The water has completely covered the vent in the wall. The sluice gates are screaming. Her body is shaking with fear and cold, but she presses on, her lungs burning. Then the roar of the water gradually begins to diminish. The gates close, and the influx stops. She gasps, aching to catch her breath. She's lost all feeling in the hand holding on to the rail. Her clothes are heavy, pulling across her thighs. She begins climbing again, unsure of what awaits her at the top.

Kennet is on the opposite side of the dry dock. He waves at her. He grips a boy by the upper arm and is marching him toward the containers.

At a distance, Simone follows them, through the containers and past the enormous tanks, until they reach the car.

Kennet's expression is strange. Simone cannot read it. The boy stands there passively, his head drooping.

"Where's Benjamin?" Simone screams before she even gets to them.

The boy doesn't respond. She grabs his shoulders and spins him around, then recoils at what she sees, gasping.

The boy's nose has been cut off.

It looks as if someone has tried to stitch up the wound, but in haste and without any medical expertise. The boy's expression is one of total apathy. The wind howls; all three of them get into the car, Kennet joining the boy in the backseat. Shivering uncontrollably, Simone turns on the engine to get the heat going. The windows quickly steam up. She finds a bar of chocolate and offers it to the boy. The inside of the car is very quiet.

"Where's Benjamin?" Kennet asks harshly.

The boy looks down at his knees. He munches the chocolate and swallows hard.

"You're going to tell us everything, you hear me?"

"You've beaten up kids, stolen their money," says Simone.

"I don't exist now," he whispers.

"Why did you do it?" Kennet asks.

"That's just the way it was when we—"

"That's just the way it was?" Kennet snaps. "Where are the others?"

"How am I supposed to know? Maybe they're in new gangs now," says the boy. "I hear Jerker is."

"Are you Wailord?"

The boy's mouth trembles. "I've stopped now," he says faintly. "I promise I've stopped."

"Where's Benjamin?" Simone asks shrilly.

"I don't know," he says quickly. "I'll never hurt him again, I promise."

"Listen to me," Simone says. "I'm his mother. I have to know."

But she is interrupted by the boy, who begins to rock back and forth, sobbing pitifully and saying over and over again, "I promise, I promise, I promise, I promise, I promise . . ."

Kennet places a hand on Simone's arm. "We need to take him in," he says emptily. "He needs help."

84

The boy who called himself Wailord was actually Birk Jansson, and his last known address was that of a foster family in Husby. At the Astrid Lindgren Children's Hospital, where Kennet took him after dropping Simone off, he was found to be suffering from dehydration and malnutrition; infected sores were found on his body, and a small amount of frostbite on his toes and fingers. Social Services were called; the boy's case worker was contacted.

As Kennet was about to leave, Birk started crying. "Please stay," he whispered, his hand covering his mutilated nose.

Kennet could feel his pulse hammering much too fast, and his nose was still bleeding from all the running. He stopped in the doorway.

"I'll wait here with you, Birk, on one condition." He sat down on a green chair next to the boy. "You have to tell me everything you know about Benjamin's disappearance."

Kennet sat there for the two hours it took for the social worker to arrive, feeling increasingly dizzy and trying to get the boy to talk. All he really managed to establish was that somebody or something had frightened Birk so much that he'd stopped hassling Benjamin. He didn't even seem to know that Benjamin had disappeared.

In the car, Kennet calls to check on Simone. She replies that she has slept for a while and is thinking of pouring herself a substantial brandy.

"Nice idea. I'm going to talk to Aida," says Kennet.

"Ask her about that picture of the grass and the fence. She wasn't telling me the truth, I'm sure of it."

Kennet parks the car in Sundbyberg in the same place as before, not far from the hot-dog stand. It's freezing now; a few sparse snowflakes drift onto the front seat when he opens the car door. He spots Aida and Nicky immediately. They sit on a park bench by an asphalt path leading down to Lake Ulvsunda. She looks on as Nicky shows her something. She has a certain air of patience that makes Kennet like her. He stands watching them for a little while. Something about the two of them strikes a chord with him; the way they seem to relate to and depend on each other. They seem so alone, so abandoned. It is almost six o'clock in the evening; bands of light from the city are reflected in the dark surface of the lake.

Kennet feels dizziness blur his vision for a moment. Carefully he crosses the icy road and walks down toward the lake across the frost-covered grass. "Hi, you two," he says.

Nicky looks up. "It's you!" he calls out, running over to hug Kennet. "Aida," he says excitedly, "Aida, it's him, the man who's really old!"

Kennet hugs the boy back, hard. "Really old, am I?"

The girl wears a pale, uneasy smile. The tip of her nose is bright red with the cold. "Benjamin?" she asks. "Have you found him?"

"No, not yet," Kennet replies, as Nicky laughs and continues to hug and jump around him.

"Aida," shouts Nicky, "he's so old they took his gun away!"

Kennet sits down on the bench next to Aida. They are surrounded by dense, dark groves of bare trees.

"I came to tell you that Wailord has been taken into care."

Aida turns to look at him, her expression sceptical.

"The others have been identified," he tells her. "There were five of them, right? Five Pokémon characters? Birk Jansson, the kid who was Wailord, has admitted everything, but he had nothing to do with Benjamin's disappearance."

Nicky has stopped dead on hearing Kennet's words and is staring open-mouthed at him. "You've beaten Wailord?" he says.

"Yes," says Kennet. "He's finished."

Nicky starts dancing around on the path again. His huge body steams with warmth in the cold air. Suddenly he stops and looks at Kennet. "You're the strongest Pokémon, you're Pikachu! You're Pikachu!"

He hugs Kennet happily and Aida laughs, her face full of surprise.

"But where's Benjamin?" she asks.

"We don't know, Aida. They might have done a lot of stupid things, but they didn't take Benjamin."

"Who else could it be?"

"I don't know." Kennet gets out the photo Aida sent to Benjamin. "Aida, tell me the truth about this picture," he says, in a kind but firm tone.

The colour leaves her face and she shakes her head. "I promised," she says quietly.

"Promises don't count when it's a matter of life and death."

But she clamps her lips together and turns away.

Nicky comes over and looks at the picture. "That's the picture his mum gave him," he says cheerfully.

"Nicky!" Aida snaps.

"Well, it is," Nicky says indignantly.

"Why can't you just keep quiet?" says Aida.

Kennet waves a hand. "Hush. Did Simone give Benjamin this photo? What do you mean, Nicky?"

But Nicky is looking anxiously at Aida, as if waiting for permission to answer. She shakes her head. Kennet's skull is aching from the impact of the accident, a pulsing, persistent throbbing.

"Answer me, Aida," he says, struggling to remain calm. "I promise you it's wrong to keep quiet in this situation."

"But the picture has nothing to do with anything," she says unhappily. "I promised Benjamin not to tell a single soul, whatever happened."

"Just tell me about this photograph!"

Kennet hears his own voice echo loudly between the buildings. Aida stubbornly compresses her lips even more tightly. Kennet studies her and forces himself to calm down. His voice sounds unsteady as he begins again.

"Aida, please listen carefully. Without his medicine, Benjamin is going to die if we don't find him. He's my only grandchild. I can't let a single clue go without investigating it."

There is total silence for a moment. Then Aida says resignedly, with tears in her voice, "Nicky's already told you." She swallows hard before going on. "His mother gave him that photo."

"What do you mean?" Kennet looks at Nicky, who nods eagerly.

"Not Simone," says Aida. "His real mother."

Kennet feels a wave of nausea sweep over him. All of a sudden his whole chest is gripped by pain; he tries to take a few deep breaths and hears his own heart pounding heavily. Not now, he thinks. You can't die just yet. He just has time to think he's having a heart attack when the pain abruptly subsides.

"His real mother?"

"Yes."

Aida gets a pack of cigarettes out of her rucksack, but before she has time to light up Kennet gently takes them from her.

"You're not allowed to smoke," he says.

"Why not?"

"You're under eighteen."

She shrugs. "Whatever."

"Fine," says Kennet, feeling as if his mind is working very slowly for some incomprehensible reason.

He fights his way into his memory, searching for facts relating to Benjamin's birth. The images flicker through his mind: Simone's face, swollen with weeping after the miscarriage, and then that midsummer when she was wearing a huge flowery tent of a dress, heavily pregnant, glowing. In the maternity ward, she showed him the baby: "Here's our little man," she said with a smile, her lips trembling. "We're going to call him Benjamin, Son of the Right Hand."

Kennet rubs his eyes hard and scratches his head beneath the bandage. "So what's the name of his . . . his real mother?"

Aida gazes out across the lake. "I don't know," she replies in a monotone. "I don't, honestly. But she told Benjamin his real name. She always called him Kasper. She was nice. She used to wait for him after school, she helped him with his homework, and I think she gave him money. I think she was really sad because she'd been forced to give him up."

Kennet holds up the photo. "And this? What's this?"

Aida glances at the printout. "That's the family grave, the grave belonging to Benjamin's real family. His relatives are buried there."

85

The few hours of daylight are already over, and darkness has settled upon the city. Advent stars glow in almost every window. A heavy aroma of grapes rises from the brandy glass on the low table in the living room. Simone is sitting in the middle of the floor, looking at some sketches. After she'd got home, she'd peeled off her wet clothes, wrapped herself in a blanket, and had instantly fallen asleep on the couch, waking up only when Kennet phoned. Then Sim Shulman had arrived.

Now, in her underwear, she places the sketches in a row: four lined sheets outlining an installation he is planning for the art gallery in Tensta.

Shulman is talking to the director of the gallery on his mobile. He paces the room as he talks. The parquet flooring that creaks beneath his feet is suddenly silent. Simone notices he has positioned himself so that he can see between her thighs. She can feel it. She gathers up the sketches, picks up her glass, and takes a sip, ignoring Shulman. She opens her thighs slightly and imagines his burning gaze boring its way in. He is shutting down the conversation now, anxious to end it. Simone lies on her back and closes her eyes. She waits, feeling the heat below, the surge of blood, the slow wetness. She needs to feel something, *anything*, to muffle the thoughts in her head, to mute the panic. Shulman has stopped speaking; he moves closer. She keeps her eyes shut, opens her legs a little more. She hears the sound of him unzipping his trousers. Suddenly she feels his hands on her hips. He rolls her onto her stomach, pulls her roughly to her knees, yanks her panties down around her thighs, and pushes into her from behind. She isn't really ready. She can see her fingers splayed on the oak floor. The nails, the veins on the back of her hand. She has to brace herself to avoid falling forwards as he thrusts into her, hard and alone. The heavy smell of the grappa is making her feel ill. She wants to ask Shulman to stop, to do it a different way, to start again in the bedroom, properly. He sighs heavily and ejaculates into her, pulls out, and goes into the bathroom. She hitches up her underwear and remains lying on the floor.

She doesn't get up until Shulman has had his shower and emerges from the bathroom with a towel wound around his hips. Her knees ache. She forces a smile as she walks past him, locking the bathroom door behind her. Her vagina feels raw and sore as she gets into the shower. A strange feeling of powerlessness threatens to overwhelm her, extinguishing her thoughts, her hopes, her happiness, even as the hot water soaks her hair, pouring down over her neck, her shoulders, and her back. She soaps herself and washes her body meticulously, then spends a long time with her face upturned beneath the gentle flow of the water.

Through the rushing sound in her ears she hears a series of thuds, and realizes Shulman is pounding on the bathroom door.

"Simone," he shouts. "Your phone's ringing."

"What?"

"Your phone."

"So answer it," she says, turning off the water.

"There's someone at the door too," he calls.

"God. I'm coming."

She steps out of the shower, catching her obscured image in the steamy mirror, a grey ghost without features. She takes a fresh towel from the shelf and dries herself, kicking her abandoned underclothes aside on the wet floor. All she can hear is a strange humming noise coming from the bathroom extractor fan.

"Sim? Who was it?"

No answer. Simone is about to yell at him, then suddenly can't. She doesn't know why, but her senses have gone on alert, have tensed up, which is why she so carefully, almost soundlessly, unlocks the bathroom door and peers out. A terrifying silence emanates from the apartment. She knows now something is wrong. She wonders if Shulman has gone home, but she dares not call out.

86

Simone hears a whispered conversation. From the kitchen, maybe. But who would Sim be talking to? She tries to brush aside her fear, but the floor creaks, and through the narrow opening Simone sees someone walk past the bathroom—and it isn't Shulman. It's a much smaller person, a woman in a bulky tracksuit. The woman comes back from the hall, and Simone doesn't have time to move away from the door. Their eyes meet in the tiny gap; the woman stiffens, and her eyes widen in fear. She quickly shakes her head at Simone and continues along the hallway, into the kitchen.

For a moment Simone stands there, processing this new information, then her gaze falls upon the bloody footprints the intruder's trainers have left on the floor. Abruptly her confusion is overridden by panic-stricken terror. She has to get out of the apartment, just get out. She opens the bathroom door and sneaks out into the passage, heading for the hall. She tries to move silently, but she can hear the sound of her own breathing and the floor creaking beneath her weight. Someone is muttering and rummaging around in the cutlery drawers in the kitchen, and something is crumpled on the floor ahead of her.

It takes a few more moments for her to understand what she is looking at. It's Shulman, on his back in front of the door. Blood is pumping from a wound in his throat, spurting wearily with the rhythm of his fading pulse. A dark red pool is spreading across the entire floor. Sim stares up at the ceiling, his eyelids trembling. His mouth is open and slack. Beside his hand, among the shoes on the doormat, lies her phone. She needs to grab it, run out of the apartment, and call the police and an ambulance. Suddenly she hears footsteps behind her in the hall. The young woman is returning. Her whole body is shaking and she raises a finger to her lips.

"We can't get out that way, the door is locked with a key," she whispers to Simone.

"Who—"

"My little brother."

"But why—"

"He thinks he killed the hypnotist. He didn't see, he thinks—"

Something crashes to the floor in the kitchen.

"Evelyn? What are you doing?" shouts Josef Ek. "Get back in here!"

"Hide," whispers the woman.

"Where are the keys?"

"He's got them in the kitchen," she says, hurrying back to her brother.

Simone creeps along the hall and into Benjamin's room. She is panting. She tries to close her mouth but can't get enough air. The floor creaks, but Josef Ek is talking loudly in the kitchen the whole time and doesn't appear to hear. She spies Benjamin's computer and hurries to turn it on, and just as she slips back into the bathroom she hears the welcome melody from the operating system.

Footsteps move rapidly up the hall. With her heart pounding, she waits a few seconds and then eases out of the bathroom and into the kitchen. The floor is covered with cutlery and bloody footprints. She can hear the two siblings moving around in Benjamin's room. Josef Ek swears and hurls things onto the floor.

"Look under the bed!" shouts Evelyn in a frightened voice.

There is a thud, the box containing Benjamin's Manga books is dragged out, and Josef hisses that there is no one there. "Help me," he says. He kicks the box as hard as he can.

"Try the closet," Evelyn suggests quickly.

He throws open the door and begins yanking clothes off hangers, throwing them behind him.

"What the fuck is this?" Josef screams.

"Hang on, Josef. He might be in the other closet." A glass shatters and heavy footsteps thump along the corridor.

Simone steps over Shulman's body. The tips of his fingers still tremble slightly. She slides the long key into the deadlock. Her hand is shaking violently.

"Josef," Evelyn shouts desperately. "Look in the bedroom! I think he's in the bedroom!"

As Simone turns the key, Josef Ek rushes into the hall and stares at her, an angry growl rumbling in his throat. Simone fumbles with the latch, her hand slips, but she manages to turn it. Josef has a carving knife in his hand. He hesitates for a moment, then moves rapidly towards her. Simone's hands are shaking so much she can't push the handle down. Evelyn rushes into the hall and hurls herself at Josef's legs, trying to restrain him, screaming for him to wait. Without looking back, he reaches behind him and slashes at her with the knife, and Evelyn loses her grip. Simone manages to get the door open, and as she stumbles out into the stairwell the bath towel slips off. Josef stops for a moment and stares at her naked body. Behind him Simone sees Evelyn rub her hand in the blood around Shulman's body, smearing it over her face and throat and sinking to the floor.

"Josef, I'm bleeding," she screams. "Darling . . . you cut me!"

She coughs and falls silent, lying on her back.

"Evelyn?" he says in a terrified voice.

He goes back into the hall, and as he bends over his sister, Simone suddenly sees the knife in Evelyn's hand. It shoots straight up as if from some kind of primitive trap and penetrates the space between two of Josef's ribs with considerable force. His body goes completely slack. His head tilts to one side, he slumps to the floor, and he is motionless.

87

Kennet passes two female police officers in the corridor at Danderyd Hospital, whispering intently to each other. In the room behind them he can see a young girl sitting on a chair staring blankly into space, a blanket draped around her shoulders. Her face and hair are spattered with blood. She is sitting with her feet slightly turned inwards, unselfconscious and childlike. He assumes this is Evelyn Ek, sister of serial killer Josef Ek. As if she hears him say her name in his mind, she looks up and gazes straight at him. There is such a strange expression in her eyes—a mixture of pain and shock, triumph and regret—that it looks almost obscene. Kennet instinctively turns away, feeling that he has caught sight of something private, something taboo. He shudders. You should be glad you're retired, glad you don't have to be the one who goes into that room, pulls out a chair, and sits down to question Evelyn Ek. Nobody should have to carry through life the things she has to tell about growing up with Josef Ek, he thinks.

A uniformed officer with a grey rectangular face is standing guard outside the closed door of Simone's room. Kennet recognizes him from his years of service but at first can't quite recall his name.

"Kennet," the man says. "Everything all right?"

"No."

"So I've heard."

415

Suddenly Kennet remembers his name, Reine, and the fact that his wife died unexpectedly just after they had their first child.

"Reine," says Kennet. "Do you know how Josef got in to see his sister?"

"It seems as if she just let him in."

"Voluntarily?"

"Not exactly."

Reine explains that Evelyn said she'd woken up in the middle of the night and gone to the front door to look through the peephole. She could see the police officer on duty sleeping on the stairs. At the change-over earlier, she'd heard him tell his colleague that he had young children at home. Evelyn didn't want to wake him, so she went and sat on the sofa, where once again she looked through the pictures in the photo album Josef had put in her box, incomprehensible glimpses of a life that had disappeared long ago. She put the album back in the box, and wondered whether it might be possible for her to change her name and move abroad. When she'd gone to the window and peeped through the venetian blind, she thought she could see someone standing on the pavement down below. She immediately pulled back, waited awhile, and peeked again. It was snowing heavily, and the street was deserted. The streetlamp suspended between the buildings was swinging wildly in the strong wind. Suddenly she got goose bumps and crept over to the front door, put her ear to the wood, and listened. She had the feeling someone was standing just outside. Josef had a particular smell about him, a smell of rage, of burning chemicals. Evelyn thought she could smell him. Perhaps she was imagining things, but she'd remained standing by the door, too afraid to look through the peephole.

After a while she leaned forward and whispered, "Josef?"

There hadn't been a sound from outside. She was just about to go back into the apartment when she heard him whisper from the other side of the door. "Open up."

She tried not to sob as she replied, "Yes."

"Did you think you could get away?"

"No," she whispered.

"Do what I tell you."

"I can't."

"Look through the peephole," he said.

"I don't want to."

"Just do it."

Trembling, she'd leaned toward the door. Through the wide angle of the lens she could see the stairwell. The police officer who had fallen asleep was still sitting on the stairs, but now a dark pool of blood was spreading beneath him on the landing. She could see that he was still breathing. She could also see Josef hiding at the outer edge of the circular field of vision provided by the lens. He pressed himself against the wall, but then leaped up and slammed his hand against the hole. Evelyn recoiled and tripped over her shoes in the hall.

"Open the door," he said. "Otherwise I'll kill the cop. Then I'll ring the neighbours' doorbells and kill them, too. I'll start with this one, right next door."

Evelyn had no strength left. She resigned herself to the situation; she would never escape Josef. She unlocked the door and let her brother in. Her only thought was that she would rather die than let him kill anyone else.

"Her police guard is going to make it," Reine says. "She saved him by doing as her brother said." He explains the sequence of events as best as he can, based on what he's been told. Josef was hiding in the house when the police returned to retrieve Evelyn's personal belongings, and he heard them speak about where to drop off the box. As for why Evelyn opened the door, Reine assumes it was because she wanted to help the wounded policeman and prevent further bloodshed.

Kennet shakes his head. "What's the matter with people?" he mutters.

"She saved your daughter's life," Reine says.

Kennet taps gently on the door of Simone's room, then pushes it open a little way. It's dark inside. On a couch he can just make out something that could be his daughter.

"Sixan," he says quietly.

"I'm here, Dad."

"Do you want it this dark? Shall I put the light on?"

"I can't cope, Dad," she whispers. "I just can't cope."

Kennet sits down on the couch and puts his arms around his daughter. She starts crying, convulsive, agonized sobs.

"Once," he whispers, rubbing her back, "when I was passing your nursery school in my patrol car, I saw you in the playground. You were standing with your face pressed to the fence, just crying: snot pouring from your nose, your face streaked and filthy, and the staff were doing nothing to console you. They were just standing there, chatting, totally indifferent."

"What did you do?" This is a story Simone has heard many times, but she always asks.

"I stopped the car and went over to you." He smiles to himself in the darkness. "You stopped crying right away, took my hand, and came with me." He pauses. "Imagine if I could take you by the hand and take you home now."

She nods, rests her head on his shoulder, and asks, "Have you heard anything about Sim?"

He strokes her cheek and wonders whether he should tell her the truth or not. The doctor has brusquely explained that Shulman was in a coma; he'd lost a lot of blood and it was unlikely he'd pull through.

"They don't really know yet," he says cautiously. "But—" He sighs. "It doesn't look good, darling."

She sobs. "I can't cope, I can't cope."

"There, there . . . I've called Erik. He's on his way."

"Thanks, Dad."

He pats her again.

"I really can't cope any more," Simone whispers.

"Don't cry, little one."

She cries even harder. At that moment the door opens and Erik switches on the light. He walks straight over, sits down on the other side of Simone, and says, "Thank God you're safe."

She presses her face into his chest. "Erik," she says, half smothered in his overcoat.

He strokes her head. He looks very tired, but his eyes are clear and sharp. She thinks he smells of home; he smells of family.

"Erik," Kennet says. "I have to tell you something very important. You too, Simone. I spoke to Aida not long ago."

"Did she tell you anything?" asks Simone.

"I wanted to let them know we'd caught Wailord and the others," says Kennet. "I didn't want them to be afraid any longer."

Erik looks at him with curiosity.

"It's a long story. I'll tell you all about it when we have time, but—"

Kennet takes a deep breath and says in a tired, harsh voice, "Someone contacted Benjamin a few days before he disappeared. Said she was his real mother, his biological mother."

Simone pulls away from Erik and stares at Kennet. She wipes her nose with the back of her hand and asks, in a voice that is high and broken from weeping, "His *real* mother?"

Kennet nods. "Aida said this woman gave Benjamin money and helped him with his homework."

"This doesn't make any sense," whispers Simone.

"She even gave him a different name."

Erik looks at Simone, then at Kennet, and asks him to continue.

"According to Aida, this woman claimed that his real name was Kasper."

Simone sees Erik's face stiffen, and the sudden rush of fear makes her feel wide awake. "What is it, Erik?"

"Kasper?" Erik asks. "She called him Kasper?"

"Yes," Kennet confirms. "Aida didn't want to say anything at first. She'd promised Benjamin that—"

He stops dead. Erik's face has lost all its colour. He stands up, takes a couple of steps backwards, bumps into an armchair, and rushes from the room.

88

Erik runs downstairs to the hospital lobby, pushes through a group of teenagers bearing flowers and Mylar balloons, dashes across the dirty floor past an old man in a wheelchair, and out through the main exit. Dodging traffic, he runs across the street and vaults the low shrubbery planted along the perimeter of the visitors' car park. The keys are already in his hand as he races along the line of grubby vehicles towards his car. He starts the engine and reverses out so violently that the side of his car scrapes the bumper of the car next to him.

His breathing is still uneven as he turns west. He drives as fast as he can, but as he approaches Edsberg School, a line of children appears, crossing the street. While he waits he takes out his mobile and calls Joona.

"It's Lydia Everson," he almost screams.

"Who?"

"Lydia has taken Benjamin!" he continues. "I told you about her. She's the one who made the complaint against me."

"We'll check her out," says Joona.

"I'm on my way."

"Give me an address."

"It's a house on Tennisvägen in Rotebro. I can't remember the number, but it's a red house, quite big."

420

"Wait for me somewhere in—"

"I'm going straight there."

"Don't rush in."

"Benjamin will die if he doesn't get his medication."

"Wait for me."

Erik ends the call, speeding up as he follows the railway line beside the long narrow lake. Recklessly, he overtakes another car by the yeast factory, passing on the right with inches to spare. As he turns off by the Co-op Forum supermarket, he feels his pulse pounding in his temples.

Not much has changed here. The pizzeria has been replaced by a sushi bar, and all the back gardens sport trampolines (they're all the rage). He parks next to the same fir hedge as ten years ago, when he and the social worker were about to visit Lydia.

As he looks at the house from inside the car, he can almost feel his presence there ten years earlier. He remembers there were no signs of a child, no toys in the garden, nothing to indicate that Lydia was a mother. On the other hand, they hadn't really looked around the house. They had only gone down the steps to the cellar and back up again, and then Lydia had rushed after him with the knife in her hand. He remembers how she looked when she drew the blade across her throat without taking her eyes off him.

Leaving the key in the ignition, he abandons the car without even closing the door behind him and rushes up the slope. He opens the gate and goes into the garden. Patches of damp snow lie amid the tall yellow grass. Icicles sparkle beneath the broken guttering. The same hanging baskets full of dead plants swing by the door.

He tries the door, but it is locked. He looks under the doormat; a few wood-lice scuttle away from the wet rectangle on the concrete steps. No key. He gropes under the wooden hand-rail: no key there, either. He walks around to the back of the house, picks up an edging stone from the flower bed, and hurls it at the patio door. The outer pane shatters, and the stone thuds back onto the grass. He picks it up and throws it again, harder this time, knocking out the entire window. He unlocks the door and walks into a bedroom where the walls are covered with pictures of angels and the Indian guru Sai Baba.

"Benjamin," he yells. "Benjamin!"

89

Erik calls to his son in spite of the fact that he can see the place is deserted; everything is dark and still in the house, with a closed-in smell of dust and old fabric. He moves quickly into the hall, opens the door leading down to the cellar, and is met by a powerful stench, a heavy smell of ash, charred wood, and burnt rubber. He races down the steps, trips, bangs into the wall with his shoulder, and regains his balance. The lights are not working, but enough sunlight comes from a high window to see that there's been a fire down here. Cinders crunch beneath his feet. Much of the room is black with soot, but some items of furniture appear to be intact. The table with its tiled surface is just slightly sooty, while the scented candles on the tray have melted, blending into a multicoloured pool of solid wax. Erik finds his way to the door leading into the other room. It hangs loosely from its hinges, and the inside of the door is completely blackened.

"Benjamin," he says, his voice full of fear.

Ash whirls up in his face and he blinks, his eyes smarting. In the middle of the floor are the remains of what looks like a cage, big enough to hold a person.

"Erik," a voice calls from upstairs.

He stops and listens. The walls creak. Burnt fragments of ceiling tiles drop to the floor. He moves slowly toward the stairs. In the distance he can hear a dog barking.

"Erik!"

It's Joona's voice. He's inside the house. Erik goes up the stairs. Joona looks at him, his expression anxious.

"What happened?"

"There's been a fire in the cellar," Erik replies.

"Nothing else?"

Erik gestures vaguely toward the stairs. "The remains of a cage."

"I brought a dog with me."

Joona moves quickly along the hall and opens the front door. He waves in the uniformed dog handler, a woman whose dark hair is braided thickly. The black Labrador, its coat groomed to a glossy sheen, walks obediently to heel. The handler nods to Erik, then crouches down in front of the dog and talks to him. The animal moves eagerly through the house, sniffing constantly, breathing quickly, seeking all the time. The dog's stomach moves as he pants, systematically searching each room. Erik suddenly feels as if he's going to throw up and leaves the house. Two police officers are chatting beside a police minibus. He goes through the gate, heads towards his car, then stops and takes out the little box with the parrot and the native. He stands there with it in his hands; then he goes over to a sewer grate and tips the contents down between the bars. His forehead covered in a cold sweat, he moistens his lips as if he is about to say something after a long silence, but then he drops the box too and hears the splash as it hits the surface of the water.

When he returns to the garden, Joona is standing outside the house. He meets Erik's gaze, and shakes his head. Erik goes inside. The dog handler is on her knees, patting the Labrador and scratching the loose skin behind his ears.

"Have you been down to the basement?" asks Erik.

"Of course," she replies, without looking at him.

"Into the inner room?"

"Yes."

"Perhaps all the ash is preventing the dog from picking up the scent."

"Rocky can find a corpse underwater, at a depth of two hundred feet," she says.

"And what about the living?"

"If there was anything here, Rocky would have found it."

"But you haven't been outside yet," says Joona, who has followed Erik inside.

"I didn't know we were supposed to," says the dog handler.

"Yes," Joona answers tersely.

She shrugs her shoulders and gets to her feet.

"Come on then," she says to the Labrador in a deep, thick voice. "Shall we go outside and have a look? Shall we go and have a look?"

Erik goes with them. The black dog moves rapidly back and forth across the overgrown lawn, sniffing around the rain barrel, where an opaque layer of ice has formed on the surface, searching among the old fruit trees. The sky is dark and cloudy. Erik notices that the neighbour has switched on Christmas lights strung in a tree. The air is bitterly cold. Joona remains close to the handler and the dog, pointing in a particular direction from time to time. Erik follows them around the back of the house. Suddenly he recognizes the mound at the far end of the garden. That's the place in the picture, he thinks. The photograph Aida sent to Benjamin before he disappeared. Erik is breathing heavily. The dog sniffs around the compost, moves over to the mound and sniffs it, pants, trots all the way around it, sniffs among the low bushes and at the back of the brown fence, comes back, trots around a leaf basket, and goes over to a small herb garden. Wooden labels with seed packets attached to them show what has been planted in the various rows. The black Labrador whines uneasily and then lies down in the middle of the little plot. He flattens himself completely on the wet, freshly dug earth. The dog's body is shaking with excitement, and the handler's expression is one of deep sadness as she praises him. Joona turns on his heel, runs back, and stands in front of Erik, refusing to let him go over to the plot. Erik has no idea what he screams, what he tries to do, but Joona moves him away from the spot and out of the garden.

"I have to know," says Erik, his voice trembling.

Joona nods. "The dog has indicated that there's a human corpse in the ground."

Erik feels his entire body give way. He sinks down onto the pavement. When he sees the police officers climb out of the bus carrying spades, he closes his eyes.

Erik Maria Bark sits alone in Joona Linna's car, looking through the windscreen. Black, sprawling branches against a dark winter sky. His mouth is dry, his head aches, and his face and scalp are itchy. He whispers something to himself, gets out of the car, climbs over the police tape cordoning off the area, and walks around the house through the tall, frosty grass. Joona is watching the uniformed officers with the shovels. They work in dogged silence, their movements almost mechanical. The whole of the small plot has been dug up. It is now only a large rectangular hole. Beside it is a plastic sheet on which muddy scraps of clothing and fragments of bone have been placed. The sound of the shovels continues, metal strikes rock, the digging stops, and the officers straighten up. Erik slowly moves closer, his footsteps heavy and reluctant. Joona turns and smiles with the whole of his tired face.

"What is it?" Erik whispers.

Joona comes to meet him, looks Erik straight in the eye, and says, "It isn't Benjamin."

"It isn't?"

"The body has been here for at least ten years."

Erik thinks for a moment. "Is it a child?"

Joona's face darkens. "Five years old, perhaps," he says.

"So Lydia had a son after all," says Erik with a shudder.

90

saturday, december 19: morning

Wet, heavy snow is falling, and a dog scurries back and forth in a rest area next door to police headquarters, barking excitedly at the snow, leaping happily among the flakes, snapping at the air and shaking itself. The sight of the animal makes Erik's heart contract. He has forgotten what it's like to simply exist. He's forgotten what it's like not to think constantly about a life without Benjamin.

He feels sick and his hands are shaking. He hasn't taken a single pill for almost twenty-four hours, and he didn't sleep at all last night.

As he walks towards the main entrance, he thinks about the old decorative woven patterns Simone had once showed him at an exhibition of women's craft. They had been like images of the sky on days like this: cloudy, dense, grey, and fluffy.

Simone waits in the corridor outside the interview room. When she catches sight of Erik, she comes to meet him and takes his hands. For some reason he is grateful for the gesture. She looks pale and composed.

"You didn't have to come," she whispers.

"Kennet said you wanted me here."

She nods almost imperceptibly. "I'm just so . . ." She pauses and clears her throat. "I've been so angry with you," she says calmly. Her eyes are moist, red-rimmed.

"I know, Simone."

"At least you've got your pills," she says acidly. She turns away and stares out the window. Erik looks at her slender figure, her arms hugging her upper body. A cold draft leaks through the air vents under the window.

The door of the interview room opens, and a stocky woman in uniform calls to them. "You can come in now." She smiles gently; her lips are glossy pink. "My name is Anja Larsson," she says to Erik and Simone. "I'll be taking your statement." The woman holds out a well-manicured hand. Her nails are long, painted red with sparkly tips. "I thought it was sort of Christmassy," she says cheerfully.

"Nice," Simone says distractedly.

Joona Linna is already sitting in the room. His jacket is on the back of the chair. His blond hair is tousled and looks unwashed. He hasn't shaved. As they sit down opposite him, he gives Erik a serious, thought-ful look.

Simone clears her throat quietly and takes a sip from her glass of water. When she puts it down, she brushes against Erik's hand. Their eyes meet, and her lips form a silent *sorry*.

Anja Larsson places the digital tape recorder on the table between them, presses RECORD, checks that the red light is showing, and then briefly states the time and date and lists those present in the room. Then she pauses, tilts her head to one side, and says in a bright, friendly voice, "OK, Simone, we'd like to hear what happened in your apartment the evening before last."

Simone nods, looks at Erik, and lowers her eyes.

"I . . . I was at home—" She stops.

"Were you alone?" asks Anja Larsson.

Simone shakes her head. "Sim Shulman was with me," she says, her tone neutral.

Joona makes a note on his pad.

"Can you tell us how you think Josef and Evelyn Ek got into the apartment?" asks Anja Larsson.

"I don't really know, because I was in the shower," Simone says slowly, and for a moment her face flushes bright red. The colour disap-pears almost immediately but leaves a warm glow on her cheeks.

"I was in the shower and Sim shouted to me that there was someone at the door . . . No, wait, he shouted that my phone was ringing."

Anja Larsson repeats. "You were in the shower and you heard Sim Shulman shout that your phone was ringing."

"Yes," Simone whispers. "I told him to answer it."

"Who was it?"

"I don't know."

"But he did answer it?"

"I think so, I'm almost sure he did."

"What time was that?" Joona suddenly asks.

Simone jumps as if she hadn't noticed him up to now. "I don't know," she says apologetically, turning to face him.

He doesn't smile, he simply insists. "Roughly."

Simone shrugs her shoulders and says hesitantly, "Five."

"Not four?" asks Joona.

"What do you mean?"

"I just want to know," he replies.

"But you already know this," Simone says to Anja.

"Five, then," says Joona, writing down the time.

"What were you doing before you took a shower?" asks Anja. "It's easier to remember times if you go through the whole day."

Simone shakes her head. She looks very tired, almost listless. She isn't looking at Erik. He is sitting quietly beside her, his heart pounding.

"I didn't know," he says suddenly, then stops. She glances at him. He tries again. "I didn't know you and Shulman were—"

She nods. "That's how it was."

He looks at her, at the woman police officer, and at Joona. "Sorry to interrupt," he stammers.

Anja turns to Simone again, her tone indulgent. "Let's go on. Sim Shulman shouted that your phone was ringing."

"He went into the hall and . . ." Simone pauses, then corrects herself once again. "No, that's not what happened. I heard Sim say, 'There's someone at the door, too,' or something along those lines. I finished my shower, dried myself, and asked him who it was. But he didn't answer. I opened the door carefully and saw—"

"Why carefully?" asks Joona.

"What?"

"Why did you open the door carefully, and not just the way you would normally open it?"

"I don't know. When he didn't answer, I felt . . . there was something in the air, it felt threatening . . . I can't explain it."

"Had you heard anything?"

"I don't think so." Simone stares straight ahead.

Anja encourages her. "Go on."

"I saw a girl through the gap in the door. There was a girl standing in the hallway, she was looking at me, she seemed scared, and she signalled to me to hide." Simone frowns. "I went into the hall and there was Sim, lying on the floor . . . There was so much blood, and more coming all the time; his eyelids were trembling, and he was trying to move his hands . . ."

Simone's voice thickens, and Erik realizes she is trying hard not to cry. He would like to comfort his wife, support her, take her hand or put his arm around her. But he doesn't know if she would get annoyed or push him away if he tried.

"Shall we take a break?" Anja asks gently.

"I . . . I . . ." Simone breaks off and lifts the glass of water to her lips, her hands shaking violently. She swallows hard and rubs her hand over her eyes. "The front door was locked." She goes on, her voice steadier now. "The girl said he had the key in the kitchen, so I sneaked into Benjamin's room and turned on the computer."

"Why did you do that?" asks Anja.

"I . . . the computer plays a little tune when it starts up. I wanted him to think I was in there. I wanted him to hear the computer and go in so I could get the key."

"Him? Who are you talking about?"

"Josef."

"Josef Ek?"

"Yes."

"How did you know it was him?"

"I didn't, at the time."

"I understand," says Anja. "Go on."

"I turned on the computer and then hid in the bathroom until I heard them go into Benjamin's room. Then I snuck into the kitchen and got the key. The girl kept trying to persuade Josef to look in different places, to delay him. I could hear them, but I think I bumped into something in the hall, because suddenly Josef came after me. The girl tried to stop him, she threw her arms around his legs and—"

She swallows hard.

"I don't know, he managed to shake her off. And then the girl pretended she'd been cut; she smeared herself with Sim's blood and lay down and played dead."

Simone goes quiet for a moment; it sounds as if she is having difficulty breathing.

Anja prompts her again. "Go on, Simone."

Simone nods. "Josef saw her and went back, and when he bent down she stabbed him in the side with the knife."

"Did you see who stabbed Sim Shulman?"

"It was Josef."

"Did you see it happen?"

"No."

The room is silent.

"Evelyn Ek saved my life," Simone whispers.

"Is there anything you'd like to add?"

"No."

"In that case, thank you for your cooperation. This interview is now concluded." And Anja reaches out a sparkling finger to stop the recording.

"Wait," says Joona, holding up a hand. "Who called you?"

Simone looks at him in confusion. It's as if she had forgotten about him already.

"On your mobile. Who was it who called?"

"I don't know." She shakes her head. "I don't even know where my phone went."

"No problem," Joona says calmly. "We'll find it."

Anja Larsson waits for a moment, looks at them inquiringly, then switches off the tape recorder.

Without looking at anyone, Simone stands up and walks slowly out of the room. Erik nods briefly at Joona and then follows her.

"Wait," he says.

She stops and turns around.

"Wait. I just want to . . ."

He pauses, sees her naked, vulnerable face, the pale, sandy freckles, the wide mouth, and the light green eyes. Without a word they hug each other, weary and sad.

"It's all right," he says. "It's all right."

He kisses her hair, her curly, strawberry-blonde hair.

"I don't know anything any more," she whispers.

"I can find out if they have a room where you can rest."

She slowly pulls away from him and shakes her head. "I'm going to look for my phone," she says earnestly. "I have to know who was calling when Shulman answered."

Joona comes out of the interview room with his jacket draped over one shoulder.

"Is Simone's phone here?" Erik asks.

Joona nods towards Anja Larsson, who is heading for the lifts farther down the hall.

"Anja should know that," he replies.

Erik is just about to hurry after her when Joona holds up his hand to stop him. He takes out his own phone and makes a call.

They see Anja stop and answer hers.

"One last thing, my treasure," says Joona. She turns around with a sullen expression and waits as they walk toward her. "Have you got the list of items we sent to the lab?"

"It's not finished. You'll have to go down and check."

They walk with her to the lift, which creaks as they travel downwards. Anja gets off at the second floor and waves to them as the doors close.

On the ground floor, Joona, Erik, and Simone head quickly down the corridor to the forensic department. The department is almost shockingly bright and antiseptically clean. Most of the staff wear white lab coats. Joona shakes hands with a very fat man who introduces himself as Erixon and takes them to another room, where a number of objects are spread out on a steel-topped table. Erik recognizes them. Two kitchen knives with black stains on them, lying in separate metal bowls. He sees a familiar towel, the hall rug, several pairs of shoes, and Simone's mobile in a plastic pocket. Joona points at the phone.

"We'd like to take a look at this," he says. "Have you finished with it?"

The fat man goes over to the list that is pinned up next to the items.

He glances at the paper and says hesitantly, "I think so . . . yes, we've finished with the outside of it."

Joona takes the phone out, wipes it on a paper towel, and casually hands it to Simone. She clicks through the list of calls, concentrating hard, mumbles something to herself, places her hand over her mouth, and suppresses a cry when she looks at the display.

"It's . . . it's Benjamin," she stammers. "The last call came from Benjamin."

They crowd around the phone. Benjamin's name flashes a couple of times before the battery gives out.

"Did Shulman speak to Benjamin?" Erik asks, raising his voice.

"I don't know," she replies feebly.

"But he answered, didn't he? I just want to clarify that."

"I was in the shower. I think he answered the phone before he—"

"Surely you can see whether it was a missed bloody call or not."

"It wasn't a missed call," she interrupts. "But I don't know if Sim had time to hear or say anything before he opened the door to Josef."

"I don't mean to sound angry," says Erik, struggling to remain calm, "but we have to know if Benjamin said anything."

Simone turns to Joona. "Aren't all mobile phone calls stored these days?"

"It could take weeks to get hold of that particular one," he replies.

Erik places a hand on Simone's arm. "We have to talk to Shulman."

"It's impossible; he's in a coma," she says, sounding upset. "I told you he was in a coma."

"Come with me," Erik says to Simone, and leaves the room.

91

Sitting beside Erik in the car, Simone glances at him from time to time. The road, a channel of brown and grey slush down the middle, rushes by, the cars ahead moving in endless flashing lines of traffic. The streetlamps flicker past monotonously. She sighs softly and looks around the car. Rubbish is strewn across the back seat and underfoot: empty water bottles, soft drink cans, a pizza box, newspapers, paper cups, empty crisp packets, discarded sweet wrappers.

Erik is driving smoothly toward Danderyd Hospital, where Sim Shulman lies in a coma, and he knows exactly what he's going to do when he gets there. He glances at Simone. She's lost weight and the corners of her mouth are turned down, her expression is anxious and unhappy.

Personally, Erik feels almost terrifyingly focused. After days of confusion, the events of the recent past are illuminated by a clear, cold light. He thinks he finally understands what has happened to him and his family.

"When we realized it couldn't be Josef who had taken Benjamin, Joona asked me to think back," he explains, and looks at her to make sure she's listening. "And I started searching the past for someone who wanted to take their revenge on me."

"And what did you find?" asks Simone.

From the corner of his eye he can see that she has turned to face him.

"I found the hypnosis group I left behind ten years ago. I hadn't

433

thought of them in a long time. That part of my life, my career, seemed to be over. But now, as I try to remember, it's as if the group never disappeared. They were just standing slightly to one side, waiting."

Simone nods. Erik keeps talking, trying to explain his theories regarding the hypnosis group, the tensions between individuals, his own balancing act, and the trust that had been shattered. "When I failed in everything, I promised never to hypnotize anyone again."

"I know, Erik."

"But then I broke my promise, because Joona persuaded me it was the only way to save Evelyn Ek."

"Do you think it's because of that, because you hypnotized Josef, that all this has happened to us?"

"I don't know, Simone. It's possible that it aroused a deeply buried and dormant hatred of me, one held in check only by my promise never to practise again. Do you remember Eva Blau?" he goes on. "She swung in and out of a psychotic state. You know she threatened me, swore she would destroy my life."

"I never understood why," Simone says quietly.

"She was afraid of someone. I thought it was paranoia, but now I'm almost certain she was being threatened by Lydia."

"Just because you're paranoid, it doesn't mean they're not out to get you," says Simone. She smiles briefly.

Erik pulls into the blue, sprawling complex of Danderyd Hospital. "It might even have been Lydia who cut Eva's face," he says, almost to himself.

Simone gives a start. "Cut her face?"

"I thought she'd done it herself. Classic self-mutilation," Erik says. "I thought she'd cut off the tip of her own nose in a desperate attempt to feel something else, to stop feeling whatever was really causing her pain—"

"Wait a minute." Simone bursts in. "Are you saying her nose had been cut off?"

"The tip of her nose."

"Erik, Dad and I found a boy with the tip of his nose cut off. Did Dad tell you? Someone had threatened the boy, frightened him and hurt him because he'd been hassling Benjamin."

"It's Lydia."

"Is she the one who's kidnapped Benjamin?"

"Yes."

"What does she want?"

Erik looks at her, his expression serious. "You already know some of this," he says. "Lydia admitted under hypnosis that she kept her son Kasper locked in a cage in the cellar and forced him to eat rotten food."

"Kasper?"

"When Kennet told me what Aida said, that this woman had told Benjamin his real name was Kasper, I knew it was Lydia."

"But she didn't really have any children."

"I'm getting to that. I went to her house in Rotebro and broke in, but the place was deserted."

He speeds along past the rows of parked cars but there are no spaces, so he heads back towards the entrance.

"There had been a fire in the basement," Erik goes on. "I assumed someone had started it deliberately, but the remains of a large cage were still there."

"But there was no cage," Simone says. "They said she had no children."

"Joona brought a dog in. He found the remains of a child buried in the garden. Ten years ago."

"Oh my God," Simone whispers.

"Yes."

"That was when—"

"I think she killed the child in the basement when she realized she'd been found out."

"So you were right all along."

"So it seems."

"Does she want to kill Benjamin?"

"I don't know. Presumably she thinks the whole thing was my fault. If I hadn't hypnotized her, she would have been able to keep the child."

Erik falls silent, thinking about Benjamin's voice when he called. How he had tried not to sound afraid, and how he had talked about the haunted house. He must have meant Lydia's haunted house. After all, that was where she had grown up, where she had carried out the abuse, and that was probably where she herself had been subjected to abuse. If she hadn't taken Benjamin to the haunted house, she could have taken him absolutely anywhere.

435

92

Erik leaves the car outside the main hospital entrance without bothering to lock it or buy a parking ticket. They hurry past the gloomy snow-filled fountain, past a few shivering smokers in robes, and dash inside and up in the lift to the ward where Sim Shulman is lying.

There's a heavy scent in the room from all the flowers. Vases filled with large fragrant bouquets stand on the windowsill. On the table is a pile of cards and letters from distraught friends and colleagues.

Erik looks at the man in the hospital bed, the sunken cheeks, the nose, the eyelids. The all-too-regular movement of Shulman's stomach follows the sucking rhythm of the respirator. He is in a permanent vegetative state, kept alive by the equipment in the room and unable to survive without it. A breathing tube has been inserted into his windpipe through an incision in his throat; he is being fed through a tube in his stomach.

"Simone, you need to speak to him when he comes round and—"

"He's not going to come round," she breaks in, her voice shrill. "He's in a coma, Erik, his brain has been damaged by the loss of blood, he's never going to come round, he's never going to speak again." She wipes the tears from her cheeks.

"We have to find out what Benjamin said—"

"Stop it!" she shouts, and begins to sob.

A nurse looks in, sees Erik with his arms around Simone's shaking body, and leaves them in peace.

"I'm going to give him an injection of Zolpidem," Erik whispers into her hair. "It's a powerful drug that can bring people out of a comatose state."

He can feel her shake her head. "What are you talking about?" she says, her words muffled by his jacket.

"It only works for a little while."

"I don't believe you," she says suspiciously.

"The sedative slows down the overactive processes in the brain that are causing the coma."

"He'll wake up? Are you serious?"

"He's never going to get better, Sixan, he's suffered severe brain damage, but with this injection he might wake up for a few seconds."

"What shall I do?"

"Sometimes patients who are given this drug can say a few words, sometimes they can only use their eyes."

"You're not allowed to do this, are you?"

"I have no intention of asking for permission, I'm just going to do it. But you have to talk to him when he comes around."

"Hurry up," she says.

Erik goes to get the equipment he needs. Simone stands by Shulman's bed and takes his hand. She looks at him. His face is calm, the dark, strong features smoothed out by relaxation. His mouth, usually so ironic, so sensual, is insignificant. Even the serious furrow between the black eyebrows has disappeared. She slowly caresses his forehead. She thinks she will continue to exhibit his work; a really good artist can never die.

Erik returns and without a word goes over to the bed and, with his back to the door, calmly pushes up the sleeve of Shulman's hospital gown. "Are you ready?" he asks.

"Yes," she replies. "I'm ready."

Erik takes the syringe, connects it to the intravenous catheter, and slowly injects a yellowish liquid. It gradually blends with the fluid in the drip, disappears down toward the needle in Shulman's arm, and enters his bloodstream. Erik pushes the syringe into his pocket, unbuttons his jacket, and transfers the electrodes from Shulman's chest to his own, takes the clamp from Shulman's finger and fastens it to his own, and carefully watches Shulman's face.

Absolutely nothing happens. Shulman's stomach continues to rise and fall regularly and mechanically with the help of the respirator.

"Should we leave?" Simone asks, after a while.

"Wait," Erik whispers.

His watch ticks slowly. On the windowsill, a petal drifts down from a flower, making a faint rustling sound as it reaches the floor. A few raindrops land on the windowpane. They can hear a woman laughing somewhere in a room far away.

A strange sighing is coming from inside Shulman's body, like a gentle breeze blowing through a half-open window.

Simone can feel the sweat from her armpits trickling down her body. She has a sense of claustrophobia, as if she is trapped in this situation. She wants to run out of the room, but she can't take her eyes off Shulman's throat. Perhaps she is imagining it, but suddenly she thinks that the artery in his neck is pulsing more quickly. Erik is breathing heavily and as he leans over Shulman, she can see that he seems nervous, biting his lower lip and looking at his watch again. The respirator continues its steady metallic sighing. Someone walks past the door. The wheels of a trolley squeak and then the room is quiet once again. The only sound comes from the machine's rhythmic work.

Suddenly they hear a faint scratching noise. Simone leans closer and sees Shulman's index finger moving over the smooth surface of the sheet. She feels her pulse speed up, and is just about to say something to Erik when Shulman opens his eyes. He stares straight at her with an odd expression. His mouth widens in a frightened grimace. His tongue moves laboriously, and saliva trickles down his chin.

"It's me, Sim. It's me," she says, taking his hand in hers. "I'm going to ask you some really important questions."

Shulman's fingers tremble. His eyes focus on her, then suddenly roll back; his mouth stretches, and the veins at his temples throb frantically.

"You answered my phone when Benjamin called, do you remember that?"

With Shulman's electrodes attached to his own chest, Erik can see on the monitor that his heart rate is increasing. Shulman's feet are vibrating under the sheet.

"Sim, can you hear me?" she asks. "It's Simone. Can you hear me, Sim?"

His eyes roll down again, but immediately slide to the side. Rapid steps can be heard in the corridor outside the door, and a woman shouts something.

"You answered my phone," she repeats.

He nods weakly.

"It was my son," she goes on. "It was Benjamin who called."

His feet begin to shake again, his eyes roll back, and his tongue flops out of his mouth.

"What did Benjamin say?"

Shulman swallows, works his jaw slowly. His eyes close.

"Sim? What did he say?"

He shakes his head.

"Didn't he say anything?"

"Not . . ." Shulman wheezes.

"What did you say?"

"Not Benjamin," he says, almost inaudibly.

"Didn't he say anything?"

"Not him," Shulman says. His voice is high, frightened.

"What?"

"Ussi?"

"What are you saying?" she asks.

"Ussi called." Shulman's mouth trembles.

Simone looks at Erik, baffled.

"Where was he?" Erik asks, looking intently at Shulman. "Ask him where Jussi was."

"Where was he?" Simone asks. "Do you know where Jussi was?"

"At home," replies Shulman in his high voice.

"Was Benjamin there too?"

Shulman's head flops to one side, his mouth goes slack, and his chin crumples. Simone looks anxiously at Erik; she doesn't know what to do.

"Was Lydia there?" Erik asks.

Shulman looks up, but his eyes slip to the side. Erik nudges Simone: You ask him.

"Was Lydia there?" Simone asks.

Shulman nods.

"Did Jussi say anything about . . ." Simone pauses as Shulman begins to whimper. Tears come to her eyes, and she strokes him gently on the cheek.

Suddenly his eyes snap into focus and he looks directly at her. "What's happened?" he asks, with complete clarity, and then slumps into a coma once again.

93

Anja walks into Joona Linna's office and silently hands him a manila folder and a glass of mulled wine. He looks up at her round, pink face. For once she looks completely serious.

"They've identified the child," she explains.

"Thanks."

There are two things he loathes, he thinks, looking at the folder. One is having to give up on a case, walking away from unidentified bodies, unsolved rapes, robberies, cases of abuse and murder. And the other thing he loathes, although in a completely different way, is when these unsolved cases are finally solved, because when the old questions are answered, it is seldom in the way one would wish.

He begins to read. The body of the child found in Lydia Everson's garden was that of a boy. He was five years old when he was killed. The cause of death is thought to be a fractured skull caused by a blunt object. In addition, a number of healed and partially healed injuries have been found, indicating repeated abuse of a serious nature. Beatings, the forensic pathologist has suggested. Abuse so serious that it caused broken bones and cracks in the skeleton. The back and the arms, especially, seem to have been the focus of violence using heavy objects. In addition, several symptoms of malnutrition on the skeleton suggest that the child was starving.

Joona looks out the window for a little while. He can't get used to this, and he has told himself that the day he does get used to it, he'll give up his job as a detective. He runs a hand through his thick hair, swallows hard, and returns to his reading.

The child has been identified. His name was Johan Samuelsson, and he had been reported missing thirteen years ago. According to her statement the mother, Isabella, had been in the garden with her son when the phone rang inside the house. She had not taken the boy with her when she went to answer, and at some point during the twenty or thirty seconds it took her to pick up the receiver, establish that there was no one there, and hang up again, the child had disappeared.

Johan was two years old at the time.

He was five years old when he was killed.

His remains then lay in Lydia Everson's garden for ten years.

The smell of the mulled wine is suddenly nauseating. Joona gets up and pushes his office window open. He looks down at the inner courtyard, the sprawling branches of the trees over by the custody area, the shining wet asphalt.

Lydia had the child with her for three years, he thinks. Three years of keeping a secret. Three years of abuse, starvation, and fear.

"Are you all right, Joona?" asks Anja, popping her head around the door.

"I'm going to go and speak to the parents," he says.

"I'm sure someone else can do that."

"No. This is my case," says Joona. "I'll go."

"I understand."

"Could you find some addresses for me in the meantime?"

"No problem."

"I'd like to know every place Lydia Everson has lived for the past thirteen years." His heart is heavy as he pulls on his fur hat and overcoat and sets off to tell Isabella and Joakim Samuelsson that their son has been found dead.

Anja calls him as he's driving out of the city.

"That was quick," he says, trying to sound cheerful but failing.

"This is my job after all, darling," chirrups Anja.

He hears her take a deep breath and he thinks of the two pictures of

Johan in the folder. In one he's dressed in a policeman's uniform, laughing out loud, his hair standing on end. And in the other: a collection of bones laid out on a metal table, neatly labelled with numbers.

"Fuck fuck fuck," he mutters to himself.

"Hey!"

"Sorry, Anja, it was another driver."

"All right, all right. But I don't want to hear that kind of language."

"No, I know," he says wearily, incapable of joining in the banter.

Anja finally seems to realize that he isn't in the mood for jokes and says neutrally, "The house where Johan Samuelsson's remains were found is Lydia Everson's mother's place. She grew up there, and that's always been her only address."

"Any family? Parents? Brothers and sisters?"

"Wait, I'm just checking it now . . . It doesn't look like it. There's no record of her father, and her mother's dead. It doesn't even look as if Lydia was in her care for very long."

"Brothers and sisters?" Joona asks again.

"No," says Anja, leafing through papers. "Sorry, yes," she calls out. "She had a little brother, but he seems to have died at an early age."

"How old was Lydia at the time?"

"She was ten."

"So she's always lived in that house?"

"No, that's not exactly what I said. She has lived elsewhere—on several occasions, in fact."

"Where?" Joona asks patiently.

"Ulleråker, Ulleråker, Ulleråker Psychiatric Clinic."

"Three stays."

"That's what it says."

"There are pieces missing," Joona remarks quietly to himself.

"What are you saying?"

"There are too many pieces missing," he answers. "I can't make sense of it, and now I have to try to explain to two parents why Lydia took their child."

94

Joona has turned onto the little street where Johan Samuelsson's parents still live. He spots their place at once, an eighteenth-century house painted Falun red, with a saddle roof. A shabby playhouse stands in the garden. Beyond the Samuelssons' hilly plot it is just possible to glimpse the black, heavy water of the Baltic Sea.

"I have to go, Anja."

He pulls his car into a raked gravel drive neatly edged with cobblestones and runs his hands over his face before getting out. He walks up to the door and rings the bell, waits, rings again. Eventually he hears someone shouting inside.

"Coming!"

The lock rattles and a teenage girl pushes open the door. Her eyes are heavily made up with kohl, and she has dyed her hair purple.

"Hey," she says.

"My name is Joona Linna," he says. "I'm from the National CID. Are your parents at home?"

The girl nods and turns to shout to them. But a middle-aged woman is already standing in the hallway, staring at Joona. "Amanda," she says in a frightened voice, "ask him . . . ask him what he wants."

Joona shakes his head. "I'd prefer not to say on the doorstep what I came to say," he says. "May I come in?"

"Yes," whispers the mother.

Joona steps inside and closes the door. He looks at the girl, whose lower lip has begun to tremble. Then he looks at Isabella Samuelsson. Her hands are pressed to her breast, and her face is deathly pale.

Joona takes a deep breath and explains quietly. "I'm so very, very sorry. We've found Johan's remains."

The mother presses her clenched fist to her mouth, making a faint whimpering sound. She leans on the wall but slips and sinks to the floor.

"Dad!" yells Amanda. "Dad!"

A man comes running down the stairs. When he sees his wife weeping on the floor, he slows down. It's as if every vestige of colour disappears from his face. He looks at his wife, his daughter, then Joona. "It's Johan," is all he says.

"We've found his remains," says Joona, his voice subdued.

They sit in the living room. The girl puts her arm around her mother, who is weeping inconsolably. The father still seems strangely calm. Joona has seen it before, these men—and sometimes women, though this is less common—who show very little reaction, who continue to talk and ask questions, whose voices take on a peculiarly vacant tone as they ask about the details. Joona knows this is not indifference but a battle, a desperate attempt to put off the moment when the pain comes.

"How did you find him?" the mother whispers, between bouts of weeping. "Where was he?"

"We were looking for another child at the home of a person suspected of kidnapping," says Joona. "Our dog picked up the scent and led us to a spot in the garden."

"In the garden?"

Joona swallows. "Johan has been buried there for ten years, according to the forensic pathologist."

Joakim Samuelsson looks up. "Ten years?" He shakes his head. "It's thirteen years since Johan disappeared," he whispers.

Joona nods, feeling utterly drained as he explains. "We have reason to believe that the person who took your child held him captive—" He looks down, making an enormous effort to sound calm when he looks up again. "Johan was held captive for three years," he goes on. "Before the perpetrator killed him. He was five when he died."

At this point the father's face breaks. His iron-hard façade is shattered into countless fragments, like a thin pane of glass. It is very painful to watch. His face crumples and tears begin to pour down his cheeks. Rough, dreadful sobs rend the air.

Joona looks around the room at the framed photographs on the walls. Recognizes the picture from the folder of little two-year-old Johan in his police uniform. Sees a confirmation photo of the girl. A picture of the parents, laughing and holding up a newborn baby. He swallows and waits. It isn't over yet.

"There's one more thing I have to ask you," he says, after giving them a moment to compose themselves. "I have to ask if you've ever heard of a woman named Lydia Everson."

The mother shakes her head in confusion. The father blinks a couple of times, then says quickly, "No, never."

Amanda whispers, "Is she . . . is she the one who took my brother?"

Joona looks at her, his expression serious. "We believe so."

When he gets up, his palms are wet with perspiration and he can feel the sweat trickling down the sides of his body.

"My condolences," he says. "I really am very, very sorry." He places his card on the table in front of them, along with the telephone numbers of a counsellor and a support group. "Call me if you think of anything, or if you just want to talk."

He is on his way out when the father suddenly gets to his feet. "Wait . . . I have to know. Have you caught her? Have you caught her yet?"

Joona clamps his jaws together. "No, we haven't caught her yet. But we're on her trail. We'll have her soon, I promise."

He calls Anja as soon as he gets in the car. She answers immediately. "Did it go well?"

"It never goes well," Joona replies steadily.

There is a brief silence at the other end of the phone.

"Did you want anything in particular?" Anja asks hesitantly.

"Yes," says Joona.

"You do know it's Saturday."

"The father is lying," Joona goes on. "He knows Lydia. He said he'd never heard of her, but he was lying."

"How do you know he was lying?"

"Something about his eyes when I asked. I'm right about this."

"I believe you. You're always right, aren't you?"

"Yes, I am."

"And if we doubt you, we have to put up with you saying, 'What did I tell you?'"

Joona smiles to himself. "You've come to know me well, Anja."

"Did you want to tell me anything else, apart from the fact that you were right?"

"Yes, I'm going over to Ulleråker."

"Now? You know it's our Christmas dinner tonight."

"Tonight?"

"Joona," Anja says chidingly. "It's our staff Christmas party, dinner at Skansen. You can't have forgotten?"

"Do I have to come?" asks Joona.

"Yes, you do," Anja replies firmly. "And you're sitting next to me."

"As long as you don't get carried away after a few drinks."

"You can cope."

"If you will be an angel and ring Ulleråker, make sure there'll be someone there I can talk to about Lydia, you can do more or less whatever you like with me," says Joona.

"Oh my God, in that case I'm already on it," says Anja cheerfully, hanging up.

95

The psychiatric clinic at Ulleråker is one of a very few still in operation in Sweden, the result of huge cuts in allocations for psychiatric care that took place in the 1990s. A complex of pale buildings set amid dark groves of trees, fields, and gardens once tended by patients, and with its own cemetery, the hospital is a world unto itself. Joona passes through an old-fashioned porte–cochère at the entrance and pulls up before the main building, an elegant old structure topped by a clock tower set directly in the centre of the complex.

Anja has done a good job as usual. When Joona walks in through the main entrance, he can see from the expression of the girl on reception that he is expected.

"Joona Linna?"

He nods and shows his ID.

"Dr. Langfeldt is waiting for you. Up the stairs, first room on the right along the hall."

Joona thanks her and begins to climb the wide stone staircase. He can hear thuds, shouts, the sound of a television coming from somewhere in the distance. There is a smell of cigarette smoke. Outside, the clinic is surrounded by an ornamental garden that resembles a church-yard, the bushes blackened and bowed down by the rain, trellises damaged by dampness with spindly climbers clinging to them. It looks gloomy, Joona thinks. A place like this isn't really aimed at recovery, it's a place for containment. He reaches the landing and looks around. To the left, through a glass door, is a long, narrow corridor. He wonders briefly where he has seen it before, then realizes it's an almost identical copy of the holding cells at Kronoberg: rows of locked doors with metal handles. An elderly woman in a long dress emerges from one of the doors. She stares at him through the glass. Joona nods to her, then opens the door leading to the other corridor. It smells strongly of bleach and antiseptic.

Dr. Langfeldt is already waiting.

"Police?" he asks rhetorically, holding out a broad, meaty hand. His handshake is surprisingly soft, perhaps the softest Joona has ever felt, and his expression gives nothing away as he says with a minimal gesture, "Please come in."

The office is large but almost entirely functional. Heavy bookshelves filled with identical files cover the walls. There are no paintings or photographs; the room is entirely free of ornamentation. The only picture is what appears to be a child's drawing in green and white chalk pinned to the door; a round face with eyes, nose, and mouth, legs and arms attached directly to it. Children of about three tend to draw adults in this way. This can be seen either as an indication that the figure has no body or that the head itself is the body.

Dr. Langfeldt goes over to his desk, which is almost entirely covered in piles of paper. He moves an old rotary telephone off the visitor's chair and makes another small gesture in Joona's direction; Joona interprets this as an invitation to sit down.

The doctor regards him thoughtfully; his face is heavy and furrowed, and there is something lifeless about his features, almost as if he is suffering from some kind of facial paralysis.

"Thank you for taking the time—" Joona begins.

"I know what you want to see me about," the doctor says. "You want information about Lydia Everson. My patient."

Joona opens his mouth, but the doctor holds up a hand to stop him.

"I presume you've heard of professional security and the confidentiality of information relating to patient records," Langfeldt continues. "In addition—"

"I'm familiar with the law," Joona interjects. "If the crime under investigation would lead to more than two years' imprisonment on conviction, then—"

"Yes, yes," says Langfeldt. The doctor turns his peculiar dead gaze on him.

"I can of course bring you in for questioning," Joona says softly. "The prosecutor is currently preparing a warrant for Lydia Everson's arrest. We will then request her patient notes, obviously."

Dr. Langfeldt taps his fingers against one another and licks his lips. "It's just . . ." he says, "I just want . . ." He pauses. "I just want a guarantee."

"A guarantee?"

Langfeldt nods. "I want my name kept out of this business."

Joona meets Langfeldt's eyes and suddenly realizes that the lifeless expression is in fact suppressed fear.

"I can't make that promise," he says harshly.

"If I plead with you?"

"I'm a stubborn man," Joona explains.

The doctor leans back, the corners of his mouth twitching slightly. It's the only sign of nerves or any other kind of vitality he has shown so far. "What is it you want to know?" he asks.

Joona leans forward. "Everything. I want to know everything."

An hour later, Joona leaves the doctor's office. He glances down the corridor opposite in passing, but the woman in the long dress has disappeared, and as he hurries down the stone staircase he notices that it's now completely dark. It's impossible to see the park and the trellises any longer. Downstairs, the girl on reception has evidently finished for the day. The desk is vacant, its surface cleared, and the office door is locked. Nothing but silence, although Joona knows that the unit houses hundreds of patients.

He shivers as he gets into his car and pulls out of the parking lot. Something is bothering him, something he can't put his finger on. He tries to remember the point at which the feeling began.

The doctor had taken out a file, identical to the other files filling the shelves. He had tapped it gently on the front and said, "Here she is."

The photograph of Lydia showed quite a pretty woman with medium-length hennaed hair and a strange, smiling expression: rage seething beneath an appealing surface.

The first time Lydia had been admitted for treatment was when she was ten years old, after she had killed her younger brother, Kasper. She had smashed in his skull one Sunday with a block of wood. She had told the doctor that her mother was forcing her to raise her brother. Kasper had been Lydia's responsibility when her mother was at work or sleeping, and it was her job to discipline him.

Lydia was taken into care; her mother was sent to prison for child abuse. Kasper Everson was three years old when he died.

"Lydia lost her family," Joona whispers, switching on the windscreen wipers as a bus coming the other way drenches his car.

Dr. Langfeldt had treated Lydia only with powerful psychopharmaceuticals; she was not offered any kind of therapy. He felt that the killing had been committed under severe pressure from her mother. With his agreement, Lydia was placed in an open residential facility for young offenders. When she turned eighteen, she moved back to her old home and lived there with a boy she had met at the residential facility, disappearing from the records.

Five years later she turned up again, this time having been admitted to a secure psychiatric unit. Lydia had gone to a playground and picked out a boy of about five, lured him to an isolated area, and hit him. She repeated this behaviour several times before she was caught. The last incident had resulted in life-threatening injuries to the child.

Dr. Langfeldt met her for the second time, and she became his patient in a unit from which she could be discharged only with the permission of the courts.

"Lydia remained in the secure unit at Ulleråker for six years. She was under treatment throughout," Langfeldt explained. "She was an exemplary patient. The only problem was that she constantly formed alliances with other inmates. She created groups around her, groups from whom she demanded unswerving loyalty."

She was making her own family, Joona thinks, as he turns off toward Fridhemsplan. He suddenly remembers the staff Christmas party at Skansen and considers pretending that he forgot about it, but he knows he owes it to Anja to appear.

Langfeldt had closed his eyes and massaged his temples as he went on. "After six years without incident, Lydia was allowed to begin spending periods away from the secure unit."

"No incidents at all?" asked Joona.

Langfeldt thought about it. "There was one thing, but it was never proven."

"What was it?"

"A patient's face was injured. She maintained she'd cut her own face, but the rumour was that Lydia Everson had done it. As far as I recall it was only gossip; there was nothing to it."

Joona nodded, blank-faced. "Go on," he said.

"She was allowed to move back to the family home. She was still under outpatient treatment, but she was looking after herself, and there was absolutely no reason," said the doctor, "to doubt her assertion that she wanted to get better. After two years it was time for Lydia to complete her treatment. She chose a form of therapy that was very fashionable at the time. She joined a hypnosis group with—"

"Erik Maria Bark," Joona supplied.

Langfeldt nodded. "It seems as if the hypnosis didn't do Lydia much good," he said superciliously. "She ended up trying to commit suicide and came back to me for the third time."

"Did she tell you about her breakdown?"

Langfeldt shook his head. "As I understand it, the whole thing was the fault of that hypnotist."

"Are you aware that she told Dr. Bark she had a son named Kasper? That she told him she had imprisoned her son?" Joona asked sharply.

Langfeldt shrugged his shoulders. "I did hear that, but I presume a hypnotist can get people to admit to just about anything."

"So you didn't take her confession seriously?"

Langfeldt smiled thinly. "She was a wreck. It was impossible even to hold a conversation with her. I had to give her electroconvulsive therapy, heavy antipsychotic drugs—it was a major task to get her back together on any level."

"So you didn't even try to investigate whether there was any basis to her confession?"

"My assessment was that such statements arose from her feelings of guilt over having murdered her brother as a child," Langfeldt replied sternly.

"When did you let her out?" Joona asked.

"Two months ago. She was definitely well."

Joona stood up, and his gaze fell on the only picture in Dr. Langfeldt's room, the childish drawing on the door. "That's you," said Joona, pointing at it. A walking head, he thought. Just a brain, no heart.

96

At five o'clock in December, the sun has been gone for two hours. The air is cold. The sparse streetlamps of Skansen provide a misty light. Down below, the city is just visible as smoky patches of light. Glassblowers and silversmiths are hard at work in the open-air museum. Joona walks through the Christmas market in Bollnäs Square. Fires are burning, horses are snorting, chestnuts are roasting. Children race through a stone maze, others drink hot chocolate. There is music everywhere, and families are dancing around a tall Christmas tree on the circular dance floor. As Joona walks toward one of the narrow gravel paths down to Solliden restaurant, he hears the laughter of children behind him and shudders.

His mobile rings. Joona answers it in front of a stall selling sausages and reindeer meat.

"It's Erik Maria Bark."

"Hi."

"I think Lydia has taken Benjamin to Jussi's haunted house. It's somewhere outside Dorotea in Västerbotten, in Lapland."

"You think?"

"I'm almost certain," Erik replies doggedly. "There are no more flights today. You don't have to come, but I've booked three tickets for first thing tomorrow morning."

"Good," says Joona. "If you can send me a text with all the information you have on Jussi, I'll contact the police in Västerbotten."

The beautiful yellow-painted restaurant is decorated with festive strings of light and branches of fir. A Christmas smorgasbord has been laid out on four huge tables; Joona spots his colleagues as soon as he walks in. They are sitting beside enormous windows that look out over the waters of Nybroviken and Södermalm, with the Gröna Lund theme park on one side and the Vasa Museum on the other.

"Here we are," Anja calls out.

She stands up and waves. Her enthusiasm gives Joona a lift. He still has an unpleasant, crawling sensation in his body after his visit to the doctor at Ulleråker. He says hello to everyone and sits down next to Anja.

Carlos Eliasson is sitting opposite him. He wears a Santa hat and nods cheerfully at Joona. "We've already drunk a toast," he confides. His normally sallow skin has a healthy flush.

Anja tries to slip her hand under Joona's arm, but he stands up and says he is going for some food.

Joona walks between the tables full of people chatting and eating, thinking that he can't really summon up the right frame of mind for a Christmas buffet. It's as if part of him is still in the living room with Johan Samuelsson's parents or at the psychiatric unit at Ulleråker, walking up the stone staircase toward the locked corridor with its rows of cells.

He takes a plate, joins the queue for herring, and contemplates his colleagues from a distance. Anja has squeezed her round, lumpy body into a red angora dress. She is still wearing her winter boots. Petter is talking intensely to Carlos; his head is newly shaven, and his scalp is shining with sweat under the chandeliers.

Joona helps himself to three different kinds of herring. He looks at a woman from another party. She is wearing a pale grey tight-fitting dress and is being led to the table by two girls with elegant hairstyles. A man in a grey suit hurries after them with a little girl in a red dress.

Joona ladles food onto his plate almost at random. There are no potatoes left in the small brass pan, and he moves on rather than wait for a waitress to come along with a fresh supply. There is no sign of his favourite dish, a Finnish turnip bake. Making his way back to the table, Joona balances his plate as he moves between officers who are now on their fourth foray to the buffet. At one table, five forensic technicians are singing *Helan går*, the traditional toast, with their small, tapering schnapps glasses raised. Joona sits down and immediately feels Anja's hand on his leg. She smiles at him.

"You remember you said I could do anything I wanted with you." She leans over and whispers loudly, "I want to dance the tango with you tonight."

Carlos hears her and shouts, "Anja Larsson, you and I will dance the tango!"

"I'm dancing with Joona," she says firmly.

Carlos tilts his head to one side and slurs, "I'll grab a ticket and wait in line."

Carlos is fast asleep on a chair in the cloakroom. Petter and his friends have gone into town to continue the celebrations at Café Opera, and Joona and Anja have promised to see that Carlos gets home safely. While they wait for their taxi, they take the opportunity to go out into the cold air. Joona leads Anja up onto the open-air dance floor, warning her about the thin film of ice he thinks he can feel on the wood beneath their feet.

Joona hums softly as they dance.

"Marry me," Anja whispers.

Joona doesn't reply; he is remembering Disa and her melancholy face. He thinks about their friendship over all these years and how he has had to disappoint her. Anja tries to stretch up and lick his ear, and he carefully moves his head a little further away.

"Joona," she whispers. "You dance so beautifully."

"I know," he replies, swinging her around.

The aroma of log fires and mulled wine surrounds them. Anja presses her body against his. It's going to be difficult to walk Carlos all the way down to the taxi stand, he thinks. Soon they'll have to make a move towards the escalator.

At that moment his phone rings in his pocket. Anja groans with disappointment as he moves to one side and answers.

"Hello," says a strained voice. "It's Joakim Samuelsson. You came to see us earlier today."

"Yes, I know. What can I do for you?" says Joona. He thinks back to how Joakim Samuelsson's pupils dilated when he was asked about Lydia Everson.

"I wonder if we could meet," says Joakim Samuelsson hesitantly. "There's something I want to tell you."

Joona looks at his watch. It's nine-thirty.

"Could we meet now?" asks Joakim, adding that his wife and daughter have gone to see his in-laws.

"That's fine," says Joona. "Can you be at police headquarters in forty-five minutes?"

"Yes," says Joakim, sounding infinitely weary.

"Sorry, my love," Joona says to Anja, who is waiting for him in the middle of the dance floor. "But there'll be no more dancing the tango tonight."

"Your loss," she says acidly.

"Spirits don't agree with me," Carlos slurs as they begin to lead him down toward the escalator and the exit.

"Don't throw up," says Anja sharply, "because if you do I'll demand a raise."

"Anja, Anja," says Carlos, cut to the quick.

97

Joakim is sitting in a white Mercedes directly opposite the entrance to National Police Headquarters. The interior light is on, and his face looks tired and lonely in its dim glow. He gives a start when Joona taps on the windscreen; he is deeply lost in thought.

"Hi," he says, opening the door. "Get in."

Joona climbs in and waits. The car smells vaguely of dog. The back-seat is covered with a hairy blanket.

"When I think about myself," says Joakim, "when I think about the way I was before Johan was born, it's like thinking about a total stranger. I had a pretty tough time when I was growing up; I ended up in an institution for young offenders. I had been fostered out, but that doesn't really mean anything; they just want you out of the system. But when I met Isabella, I pulled myself together and started studying properly. I qualified as an engineer the year Johan was born. I remember once we took a holiday. I'd never been on holiday before. We went to Greece. Johan had just learned to walk." Joakim Samuelsson shuts his eyes, shakes his head. "So long ago. He was so much like me . . . the same . . ."

He falls silent. A rat, damp and grey, scuttles along the dark pavement by bushes littered with rubbish.

"What did you want to tell me?" asks Joona after a while.

Joakim rubs his eyes. "Are you sure it was Lydia Everson who did this?" he asks, his voice weak.

Joona nods. "I'm absolutely sure."

"Right," whispers Joakim Samuelsson. He turns his exhausted, furrowed face toward Joona. "I do know her," he says simply. "I know her very well. We were in the youth offenders' institution together. When Lydia was only fourteen they found out she was pregnant. They were shit-scared at first: then they forced her to have an abortion. It was supposed to be kept quiet, but they botched the job. There were all sorts of complications, infections. But after a while she recovered."

Joakim's hands are shaking as he places them on the steering wheel.

"We moved in together when we left the institution. We lived in her house in Rotebro and tried to have a baby. She was completely obsessed with the idea. But nothing happened. So she went to see a gynaecologist. I'll never forget that day, when she came back from the doctor's." He runs his shaking hands through his hair. "They said there was too much scarring from the abortion and the aftermath. The doctor told her she could never get pregnant."

"And the one time she *was* pregnant," says Joona, "was it yours?"

"Yes."

"So you owed her a child," Joona says, almost to himself.

98

The terminal buildings at Arlanda Airport are covered with dense, heavy snow that falls ceaselessly from the dark sky. The runways are constantly being cleared. Erik stands by the huge window in the cafeteria, watching luggage swing around and around in a slow circle on the carousel.

Simone arrives with coffee and a plate of saffron Lucia buns and Christmas ginger cookies. She puts the two cups down in front of Erik, then looks out at the runways. They watch a crew of flight attendants heading across the tarmac on their way to one of the smaller jets. They are all wearing red Santa hats, the women in their heels jogging on tiptoe through the deep slush underfoot.

On the windowsill in the cafeteria, a mechanical Father Christmas is moving his hips rhythmically. His batteries seem to be running out; his movements are becoming increasingly spasmodic. Simone meets Erik's gaze, and raises her eyebrows ironically at the sight of the thrusting Santa.

"The buns were free," she says, staring blankly into space; then she remembers. "The fourth Sunday in Advent. It's the fourth Sunday in Advent today."

They look at each other, not knowing what to say. Suddenly Simone gives a start and looks upset.

"What's the matter?" Erik asks.

"The factor concentrate," she says, her voice choked. "We forgot . . . If he's there, if he's alive . . . It's been too long. He won't be able to stand up."

"Simone, I've got it," says Erik. "I've brought it with me."

She looks at him, her eyes red-rimmed. "Really?"

"Kennet reminded me. He called from the hospital."

Kennet. Simone thinks about how she drove her father home, watched him get out of the car—and fall head first into the slush. She thought he'd tripped, but when she ran around to help him up, he was almost unconscious. She drove him back to the hospital, where they took him in on a stretcher; his reflexes were weak and his pupils slow to react. The doctor thought it was a combination of the after-effects of the concussion and the fact that he had seriously over-exerted himself.

"How is he?" Erik asks.

"He was asleep when I was there yesterday. The doctor doesn't seem to think it's too serious, but he wants to keep Dad there until his condition stabilizes."

"Good," says Erik. He contemplates the mechanical Santa; then, without a word, he picks up his red Christmas napkin and places it over Santa's head.

The napkin waggles rhythmically back and forth. Simone starts to laugh, spraying Erik's jacket with biscuit crumbs.

"Sorry," she whimpers, "it just looks so sick. A sex-crazed Santa . . ."

She succumbs to a fresh attack of the giggles and ends up bent double over the table. Then she begins to cry. After a while she stops, blows her nose, wipes her face, and drinks her coffee. Her mouth has just begun to twitch again when Joona Linna comes over to their table.

"The Umeå police are on their way there now," he says, without preamble.

"Are you in radio contact with them?" Erik asks.

"I'm not, but they're in touch with—"

Joona stops abruptly when he catches sight of the napkin covering the thrusting Santa. A pair of brown plastic boots is protruding from beneath the paper. Simone turns her head away, her body shaking with laughter or weeping or a combination of both. It sounds as if she's choking. Erik quickly gets up and leads her away.

"Let go of me," she says, between convulsions.

"I just want to help you, Simone. Come outside."

They open a door leading onto a balcony and stand in the chilly air.

"I'm all right now, thank you," she whispers.

Erik brushes the snow off the railing and holds her naked wrist against the cold metal.

"All right now," she repeats. "All right . . . now."

She closes her eyes and wobbles. Erik catches her. He can see Joona looking at them from inside the cafeteria.

"How are you really, Simone?" Erik whispers.

She peers at him. "Nobody believes me when I tell them I'm just so tired."

"I'm tired too; I believe you."

"But you've got your pills, haven't you?"

"Yes," he replies, without even thinking of defending himself.

Simone's face crumples and Erik suddenly feels hot tears trickling down his cheeks. Since he's stopped taking drugs he feels more defence-less than he has in years, totally open and without protection.

"All this time," he goes on, his lips trembling, "I've only had one thought: he can't be dead."

They stand there motionless, their arms around each other. The snow falls on them in large, fluffy flakes. A plane takes off in the distance with a low roar. When Joona taps on the glass, they both jump. Erik opens the door and Joona comes out. He clears his throat. "I thought you should know that we have identified the body on Lydia's property."

"Who was it?"

"It wasn't Lydia's child . . . The boy had disappeared from his family thirteen years ago."

Erik nods and waits. Joona sighs deeply. "Remains of excrement and urine show that . . ." He shakes his head. ". . . show that the child lived there for a fairly long time, probably three years, before he was killed."

He waits as the information sinks in. Another plane roars in the dis-tance, on its way up into the sky.

"In other words, Erik, you were right the whole time. Lydia did have a child in a cage, and she regarded that child as her own."

"Yes," Erik says.

"She killed the boy when she realized what she had said under hyp-nosis, what that meant and what it was going to mean."

"I actually thought I was wrong. I accepted it," says Erik dully, gazing out at the wintry runways.

"Was that why you stopped?" asks Joona.

"Yes."

Simone runs a shaky hand over her forehead. "Lydia spotted you when you broke your promise. She saw Benjamin," she says quietly.

"No, she must have been following us all the time," Erik whispers.

"Lydia was released from Ulleråker two months ago," Joona says. "She approached Benjamin cautiously. Perhaps your promise never to use hypnosis again was holding her back."

Joona thinks that Lydia held Joakim Samuelsson responsible for the abortion that led to her inability to have children, so she took his son, Johan. And by the same twisted process of reasoning, Lydia held Erik responsible for her having murdered Johan, so she took Benjamin when Erik began to practise hypnosis again.

Erik's expression is grave, his face hard and closed. He opens his mouth to explain that he actually saved Evelyn's life by breaking his promise but is forestalled by the arrival of a police officer.

"We have to go now," the officer says. "The plane is taking off in ten minutes."

"Have you spoken to the police up in Dorotea?" Joona asks.

"It's not possible to make contact with the patrol who went to the house," the officer replies.

"Why not?"

"I don't know. They said they've been trying for fifty minutes."

"What the hell. Then they need to send backup," says Joona.

"That's what I told them, but they said they wanted to wait and see what happened."

As they set off to walk the short distance to the plane that is waiting to take them to Vilhelmina Airport in southern Lapland, Erik suddenly feels a brief, strange surge of relief: he was right all along.

He lifts his face to the falling snow. The flakes whirl and swirl, heavy and light at the same time. Simone turns and takes his hand.

99

thursday, december 17: evening

Benjamin is lying on the floor, listening to the rocking chair creak stickily against the shiny surface of the plastic mat. His joints ache painfully, an ache that has intensified over the past few days. The chair rocks slowly back and forth. The wind blows across the tin roof. Suddenly the crude hinge on the porch door sings its metallic song. Heavy footsteps approach down the hall. Someone stamps the snow off their boots. Benjamin raises his head, but the dog leash tightens around his neck when he tries to see who has come into the room.

"Lie down," Lydia murmurs.

He lowers his head to the floor, once again feeling the long coarse pile of the woven rug against his cheek, the dry smell of dust filling his nose.

"It's the fourth Sunday in Advent in three days," says Jussi. "We ought to make ginger biscuits."

"Sundays are for discipline and nothing else," says Lydia, continuing to rock.

Marek grins at something but doesn't speak.

"Go on, laugh," says Lydia.

"It was nothing."

"Laugh," says Lydia, her voice subdued. "I want my family to be happy."

"We are," Marek replies.

464

The floor is cold, and a cold draft seeps through the walls. The dust bunnies among the cables behind the television are drifting around. Benjamin is still wearing only his pyjamas. He thinks back to their arrival at Jussi's haunted house. There was already snow on the ground, and since then it has snowed, thawed, and frozen hard again. Marek led him through an area crammed with dilapidated vehicles at the front of the house, old buses covered in snow and scrap cars piled high. The snow burned Benjamin's bare feet. It felt like walking in a dry moat between the great heaps of snow-covered cars in the failing light.

There was a light on in the house, and when Jussi came out onto the porch, his elk gun over his arm, and caught sight of Lydia, it was as if all his determination abandoned him. She was not expected, nor was she welcome. But he was not about to offer any resistance, he would simply submit to her will, as usual. He merely shook his head when Marek took the gun from him.

Then there were footsteps on the porch, and Annbritt came out. Jussi had mumbled that Annbritt was his partner and they ought to let her go. When Annbritt saw the dog collar and leash around Benjamin's neck, the colour drained from her face and she tried to go back into the house and shut the door, but Marek stopped her by inserting the barrel of the gun between the door and the frame and asked her with a smile if they might come in.

"Shall we discuss Christmas dinner?" Annbritt asks now, her voice uncertain.

"The most important things are the herring and the boar," says Jussi.

Lydia sighs irritably. Benjamin gazes up at the gold-coloured ceiling fan, four gold lamps clustered beneath the blades. Its shadow looks like a grey flower against the white ceiling.

"I expect the boy will want meatballs," says Jussi.

"We'll see," Lydia replies.

Marek spits into a potted plant and looks out into the darkness. "I'm getting hungry," he says.

"We've got plenty of elk and venison in the freezer," says Jussi.

Marek goes over to the table, pokes about in the bread basket, breaks off a piece, and stuffs it in his mouth.

When Benjamin looks up, Lydia automatically yanks the leash. He coughs and puts his head down again. He is hungry and tired.

"I need my medicine soon," he says.

"You'll be just fine," replies Lydia.

"I have to have an injection once a week, and it's been more than a week since—"

"Shut up."

"I'll die if I don't."

Lydia jerks the leash so hard that Benjamin whimpers with pain. He starts to cry, and she jerks it again to shut him up.

Marek switches on the television; it makes a crackling noise and a distant voice can be heard; it could be a soccer game. Marek flicks between the channels without getting a picture and switches it off.

"I should have brought the TV from the other house," he says.

"It's not the TV. There just aren't any cable channels up here," says Jussi.

"You're an idiot," says Lydia.

"Why doesn't the dish work?" asks Marek.

"I don't know," says Jussi. "It gets very windy here. It's probably twisted."

"Fix it then," says Marek.

"You fix it!"

"Shut up," says Lydia.

"There's nothing but crap on television anyway," Jussi mutters.

"I like *Let's Dance*," says Marek.

"Can I go to the toilet?" Benjamin asks quietly.

"You piss outside," says Lydia.

"All right."

"Take him out, Marek," Lydia instructs.

"Jussi can do it," he replies.

"Why can't he go by himself?" complains Jussi. "He can't run away, it's minus five out there, and it's a long way to—"

"Get off your ass and go with him," Lydia breaks in. "I'll keep an eye on Annbritt in the meantime."

Sitting up makes Benjamin feel dizzy. He sees that Jussi has taken the dog leash from Lydia. Benjamin's knees are stiff, and a sharp pain shoots up his thighs when he starts to walk. Every step is unbearable, but he grits his teeth in an effort to remain silent. He doesn't want to annoy Lydia.

There are diplomas hanging along the wall in the hall. Dim light comes from a brass sconce with a frosted glass shade. A plastic bag from the ICA supermarket with the words QUALITY, COURTESY, SERVICE has been dropped on the cork-coloured vinyl floor.

"I need to take a shit," says Jussi, letting go of the leash. "Wait on the porch when you come back."

Jussi clutches his belly, disappears into the bathroom, puffing and blowing, and locks the door behind him. Benjamin can see Annbritt's curved, strong back through the gap in the door. He hears Marek rhapsodizing about Greek pizza.

Lydia's dark green padded jacket is hanging on a hook in the hallway. Benjamin looks around and then goes through the pockets rapidly, finding the house keys, a gold-coloured purse, and his own mobile. The battery is very low, but there should be enough life in it for at least one call. His heart quickening, he creeps out into the bitter cold. The snow has been cleared from the path leading down to the woodshed, and he sets off on his bare feet, trying to ignore the pain in his aching joints. In the darkness he can just make out the round shapes of the snow-covered cars and old buses in the yard. His hands are stiff and shaking with cold.

Reception is poor. He calls his mother's number and presses the phone to his ear, his hand trembling. He hears the first crackling signal just as the door opens. It's Jussi. They stare at each other. It doesn't occur to Benjamin to hide the phone. Perhaps he ought to run, but where would he go? Jussi strides toward him, his face pale and agitated.

"Are you finished?" he asks loudly, looking behind him.

Jussi reaches Benjamin and looks him in the eye; they have made an agreement. He takes Benjamin's phone and continues on down to the woodshed as Lydia emerges from the house.

"What are you two up to?" she asks, her voice oddly cheerful.

"I'm fetching some more wood," Jussi shouts, hiding the phone in his inside pocket.

"I'm finished," says Benjamin.

Lydia stands in the doorway and lets Benjamin into the house.

It's almost pitch dark inside the woodshed. The only light comes from the pale blue display of the phone. Jussi sees that it shows MUM. He puts it to his ear in time to hear someone answer.

"Hello?" says a man's voice. "Hello?"

"Is that Erik?" asks Jussi.

"No, this is—"

"My name is Jussi. Can you give Erik a message? This is important; we're up here at my house, me and Lydia and Marek and—"

A sudden guttural scream comes from the person who answered the phone. There is a sound of crashing and crackling, someone coughs, a woman whimpers and weeps; then there is silence. The connection is broken. Jussi stares at the phone in astonishment. Just as he thinks he might try someone else and begins scrolling through the numbers, the battery gives out. And then the woodshed door opens and Lydia steps inside.

"I could see your aura through the open door. It was completely blue," she announces.

Jussi slips the phone into his back pocket and starts piling wood into a basket.

"You go on inside," says Lydia. "I'll do this."

"Thanks," he replies, leaving the shed.

On the way up to the house, he can see ice crystals in the snow sparkling in the light from the window. The snow makes a dry, creaking sound beneath his boots. Behind him he can hear an irregular shuffling, accompanied by a panting, sighing sound. Jussi just has time to think of his dog, Castro. He remembers when Castro was a puppy, the way he used to chase mice beneath the light, freshly fallen snow. Jussi is smiling to himself when a sudden blow to the back of his head makes him lurch forwards. He would land on his stomach, were it not for the fact that the axe, stuck in the back of his head, is pulling him backwards. He stands still, his arms dangling at his sides. Lydia jerks the axe and manages to pull it out. Jussi can feel the warmth of his own blood pouring down his neck and back. He drops to his knees, falls forwards, feels the snow against his face, kicks out with his legs, and rolls over onto his back so that he can stand. His field of vision is shrinking fast, but during his last conscious seconds he sees Lydia raising the axe above him again.

100

Benjamin is curled up against the wall behind the television. He feels scarily dizzy; he's having trouble focusing his eyes. But the worst thing is the thirst. He's thirstier than he's ever been in his life. The hunger has abated. It hasn't gone, it's still there, a nagging ache in his gut. But it is completely overshadowed by thirst—thirst and the pain in his joints. The thirst is like being stabbed, as if his throat were full of open sores. He can barely swallow now; there is no saliva in his mouth. How many days has he been here, lying on this floor, in this house? Benjamin, Lydia, Marek, and Annbritt, in this one furnished room, doing nothing.

Benjamin listens to the faint tapping of the snow as it lands on the roof. He thinks about how Lydia made her way into his life, running after him one day as he was walking home from school.

"You forgot this," she'd called, and handed him his hat.

He'd stopped and thanked her. She'd given him a strange look and said, "You're Benjamin, aren't you?"

He asked her how she knew his name.

She'd stroked his hair. "Oh, dear boy. I called you Kasper." And when he'd looked at her uncomprehendingly, she'd added, "I'm your real mother. I gave birth to you. Haven't they told you?" She opened her bag and gave him a little pale-blue crocheted outfit. "I made this for you when you were in my belly," she whispered.

He explained that his name was Benjamin Peter Bark and he couldn't be her child. He'd tried to speak to her calmly and kindly. She listened with a smile on her face, then shook her head sorrowfully.

"Ask your parents," she had said to him. "Ask them if you really are their child. You can ask, but they won't tell you the truth. They couldn't have children. You'll be able to tell that they're lying. They'll lie because they're afraid of losing you. You're not their biological child. I can tell you about your real background. You're mine. Can't you see how alike we are? I was forced to give you up for adoption."

"But I'm not adopted."

"I knew it. I knew they wouldn't tell you," she said.

He thought about it and suddenly realized that she could actually be telling the truth; he had felt different for a long time.

Lydia smiled at him. "I can't prove it to you. You have to trust your own instincts, you have to explore your feelings. Then you'll realize it's true."

They parted, but he'd met up with her again the following day. They went to a café and sat talking for a long time. She told him how she had been forced to give him up for adoption but had never forgotten him. She had thought about him every day since he was born and was taken away from her. She had yearned for him every minute of her life.

Benjamin had told Aida everything, and they'd agreed that it was best if Erik and Simone knew nothing about what he'd learned until he had thought the whole thing through. He wanted to get to know Lydia first. It could be true, couldn't it? Lydia contacted him via Aida's e-mail and sent him the picture of the family grave.

"I want you to know who you are, Kasper," she said. "This is the resting place of your family. One day we'll go there together, just you and me."

Benjamin started to believe her. He wanted to. She was exciting. It felt strange for him to be so wanted, so loved. She had given him money and small mementoes from her childhood, she had given him books and a camera, and he had given her drawings and things he had collected when he was a child.

She had even stopped Wailord from hassling him. One day she simply handed him a piece of paper on which Wailord had written that he gave his word never to come near Benjamin or his friends again. His parents would never have been able to achieve something like that. He was becoming more and more convinced that Erik and Simone—people he had believed throughout his whole life—were liars. It annoyed him that they never talked to him, never really showed him what he meant to them.

He had been so incredibly stupid.

Then Lydia had started to talk about coming to the apartment, about visiting him at home. She wanted his keys. He didn't really understand why. He said he could let her in if she rang the doorbell, but she got angry with him. She said she would have to punish him if he didn't do as he was told. Her outburst surprised and scared him. She explained that when he was very small she had given his adoptive parents something called a ferrule as a sign that she wanted them to give him a proper upbringing. Then she took his keys out of his backpack and said the whole conversation was ridiculous; she would be the one to decide when she visited her own child.

That was when he realized there was something not quite right about Lydia.

The next day when she was waiting for him, he simply went up to her and told her as calmly as he could that he wanted his keys back and he didn't want to see her again.

"Of course, Kasper," she'd said. "You must have your keys." She reached into her bag and handed them to him.

He headed off, but she followed him. He stopped and waited for her and told her she hadn't understood: he didn't want to see her again.

Benjamin peers down at his body. A large bruise has appeared on his knee. If his mother saw that, she'd go crazy, he thinks.

Marek is staring out the window as usual. He inhales deeply through his nose and spits on the window in the direction of Jussi's body, out in the snow. Annbritt is slumped at the table. She is trying to stop crying; she swallows, clears her throat, and makes a hiccuping sound. When she came out and saw Lydia kill Jussi, she screamed and screamed until Marek pointed the gun at her and said he would kill her if she made one more sound.

There is no sign of Lydia. Benjamin thinks hard for a moment, then painfully raises himself into a sitting position. He says hoarsely, "Marek, I need to tell you something."

Marek looks over at Benjamin with eyes as black as peppercorns; then he gets down on the floor and starts doing push-ups. "What do you want, you little shit?"

Benjamin swallows, his throat agonizingly sore. "Jussi told me Lydia's going to kill you," he says. "She was going to take him first, then Annbritt, then you."

Marek continues with his push-ups, counting under his breath, and gets up with a sigh. "You're a funny little shit, aren't you."

"He said she only wants me. She wants to be alone with me. It's true."

"Oh, is it really?"

"Yes. Jussi said she told him what she was going to do. She was going to start by killing him, and now he's—"

"Shut the fuck up."

"Are you just going to sit here waiting until it's your turn?" Benjamin asks. "She doesn't care about you. She thinks this would be a better family if it was just me and her."

"Did Jussi really say she was going to kill me?" Marek asks.

"I promise, she's going to—"

Marek laughs loudly. "I've already heard everything anyone can say to avoid pain," he says with a grin. "All the promises, all the tricks, all the deals, and all the ruses." He turns indifferently to face the window.

Benjamin sighs. He's trying to come up with something else to say when Lydia walks in. Her mouth is a thin, strained line and her face is pale. She is holding something behind her back.

"So a week has passed and it's Sunday again," she states ceremoniously, closing her eyes.

"The fourth Sunday in Advent," Annbritt whispers.

"I would like us to relax and reflect upon the past week," Lydia says slowly. "Jussi left us three days ago. He is no longer among the living; his soul is travelling on one of the seven wheels of heaven. He will be torn to pieces for his treachery, through thousands of incarnations as a beast of slaughter and an insect." She pauses. "Have you reflected?" she asks, after a while. They nod, and Lydia smiles contentedly. "Kasper, come here," she says quietly.

Benjamin tries to get to his feet, making a real effort not to grimace with the pain, but still Lydia asks, "Are you making faces at me?"

"No," he whispers.

"We are a family, and we respect one another."

"Yes," he replies, his voice full of tears.

Lydia smiles and produces the object she has been hiding behind her back.

101

With no sign of emotion, Lydia holds up a pair of scissors in front of Benjamin. They are tailoring scissors, sharp, with broad blades.

"In that case," she says calmly, "it will be no problem for you to accept your punishment." With an expression of utter serenity she places the scissors on the table.

"I'm only a kid," says Benjamin, swaying.

"Stand still," she snaps at him. "It's never enough, is it? You never, ever understand. I struggle and try my hardest, I wear myself out so this family will work, will be whole and pure. I just want it to *work*."

Benjamin is looking at the floor and crying: rough, heavy sobs.

"Aren't we a family? Aren't we?"

"Yes," he says. "Yes. We are."

"So why do you behave like this? Sneaking around behind our backs, betraying us, deceiving us, stealing from us, giving us lip. Why do you behave like this toward me? Poking your nose into everything, talking behind my back."

"I don't know," Benjamin whispers. "I'm sorry."

Lydia picks up the scissors. She is breathing heavily now, and her face is sweaty. Red blotches have appeared on her cheeks and throat. "You will receive a punishment so that we can put all this behind us," she says. She looks from Annbritt to Marek and back again. "Annbritt, come here."

Annbritt, who has been staring at the wall, moves forward hesitantly. Her expression is strained, her eyes shift around the room, her narrow chin trembles.

"Cut off his nose," says Lydia.

Annbritt looks at Lydia and then at Benjamin. She shakes her head.

Lydia slaps her hard across the face. She grabs hold of Annbritt's stout upper arm and shoves her closer to Benjamin.

"Kasper has been poking his nose into everything, and now he's going to lose it."

Annbritt picks up the scissors. Marek seizes Benjamin's head in a firm grip, angling his face toward her. The blades of the scissors glint before Benjamin's eyes, and he sees the terrified look in the woman's eye.

"Get on with it!" Lydia yells.

Annbritt tentatively extends the hand holding the scissors towards Benjamin. Her face contorts and she begins to weep openly.

"I have a blood disorder," Benjamin whimpers. "My blood doesn't coagulate! Please. I'll die if you do that!"

Annbritt brings the blades together in the air in front of him and drops the scissors on the floor. "I can't," she sobs. "I just can't. It hurts my hand to hold the scissors."

"This is a family," says Lydia with weary inflexibility, as she laboriously bends down and picks up the scissors. "You will obey and respect me—do you hear me?"

"They hurt my hand, I told you! Those scissors are too big for—"

"Shut up!" Lydia snaps, striking her hard across the mouth with the handle of the scissors. Annbritt gasps with pain and staggers to one side. Leaning against the wall, she puts a hand to her bleeding lips.

"Sundays are for discipline," Lydia says.

"I don't want to." She cowers. "Please. I don't want to."

"Get on with it," Lydia says impatiently. She cocks her head suddenly. "What did you say? Did you say *cunt* to me?" She lifts the scissors menacingly.

"No, no." Annbritt sobs, holding out her hand. "I'll do it. I'll cut off his nose. I'll help you. It won't hurt; it'll soon be over."

Lydia looks satisfied and hands her the scissors. Annbritt goes over to Benjamin, pats him on the head, and whispers quickly, "Don't be scared. Just get out, get out as fast as you can."

Benjamin looks at her with a puzzled expression, trying to read her frightened eyes and trembling mouth. Annbritt raises the scissors but turns and stabs weakly at Lydia instead. Benjamin sees Lydia defend herself against Annbritt's attack, sees Marek grasp her wrist, yank at her arm, and dislocate her shoulder. Annbritt screams with pain. Benjamin is already out of the room by the time Lydia picks up the scissors and sits down astride Annbritt's chest. Annbritt shakes her head from side to side, trying to escape.

As Benjamin passes through the chilly porch and emerges into the burning cold out on the steps, he hears Annbritt screaming and coughing.

Lydia wipes the blood from her cheek and looks around for the boy; Benjamin is moving quickly along the cleared path. Marek takes the elk gun down from the wall, but Lydia stops him. "It'll do him good," she says. "Kasper has no shoes, and he's wearing nothing but his pyjamas. He'll come back to Mummy when he gets cold."

"Otherwise he'll die," says Marek.

Benjamin ignores the pain in his joints as he runs between the rows of derelict vehicles. He crouches behind an old Volvo sedan and eats some snow, slaking the terrible thirst he feels, and then begins to run again. Soon, he is no longer able to feel his feet. Marek is yelling something at him from the steps of the house, and Benjamin begins looking for a place to hide in the darkness. Maybe he can make his way down to the lake when things quiet down. Jussi said you could always find a fisherman there, sitting patiently over a hole drilled in the ice.

He has to stop; leaning on a pick-up, he listens for footsteps, glances up at the dark edge of the forest, and moves on. He won't be able to keep going much longer. He crawls under a stiff tarpaulin covering a tractor, slides along the frosty grass beneath the next car, stands up, and finds himself between two buses. He gropes along the side of one of the enormous vehicles until he locates an open window, and scrambles inside. Moving through the dark, musty coach by feel, he finds a pile of old rugs on a seat and wraps himself up in them.

102

The red-painted airport at Vilhelmina is a desolate sight in the midst of the vast white landscape. It is only ten o'clock in the morning, but it is still quite dark. The concrete landing strip is illuminated by floodlights. After a flight lasting one and a half hours, they are now taxiing slowly toward the terminal building.

Inside the waiting area it is surprisingly warm and cosy. Christmas music is playing, and the aroma of coffee drifts out from a shop that appears to be a mixture of news-stand, information desk, and cafeteria. Outside hang wide rows of Sami handicrafts: butter knives, wooden drinking scoops, baskets made of birch bark. Simone stares blankly at some Sami hats on a counter. She feels a brief pang of sorrow for this ancient hunting culture that is now compelled to reinvent itself in the form of brightly coloured hats with red tassels for tourists who regard the whole thing as a bit of a joke. Time has driven away the shamanism of the Sami; people hang the ceremonial drum, *meavrresgárri*, on the wall above their sofas, and the herding of reindeer is well on the way to becoming a performance for the benefit of tourists.

Joona takes out his phone and makes a call. He shakes his head with growing irritation. Erik and Simone can hear a tinny voice at the other end responding to his terse questions. When Joona flicks his phone shut, his expression is tense and serious.

"What is it?" Erik asks.

Joona stretches up to look out the window. "They still haven't heard from the patrol that went out to the house," he says, sounding distracted.

"That's not good," Erik says quietly.

"I'll call the station."

"But we can't just sit and wait for them."

"We're not going to," Joona replied. "We've got a car—it should be here already."

"God," Simone says. "Everything takes such a bloody long time."

"The distances are a little different up here," says Joona. He shrugs his shoulders and they follow him as he heads for the exit. Once through the doors, a different, dry cold suddenly hits them, a cold of another magnitude entirely.

Two dark-blue cars pull up in front of them, and two men dressed in the bright yellow uniforms of the Mountain Rescue Service get out.

"Joona Linna?" asks one of them.

Joona nods briefly.

"We were told to deliver a car to you."

"Mountain Rescue?" Erik asks anxiously. "Where are the police?"

One of the men straightens up and explains tersely. "There isn't that much difference up here. Police, Customs, Mountain Rescue—we usually work together as necessary."

The other man chips in. "We're a bit short-staffed at the moment, with Christmas just around the corner."

No one says anything for a moment. Erik looks desperate by this stage. He opens his mouth to speak, but Joona gets there first. "Have you heard anything from the patrol that went out to the cottage?" he asks.

"Not since seven o'clock this morning."

"How long does it take to get up there?"

"Oh, you'd need an hour or two."

"Two and a half," says the other man. "Bearing in mind the time of year."

"Which car?" Joona asks impatiently, moving towards one of them.

"Doesn't make a difference," replies one of the men.

"Give us the one with more fuel in it," says Joona, and they climb inside. Joona takes the keys and asks Erik to enter their destination into the brand-new GPS system.

"Wait," Joona calls after the men, who are heading for the other car. They stop.

"The patrol that went out to the cottage this morning—were they Mountain Rescue as well?"

"Yes, I'm sure they were."

They follow the shore of Lake Volgsjö and then, just a few miles farther on, they come out onto the main road, driving west in a straight line for about six miles before turning off onto the winding road that means fifty miles more. They travel in silence. Once they have left Vilhelmina far behind, they notice that the sky seems to lighten and a strange, soft glow appears to open up the view. They become aware of the contours of mountains and lakes around them.

"You see?" says Erik. "It's getting lighter."

"It won't get lighter for several weeks," Simone replies.

"The snow catches the light through the clouds," says Joona.

Simone rests her head against the window. They drive through snow-covered forests, immense white fields that have been cleared of trees, dark boggy areas, and lakes that look like enormous plains. In the darkness they can just make out a strangely beautiful lake, with steep shores, cold and frozen, sparkling darkly by the light of the snow.

After almost one and a half hours, sometimes heading north, sometimes west, the road begins to narrow. They are now in Dorotea, approaching the Norwegian border, and high, jagged mountains tower above them. Suddenly a car coming in the opposite direction flashes its headlights at them. They pull over to the side of the road, watching as the other car stops and reverses toward them.

"Mountain Rescue," says Joona dryly, when they see that the car is the same as theirs. He rolls down the window, and crisp ice-cold air sucks all the heat out of the car.

"Are you the lot from Stockholm?" shouts one of the men in the car in Finnish.

"We are," Joona replies in Finnish. "City slickers, that's us." They laugh, then Joona reverts to Swedish. "Was it you who went out to the house? Nobody has been able to get hold of you."

"No radio coverage," replies the man. "But it was a waste of petrol. There's nothing up there."

"Nothing? No tracks around the house?"

The man shakes his head. "We went through the layers of snow."

"What do you mean?" asks Erik.

"It's snowed five times since the twelfth—so we searched for tracks through five layers of snow."

"Well done," says Joona.

"That's why it took a while."

"But no one's been there?" asks Simone.

The man shakes his head. "Not since the twelfth, like I said."

"Shit," Joona says quietly.

"So are you coming back with us, then?" asks the man.

Joona shakes his head. "We've come all the way from Stockholm. We're not turning back now."

The man shrugs his shoulders. "Suit yourself." They wave and head off to the east.

"No radio coverage," Simone whispers. "But Jussi said he was calling from there."

They drive on in silence. Simone is thinking the same thing as the others. This trip may be a disastrous mistake. They could have been lured in the wrong direction, up into a crystal world of snow and ice, of wilderness and darkness, while Benjamin is somewhere else altogether, without protection, without his medication, perhaps no longer even alive.

It's the middle of the day, but this far north, deep in the forests, day is like night at this time of year, an immense night that overshadows the dawn from December to January, that refuses to crack and let in the light.

103

They reach Jussi's house, driving the last part across the hard crust on the snow. The air is freezing, utterly still and fragile. Joona draws his gun. It's been a long time since he saw real snow and experienced this dry feeling in his nose from severe cold.

Three small buildings face one another in a U-shaped formation. The snow has formed a huge, softly curved dome over each of the roofs, and there are drifts against the walls, right up to the windowsills. Erik gets out of the car and looks around. The Mountain Rescue team's tyre tracks are clearly visible, as are their footprints around the buildings.

"Oh God," Simone whispers, hurrying forward.

"Wait," says Joona.

"There's no one here, it's empty, we've—"

"It *seems* to be empty," Joona says. "That's all we know."

Simone waits, shivering, as Joona crunches across the snow. He stops by one of the small windows, leans forward, and can make out a wooden chest and some rag rugs on the floor. The chairs have been placed upside down on the dining table, and the refrigerator is empty and switched off, with the door wide open.

Simone looks at Erik, who has stopped in the middle of the yard, looking around as if perplexed. She is about to ask him what's wrong when he says loudly and clearly, "He isn't here."

"There's nobody here," Joona replies wearily.

"I mean," Erik says, "this isn't his haunted house."

"What are you saying?"

"This is the wrong cottage. Jussi's haunted house is pale green. I've heard him describe it: there's a larder off the porch, a tin roof with rusty nails, a satellite dish near the gable end, and the yard is full of old cars, buses, and tractors."

Joona waves his hand. "This is his address. This is where he's registered."

"But it's the wrong place."

Erik takes a few steps towards the house again; then he looks at Simone and Joona, his expression deadly serious, and says stubbornly, "This is not the haunted house."

Joona swears and takes out his cell phone, then swears even more when he remembers there is no coverage.

"We're not likely to find anyone we can ask out here, so we'll have to drive until we pick up a signal again," he says, getting back in the car. They reverse up the drive and are about to pull out onto the road when Simone spots a dark figure among the trees. He is standing there motionless with his arms by his sides, watching them.

"There!" she shouts. "There's someone over there!"

104

The edge of the forest on the other side of the road is dense and dark, the snow packed tightly between the trunks, the branches overloaded. She gets out of the car, even though Joona tells her to wait, and tries to see between the trees. The headlights are reflected in the windows of the house. Erik catches up with her.

"I saw someone," she whispers.

Joona gets out of the car, draws his gun, and follows them. Simone hurries toward the edge of the forest and spots the man once again among the trees, farther in this time.

"Wait, please!" she shouts.

She runs a little way but stops when she meets his gaze. It's an old man with a furrowed, utterly serene face. He is very short, he hardly reaches up to her chest, and he is wearing a thick, stiff anorak and trousers made of reindeer skin. A couple of dead ptarmigans are slung over his shoulder.

"Sorry to bother you," Simone says.

He says something she doesn't understand, then looks down and mumbles something. Erik and Joona approach cautiously. Joona has already concealed his gun inside his jacket.

"I guess he's speaking Finnish," says Simone.

"Hang on," says Joona, turning to the man.

Erik hears Joona introduce himself, point to the car, then mention Jussi's name. He is speaking Finnish in a steady, muted way. The old man nods slowly, pulls out a pipe, and lights it. He listens to Joona with his face upturned, as if he were looking for something and listening at the same time. Taking a puff of his pipe, he asks Joona something in a calm, melodic, clucking voice; Joona replies, and the man shakes his head regretfully. He looks at Erik and Simone with an expression of sympathy. When he offers them the pipe, Erik has enough presence of mind to accept it, take a puff, and pass it back. The tobacco is bitter and strong; Erik wills himself not to cough.

Simone hears the Sami explain something at length to Joona. He breaks a twig from a tree and draws a few lines in the snow. Joona leans over the snow map, pointing and asking questions. He takes a small note-pad out of his inside pocket and copies the map. Simone whispers "thank you" as they walk back to the car. The little man turns away, points into the forest, and sets off along a narrow track between the trees.

They have left the car doors open, and the seats are so cold they burn their backs and legs when they get in.

Joona hands Erik the piece of paper onto which he copied the old man's directions.

"He was speaking an odd kind of Umeå Lappish, so I didn't really understand everything. He was talking about the Kroik family place."

"But he knew Jussi?"

"Yes. If I understood him correctly, Jussi has another house, a hunting lodge even deeper in the forest. There's supposed to be a lake up ahead on the left. We can drive as far as a place where three big stones have been raised in memory of the fact that the Sami used to spend their summers here. The snow-ploughs don't go any further, so we have to walk north across the snow from there until we see an old trailer."

Joona looks at Simone and Erik with an ironic expression and adds, "The old man said that if we fall through the ice on Lake Djuptjärnen, we've gone too far."

They drive for forty minutes, slowing down to pause at the three standing stones hewn and raised by the community of Dorotea. The headlights make everything look grey and shadowy. The stones appear for a few seconds, then disappear into the darkness again.

Joona parks the car by the edge of the forest and says he probably

484

ought to camouflage it; he cuts a few branches but changes his mind. He glances up at the starlit sky and sets off as quickly as he can. The others follow, as quietly as possible. The hard crust lies like a heavy board over the deep snow. The old man's directions are correct; after a third of a mile, they see a rusty trailer half buried in the snow and turn off the path. Others have walked along the track they are on. Below them lies a house surrounded by snow. Smoke is rising from the chimney. In the light from the windows, the outside walls appear to be mint green.

This is Jussi's house, Erik thinks. *This* is the haunted house.

In the yard they can just make out big dark snow-covered shapes that form a strange labyrinth. As they head slowly towards the house, they move along narrow passageways between these great heaps of snow-covered vehicles—scrap cars, buses, combine harvesters, ploughs, and scooters—their feet crunching on the snow.

Inside the house, they see a figure moving past the window. Something's happening over there; the movements are rapid, violent. Erik can't wait any longer, he starts running towards the house; he doesn't give a damn about the consequences. Simone runs alongside him, panting. As they close the distance, running across the hard snow, they suddenly hear a muffled scream, followed by rapid, floundering thuds. A figure appears in the window again. A branch snaps off at the edge of the forest. The door of the woodshed bangs. Simone is breathing fast. They stop at the edge of a path that has been shovelled out of the snow, just before reaching the house.

105

The person at the window has disappeared. The wind sighs in the tree-tops. Light snow swirls across the ground. Suddenly the door is flung open, and they are dazzled; someone is shining a powerful torch in their faces. They shade their eyes with their hands and squint in order to try and see.

"Benjamin?" Erik calls out.

When the beam of light is lowered to the ground, Erik recognizes Lydia. In one hand she is holding the torch, in the other, a large pair of scissors. The light illuminates a figure in the snow. It's Jussi. His face is an icy bluish-grey, his eyes are closed, he is covered in frozen blood, and an axe sticks out of his chest. Simone stands next to Erik in silence. He can tell by her shallow, rapid breathing that she has also seen the body. At the same moment he realizes that Joona is no longer with them. He must have gone a different way, thinks Erik. He'll creep up on Lydia from behind if I can just keep her busy for long enough.

"Lydia," says Erik. "Good to see you again."

She stands there motionless, watching them but saying nothing. The scissors glint in her hand, swinging loosely. The beam of the torch shines on the grey path.

"We've come to pick up Benjamin," Erik explains calmly.

"Benjamin," Lydia replies. "Who's Benjamin?"

"He's my child," says Simone, her voice half suffocated.

Erik tries to gesture to her to keep quiet; perhaps she sees him, because she takes a step back and tries to steady her breathing.

"I haven't seen anyone else's child, only my own," Lydia says slowly.

"Lydia, listen to me," says Erik. "If we can take Benjamin, we'll go away and forget all about this. I promise never to hypnotize anyone ever again—"

"But I haven't seen him," Lydia insists, glancing at the scissors. "There's only me and my Kasper here."

Lydia is in the perfect spot right now, Erik thinks feverishly. She's focused on us and her back is to the house. All Joona has to do is creep around and overpower her from behind.

"I'd like you to leave now," she says firmly.

"Please, just let us give him his medication," Erik begs. His voice has begun to shake. Suddenly, he thinks he can see someone moving along the line of vehicles diagonally behind the house. A jolt of relief shoots through his heart. But Lydia's expression becomes alert, and she lifts the torch and shines it towards the woodshed and out across the snow.

"Kasper needs his medication," says Erik.

Lydia lowers the torch again. Her voice is cold and harsh. "I'm his mother. I know what he needs," she says.

"You're right, of course you are," Erik says quickly. "But if you let us give Kasper a little bit of medicine, you can show him what's right and wrong; you can discipline him. I mean, it *is* Sunday—"

Erik pauses involuntarily as he sees the figure behind the house move closer, then disappear from view.

"On Sundays," he goes on, "you usually—"

Two people appear around the side of the house. Joona is moving stiffly and reluctantly toward them. Behind him is Marek, with the elk gun pressed into Joona's back.

Lydia smiles and steps up onto the hard snow from the cleared path.

"Shoot them," she says tersely. Lydia nods in Simone's direction. "Start with her."

"I've only got two cartridges," Marek replies.

"Do what you like, just get it done," she says.

"Marek," says Erik. "They stopped me from working. I wanted to help you—"

"Shut your fucking mouth."

"You'd started talking about what happened in the big house out in the country in Zenica-Doboj."

"I can show you what happened," says Marek, looking at Simone with calm, empty eyes.

"Just get on with it," sighs Lydia, looking impatient.

"Lie down," Marek says to Simone. "And take off your jeans."

She doesn't move. Marek turns the gun on her, and she backs away. Erik moves forward and Marek quickly aims at him.

"I'll shoot him in the stomach," says Marek. "Then he'll be able to watch while we're having fun."

"Do it, already," says Lydia.

"Wait," says Simone, starting to unzip her jeans.

Marek spits into the snow and takes a step towards her, but he doesn't really seem to know what to do. He looks at Erik and waves the gun in his direction. Simone won't meet his eyes. He points the gun at her, aiming the barrel first at her head, then at her stomach.

"Don't do this," says Erik.

Marek lowers the elk gun and moves towards Simone. Lydia steps back. Simone starts to pull down her jeans and underwear.

"Hold the gun," Marek says quietly to Lydia.

She is moving towards him when a noise comes from among the maze of junked vehicles—a metallic knocking, over and over again. Suddenly, there's a roar as an engine kicks into life, with the sharp sound of the pistons working. The engine revs deafeningly, the gearbox screams, snow is churned into the air, and a bright light blanches the front of the house. An old bus with a huge tarpaulin over the roof rumbles forward out of the formation, tearing free of the hard crust of snow that covers it and heading straight for them.

106

sunday, december 20 (fourth sunday of advent): afternoon

When Marek turns his head to look over at the bus, Joona moves forward with remarkable speed and grabs the stock of the gun. Marek holds on tight but is forced to take a step forward. Joona hits him hard across the chest and tries to kick his legs out from under him, but the powerfully built Marek remains on his feet and, using all the strength in his arms, tries to turn the gun around, the butt grazing Joona's head and sending him to his knees. But Marek's fingers are so cold he loses his grip, and the gun spins through the air to land in front of Lydia. Simone rushes towards it, but a snarling Marek seizes her hair and yanks her back.

The bus has run into a fir tree and become stuck, its engine roaring in protest; it is surrounded by a miasma of exhaust fumes and churned-up snow as it bumps stubbornly into the trunk of the tree, scraping off the bark, the wheels spinning without traction. The engine revs once again, the tree sways, and snow tumbles from its dark branches. The front door of the bus opens and closes over and over again with a gentle hiss. Benjamin's bewildered face is visible within. His nose is bleeding.

"Benjamin!" Simone screams. "Benjamin!"

Lydia runs toward the bus with Marek's gun, Erik following. Screaming, Lydia climbs aboard the bus, lashing out at Benjamin with the butt of the gun and shoving him out of the driver's seat. She settles behind the wheel and manipulates the tall gearshift. With a shrieking grinding

489

of gears, the bus begins to roll back, picking up speed as it rattles down the slope toward the lake. Erik yells at Lydia to stop, racing after them in the tracks dug by the wheels.

Marek is still holding Simone by the hair. She is screaming and trying to pry his fingers loose. Joona tenses, shifting from a kneeling position to a poised crouch, then leaps to his feet. As Marek begins to turn in his direction, Joona drops his shoulder and twists his body, driving his fist into Marek's armpit. Marek's arm flaps as if it had been jarred loose from its socket, and his grip on Simone's hair loosens. She pulls away and scrambles for the scissors in the snow. Marek lashes out with his other hand, but Joona dodges the blow and jabs his right elbow down towards the side of Marek's neck with all his strength, breaking the collarbone with a dull crack. Marek falls to the ground, screaming with pain. Simone dives for the scissors, but Marek kicks her in the stomach, grabbing the scissors and making a sweeping backwards slash with his functioning arm. Simone screams and sees Joona's face stiffen as the scissors penetrate his right thigh, blood splashing onto the snow. Grimacing fiercely, Joona swings down with the handcuffs he's taken out and smashes Marek's skull over the left ear. It is a hard blow. Marek stops moving; he simply stares straight ahead, trying to say something. Blood is pouring from his nose and ear. Joona bends over him, panting, and fastens the handcuffs around Marek's slack wrists.

Erik has raced after the bus in the darkness, his breath tearing at his lungs. The tail-lights glow red up ahead, and the pale beam of the headlights flickers over the forest. There is a sharp crack as one of the side mirrors smashes into a tree.

Erik hopes that the cold will protect his son. Temperatures below zero can lower his body temperature by perhaps ten per cent, enough to make Benjamin's blood flow more slowly, maybe enough to enable him to survive in spite of the fact that he has been hurt.

The ground slopes sharply behind the house. Erik stumbles and gets back up. The hazards of the terrain, tree stumps and hillocks hidden beneath the deep snow, have been unearthed by the bus's crazed advance. The bus is a shadow in the distance, a silhouette with a blurred glow surrounding it. It looks as if Lydia will attempt to drive along the shoreline, making her way around the lake to the old logging road Eric had seen on

Joona's copy of the Sami's map. Instead, the bus brakes suddenly and pulls out onto the frozen surface of the lake.

Erik yells at Lydia to stop. As it shoots past the jetty, a rope dragging behind the bus catches on the rocks, and the tarpaulin is ripped from the roof.

The air is thick with the smell of diesel. By the time Erik reaches the edge of the lake, the bus is already sixty feet out onto the ice. Suddenly, it stops. There's a loud rumbling and cracking sound. Erik's throat constricts with panic as he watches the red tail-lights of the bus tilt upward, as if someone were slowly raising their eyes. The ice has given way and the bus has fallen through. Its wheels are spinning backward but serve only to make the hole in the ice bigger.

Erik grabs a life belt from the jetty and begins running across the ice, his heart pounding. The lights inside the bus, which is still floating, make it glow like a frosted bell jar. There is a splashing sound, and heavy lumps of ice break off and whirl around in the black water.

Erik thinks he can see a white face in the rolling water behind the bus.

"Benjamin!" he screams.

The swell from the bus surges over the ice, making it treacherous beneath his feet. He knots the line from the life belt around his waist, so he won't drop it, and hurls it into the dark water, but he no longer sees anything there. The engine roars. The bloody red glow from the tail-lights spreads across churned-up ice and snow.

The front of the bus sinks deeper, headlights disappearing beneath the water. Only the roof is visible now. The engine dies. There is no sound apart from the cracking and crunching of the ice and the lazy bubbling of the water. Suddenly Erik sees that both Benjamin and Lydia are still inside the bus. The floor tilts forward and they move towards the back. Benjamin clings to a pole. The roof over the driver's seat is almost on a level with the ice.

Erik races toward the hole in the ice and jumps onto the bus. The whole vehicle bobs underneath him. From a distance he can hear Simone shouting something; she has reached the shoreline. Erik crawls over to the emergency exit set in the roof, stands up, and stamps hard on the glass. Shards of glass cascade over the seats and floor. All he can think of is getting Benjamin out of the sinking bus. He clambers down, swinging by his arms, manages to find a foothold on the back of a seat, and jumps onto the floor. Benjamin looks terrified; he is wearing nothing but pyjamas, and blood is trickling from his nose and from a small cut on his cheek.

"Dad," he whispers.

Erik follows his gaze to Lydia. She is standing at the back of the bus, her face bloodied and completely closed down. She is holding the gun. The driver's seat is now underwater. The floor tilts more sharply. Water pours steadily in between the rubber seals on the exit doors.

"Lydia, we have to get out of here!" Erik shouts.

Lydia merely shakes her head.

"Benjamin," he says, without taking his eyes off Lydia, "climb up on top of me and get out through the roof."

Benjamin doesn't reply but follows Erik's instructions. He moves unsteadily along the aisle, climbs up onto a seat, and then onto Erik's back and shoulders. When he reaches the open hatch with his hands, Lydia raises the gun and fires. Erik feels no pain, just a blow to his shoulder so powerful that he is knocked off his feet. Only when he stands up again does he feel the pain and the warm blood trickling down.

Overhead, Benjamin dangles from the opening in the roof. Erik moves over and pushes him up with his uninjured arm, even though he can see Lydia pointing the gun at him once again. Benjamin is already out on the roof when the next shot comes. Lydia misses. The bullet whizzes past Erik's hip and shatters a window beside him; icy water comes flooding in. As Erik tries to reach up to the roof hatch, the bus tips over onto its side and he ends up beneath the surging water.

107

The shock of the freezing water makes Erik lose consciousness for a few seconds. He kicks out with his legs in a panic, breaks the surface, and fills his lungs with air. Slowly and with a metallic creaking sound, the bus begins to roll and sink beneath the black water. It lurches; he feels a blow to his head and then is underwater once again. Through the window he can see the headlights still shining deep in the lake. His heart is pounding. His face and head feel as if they are being squeezed in a vice. He can see Lydia under the water, clinging to a pole with her back to the rear seats. His ears are filled with a roaring sound, and he is immobilized by the incomprehensible cold. He sees the open hatch and the shattered window; he knows the bus is sinking fast, knows he has to swim out. He has to fight, but his arms won't work and he has no feeling in his legs. He is almost weightless. He tries to edge forward but finds it difficult to synchronize his movements.

Now Erik sees he is surrounded by a cloud of blood from the cut on his shoulder. Suddenly Lydia meets his gaze, staring calmly into his eyes. They hang there in the icy water, looking at each other. Her hair floats with the movement of the current, and small air bubbles emerge from her nose like a string of pearls.

Erik needs to breathe, his throat tightens, but he is fighting against his lungs as they struggle to take in oxygen. His temples are throbbing and a white light is flashing inside his head. His body temperature is so low he is on the point of losing consciousness. The ringing in his ears gets louder, rising and falling.

Erik thinks about Simone, about the fact that Benjamin is going to make it. It feels like a dream, floating freely in the icy water. With remarkable clarity, he realizes that this is the moment of his death, and his stomach contracts with fear.

He has lost all sense of direction, of his own body, of light and darkness. The water feels warm, almost hot. He thinks that soon he will have to open his mouth and simply give in, simply let the end come as his lungs fill with water.

New, strange thoughts run through his mind as something suddenly happens. He feels the rope around his waist tighten. He has forgotten that he knotted the long line attached to the life belt around his body. It seems to be tangled in something. He is being dragged to the side. It is impossible to resist, he has no strength left. His slack body is hauled inexorably around a pillar and then up through the roof hatch. The back of his head thumps against something, one shoe comes off, and then he is out in the black water. He is carried upwards while the bus continues without him into the depths, Lydia inside the glowing cage as it drifts silently to the bottom of the lake.

108

Simone, Erik, and Benjamin return to a grey Stockholm beneath a sky that is already dark. The air is heavy with rain, and the city is enveloped in a purplish mist. Everywhere, colourful lights are shining, on Christmas trees and garland-looped balcony railings. Advent stars glow in virtually every window. Santa and his elves are everywhere.

The taxi driver who drops them at the Birger Jarl Hotel has his Santa hat on. He waves at them gloomily in the rear-view mirror; they notice he even has a plastic Santa on his roof.

Simone glances at the lobby and the dark windows of the hotel restaurant, and says it feels odd to be staying in a hotel when they're only a few hundred feet away from home.

"But I really don't want to go back to our apartment," she says.

"No, of course not," Erik agrees.

"Not ever again."

"Me neither," says Benjamin.

"What shall we do?" Erik asks. "How about the cinema?"

"I'm hungry," Benjamin says quietly.

By the time the helicopter arrived at the hospital in Umeå, the bullet had gone straight through Erik's left shoulder muscle, causing only su-

495

perficial damage to the outer part of his upper arm. Once they stabilized his condition, he underwent surgery. Afterwards, he shared a room with Benjamin, who had been admitted for observation and rehydration, so his medication could be regulated. After only one day in the hospital, Benjamin started to ask about going home.

The psychologist assigned to assess Benjamin's condition seemed unable to grasp the level of danger to which Benjamin had been exposed. After talking to Benjamin for forty-five minutes, she met with Erik and Simone and blandly announced that the boy seemed fine, under the circumstances; they should just keep an eye on him and give him time.

Did the woman just want to reassure them? His parents realized that Benjamin was going to need real help; they could already see him searching among his memories, as if he had already decided to ignore some of them, and they sensed that if he were left alone he would close up around what had happened like bedrock around a fossil.

"I know two really good specialists in adolescent psychology," said Erik. "We'll call them as soon as we get back to Stockholm."

"Good." Simone shuddered.

"And how are *you* feeling?" he asked her.

"There's this hypnotist I've heard about," Simone said.

"Just be careful of him."

"I will." Simone smiled.

"But seriously," Erik said. "All of us are going to need to work through this."

She nodded, and her expression grew very thoughtful.

"Little Benjamin," she said softly.

Erik went and lay down again in the bed next to Benjamin's, and Simone sat on a chair between the two. They looked at their son, lying there so pale and thin. They never tired of gazing at his face, as if he were their newborn baby.

"How are you feeling, little man?" Erik asked him tentatively.

Benjamin stared out the window. The darkness outside turned the glass into a vibrating reflection as the wind pushed and tapped at the pane.

109

Benjamin had just scrambled up onto the roof of the bus when he'd heard the second shot. He'd slipped and almost fallen into the water. At the same moment he had seen Simone in the darkness on the edge of the huge hole in the ice. She'd yelled to him that the bus was sinking and he had to get onto the ice. Spotting the orange life belt bobbing in the black water behind the bus, he'd jumped, grabbed hold of it, slipped it over his arms, and kicked toward the edge of the ice, even as he'd felt his legs growing numb. Lying flat on the ice, Simone had reached out toward the freezing water to find his hand and pulled him out, then dragged him a little way from the edge. She'd taken off her jacket and wrapped it around him, hugging him and telling him that a helicopter was on the way.

Benjamin sobbed. "Dad's still in there!"

The bus had sunk quickly, disappearing beneath the surface with a groan, and they had been left in darkness. They could hear the splash of the churned-up water and the clucking of huge air bubbles, the sheets of ice shifting back into place. Simone held Benjamin tightly, shivering, trying to keep from screaming. All of a sudden, he had been yanked out of her arms. He'd tried to get up but had slipped and fallen. The line attached to the life belt lay taut across the ice, running down into the water, and Benjamin was being pulled towards the hole in the ice. He was struggling, sliding on his bare feet, and screaming. Simone had grabbed hold of him, and together they slithered inexorably toward the edge.

"It's Dad!" Benjamin had suddenly shouted. "He had the rope around his waist!"

Simone's face suddenly became hard and resolute. She grabbed hold of the life belt, hooked both arms through it, and dug in her heels. Benjamin grimaced with pain as they edged closer and closer to the water. The line was so tight it made a singing sound as it scraped over the edge of the ice, like a bow being drawn across the taut string of a violin. Then suddenly the tug-of-war shifted: it was still hard work, but they were able to move backwards, step by step, away from the water. And then there was almost no resistance at all. They hauled Erik up through the opening in the roof, and now he floated free of the doomed vehicle. A few seconds later, Simone was able to drag him up onto the ice. He lay there face down, coughing and breathing hard as a red stain spread beneath him.

When the police and paramedics arrived at Jussi's house, they found Joona lying in the snow with a provisional pressure bandage around his thigh, his gun trained on a bellowing, handcuffed Marek. Jussi's frozen corpse lay at the bottom of the porch steps with an axe in the chest. One survivor was found in the house: Annbritt had been hiding in the wardrobe in the bedroom. She was covered in blood, curled up behind the clothes like a child. The paramedics carried her out to the helicopter on a stretcher and gave her emergency treatment during the flight.

Two days later, Mountain Rescue divers went down into the lake to recover Lydia's body. The bus stood solidly on its six wheels at a depth of two hundred feet, as if it had just stopped to pick up some passengers. One diver entered through the front door and shone his torch around the empty seats. The gun was on the floor at the back of the aisle. It was only when he directed the beam upward that the diver saw Lydia. She lay with her back pressed against the ceiling of the bus, her arms dangling down and her neck bowed. The skin on her face had already begun to loosen and come away. Her hennaed hair billowed gently with the movement of the water, her mouth was calm, her eyes were closed as if she was asleep.

Benjamin had no idea where he had been for the first few days after the kidnapping. Possibly, Lydia had kept him at her house or at Marek's, but he had been so dazed from the sedative with which he had been injected that he hadn't really grasped what was going on. He might have been given further injections as he started to come round. Those first days were simply dark and lost.

It was in the car heading north that he had regained consciousness and found his mobile still around his neck. It was night when they'd taken him; it wouldn't have occurred to them he would have one. Although he'd managed to call Erik, they'd heard his voice and the phone had been confiscated.

Then came a series of long, terrible days. Erik and Simone only managed to coax fragments from him. All they really knew was that he had been forced to lie on the floor of Jussi's house with a dog collar and leash around his neck. Judging by his condition when he was admitted to the hospital, he had been given nothing to eat or drink for several days. He had managed to get away with the help of Jussi and Annbritt, he told them, then fell silent. Eventually he was able to explain how Jussi had saved him when he was trying to call home, and the terrible price he had paid for it; how Annbrit had attacked Lydia to allow him a chance to escape, and that he had heard Annbritt screaming as Lydia cut off her nose. Benjamin had hidden by crawling through an open window of one of the snow-covered buses. There he'd found some rugs and a mouldy blanket, which probably saved him from freezing to death. He'd curled up on a passenger seat and fallen asleep. He had been awakened a few hours later by the sound of his parents' voices.

"I didn't know I was alive," whispered Benjamin.

Then he'd heard Marek threaten his parents. And he realized he was staring at a key in the ignition of the bus, and without even thinking, he'd clambered over the seat and turned it. And the headlights had come on, and the engine had roared furiously as he headed for the spot where he thought Marek was.

Benjamin stopped speaking, a few fat tears caught in his eyelashes.

110

After two days in the hospital at Umeå, Benjamin was strong enough to walk. He went with Erik and Simone to see Joona Linna, who was in the post-operative ward. His thigh had been badly damaged by Marek's attack with the scissors, but three weeks' rest would probably lead to a full recovery. A beautiful woman with her hair in a soft braid over her shoulder was sitting with him, reading aloud from a book, when they walked in. Putting it down, she rose and introduced herself as Disa, a friend of Joona's for many years.

"We have a reading group, so of course I have to make sure he keeps up," she said, in the same pleasing dialect as Joona's.

Simone saw that she was reading Virginia Woolf's *To the Lighthouse*.

"Mountain Rescue has lent me a small apartment," said Disa with a smile.

"And you," said Joona. "You'll be given a police escort from Arlanda."

Simone and Erik declined the offer. They wanted to be alone with their son rather than spend time with more police officers.

When Benjamin was discharged on the fourth day, Simone immediately booked tickets for the flight home. She went to get coffee for them all, but for the first time the hospital cafeteria was closed. In the day room there was nothing but a jug of apple juice and some biscuits. She went out in search of a café, but everything seemed strangely deserted.

There was a peaceful calm over the whole town. She stopped by a railway line and followed the gleaming track with her eyes, seeing the snow covering the embankment. Far away in the darkness she could just make out the wide River Ume, striped with white ice and black water.

Only now did something inside her begin to relax. It was over. They had got Benjamin back.

Now they are standing uncertainly outside the Birger Jarl Hotel in Stockholm. Benjamin is wearing a tracksuit from the police Lost and Found that is far too big for him, a woolly hat—of the Sami tourist variety—that Simone bought for him at the airport, and a pair of mittens that are slightly too small. The city is deserted, with not a soul in sight. The underground station is closed, there are no buses, the restaurants are dark and silent.

Erik looks at his watch, perplexed. It's four o'clock in the afternoon. A woman hurries along, carrying a large bag.

"It's Christmas Eve," Simone says suddenly. "Today is Christmas Eve."

Benjamin looks at her in surprise.

"That would explain why people keep wishing us a Merry Christmas," says Erik with a smile.

"What shall we do?" Benjamin asks.

"McDonald's is open," Erik says.

"Are you suggesting we have Christmas dinner at McDonald's?" asks Simone.

A thin freezing rain begins to fall on them as they hurry towards the restaurant. It's an ugly, squat building, pressing itself to the ground beneath the ochre-coloured rotunda of the library. A woman in her sixties is standing behind the counter. There are no other customers to be seen.

"I'd like a glass of wine," says Simone. "But I guess that's out of the question."

"How about a milkshake?" says Erik.

"Vanilla, strawberry, or chocolate?" the woman asks sourly.

Simone looks as if she's about to burst out laughing, but she pulls herself together. "Strawberry, of course."

"Me too," Benjamin chips in.

The woman taps in their order with small, angry movements. "Will that be all?" she asks.

"Get a selection," Simone says to Erik. "We'll go and sit down." She and Benjamin thread their way among the empty tables. "A table by the window," she whispers, smiling at Benjamin.

She sits down next to her son, puts her arm around him, and feels the tears running down her cheeks. Outside, a lone skateboarder whizzes along between the patches of ice with harsh scraping, rattling noises. A woman is sitting on her own on a bench on the edge of the playground behind the School of Economics, an empty shopping trolley beside her. The tyre seats on the children's swings are blowing back and forth in the wind.

"Are you cold?" she asks.

Benjamin doesn't reply; he just rests his face against her chest, allowing her to kiss his head over and over again.

Erik puts a tray down on the table and returns to the counter to fetch another before sitting down and beginning to distribute cartons, paper bags, and drinks around the table. "When you eat at McDonald's, you need to go all the way."

"*Nice*," says Benjamin, sitting up.

"Wait," Erik says. He holds out a Happy Meal toy. "Merry Christmas," he says.

"Thanks, Dad." Benjamin grins, looking at the plastic packaging.

Simone looks at her child. He's lost so much weight. But there's something else, she thinks. It's as if he still has a weight within him, something that is pulling at his thoughts, worrying him and dragging him down. He's not really with them; his gaze is turned inwards.

When she sees Erik reach out and pat his son on the cheek, she begins to cry again. She turns away with a whispered apology and sees a plastic bag whisked out of a rubbish bin by the wind and pressed against the window.

"Come on, dig in," Erik says.

Benjamin is unwrapping a Big Mac when Erik's phone rings. It's Joona.

"Merry Christmas, Joona," he says.

"Same to you, Erik," says Joona. "Are you back in Stockholm?"

"We're actually having Christmas dinner right now."

"Do you remember I said we would find your son?"

"Yes, I remember."

"You had your doubts from time to time."

"Yes," says Erik. "I admit it."

"But I knew it would all work out," Joona goes on.

"I didn't."

"I know, I noticed," says Joona. "That's why there's something I need to say to you."

"Yes?"

"What did I tell you?" asks Joona.

"What?"

"I was right, wasn't I?"

"Yes, you were right," Erik replies.

"Merry Christmas," says Joona, ending the call.

Erik stares at the phone with a surprised expression, then turns to Simone. He looks at her transparent skin and wide mouth. Webs of worry lines have appeared around her eyes lately. She smiles at him, and he follows her gaze as she looks at Benjamin.

Erik watches his son for a long time. His throat aches with love. Benjamin is eating French fries, his expression serious. He has disappeared into his thoughts. His eyes stare vacantly, as if he has been sucked into his memories and the spaces between them. Erik reaches out with his uninjured arm, squeezes his son's fingers, and sees him look up.

"Merry Christmas, Dad," says Benjamin with a smile. "Here, have some fries."

"What about taking some of this food over to see Granddad?" Erik suggests.

"Are you serious?" asks Simone.

"How much fun is it being in the hospital at Christmas?"

Simone smiles at him and calls for a taxi. Benjamin goes over to the counter for a bag to put the food in.

As their taxi slowly drives past Odenplan, Erik sees his family reflected in the window, superimposed over the enormous decorated Christmas tree in the square. They slip past the branches as if they were dancing together around it. There it stands, tall and wide, hundreds of tiny glowing lights curling up towards the bright shining star.